Great German Short Stories

· DOVER · THRIFT · EDITIONS ·

Great German Short Stories

EDITED BY

EVAN BATES

DOVER PUBLICATIONS, INC.
Mineola, New York

DOVER THRIFT EDITIONS

GENERAL EDITOR: PAUL NEGRI
EDITOR OF THIS VOLUME: EVAN BATES

Bibliographical Note

This Dover edition, first published in 2003, is a new selection of eight short stories reprinted from standard sources. "The Story of the Just Casper and Fair Annie" by Clemens Brentano is reprinted from *Fiction and Fantasy of German Romance* by Frederick Pierce and Carl F. Schreiber, copyright © 1928 by Oxford University Press, Inc. Used by permission of Oxford University Press, Inc. A new introductory Note has been specially prepared for this edition.

Translations used are those of Stanley Appelbaum (Kafka's "In the Penal Colony," Rilke's "How Old Timofei Died with a Song," Kleist's "The Earthquake in Chile," Schnitzler's "Lieutenant Gustl"); Kenneth Burke (Mann's "Death in Venice"); Adele S. Seltzer (Hauptmann's "Flagman Thiel"); Carl F. Schreiber (Brentano's "The Story of the Just Casper and Fair Annie"); and Thomas Carlyle (Hoffmann's "The Golden Pot").

Library of Congress Cataloging-in-Publication Data

Great German short stories / edited by Evan Bates.
     p. cm. — (Dover thrift editions)
    Contents: Death in Venice / Thomas Mann—Flagman Thiel / Gerhart Hauptmann—In the penal colony / Franz Kafka—The golden pot / E.T.A. Hoffmann—How Old Timofei died with a song / Rainer Maria Rilke—The earthquake in Chile / Heinrich von Kleist—Lieutenant Gustl / Arthur Schnitzler—The story of the Just Casper and Fair Annie / Clemens Brentano.
    ISBN 0-486-43205-X (pbk.)
    1. German fiction—Translations into English. 2. Short stories, German—Translations into English. I. Bates, Evan. II. Series.

PT1327.G74 2003
833'.0108—dc21

    2003055218

Manufactured in the United States of America
Dover Publications, Inc., 31 East 2nd Street, Mineola, N.Y. 11501

Note

Counting the shorter works of Schiller and Goethe among its precursors, German short fiction[1] attained its characteristically modern form and became widely read around the turn of the nineteenth century. Since that time, the form's inherent possibilities have attracted most of the prominent writers in the language. This collection of eight narratives includes a contribution by one of the earliest adepts of modern German short fiction, Heinrich von Kleist, and contains many of the best examples of the genre from the next hundred years, including the work of Franz Kafka and Thomas Mann in the early twentieth century. The featured authors share the ability to communicate resonant social, political, and artistic matters, but differ radically in their thematic and aesthetic approaches, thus providing a sampling of the myriad literary achievements that the genre has inspired since its inception.

"Death in Venice" (1912) is Mann's well-known literary investigation of the social and physical conditions necessary for artistic production, a contemplation of the relationship between art and experience. It is far from purely philosophical, however, as Mann exquisitely draws Venice as experienced by his main character, who suffers from an obsession.

Gerhart Hauptmann received the 1912 Nobel Prize for Literature, and his "Flagman Thiel" (1887) is one of the most widely read German

---

[1]For the sake of brevity, the contents of this volume have been gathered under the term *short stories*, although many of the included texts are usually referred to as *novellas* or *short novels*. Discussions as to the differences between a short story and novella become quite technical and are more subtle than questions of length or date of origin. Generally, the descriptive term *novella* appeared long before "short story" was used (Friedrich Schlegel, writing in 1801, contributed the first theory of the novella in German). Both terms continue to be used, however, interchangeably in many cases. (See *History of the German Novelle* by E. K. Bennett and revised by H. M. Waidson, Cambridge University Press, 1961.)

short stories of all time. An exploration of the deadening (and deadly) effects of routine and denial, its naturalistic narrative is captivating.

"In the Penal Colony" (1919) is possibly the most significant story of Kafka's oeuvre. The narrative centers on a cryptic "machine," one of the most brilliant symbols in modern literature. The rules for the operation of this apparatus, and the enigmatic effects it has on its victim as well as bystanders, are highly inventive.

Hoffmann's "The Golden Pot" (1814) is distinguished from the other stories in this volume by its comical atmosphere and enormously fantastic elements. It features the student Anselmus, who is infatuated with two women—the mysterious Serpentina and the attractive Veronica—the first offering artistic inspiration and the second material comfort.

"How Old Timofei Died with a Song" (1900) is excerpted from a larger cycle, *Stories from the Good Lord*, which Rilke first published in 1900 and was the most successful of his story volumes, going through twelve editions in his lifetime. A framed story that depicts the transmission of artistic capital from one generation to the next, it is Rilke's celebration of the Russian fairy tales and legends that he encountered on a trip there.

Kleist's "The Earthquake in Chile" (1807) propels the reader at a rapid pace through a brief and spectacular narrative. Taking place in seventeenth-century Chile, where both nature and public opinion (fueled by religious dogma) are capable of causing random and incredibly violent acts, it demonstrates Kleist's ability to condense an elaborate experience and social texture into a short, highly charged form. Kleist's powerful brevity influenced many later writers, including Kafka.

Schnitzler's "Lieutenant Gustl" (1900) takes place almost entirely in the mind of a military officer as he visits an opera and contemplates the appropriate reaction to an insult received there. Considered to be the first purely interior monologue in European literature, its claustrophobic effect on the reader is well suited to the short-story form. As a result of its publication, Schnitzler was deprived of his medical officer's rank in the army, having offended the Austrian military administration with this portrayal of the intellectual and emotional narrowness of one of its elite.

"The Story of the Just Casper and Fair Annie" (1817) is Brentano's best short story. A study of guilt and honor, and their effects on human behavior, it incorporates myriad literary forms, including the folk song and the hymn.

Contents

DEATH IN VENICE

Thomas Mann

I

ON A spring afternoon of the year 19—, when our continent lay under such threatening weather for whole months, Gustav Aschenbach, or von Aschenbach as his name read officially after his fiftieth birthday, had left his apartment on the Prinzregentenstrasse in Munich and had gone for a long walk. Overwrought by the trying and precarious work of the forenoon—which had demanded a maximum wariness, prudence, penetration, and rigor of the will—the writer had not been able even after the noon meal to break the impetus of the productive mechanism within him, that *motus animi continuus* which constitutes, according to Cicero, the foundation of eloquence; and he had not attained the healing sleep which—what with the increasing exhaustion of his strength—he needed in the middle of each day. So he had gone outdoors soon after tea, in the hopes that air and movement would restore him and prepare him for a profitable evening.

It was the beginning of May, and after cold, damp weeks a false midsummer had set in. The English Gardens, although the foliage was still fresh and sparse, were as pungent as in August, and in the parts nearer the city had been full of conveyances and promenaders. At the Aumeister, which he had reached by quieter and quieter paths, Aschenbach had surveyed for a short time the Wirtsgarten with its lively crowds and its border of cabs and carriages. From here, as the sun was sinking, he had started home, outside the park, across the open fields; and since he felt tired and a storm was threatening from the direction of Föhring, he waited at the North Cemetery for the tram which would take him directly back to the city.

It happened that he found no one in the station or its vicinity. There was not a vehicle to be seen, either on the paved Ungererstrasse, with its solitary glistening rails stretching out towards Schwabing, or on the Föhringer Chaussee. Behind the fences of the stone-masons' establishments, where the crosses, memorial tablets, and monuments standing for sale formed a second, uninhabited burial ground, there was no sign of life; and opposite him the Byzantine structure of the Funeral Hall lay silent in the reflection of the departing day, its façade ornamented in luminous colors with Greek crosses and hieratic paintings, above which were displayed inscriptions symmetrically arranged in gold letters, and texts chosen to bear on the life beyond, such as, "They enter into the dwelling of the Lord," or, "The light of eternity shall shine upon them." And for some time, as he stood waiting, he found a grave diversion in spelling out the formulas and letting his mind's eye lose itself in their transparent mysticism, when, returning from his reveries, he noticed in the portico, above the two apocalyptic animals guarding the steps, a man whose somewhat unusual appearance gave his thoughts an entirely new direction.

Whether he had just now come out from the inside through the bronze door, or had approached and mounted from the outside unobserved, remained uncertain. Aschenbach, without applying himself especially to the matter, was inclined to believe the former. Of medium height, thin, smooth-shaven, and noticeably pug-nosed, the man belonged to the red-haired type and possessed the appropriate fresh milky complexion. Obviously, he was not of Bavarian extraction, since at least the white and straight-brimmed straw hat that covered his head gave his appearance the stamp of a foreigner, of some one who had come from a long distance. To be sure, he was wearing the customary knapsack strapped across his shoulders, and a belted suit of rough yellow wool; his left arm was resting on his thigh, and his gray storm cape was thrown across it. In his right hand he held a cane with an iron ferrule, which he had stuck diagonally into the ground, while, with his feet crossed, he was leaning his hip against the crook. His head was raised so that the Adam's-apple protruded hard and bare on a scrawny neck emerging from a loose sport-shirt. And he was staring sharply off into the distance, with colorless, red-lidded eyes between which stood two strong, vertical wrinkles peculiarly suited to his short turned-up nose. Thus—and perhaps his elevated position helped to give the impression—his bearing had something majestic and commanding about it, something bold, or even savage. For whether he was grimacing because he was blinded by the setting sun, or whether it was a case of a permanent distortion of the physiognomy, his lips seemed too short, they were so completely pulled back from his teeth that these were exposed even to the gums, and stood out white and long.

It is quite possible that Aschenbach, in his half-distracted, half-inquisitive examination of the stranger, had been somewhat inconsiderate, for he suddenly became aware that his look was being answered, and indeed so militantly, so straight in the eye, so plainly with the intention of driving the thing through to the very end and compelling him to capitulate, that he turned away uncomfortably and began walking along by the fences, deciding casually that he would pay no further attention to the man. The next minute he had forgotten him. But perhaps the exotic element in the stranger's appearance had worked on his imagination; or a new physical or spiritual influence of some sort had come into play. He was quite astonished to note a peculiar inner expansion, a kind of roving unrest, a youthful longing after far-off places: a feeling so vivid, so new, or so long dormant and neglected, that, with his hands behind his back and his eyes on the ground, he came to a sudden stop, and examined into the nature and purport of this emotion.

It was the desire for travel, nothing more; although, to be sure, it had attacked him violently, and was heightened to a passion, even to the point of an hallucination. His yearnings crystallized; his imagination, still in ferment from his hours of work, actually pictured all the marvels and terrors of a manifold world which it was suddenly struggling to conceive. He saw a landscape, a tropical swampland under a heavy, murky sky, damp, luxuriant and enormous, a kind of prehistoric wilderness of islands, bogs, and arms of water, sluggish with mud; he saw, near him and in the distance, the hairy shafts of palms rising out of a rank lecherous thicket, out of places where the plant-life was fat, swollen, and blossoming exorbitantly; he saw strangely misshapen trees lowering their roots into the ground, into stagnant pools with greenish reflections; and here, between floating flowers which were milk-white and large as dishes, birds of a strange nature, high-shouldered, with crooked bills, were standing in the muck, and looking motionlessly to one side; between dense, knotted stalks of bamboo he saw the glint from the eyes of a crouching tiger—and he felt his heart knocking with fear and with puzzling desires. Then the image disappeared: and with a shake of his head Aschenbach resumed his walk along past the fences of the stone-masons' establishments.

Since the time, at least, when he could command the means to enjoy the advantages of moving about the world as he pleased, he had considered traveling simply as a hygienic precaution which must be complied with now and then despite one's feelings and one's preferences. Too busy with the tasks arranged for him by his interest in his own ego and in the problems of Europe, too burdened with the onus of production, too little prone to diversion, and in no sense an amateur of the varied amusements of the great world, he had been thoroughly satisfied with such knowledge of the earth's surface as any one can get without moving far out of his own circle; and he had never even been tempted to leave Europe. Especially now that his life was slowly on the decline, and that the artist's fear of not having finished—this uneasiness lest the clock run down before he had done his part and given himself completely—could no longer be waved aside as a mere whim, he had confined his outer existence almost exclusively to the beautiful city which had become his home and to the rough country-house which he had built in the mountains and where he spent the rainy summers.

Further, this thing which had laid hold of him so belatedly, but with such suddenness, was very readily moderated and adjusted by the force of his reason and of a discipline which he had practiced since youth. He had intended carrying his life-work forward to a certain point before removing to the country. And the thought of knocking about the world for months and neglecting his work during this time, seemed much too lax and contrary to his plans; it really could not be considered seriously. Yet he knew only too well what the reasons were for this unexpected temptation. It was the urge to escape—he admitted to himself—this yearning for the new and the remote, this appetite for freedom, for unburdening, for forgetfulness; it was a pressure away from his work, from the steady drudgery of a coldly passionate service. To be sure, he loved his work and almost loved the enervating battle that was fought daily between a proud tenacious will—so often tested—and this growing weariness which no one was to suspect and which must not betray itself in his productions by any sign of weakness or negligence. But it seemed wise not to draw the bow overtightly, and not to strangle by sheer obstinacy so strongly persistent an appetite. He thought of his work, thought of the place at which yesterday and now again today he had been forced to leave off, and which, it seemed, would yield neither to patience and coaxing nor to a definite attack. He examined it again, trying to break through or to circumvent the deadlock, but he gave up with a shudder of repugnance. There was no unusual difficulty here; what balked him were the scruples of aversion, which took the form of a fastidious insatiability. Even as a young man this insatiability had meant to him the very nature, the fullest essence, of talent; and for that reason he had restrained and chilled his emotions, since he was aware that they incline to content themselves with a happy approximate, a state of semi-completion. Were these enslaved emotions now taking their vengeance on him, by leaving him in the lurch, by refusing to forward and lubricate his art; and were they bearing off with them every enjoyment, every live interest in form and expression?

Not that he was producing anything bad; his years gave him at least this advantage, that he felt himself at all times in full and easy possession of his craftsmanship. But while the nation honored him for this, he himself was not content; and it seemed to him that his work lacked the marks of that fiery and fluctuating emotionalism which is an enormous thing in one's favor, and which, while it argues an enjoyment on the part of the author, also constitutes, more than any depth of content, the enjoyment of the amateur. He feared the summer in the country, alone in the little house with the maid who prepared his meals, and the servant who brought them to him. He feared the familiar view of the mountain peaks and the slopes which would stand about him in his boredom and his discontent. Consequently there was need of a break in some new direction. If the summer was to be endurable and productive, he must attempt something out of his usual orbit; he must relax, get a change of air, bring an element of freshness into the blood. To travel, then—that much was settled. Not far, not all the way to the tigers. But one night on the sleeper, and a rest of three or four weeks at some pleasant popular resort in the South. . . .

He thought this out while the noise of the electric tram came nearer along the Ungererstrasse; and as he boarded it, he decided to devote the evening to the study of maps and time-tables. On the platform it occurred to him to look around for the man in the straw hat, his companion during that most significant time spent waiting at the station. But his whereabouts remained uncertain, as he was not to be seen either at the place where he was formerly standing, or anywhere else in the vicinity of the station, or on the car itself.

II

The author of that lucid and powerful prose epic built around the life of Frederick of Prussia; the tenacious artist who, after long application, wove rich, varied strands of human destiny together under one single predominating theme in the fictional tapestry known as "Maya"; the creator of that stark tale which is called "The Wretch" and which pointed out for an entire oncoming generation the possibility of some moral certainty beyond pure knowledge; finally, the writer (and this sums up briefly the works of his mature period) of the impassioned treatise on "Art and the Spirit," whose capacity for mustering facts, and, further, whose fluency in their presentation, led cautious judges to place this treatise alongside Schiller's conclusions on naïve and sentimental poetry—Gustav Aschenbach, then, was the son of a higher law official, and was born in L——, a leading city in the Province of Silesia. His forebears had been officers, magistrates, government functionaries, men who had led severe, steady lives serving their king, their state. A deeper strain of spirituality had been manifest in them once, in the person of a preacher; the preceding generation had brought a brisker, more sensuous blood into the family through the author's mother, daughter of a Bohemian bandmaster. The traces of foreignness in his features came from her. A marriage of sober painstaking conscientiousness with impulses of a darker, more fiery nature had had an artist as its result, and this particular artist.

Since his whole nature was centered around acquiring a reputation, he showed himself, if not exactly precocious, at least (thanks to the firmness and pithiness of his personality, his accent) ripened and adjusted to the public at an early age. Almost as a schoolboy he had made a name for himself. Within ten years he had learned to face the world through the medium of his writing-table, to discharge the obligations of his fame in a correspondence which (since many claims are pressed on the successful, the trustworthy) had to be brief as well as pleasant and to the point. At forty, wearied by the vicissitudes and the exertion of his own work, he had to manage a daily mail which bore the postmarks of countries in all parts of the world.

Equally removed from the banal and the eccentric, his talents were so constituted as to gain both the confidence of the general public and the stable admiration and sympathy of the critical. Thus even as a young man continually devoted to the pursuit of craftsmanship—and that of no ordinary kind—he had never known the careless freedom of youth. When, around thirty-five years of age, he had been taken ill in Vienna, one sharp observer said of him in company: "You see, Aschenbach has always lived like this," and the speaker contracted the fingers of his left hand into a fist: "never like this," and he let his open hand droop comfortably from the arm of his chair. That hit the mark; and the heroic, the ethical about it all was that he was not of a strong constitution, and though he was pledged by his nature to these steady efforts, he was not really born to them.

Considerations of ill health had kept him from attending school as a boy, and had compelled him to receive instruction at home. He had grown up alone, without comrades—and he was forced to realize soon enough that he belonged to a race which often lacked, not talent, but that physical substructure which talent relies on for its fullest fruition: a race accustomed to giving its best early, and seldom extending its faculties over the years. But his favorite phrase was "carrying through"; in his novel on Frederick he saw the pure apotheosis of this command, which struck him as the essential concept of the virtuous in action and passion. Also, he wished earnestly to grow old, since he had always maintained that the only artistry which can be called truly great, comprehensive—yes, even truly admirable—is that which is permitted to bear fruits characteristic of each stage in human development.

Since he must carry the responsibilities of his talent on frail shoulders, and wanted to go a long way, the primary requirement was discipline—and fortunately discipline was his direct inheritance from his father's side. By forty, fifty, or at an earlier age when others are still slashing about with enthusiasm, and are contentedly putting off to some later date the execution of plans on a large scale, he would start the day early, dashing cold water over his chest and back, and then, with a couple of tall wax candles in silver candlesticks at the head of his manuscript, he would pay out to his art, in two or three eager, scrupulous morning hours, the strength which he had accumulated in sleep. It was pardonable, indeed it was a direct tribute to the effectiveness of his moral scheme, that the uninitiated took his "Maya" world, and the massive epic machinery upon which the life of the hero Frederick was unrolled, as evidence of long breath and sustaining power. While actually they had been built up layer by layer, in small daily allotments, through hundreds and hundreds of single inspirations. And if they were so excellent in both composition and texture, it was solely because their creator had held out for years under the strain of one single work, with a steadiness of will and a tenacity comparable to that which conquered his native province; and because, finally, he had turned over his most vital and valuable hours to the problem of minute revision.

In order that a significant work of the mind may exert immediately some broad and deep effect, a secret relationship, or even conformity, must exist between the personal destiny of the author and the common destiny of his contemporaries. People do not know why they raise a work of art to fame. Far from being connoisseurs, they believe that they see in it hundreds of virtues which justify so much interest; but the true reason for their applause is an unconscious sympathy. Aschenbach had once stated quite plainly in some remote place that nearly everything great which comes into being does so in spite of something—in spite of sorrow or suffering, poverty, destitution, physical weakness, depravity, passion, or a thousand other handicaps. But that was not merely an observation; it was a discovery, the formula of his life and reputation, the key to his work. And what wonder, then, that it was also the distinguishing moral trait, the dominating gesture, of his most characteristic figures?

Years before, one shrewd analyst had written of the new hero-type to which this author gave preference, and which kept turning up in variations of one sort or another: he called it the conception of "an intellectual and youthful masculinity" which "stands motionless, haughty, ashamed, with jaw set, while swords and spear-points beset the body." That was beautiful and ingenious; and it was exact, although it may have seemed to suggest too much passivity. For to be poised against fatality, to meet adverse conditions gracefully, is more than simple endurance; it is an act of aggression, a positive triumph—and the figure of Sebastian is the most beautiful figure, if not of art as a whole, at least of the art of literature. Looking into this fictional world, one saw: a delicate self-mastery by which any inner deterioration, any biological decay was kept concealed from the eyes of the world; a crude, vicious sensuality capable of fanning its rising passions into pure flame, yes, even of mounting to dominance in the realm of beauty; a pallid weakness which draws from the glowing depths of the soul the strength to bow whole arrogant peoples before the foot of the cross, or before the feet of weakness itself; a charming manner maintained in his cold, strict service to form; a false, precarious mode of living, and the keenly enervating melancholy and artifice of the born deceiver—to observe such trials as this was enough to make one question whether there really was any heroism other than weakness. And, in any case, what heroism could be more in keeping with the times? Gustav Aschenbach was the one poet among the many workers on the verge of exhaustion: the over-burdened, the used-up, the clingers-on, in short all those moralists of production who, delicately built and destitute of means, can rely for a time at least on will-power and the shrewd husbandry of their resources to secure the effects of greatness. There are many such: they are the heroes of the period. And they all found themselves in his works; here they were indeed, upheld, intensified, applauded; they were grateful to him, they acclaimed him.

In his time he had been young and raw; and, misled by his age, he had blundered in public. He had stumbled, had exposed himself; both in writing and in talk he had offended against caution and tact. But he had acquired the dignity which, as he insisted, is the innate goad and craving of every great talent; in fact, it could be said that his entire development had been a conscious undeviating progression away from the embarrassments of skepticism and irony, and towards dignity.

The general masses are satisfied by vigor and tangibility of treatment rather than by any close intellectual processes; but youth, with its passion for the absolute, can be arrested only by the problematical. And Aschenbach had been absolute, problematical, as only a youth could be. He had been a slave to the intellect, had played havoc with knowledge had ground up his seed crops, had divulged secrets, had discredited talent, had betrayed art—yes, while his modelings were entertaining the faithful votaries, filling them with enthusiasm, making their lives more keen, this youthful artist was taking the breath away from the generation then in its twenties by his cynicisms on the questionable nature of art, and of artistry itself.

But it seems that nothing blunts the edge of a noble, robust mind more quickly and more thoroughly than the sharp and bitter corrosion of knowledge; and certainly the moody radicalism of the youth, no matter how conscientious, was shallow in comparison with his firm determination as an older man and a master to deny knowledge, to reject it, to pass it with raised head, in so far as it is capable of crippling, discouraging, or degrading to the slightest degree, our will, acts, feelings, or even passions. How else could the famous story of "The Wretch" be understood than as an outburst of repugnance against the disreputable psychologism of the times: embodied in the figure of that soft and stupid half-clown who pilfers a destiny for himself by guiding his wife (from powerlessness, from lasciviousness, from ethical frailty) into the arms of an adolescent, and believes that he may through profundity commit vileness? The verbal pressure with which he here cast out the outcast announced the return from every moral skepticism, from all fellow-feeling with the engulfed: it was the counter-move to the laxity of the sympathetic principle that to understand all is to forgive all—and the thing that was here well begun, even nearly completed, was that "miracle of reborn ingenuousness" which was taken up a little later in one of the author's dialogues expressly and not without a certain discreet emphasis. Strange coincidences! Was it as a result of this rebirth, this new dignity and sternness, that his feeling for beauty—a discriminating purity, simplicity, and evenness of attack which henceforth gave his productions such an obvious, even such a deliberate stamp of mastery and classicism—showed an almost excessive strengthening about this time? But ethical resoluteness in the exclusion of science, of emancipatory and restrictive knowledge—does this not in turn signify a simplification, a reduction morally of the world to too limited terms, and thus also a strengthened capacity for the forbidden, the evil, the morally impossible? And does not form have two aspects? Is it not moral and unmoral at once—moral in that it is the result and expression of discipline, but unmoral, and even immoral, in that by nature it contains an indifference to morality, is calculated, in fact, to make morality bend beneath its proud and unencumbered scepter?

Be that as it may. An evolution is a destiny; and why should his evolution, which had been upheld by the general confidence of a vast public, not run through a different course from one accomplished outside the luster and the entanglements of fame? Only chronic vagabondage will find it tedious and be inclined to scoff when a great talent outgrows the libertine chrysalis-stage, learns to seize upon and express the dignity of the mind, and superimposes a formal etiquette upon a solitude which had been filled with unchastened and rigidly isolated sufferings and struggles and had brought all this to a point of power and honor among men. Further, how much sport, defiance, indulgence there is in the self-formation of a talent! Gradually something official, didactic, crept into Gustav Aschenbach's productions, his style in later life fought shy of any abruptness and boldness, any subtle and unexpected contrasts; he inclined towards the fixed and standardized, the conventionally elegant, the conservative, the formal, the formulated, nearly. And, as is traditionally said of Louis XIV, with the advancing years he came to omit every common word from his vocabulary. At about this time it happened that the educational authorities included selected pages by him in their prescribed school readers. This was deeply sympathetic to his nature, and he did not decline when a German prince who had just mounted the throne raised the author of the "Frederick" to knighthood on the occasion of his fiftieth birthday. After a few years of unrest, a few tentative stopping-places here and there, he soon chose Munich as his permanent home, and lived there in a state of middle-class respectability such as fits in with the life of the mind in certain individual instances. The marriage which, when still young, he had contracted with a girl of an educated family came to an end with her death after a short period of happiness. He was left with a daughter, now married. He had never had a son.

Gustav von Aschenbach was somewhat below average height, dark, and smooth-shaven. His head seemed a bit too large in comparison with his almost dapper figure. His hair was brushed straight back, thinning out towards the crown, but very full about the temples, and strongly marked with gray; it framed a high, ridged forehead. Gold spectacles with rimless lenses cut into the bridge of his bold, heavy nose. The mouth was big, sometimes drooping, sometimes suddenly pinched and firm. His cheeks were thin and wrinkled, his well-formed chin had a slight cleft. This head, usually bent patiently to one side, seemed to have gone through momentous experiences, and yet it was his art which had produced those effects in his face, effects which are elsewhere the result of hard and agitated living. Behind this brow the brilliant repartee of the dialogue on war between Voltaire and the king had been born; these eyes, peering steadily and wearily from behind their glasses, had seen the bloody inferno of the lazaret in the Seven Years' War. Even as it applies to the individual, art is a heightened mode of existence. It gives deeper pleasures, it consumes more quickly. It carves into its servants' faces the marks of imaginary and spiritual adventures, and though their external activities may be as quiet as a cloister, it produces a lasting voluptuousness, overrefinement, fatigue, and curiosity of the nerves such as can barely result from a life filled with illicit passions and enjoyments.

III

Various matters of a literary and social nature delayed his departure until about two weeks after that walk in Munich. Finally he gave orders to have his country-house ready for occupancy within a month; and one day between the middle and the end of May he took the night train for Trieste, where he made a stop-over of only twenty-four hours, and embarked the following morning for Pola.

What he was hunting was something foreign and unrelated to himself which would at the same time be quickly within reach; and so he stopped at an island in the Adriatic which had become well known in recent years. It lay not far off the Istrian coast, with beautifully rugged cliffs fronting the open sea, and natives who dressed in variegated tatters and made strange sounds when they spoke. But rain and a heavy atmosphere, a provincial and exclusively Austrian patronage at the hotel, and the lack of that restfully intimate association with the sea which can be gotten only by a soft, sandy beach, irritated him, and prevented him from feeling that he had found the place he was looking for. Something within was disturbing him, and drawing him he was not sure where. He studied sailing dates, he looked about him questioningly, and of a sudden, as a thing both astounding and self-evident, his goal was before him. If you wanted to reach over night the unique, the fabulously different, where did you go? But that was plain. What was he doing here? He had lost the trail. He had wanted to go there. He did not delay in giving notice of his mistake in stopping here. In the early morning mist, a week and a half after his arrival on the island, a fast motor-boat was carrying him and his luggage back over the water to the naval port, and he landed there just long enough to cross the gangplank to the damp deck of a ship which was lying under steam ready for the voyage to Venice.

It was an old hulk flying the Italian flag, decrepit, sooty, and mournful. In a cave-like, artificially lighted inside cabin where Aschenbach, immediately upon boarding the ship, was conducted by a dirty hunchbacked sailor, who smirked politely, there was sitting behind a table, his hat cocked over his forehead and a cigarette stump in the corner of his mouth, a man with a goatee, and with the face of an old-style circus director, who was taking down the particulars of the passengers with professional grimaces and distributing the tickets. "To Venice!" he repeated Aschenbach's request, as he extended his arm and plunged his pen into the pasty dregs of a precariously tilted inkwell. "To Venice, first class! At your service, sir." And he wrote a generous scrawl, sprinkled it with blue sand out of a box, let the sand run off into a clay bowl, folded the paper with sallow, bony fingers, and began writing again. "A happily chosen destination!" he chatted on. "Ah, Venice! A splendid city! A city of irresistible attractiveness for the educated on account of its history as well as its present-day charms." The smooth rapidity of his movements and the empty words accompanying them had something anæsthetic and reassuring about them, much as though he feared lest the traveler might still be vacillating in his decision to go to Venice. He handled the cash briskly, and let the change fall on the spotted table-cover with the skill of a croupier. "A pleasant journey, sir!" he said with a theatrical bow. "Gentlemen, I have the honor of serving you!" he called out immediately after, with his arm upraised, and he acted as if business were in full swing, although no one else was there to require his attention. Aschenbach returned to the deck.

With one arm on the railing, he watched the passengers on board and the idlers who loitered around the dock waiting for the ship to sail. The second-class passengers, men and women, were huddled together on the foredeck, using boxes and bundles as seats. A group of young people made up the travelers on the first deck, clerks from Pola, it seemed, who had gathered in the greatest excitement for an excursion to Italy. They made a considerable fuss about themselves and their enterprise, chattered, laughed, enjoyed their own antics self-contentedly, and, leaning over the hand-rails, shouted flippantly and mockingly at their comrades who, with portfolios under their arms, were going up and down the waterfront on business and kept threatening the picnickers with their canes. One, in a bright yellow summer suit of ultra-fashionable cut, with a red necktie, and a rakishly tilted Panama, surpassed all the others in his crowning good humor. But as soon as Aschenbach looked at him a bit more carefully, he discovered with a kind of horror that the youth was a cheat. He was old, that was unquestionable. There were wrinkles around his eyes and mouth. The faint crimson of the cheeks was paint, the hair under his brilliantly decorated straw hat was a wig; his neck was hollow and stringy, his turned-up mustache and the imperial on his chin were dyed; the full set of yellow teeth which he displayed when he laughed, a cheap artificial plate; and his hands, with signet rings on both index fingers, were those of an old man. Fascinated with loathing, Aschenbach watched him in his intercourse with his friends. Did they not know, did they not observe that he was old, that he was not entitled to wear their bright, foppish clothing, that he was not entitled to play at being one of them? Unquestioningly, and as quite the usual thing, it seemed, they allowed him among them, treating him as one of their own kind and returning his jovial nudges in the ribs without repugnance. How could that be? Aschenbach laid his hand on his forehead and closed his eyes; they were hot, since he had had too little sleep. He felt as though everything were not quite the same as usual, as though some dream-like estrangement, some peculiar distortion of the world, were beginning to take possession of him, and perhaps this could be stopped if he hid his face for a time and then looked around him again. Yet at this moment he felt as though he were swimming; and looking up with an unreasoned fear, he discovered that the heavy, lugubrious body of the ship was separating slowly from the walled bank. Inch by inch, with the driving and reversing of the engine, the strip of dirty glistening water widened between the dock and the side of the ship; and, after cumbersome maneuvering, the steamer finally turned its nose towards the open sea. Aschenbach crossed to the starboard side, where the hunchback had set up a deck-chair for him, and a steward in a spotted dress-coat asked after his wants.

The sky was gray, the wind damp. Harbor and islands had been left behind, and soon all land was lost in the haze. Flakes of coal dust, bloated with moisture, fell over the washed deck, which would not dry. After the first hour an awning was spread, since it had begun to rain.

Bundled up in his coat, a book in his lap, the traveler rested, and the hours passed unnoticed. It stopped raining; the canvas awning was removed. The horizon was unbroken. The sea, empty, like an enormous disk, lay stretched under the curve of the sky. But in empty inarticulate space our senses lose also the dimensions of time, and we slip into the incommensurate. As he rested, strange shadowy figures, the old dandy, the goatee from the inside cabin, passed through his mind, with vague gestures, muddled dream-words—and he was asleep.

About noon he was called to a meal down in the corridor-like dining-hall into which the doors opened from the sleeping-cabins; he ate near the head of a long table, at the other end of which the clerks, including the old man, had been drinking with the boisterous captain since ten o'clock. The food was poor, and he finished rapidly. He felt driven outside to look at the sky, to see if it showed signs of being brighter above Venice.

He had kept thinking that this had to occur, since the city had always received him in full blaze. But sky and sea remained dreary and leaden, at times a misty rain fell, and here he was reaching by water a different Venice than he had ever found when approaching on land. He stood by the forestays, looking in the distance, waiting for land. He thought of the heavy-hearted, enthusiastic poet for whom the domes and bell towers of his dreams had once risen out of these waters; he relived in silence some of that reverence, happiness and sorrow which had been turned then into cautious song; and easily susceptible to sensations already molded, he asked himself wearily and earnestly whether some new enchantment and distraction, some belated adventure of the emotions, might still be held in store for this idle traveler.

Then the flat coast emerged on the right; the sea was alive with fishing-smacks; the bathers' island appeared; it dropped behind to the left, the steamer slowly entered the narrow port which is named after it;

and on the lagoon, facing gay ramshackle houses, it stopped completely, since it had to wait for the barque of the health department.

An hour passed before it appeared. He had arrived, and yet he had not; no one was in any hurry, no one was driven by impatience. The young men from Pola, patriotically attracted by the military bugle calls which rang over the water from the vicinity of the public gardens, had come on deck and, warmed by their Asti, they burst out with cheers for the drilling *bersagliere*. But it was repulsive to see what a state the primped-up old man had been brought to by his comradeship with youth. His old head was not able to resist its wine like the young and robust: he was painfully drunk. With glazed eyes, a cigarette between his trembling fingers, he stood in one place, swaying backwards and forwards from giddiness, and balancing himself laboriously. Since he would have fallen at the first step, he did not trust himself from the spot—yet he showed a deplorable insolence, buttonholed every one who came near him, stammered, winked and tittered, lifted his wrinkled, ornamented index finger in a stupid attempt at bantering, while he licked the corners of his mouth with his tongue in the most abominably suggestive manner. Aschenbach observed him darkly, and a feeling of numbness came over him again, as though the world were displaying a faint but irresistible tendency to distort itself into the peculiar and the grotesque: a feeling which circumstances prevented him from surrendering himself to completely, for just then the pounding activity of the engines commenced again, and the ship, resuming a voyage which had been interrupted so near its completion, passed through the San Marco canal.

So he saw it again, the most remarkable of landing-places, that blinding composition of fantastic buildings which the Republic lays out before the eyes of approaching seafarers: the soft splendor of the palace, the Bridge of Sighs, on the bank the columns with lion and saint, the advancing, showy flank of the enchanted temple, the glimpse through to the archway, and the giant clock. And as he looked on he thought that to reach Venice by land, on the railroad, was like entering a palace from the rear, and that this most unreal of cities should not be approached except as he was now doing, by ship, over the high seas.

The engine stopped, gondolas pressed in, the gangway was let down, customs officials climbed on board and discharged their duties perfunctorily; the disembarking could begin. Aschenbach made it understood that he wanted a gondola to take him and his luggage to the dock of those little steamers which ply between the city and the Lido, since he intended to locate near the sea. His plans were complied with, his wants were shouted down to the water, where the gondoliers were wrangling with one another in dialect. He was still hindered from descending; he was hindered by his trunk, which was being pulled and dragged with difficulty down the ladder-like steps. So that for some minutes he was not able to avoid the importunities of the atrocious old man, whose drunkenness gave him a sinister desire to do the foreigner parting honors. "We wish you a very agreeable visit," he bleated as he made an awkward bow. "We leave with pleasant recollections! *Au revoir, excusez*, and *bon jour*, your excellency!" His mouth watered, he pressed his eyes shut, he licked the corners of his mouth, and the dyed imperial turned up about his senile lips. "Our compliments," he mumbled, with two fingertips on his mouth, "our compliments to our sweetheart, the dearest, prettiest sweetheart . . ." And suddenly his false upper teeth fell down on his lower lip. Aschenbach was able to escape. "To our sweetheart, our handsome sweetheart," he heard the cooing, hollow, stuttering voice behind him while, supporting himself against the hand-rail, he went down the gangway.

Who would not have to suppress a fleeting shudder, a vague timidity and uneasiness, if it were a matter of boarding a Venetian gondola for the first time or after several years? The strange craft, an entirely unaltered survival from the times of balladry, with that peculiar blackness which is found elsewhere only in coffins—it suggests silent, criminal adventures in the rippling night, it suggests even more strongly death itself, the bier and the mournful funeral, and the last silent journey. And has it been observed that the seat of such a barque, this arm-chair of coffin-black veneer and dull black upholstery, is the softest, most luxuriant, most lulling seat in the world? Aschenbach noted this when he had relaxed at the feet of the gondolier, opposite his luggage, which lay neatly assembled on the prow. The rowers were still wrangling, harshly, incomprehensibly, with threatening gestures. But the strange silence of this canal city seemed to soften their voices, to disembody them, and dissipate them over the water. It was warm here in the harbor. Touched faintly by the warm breeze of the sirocco, leaning back against the limber portions of the cushions, the traveler closed his eyes in the enjoyment of a lassitude which was as unusual with him, as it was sweet. The trip would be short, he thought; if only it went on for ever! He felt himself glide with a gentle motion away from the crowd and the confusion of voices.

It became quieter and quieter around him! There was nothing to be heard but the splashing of the oar, the hollow slapping of the waves against the prow of the boat as it stood above the water black and bold and armed with its halberd-like tip, and a third sound, of speaking, of whispering—the whispering of the gondolier, who was talking to himself between his teeth, fitfully, in words that were pressed out by the exertion of his arms. Aschenbach looked up, and was slightly astonished to discover that the lagoon was widening, and he was headed for the open sea. This seemed to indicate that he ought not to rest too much, but should see to it that his wishes were carried out.

"To the steamer dock!" he repeated, turning around completely and looking into the face of the gondolier who stood behind on a raised platform and towered up between him and the dun-colored sky. He was a man of unpleasant, even brutal appearance, dressed in sailor-blue, with a yellow sash; a formless straw hat, its weave partially unraveled, was tilted insolently on his head. The set of his face, the blond curly mustache beneath a curtly turned-up nose, undoubtedly meant that he was not Italian. Although of somewhat frail build, so that one would not have thought him especially well suited to his trade, he handled the oar with great energy, throwing his entire body into each stroke. Occasionally he drew back his lips from the exertion, and disclosed his white teeth. Wrinkling his reddish brows, he gazed on past his passenger, as he answered deliberately, almost gruffly: "You are going to the Lido." Aschenbach replied: "Of course. But I have just taken the gondola to get me across to San Marco. I want to use the *vaporetto*."

"You cannot use the *vaporetto*, sir."

"And why not?"

"Because the *vaporetto* will not haul luggage."

That was so; Aschenbach remembered. He was silent. But the fellow's harsh, presumptuous manner, so unusual towards a foreigner here, seemed unbearable. He said: "That is my affair. Perhaps I want to put my things in storage. You will turn back."

There was silence. The oar splashed, the water thudded against the bow. And the talking and whispering began again. The gondolier was talking to himself between his teeth.

What was to be done? This man was strangely insolent, and had an uncanny decisiveness; the traveler, alone with him on the water, saw no way of getting what he wanted. And besides, how softly he could rest, if only he did not become excited! Hadn't he wanted the trip to go on and on for ever? It was wisest to let things take their course, and the main thing was that he was comfortable. The poison of inertia seemed to be issuing from the seat, from this low, black-upholstered arm-chair, so gently cradled by the oarstrokes of the imperious gondolier behind him. The notion that he had fallen into the hands of a criminal passed dreamily across Aschenbach's mind—without the ability to summon his thoughts to an active defense. The possibility that it was all simply a plan for cheating him seemed more abhorrent. A feeling of duty or pride, a kind of recollection that one should prevent such things, gave him the strength to arouse himself once more. He asked: "What are you asking for the trip?"

Looking down upon him, the gondolier answered: "You will pay."

It was plain how this should be answered. Aschenbach said mechanically: "I shall pay you nothing, absolutely nothing, if you don't take me where I want to go."

"You want to go to the Lido."

"But not with you."

"I am rowing you well."

That is so, Aschenbach thought, and relaxed. That is so, you are rowing me well. Even if you do have designs on my cash, and send me down to Pluto with a blow of your oar from behind, you will have rowed me well.

But nothing like that happened. They were even joined by others: a boatload of musical brigands, men and women, who sang to guitar and mandolin, riding persistently side by side with the gondola and filling the silence over the water with their covetous foreign poetry. A hat was held out, and Aschenbach threw in money. Then they stopped singing, and rowed away. And again the muttering of the gondolier could be heard as he talked fitfully and jerkily to himself.

So they arrived, tossed in the wake of a steamer plying towards the city. Two municipal officers, their hands behind their backs, their faces turned in the direction of the lagoon, were walking back and forth on the bank. Aschenbach left the gondola at the dock, supported by that old man who is stationed with his grappling-hook at each one of Venice's landing-places. And since he had no small money, he crossed over to the hotel by the steamer wharf to get change and pay the rower what was due him. He got what he wanted in the lobby, he returned and found his traveling-bags in a cart on the dock, and gondola and gondolier had vanished.

"He got out in a hurry," said the old man with the grappling-hook. "A bad man, a man without a license, sir. He is the only gondolier who doesn't have a license. The others telephoned here."

Aschenbach shrugged his shoulders.

"The gentleman rode for nothing," the old man said, and held out his hat. Aschenbach tossed in a coin. He gave instructions to have his luggage taken to the beach hotel, and followed the cart through the avenue, the white-blossomed avenue which, lined on both sides with taverns, shops, and boarding-houses, runs across the island to the shore.

He entered the spacious hotel from the rear, by the terraced garden, and passed through the vestibule and the lobby until he reached the desk. Since he had been announced, he was received with obliging promptness. A manager, a small, frail, flatteringly polite man with a black mustache and a French style frock-coat, accompanied him to the third floor in the lift, and showed him his room, an agreeable place furnished in cherry wood. It was decorated with strong-smelling flowers, and its high windows afforded a view out across the open sea. He stepped up to one of them after the employee had left; and while his luggage was being brought up and placed in the room behind him, he looked down on the beach (it was comparatively deserted in the afternoon) and on the sunless ocean which was at flood-tide and was sending long low waves against the bank in a calm regular rhythm.

The experiences of a man who lives alone and in silence are both vaguer and more penetrating than those of people in society; his thoughts are heavier, more odd, and touched always with melancholy. Images and observations which could easily be disposed of by a glance, a smile, an exchange of opinion, will occupy him unbearably, sink deep into the silence, become full of meaning, become life, adventure, emotion. Loneliness ripens the eccentric, the daringly and estrangingly beautiful, the poetic. But loneliness also ripens the perverse, the disproportionate, the absurd, and the illicit.—So, the things he had met with on the trip, the ugly old fop with his twaddle about sweethearts, the lawbreaking gondolier who was cheated of his pay, still left the traveler uneasy. Without really providing any resistance to the mind, without offering any solid stuff to think over, they were nevertheless profoundly strange, as it seemed to him, and disturbing precisely because of this contradiction. In the meanwhile, he greeted the sea with his eyes, and felt pleasure at the knowledge that Venice was so conveniently near. Finally he turned away, bathed his face, left orders to the chambermaid for a few things he still needed done to make his comfort complete, and let himself be taken to the ground floor by the green-uniformed Swiss who operated the lift.

He took his tea on the terrace facing the ocean, then descended and followed the boardwalk for quite a way in the direction of the Hotel Excelsior. When he returned it seemed time to dress for dinner. He did this with his usual care and slowness, since he was accustomed to working over his toilet. And yet he came down a little early to the lobby, where he found a great many of the hotel guests assembled, mixing distantly and with a show of mutual indifference to one another, but all waiting for meal-time. He took a paper from the table, dropped into a leather chair, and observed the company; they differed agreeably from the guests where he had first stopped.

A wide and tolerantly inclusive horizon was spread out before him. Sounds of all the principal languages formed a subdued murmur. The accepted evening dress, a uniform of good manners, brought all human varieties into a fitting unity. There were Americans with their long wry features, large Russian families, English ladies, German children with

French nurses. The Slavic element seemed to predominate. Polish was being spoken nearby.

It was a group of children gathered around a little wicker table, under the protection of a teacher or governess: three young girls, apparently fifteen to seventeen, and a long-haired boy about fourteen years old. With astonishment Aschenbach noted that the boy was absolutely beautiful. His face, pale and reserved, framed with honey-colored hair, the straight sloping nose, the lovely mouth, the expression of sweet and godlike seriousness, recalled Greek sculpture of the noblest periods; and the complete purity of the form was accompanied by such a rare personal charm that, as he watched, he felt that he had never met with anything equally felicitous in nature or the plastic arts. He was further struck by the obviously intentional contrast with the principles of upbringing which showed in the sisters' attire and bearing. The three girls, the eldest of whom could be considered grown up, were dressed with a chasteness and severity bordering on disfigurement. Uniformly cloister-like costumes, of medium length, slate-colored, sober, and deliberately unbecoming in cut, with white turned-down collars as the only relief, suppressed every possible appeal of shapeliness. Their hair, brushed down flat and tight against the head, gave their faces a nun-like emptiness and lack of character. Surely this was a mother's influence, and it had not even occurred to her to apply the pedagogical strictness to the boy which she seemed to find necessary for her girls. It was clear that in his existence the first factors were gentleness and tenderness. The shears had been resolutely kept from his beautiful hair; like a Prince Charming's, it fell in curls over his forehead, his ears, and still deeper, across his neck. The English sailor suit, with its braids, stitchings, and embroideries, its puffy sleeves narrowing at the ends and fitting snugly about the fine wrists of his still childish but slender hands, gave the delicate figure something rich and luxurious. He was sitting, half profile to the observer, one foot in its black patent-leather shoe placed before the other, an elbow resting on the arm of his wicker chair, a cheek pressed against his fist, in a position of negligent good manners, entirely free of the almost subservient stiffness to which his sisters seemed accustomed. Did he have some illness? For his skin stood out as white as ivory against the golden darkness of the surrounding curls. Or was he simply a pampered favorite child, made this way by a doting and moody love? Aschenbach inclined to believe the latter. Almost every artist is born with a rich and treacherous tendency to recognize injustices which have created beauty, and to meet aristocratic distinction with sympathy and reverence.

A waiter passed through and announced in English that the meal was ready. Gradually the guests disappeared through the glass door into the dining-hall. Stragglers crossed, coming from the entrance, or the lifts. Inside, they had already begun serving, but the young Poles were still waiting around the little wicker table; and Aschenbach, comfortably propped in his deep chair, and with this beauty before his eyes, stayed with them.

The governess, a small corpulent middle-class woman with a red face, finally gave the sign to rise. With lifted brows, she pushed back her chair and bowed, as a large woman dressed in gray and richly jeweled with pearls entered the lobby. This woman was advancing with coolness and precision; her lightly powdered hair and the lines of her dress were arranged with the simplicity which always signifies taste in those quarters where devoutness is taken as one element of dignity. She might have been the wife of some high German official. Except that her jewelry added something fantastically lavish to her appearance; indeed, it was almost priceless, and consisted of ear pendants and a very long triple chain of softly glowing pearls, as large as cherries.

The children had risen promptly. They bent over to kiss the hand of their mother who, with a distant smile on her well-preserved though somewhat tired and peaked features, looked over their heads and directed a few words to the governess in French. Then she walked to the glass door. The children followed her: the girls in the order of their age, after them the governess, the boy last. For some reason or other he turned around before crossing the sill, and since no one else was in the lobby his strange dusky eyes met those of Aschenbach, who, his newspaper on his knees, lost in thought, was gazing after the group.

What he saw had not been unusual in the slightest detail. They had not preceded the mother to the table; they had waited, greeted her with respect, and observed the customary forms on entering the room. But it had taken place so pointedly, with such an accent of training, duty, and self-respect, that Aschenbach felt peculiarly touched by it all. He delayed for a few moments, then he too crossed into the dining-room, and was assigned to his table, which, as he noted with a brief touch of regret, was very far removed from that of the Polish family.

Weary, and yet intellectually active, he entertained himself during the lengthy meal with abstract, or even transcendental things; he thought over the secret union which the lawful must enter upon with the individual for human beauty to result, from this he passed into general problems of form and art, and at the end he found that his thoughts and discoveries were like the seemingly felicitous promptings of a dream which, when the mind is sobered, are seen to be completely empty and unfit. After the meal, smoking, sitting, taking an occasional turn in the park with its smell of nightfall, he went to bed early and spent the night in a sleep deep and unbroken, but often enlivened with the apparitions of dreams.

The weather did not improve any the following day. A land breeze was blowing. Under a cloudy ashen sky, the sea lay in dull peacefulness; it seemed shriveled up, with a close, dreary horizon, and it had retreated from the beach, baring the long ribs of several sandbanks. As Aschenbach opened his window, he thought that he could detect the foul smell of the lagoon.

He felt depressed. He thought already of leaving. Once, years ago, after several weeks of spring here, this same weather had afflicted him, and impaired his health so seriously that he had to abandon Venice like a fugitive. Was not this old feverish unrest again setting in, the pressure in the temples, the heaviness of the eyelids? It would be annoying to change his residence still another time; but if the wind did not turn, he could not stay here. To be safe, he did not unpack completely. He breakfasted at nine in the buffet-room provided for this purpose between the lobby and the dining-room.

That formal silence reigned here which is the ambition of large hotels. The waiters who were serving walked about on soft soles. Nothing was audible but the tinkling of the tea-things, a word half whispered. In one corner, obliquely across from the door, and two tables removed from his own, Aschenbach observed the Polish girls with their governess. Erect and red-eyed, their ash-blond hair freshly smoothed down, dressed in stiff blue linen with little white cuffs and turned-down collars — they were sitting there, handing around a glass of marmalade. They had almost finished their breakfast. The boy was missing.

Aschenbach smiled. "Well, little Phæacian!" he thought. "You seem to be enjoying the pleasant privilege of having your sleep out." And, suddenly exhilarated, he recited to himself the line: "A frequent change of dress, warm baths, and rest."

He breakfasted without haste. From the porter, who entered the hall holding his braided cap in his hand, he received some forwarded mail; and while he smoked a cigarette he opened a few letters. In this way it happened that he was present at the entrance of the late sleeper who was being waited for over yonder.

He came through the glass door and crossed the room in silence to his sisters' table. His approach — the way he held the upper part of his body, and bent his knees, the movement of his white-shod feet — had an extraordinary charm; he walked very lightly, at once timid and proud, and this became still more lovely through the childish embarrassment with which, twice as he proceeded, he turned his face towards the center of the room, raising and lowering his eyes. Smiling, with something half muttered in his soft vague tongue, he took his place; and now, as he turned his full profile to the observer, Aschenbach was again aston-ished, terrified even, by the really godlike beauty of this human child. Today the boy was wearing a light blouse of blue and white striped cotton goods, with a red silk tie in front, and closed at the neck by a plain white high collar. This collar lacked the distinctiveness of the blouse, but above it the flowering head was poised with an incomparable seductiveness—the head of an Eros, in blended yellows of Parian marble, with fine serious brows, the temples and ears covered softly by the abrupt encroachment of his curls.

"Good, good!" Aschenbach thought, with that deliberate expert appraisal which artists sometimes employ as a subterfuge when they have been carried away with delight before a masterwork. And he thought further: "Really, if the sea and the beach weren't waiting for me, I should stay here as long as you stayed!" But he went then, passed through the lobby under the inspection of the servants, down the wide terrace, and straight across the boardwalk to the section of the beach reserved for the hotel guests. The barefoot old man in dungarees and straw hat who was functioning here as bathing-master assigned him to the bath-house he had rented; a table and a seat were placed on the sandy board platform, and he made himself comfortable in the lounge chair which he had drawn closer to the sea, out into the waxen yellow sand.

More than ever before, he was entertained and amused by the sights on the beach, this spectacle of carefree, civilized people getting sensuous enjoyment at the very edge of the elements. The gray flat sea was already alive with wading children, swimmers, a motley of figures lying on the sandbanks with arms bent behind their heads. Others were rowing about in little red and blue striped boats without keels; they were continually upsetting, amid laughter. Before the long stretches of bathing-houses, where people were sitting on the platforms as though on small verandas, there was a play of movement against the line of rest and inertness behind—visits and chatter, fastidious morning elegance alongside the nakedness which, boldly at ease, was enjoying the freedom which the place afforded. Farther in front, on the damp firm sand, people were parading about in white bathing-cloaks, in ample, brilliantly colored wrappers. An elaborate sand pile to the right, erected by children, had flags in the colors of all nations planted around it. Venders of shells, cakes, and fruit spread out their wares, kneeling. To the left, before one of the bathing-houses which stood at right angles to the others and to the sea, a Russian family was encamped: men with beards and large teeth, slow delicate women, a Baltic girl sitting by an easel and painting the sea amidst exclamations of despair, two ugly good-natured children, an old maidservant who wore a kerchief on her head and had the alert scraping manners of a slave. Delighted and appreciative, they were living there, patiently calling the names of the two rowdy disobedient children, using their scanty Italian to joke with the humorous old man from whom they were buying candy, kissing one another on the cheek, and not in the least concerned with any one who might be observing their community.

"Yes, I shall stay," Aschenbach thought. "Where would things be better?" And, his hands folded in his lap, he let his eyes lose themselves in the expanses of the sea, his gaze gliding, swimming, and failing in the monotone mist of the wilderness of space. He loved the ocean for deep-seated reasons: because of that yearning for rest, when the hard-pressed artist hungers to shut out the exacting multiplicities of experience and hide himself on the breast of the simple, the vast; and because of a forbidden hankering—seductive, by virtue of its being directly opposed to his obligations—after the incommunicable, the incommensurate, the eternal, the non-existent. To be at rest in the face of perfection is the hunger of every one who is aiming at excellence; and what is the non-existent but a form of perfection? But now, just as his dreams were so far out in vacancy, suddenly the horizontal fringe of the sea was broken by a human figure; and as he brought his eyes back from the unbounded, and focused them, it was the lovely boy who was there, coming from the left and passing him on the sand. He was barefooted, ready for wading, his slender legs exposed above the knees; he walked slowly, but as lightly and proudly as though it were the customary thing for him to move about without shoes; and he was looking around him towards the line of bathing-houses opposite. But as soon as he had noticed the Russian family, occupied with their own harmony and contentment, a cloud of scorn and detestation passed over his face. His brow darkened, his mouth was compressed, he gave his lips an embittered twist to one side so that the cheek was distorted and the forehead became so heavily furrowed that the eyes seemed sunken beneath its pressure: malicious and glowering, they spoke the language of hate. He looked down, looked back once more threateningly, then with his shoulder made an abrupt gesture of disdain and dismissal, and left the enemy behind him.

A kind of pudency or confusion, something like respect and shyness, caused Aschenbach to turn away as though he had seen nothing. For the earnest-minded who have been casual observers of some passion, struggle against making use, even to themselves, of what they have seen. But he was both cheered and unstrung—which is to say, he was happy. This childish fanaticism, directed against the most good-natured possible aspect of life—it brought the divinely arbitrary into human relationships; it made a delightful natural picture which had appealed only to the eye now seem worthy of a deeper sympathy; and it gave the figure of this half-grown boy, who had already been important enough by his sheer beauty, something to offset him still further, and to make one take him more seriously than his years justified. Still looking away, Aschenbach could hear the boy's voice, the shrill, somewhat weak voice with which, in the distance now, he was trying to call hello to his playfellows busied around the sand pile. They answered him, shouting back his name, or some affectionate nickname; and Aschenbach listened with a certain curiosity, without being able to catch anything more definite than two melodic syllables like "Adgio," or still more frequently "Adgiu," with a ringing *u*-sound prolonged at the end. He was pleased with the resonance of this; he found it adequate to the subject. He repeated it silently and, satisfied, turned to his letters and manuscripts.

His small portable writing-desk on his knees, he began writing with his fountain pen an answer to this or that bit of correspondence. But after the first fifteen minutes he found it a pity to abandon the situation—the most enjoyable he could think of—in this manner and waste it in activities which did not interest him. He tossed the writing materials to one side, and he faced the ocean again; soon afterwards, diverted by the childish voices around the sand heap, he revolved his head comfortably along the back of the chair towards the right, to discover where that excellent little Adgio might be and what he was doing.

He was found at a glance; the red tie on his breast was not to be overlooked. Busied with the others in laying an old plank across the damp moat of the sand castle, he was nodding, and shouting instructions for this work. There were about ten companions with him, boys and girls of his age, and a few younger ones who were chattering with one another in Polish, French, and in several Balkan tongues. But it was his name which rang out most often. He was openly in demand, sought after, admired. One boy especially, like him a Pole, a stocky fellow who was called something like "Jaschu," with sleek black hair and a belted linen coat, seemed to be his closest vassal and friend. When the work on the sand structure was finished for the time being, they walked arm-in-arm along the beach and the boy who was called "Jaschu" kissed the beauty.

Aschenbach was half minded to raise a warning finger. "I advise you, Cristobulus," he thought, smiling, "to travel for a year! For you need that much time at least to get over it." And then he breakfasted on large ripe strawberries which he got from a peddler. It had become very warm, although the sun could no longer penetrate the blanket of mist in the sky. Laziness clogged his brain, even while his senses delighted in the numbing, drugging distractions of the ocean's stillness. To guess, to puzzle out just what name it was that sounded something like "Adgio," seemed to the sober man an appropriate ambition, a thoroughly comprehensive pursuit. And with the aid of a few scrappy recollections of Polish he decided that they must mean "Tadzio," the shortened form of "Tadeusz," and sounding like "Tadziu" when it is called.

Tadzio was bathing. Aschenbach, who had lost sight of him, spied his head and the arm with which he was propelling himself, far out in the water; for the sea must have been smooth for a long distance out. But already people seemed worried about him; women's voices were calling after him from the bathing-houses, uttering this name again and again. It almost dominated the beach like a battle-cry, and with its soft consonants, its long-drawn *u*-note at the end, it had something at once sweet and wild about it: "Tadziu! Tadziu!" He turned back; beating the resistant water into a foam with his legs, he hurried, his head bent down over the waves. And to see how this living figure, graceful and clean-cut in its advance, with dripping curls, and lovely as some frail god, came up out of the depths of sky and sea, rose and separated from the elements—this spectacle aroused a sense of myth, it was like some poet's recovery of time at its beginning, of the origin of forms and the birth of gods. Aschenbach listened with closed eyes to this song ringing within him, and he thought again that it was pleasant here, and that he would like to remain.

Later Tadzio was resting from his bath; he lay in the sand, wrapped in his white robe, which was drawn under the right shoulder, his head supported on his bare arm. And even when Aschenbach was not observing him, but was reading a few pages in his book, he hardly ever forgot that this boy was lying there and that it would cost him only a slight turn of his head to the right to behold the mystery. It seemed that he was sitting here just to keep watch over his repose—busied with his own concerns, and yet constantly aware of this noble picture at his right, not far in the distance. And he was stirred by a paternal affection, the profound leaning which those who have devoted their thoughts to the creation of beauty feel towards those who possess beauty itself.

A little past noon he left the beach, returned to the hotel, and was taken up to his room. He stayed there for some time in front of the mirror, looking at his gray hair, his tired, sharp features. At this moment he thought of his reputation, and of the fact that he was often recognized on the streets and observed with respect, thanks to the sure aim and the appealing finish of his words. He called up all the exterior successes of his talent which he could think of, remembering also his elevation to the knighthood. Then he went down to the dining-hall for lunch, and ate at his little table. As he was riding up in the lift, after the meal was ended, a group of young people just coming from breakfast pressed into the swaying cage after him, and Tadzio entered too. He stood quite near to Aschenbach, for the first time so near that Aschenbach could see him, not with the aloofness of a picture, but in minute detail, in all his human particularities. The boy was addressed by some one or other, and as he was answering with an indescribably agreeable smile he stepped out again, on the second floor, walking backwards, and with his eyes lowered. "Beauty makes modest," Aschenbach thought, and he tried insistently to explain why this was so. But he had noticed that Tadzio's teeth were not all they should be; they were somewhat jagged and pale. The enamel did not look healthy; it had a peculiar brittleness and transparency, as is often the case with anæmics. "He is very frail, he is sickly," Aschenbach thought. "In all probability he will not grow old." And he refused to reckon with the feeling of gratification or reassurance which accompanied this notion.

He spent two hours in his room, and in the afternoon he rode in the *vaporetto* across the foul-smelling lagoon to Venice. He got off at San Marco, took tea on the Piazza, and then, in accord with his schedule for the day, he went for a walk through the streets. Yet it was this walk which produced a complete reversal in his attitudes and his plans.

An offensive sultriness lay over the streets. The air was so heavy that the smells pouring out of homes, stores, and eating-houses became mixed with oil, vapors, clouds of perfumes, and still other odors—and these would not blow away, but hung in layers. Cigarette smoke remained suspended, disappearing very slowly. The crush of people along the narrow streets irritated rather than entertained the walker. The farther he went, the more he was depressed by the repulsive condition resulting from the combination of sea air and sirocco, which was at the same time both stimulating and enervating. He broke into an uncomfortable sweat. His eyes failed him, his chest became tight, he had a fever, the blood was pounding in his head. He fled from the crowded business streets across a bridge into the walks of the poor. On a quiet square, one of those forgotten and enchanting places which lie in the interior of Venice, he rested at the brink of a well, dried his forehead, and realized that he would have to leave here.

For the second and last time it had been demonstrated that this city in this kind of weather was decidedly unhealthy for him. It seemed foolish to attempt a stubborn resistance, while the prospects for a change of wind were completely uncertain. A quick decision was called for. It was not possible to go home this soon. Neither summer nor winter quarters were prepared to receive him. But this was not the only place where there were sea and beach; and elsewhere these could be found without the lagoon and its malarial mists. He remembered a little watering-place not far from Trieste which had been praised to him. Why not there? And without delay, so that this new change of location would still have time to do him some good. He pronounced this as good as settled, and stood up. At the next gondola station he took a boat back to San Marco, and was led through the dreary labyrinth of canals, under fancy marble balconies flanked with lions, around the corners of smooth walls, past the sorrowing façades of palaces which mirrored large dilapidated business-signs in the pulsing water. He had trouble arriving there, for the gondolier, who was in league with lace-makers and glass-blowers, was always trying to land him for inspections and purchases; and just as the bizarre trip through Venice would begin to cast its spell, the greedy business sense of the sunken Queen did all it could to destroy the illusion.

When he had returned to the hotel, he announced at the office before dinner that unforeseen developments necessitated his departure the following morning. He was assured of their regrets. He settled his accounts. He dined and spent the warm evening reading the newspapers in a rocking-chair on the rear terrace. Before going to bed he got his luggage all ready for departure.

He did not sleep so well as he might, since the impending break-up made him restless. When he opened the window in the morning, the sky was as overcast as ever, but the air seemed fresher, and he was already beginning to repent. Hadn't his decision been somewhat hasty and uncalled for, the result of a passing diffidence and indisposition? If he had delayed a little, if, instead of surrendering so easily, he had made some attempt to adjust himself to the air of Venice or to wait for an improvement in the weather, he would not be so rushed and inconvenienced, but could anticipate another forenoon on the beach like yesterday's. Too late. Now he would have to go on wanting what he had wanted yesterday. He dressed, and at about eight o'clock rode down to the ground-floor for breakfast.

As he entered, the buffet-room was still empty of guests. A few came in while he sat waiting for his order. With his tea-cup to his lips, he saw the Polish girls and their governess appear: rigid, with morning freshness, their eyes still red, they walked across to their table in the corner by the window. Immediately afterwards, the porter approached him, cap in hand, and warned him that it was time to go. The automobile is ready to take him and the other passengers to the Hotel Excelsior, and from here the motorboat will bring the ladies and gentlemen to the station through the company's private canal. Time is pressing.— Aschenbach found that it was doing nothing of the sort. It was still over an hour before his train left. He was irritated by this hotel custom of hustling departing guests out of the house, and indicated to the porter that he wished to finish his breakfast in peace. The man retired hesitatingly, to appear again five minutes later. It is impossible for the car to wait any longer. Then he would take a cab, and carry his trunk with him, Aschenbach replied in anger. He would use the public steamboat at the proper time, and he requested that it be left to him personally to worry about his departure. The employee bowed himself away. Pleased with the way he had warded off these importunate warnings, Aschenbach finished his meal at leisure; in fact, he even had the waiter bring him a newspaper. The time had become quite short when he finally arose. It was fitting that at the same moment Tadzio should come through the glass door.

On the way to his table he walked in the opposite direction to Aschenbach, lowering his eyes modestly before the man with the gray hair and high forehead, only to raise them again, in his delicious manner, soft and full upon him—and he had passed. "Good-by, Tadzio!" Aschenbach thought. "I did not see much of you." He did what was unusual with him, really formed the words on his lips and spoke them to himself; then he added: "God bless you!"—After this he left, distributed tips, was ushered out by the small gentle manager in the French frock-coat, and made off from the hotel on foot, as he had come, going along the white blossoming avenue which crossed the island to the steamer bridge, accompanied by the house servant carrying his hand luggage. He arrived, took his place—and then followed a painful journey through all the depths of regret.

It was the familiar trip across the lagoon, past San Marco, up the Grand Canal. Aschenbach sat on the circular bench at the bow, his arm supported against the railing, shading his eyes with his hand. The public gardens were left behind, the Piazzetta opened up once more in princely splendor and was gone, then came the great flock of palaces, and as the channel made a turn the magnificently slung marble arch of the Rialto came into view. The traveler was watching; his emotions were in conflict. The atmosphere of the city, this slightly foul smell of sea and swamp which he had been so anxious to avoid—he breathed it now in deep, exquisitely painful draughts. Was it possible that he had not known, had not considered, just how much he was attached to all this? What had been a partial misgiving this morning, a faint doubt as to the advisability of his move, now became a distress, a positive misery, a spiritual hunger, and so bitter that it frequently brought tears to his eyes, while he told himself that he could not possibly have foreseen it. Hardest of all to bear, at times completely insufferable, was the thought that he would never see Venice again, that this was a leave-taking for ever. Since it had been shown for the second time that the city affected his health, since he was compelled for the second time to get away in all haste, from now on he would have to consider it a place impossible and forbidden to him, a place which he was not equal to, and which it would be foolish for him to visit again. Yes, he felt that if he left now, he would be shamefaced and defiant enough never to see again the beloved city which had twice caused him a physical breakdown. And of a sudden this struggle between his desires and his physical strength seemed to the aging man so grave and important, his physical defeat seemed so dishonorable, so much a challenge to hold out at any cost, that he could not understand the ready submissiveness of the day before, when he had decided to give in without attempting any serious resistance.

Meanwhile the steamboat was nearing the station; pain and perplexity increased, he became distracted. In his affliction, he felt that it was impossible to leave, and just as impossible to turn back. The conflict was intense as he entered the station. It was very late; there was not a moment to lose if he was to catch the train. He wanted to, and he did not want to. But time was pressing; it drove him on. He hurried to get his ticket, and looked about in the tumult of the hall for the officer on duty here from the hotel. The man appeared and announced that the large trunk had been transferred. Transferred already? Yes, thank you — to Como. To Como? And in the midst of hasty running back and forth, angry questions and confused answers, it came to light that the trunk had already been sent with other foreign baggage from the express office of the Hotel Excelsior in a completely wrong direction.

Aschenbach had difficulty in preserving the expression which was required under these circumstances. He was almost convulsed with an adventurous delight, an unbelievable hilarity. The employee rushed off to see if it were still possible to stop the trunk, and, as was to be expected, he returned with nothing accomplished. Aschenbach declared that he did not want to travel without his trunk, but had decided to go back and wait at the beach hotel for its return. Was the company's motorboat still at the station? The man assured him that it was lying at the door. With Italian volubility he persuaded the clerk at the ticket window to redeem the canceled ticket, he swore that they would act speedily, that no time or money would be spared in recovering the trunk promptly, and — so the strange thing happened that, twenty minutes after his arrival at the station, the traveler found himself again on the Grand Canal, returning to the Lido.

Here was an adventure, wonderful, abashing, and comically dreamlike, beyond belief: places which he had just bid farewell to for ever in the most abject misery — yet he had been turned and driven back by fate, and was seeing them again in the same hour! The spray from the prow washing between gondolas and steamers with an absurd agility, the speedy little craft shot ahead to its goal, while the lone passenger was hiding the nervousness and ebullience of a truant boy under a mask of resigned anger. From time to time he shook with laughter at this mishap which, as he told himself, could not have turned out better for a child of destiny. There were explanations to be given, expressions of astonishment to be faced—and then, he told himself, everything would be all right; then a misfortune would be avoided, a grave error rectified. And all that he had thought he was leaving behind him would be open to him again, there at his disposal. . . . And, to cap it all, was the rapidity of the ride deceiving him, or was the wind really coming from the sea?

The waves beat against the walls of the narrow canal which runs through the island to the Hotel Excelsior. An automobile omnibus was awaiting his return there, and took him above the rippling sea straight to the beach hotel. The little manager with mustache and long-tailed frock-coat came down the stairs to meet him.

He ingratiatingly regretted the episode, spoke of it as highly painful to him and the establishment, but firmly approved of Aschenbach's decision to wait here for the baggage. Of course his room had been given up, but there was another one, just as good, which he could occupy immediately. *"Pas de chance, Monsieur,"* the Swiss elevator boy smiled as they were ascending. And so the fugitive was established again, in a room almost identical with the other in its location and furnishings.

Tired out by the confusion of this strange forenoon, he distributed the contents of his hand-bag about the room and dropped into an armchair by the open window. The sea had become a pale green, the air seemed thinner and purer; the beach with its cabins and boats, seemed to have color, although the sky was still gray. Aschenbach looked out, his hands folded in his lap; he was content to be back, but shook his head disapprovingly at his irresolution, his failure to know his own mind. He sat here for the better part of an hour, resting and dreaming vaguely. About noon he saw Tadzio in a striped linen suit with a red tie, coming back from the sea across the private beach and along the boardwalk to the hotel. Aschenbach recognized him from this altitude before he had actually set eyes on him; he was about to think some such words as "Well, Tadzio, there you are again!" but at the same moment he felt this careless greeting go dumb before the truth in his heart. He felt the exhilaration of his blood, a conflict of pain and pleasure, and he realized that it was Tadzio who had made it so difficult for him to leave.

He sat very still, entirely unobserved from this height, and looked within himself. His features were alert, his eyebrows raised, and an attentive, keenly inquisitive smile distended his mouth. Then he raised his head, lifted both hands, which had hung relaxed over the arms of

the chair, and in a slow twisting movement turned the palms upward —
as though to suggest an opening and spreading outward of his arms. It
was a spontaneous act of welcome, of calm acceptance.

IV

Day after day now the naked god with the hot cheeks drove his fire-
breathing quadriga across the expanses of the sky, and his yellow locks
fluttered in the assault of the east wind. A white silk sheen stretched
over the slowly simmering Ponto. The sand glowed. Beneath the quak-
ing silver blue of the ether, rust-colored canvases were spread in front
of the bathing-houses, and the afternoons were spent in the sharply de-
marcated spots of shade which they cast. But it was also delightful in
the evening, when the vegetation in the park had the smell of balsam,
and the stars were working through their courses above, and the soft
persistent murmur of the sea came up enchantingly through the night.
Such evenings contained the cheering promise that more sunny days
of casual idleness would follow, dotted with countless closely interspersed possibilities of well-timed accidents.

The guest who was detained here by such an accommodating
mishap did not consider the return of his property as sufficient grounds
for another departure. He suffered some inconvenience for two days,
and had to appear for meals in the large dining-room in his traveling-
clothes. When the strayed luggage was finally deposited in his room
again, he unpacked completely and filled the closet and drawers with
his belongings; he had decided to remain here indefinitely, content
now that he could pass the hours on the beach in a silk suit and appear
for dinner at his little table again in appropriate evening dress.

The comfortable rhythm of this life had already cast its spell over
him; he was soon enticed by the ease, the mild splendor, of his program. Indeed, what a place to be in, when the usual allurement of living in watering-places on southern shores was coupled with the immediate nearness of the most wonderful of all cities! Aschenbach was not
a lover of pleasure. Whenever there was some call for him to take a holiday, to indulge himself, to have a good time — and this was especially
true at an earlier age — restlessness and repugnance soon drove him
back to his rigorous toil, the faithful sober efforts of his daily routine.
Except that this place was bewitching him, relaxing his will, making
him happy. In the mornings, under the shelter of his bathing-house,
letting his eyes roam dreamily in the blue of the southern sea; or on a
warm night as he leaned back against the cushions of the gondola carrying him under the broad starry sky home to the Lido from the Piazza
di San Marco after long hours of idleness — and the brilliant lights, the

melting notes of the serenade were being left behind—he often recalled his place in the mountains, the scene of his battles in the summer, where the clouds blew low across his garden, and terrifying storms put out the lamps at night, and the crows which he fed were swinging in the tops of the pine-trees. Then everything seemed just right to him, as though he were lifted into the Elysian fields, on the borders of the earth, where man enjoys the easiest life, where there is no snow or winter, nor storms and pouring rains, but where Oceanus continually sends forth gentle cooling breezes, and the days pass in a blessed inactivity, without work, without effort, devoted wholly to the sun and to the feast-days of the sun.

Aschenbach saw the boy Tadzio frequently, almost constantly. Owing to the limited range of territory and the regularity of their lives, the beauty was near him at short intervals throughout the day. He saw him, met him, everywhere: in the lower rooms of the hotel, on the cooling water trips to the city and back, in the arcades of the square, and at times when he was especially lucky ran across him on the streets. But principally, and with the most gratifying regularity, the forenoon on the beach allowed him to admire and study this rare spectacle at his leisure. Yes, it was this guaranty of happiness, this daily recurrence of good fortune, which made his stay here so precious, and gave him such pleasure in the constant procession of sunny days.

He was up as early as he used to be when under the driving pressure of work, and was on the beach before most people, when the sun was still mild and the sea l ay blinding white in the dreaminess of morning. He spoke amiably to the guard of the private beach, and also spoke familiarly to the barefoot, white-bearded old man who had prepared his place for him, stretching the brown canopy and bringing the furniture of the cabin out on the platform. Then he took his seat. There would now be three or four hours in which the sun mounted and gained terrific strength, the sea a deeper and deeper blue, and he might look at Tadzio.

He saw him approaching from the left, along the edge of the sea; he saw him as he stepped out backwards from among the cabins; or he would suddenly find, with a shock of pleasure, that he had missed his coming, that he was already here in the blue and white bathing-suit which was his only garment now while on the beach, that he had already commenced his usual activities in the sun and the sand—a pleasantly trifling, idle, and unstable manner of living, a mixture of rest and play. Tadzio would saunter about, wade, dig, catch things, lie down, go for a swim, all the while being kept under surveillance by the women on the platform who made his name ring out in their falsetto voices: "Tadziu! Tadziu!" Then he would come running to them with a look of eagerness, to tell them what he had seen, what he had experienced, or to show them what he had found or caught: mussels, sea-horses, jelly-fish, and crabs that ran sideways. Aschenbach did not understand a word he said, and though it might have been the most ordinary thing in the world, it was a vague harmony in his ear. So the foreignness of the boy's speech turned it into music, a wanton sun poured its prodigal splendor down over him, and his figure was always set off against the background of an intense sea-blue.

This piquant body was so freely exhibited that his eyes soon knew every line and posture. He was continually rediscovering with new pleasure all this familiar beauty, and his astonishment at its delicate appeal to his senses was unending. The boy was called to greet a guest who was paying his respects to the ladies at the bathing-house. He came running, running wet perhaps out of the water, tossed back his curls, and as he held out his hand, resting on one leg and raising his other foot on the toes, the set of his body was delightful; it had a charming expectancy about it, a well-meaning shyness, a winsomeness which showed his aristocratic training. . . . He lay stretched full length, his bath towel slung across his shoulders, his delicately chiseled arm supported in the sand, his chin in his palm; the boy called Jaschu was squatting near him and making up to him—and nothing could be more enchanting than the smile of his eyes and lips when the leader glanced up at his inferior, his servant. . . . He stood on the edge of the sea, alone, apart from his people, quite near to Aschenbach—erect, his hands locked across the back of his neck, he swayed slowly on the balls of his feet, looked dreamily into the blueness of sea and sky, while tiny waves rolled up and bathed his feet. His honey-colored hair clung in rings about his neck and temples. The sun made the down on his back glitter; the fine etching of the ribs, the symmetry of the chest, were emphasized by the tightness of the suit across the buttocks. His armpits were still as smooth as those of a statue; the hollows of his knees glistened, and their bluish veins made his body seem built of some clearer stuff. What rigor, what precision of thought were expressed in this erect, youthfully perfect body! Yet the pure and strenuous will which, darkly at work, could bring such godlike sculpture to the light—was not he, the artist, familiar with this? Did it not operate in him too when he, under the press of frugal passions, would free from the marble mass of speech some slender form which he had seen in the mind and which he put before his fellows as a statue and a mirror of intellectual beauty?

Statue and mirror! His eyes took in the noble form there bordered with blue; and with a rush of enthusiasm he felt that in this spectacle he was catching the beautiful itself, form as the thought of God, the one pure perfection which lives in the mind, and which, in this symbol and likeness, had been placed here quietly and simply as an object of devotion. That was drunkenness; and eagerly, without thinking, the aging artist welcomed it. His mind was in travail; all that he had learned dropped back into flux; his understanding threw up age-old thoughts which he had inherited with youth though they had never before lived with their own fire. Is it not written that the sun diverts our attention from intellectual to sensual things? Reason and understanding, it is said, become so numbed and enchanted that the soul forgets everything out of delight with its immediate circumstances, and in astonishment becomes attached to the most beautiful object shined on by the sun; indeed, only with the aid of a body is it capable then of raising itself to higher considerations. To be sure, Amor did as the instructors of mathematics who show backward children tangible representations of the pure forms—similarly the god, in order to make the spiritual visible for us, readily utilized the form and color of man's youth, and as a reminder he adorned these with the reflected splendor of beauty which, when we behold it, makes us flare up in pain and hope.

His enthusiasm suggested these things, put him in the mood for them. And from the noise of the sea and the luster of the sun he wove himself a charming picture. Here was the old plane-tree, not far from the walls of Athens—a holy, shadowy place filled with the smell of *agnus castus* blossoms and decorated with ornament and images sacred to Achelous and the Nymphs. Clear and pure, the brook at the foot of the spreading tree fell across the smooth pebbles; the cicadas were fiddling. But on the grass, which was like a pillow gently sloping to the head, two people were stretched out, in hiding from the heat of the day: an older man and a youth, one ugly and one beautiful, wisdom next to loveliness. And amid gallantries and skillfully engaging banter, Socrates was instructing Phædrus in matters of desire and virtue. He spoke to him of the hot terror which the initiate suffer when their eyes light on an image of the eternal beauty; spoke of the greed of the impious and the wicked who cannot think beauty when they see its likeness, and who are incapable of reverence; spoke of the holy distress which befalls the noble-minded when a god-like countenance, a perfect body, appears before them; they tremble and grow distracted, and hardly dare to raise their eyes, and they honor the man who possesses this beauty, yes, if they were not afraid of being thought downright madmen they would sacrifice to the beloved as to the image of a god. For beauty, my Phædrus, beauty alone is both lovely and visible at once; it is, mark me, the only form of the spiritual which we can receive through the senses. Else what would become of us if the divine, if reason and virtue and truth, should appear to us through the senses? Should we not perish and be consumed with love, as Semele once was with Zeus? Thus, beauty is the sensitive man's access to the spirit—but only a road, a means simply, little Phædrus. . . . And then this crafty suitor made the neatest remark of all; it was this, that the lover is more divine than the beloved, since the god is in the one, but not in the other—perhaps the most delicate, the most derisive thought which has ever been framed, and the one from which spring all the cunning and the profoundest pleasures of desire.

Writers are happiest with an idea which can become all emotion, and an emotion all idea. Just such a pulsating idea, such a precise emotion, belonged to the lonely man at this moment, was at his call. Nature, it ran, shivers with ecstasy when the spirit bows in homage before beauty. Suddenly he wanted to write. Eros loves idleness, they say, and he is suited only to idleness. But at this point in the crisis the affliction became a stimulus towards productivity. The incentive hardly mattered. A request, an agitation for an open statement on a certain large burning issue of culture and taste, was going about the intellectual world, and had finally caught up with the traveler here. He was familiar with the subject, it had touched his own experience; and suddenly he felt an irresistible desire to display it in the light of his own version. And he even went so far as to prefer working in Tadzio's presence, taking the scope of the boy as a standard for his writing, making his style follow the lines of this body which seemed godlike to him, and carrying his beauty over into the spiritual just as the eagle once carried the Trojan stag up into the ether. Never had his joy in words been more sweet. He had never been so aware that Eros is in the word as during those perilously precious hours when, at his crude table under the canopy, facing the idol and listening to the music of his voice, he followed Tadzio's beauty in the forming of his little tract, a page and a half of choice prose which was soon to excite the admiration of many through its clarity, its poise, and the vigorous curve of its emotion. Certainly it is better for people to know only the beautiful product as finished, and not in its conception, its conditions of origin. For knowledge of the sources from which the artist derives his inspiration would often confuse and alienate, and in this way detract from the effects of his mastery. Strange hours! Strangely enervating efforts! Rare creative intercourse between the spirit and body! When Aschenbach put away his work and started back from the beach, he felt exhausted, or in dispersion even; and it was as though his conscience were complaining after some transgression.

The following morning, as he was about to leave the hotel, he looked off from the steps and noticed that Tadzio, who was alone and was already on his way towards the sea, was just approaching the private beach. He was half tempted by the simple notion of seizing this opportunity to strike up a casual friendly acquaintanceship with the boy who had been the unconscious source of so much agitation and upheaval; he wanted to address him, and enjoy the answering look in his eyes. The boy was sauntering along, he could be overtaken; and Aschenbach quickened his pace. He reached him on the boardwalk behind the bathing-houses; was about to lay a hand on his head and shoulders; and some word or other, an amiable phrase in French, was on the tip of his tongue. But he felt that his heart, due also perhaps to his rapid stride, was beating like a hammer; and he was so short of breath that his voice would have been tight and trembling. He hesitated, he tried to get himself under control. Suddenly he became afraid that he had been walking too long so close behind the boy. He was afraid of arousing curiosity and causing him to look back questioningly. He made one more spurt, failed, surrendered, and passed with bowed head.

"Too late!" he thought immediately. Too late! Yet was it too late? This step which he had just been on the verge of taking would very possibly have put things on a sound, free and easy basis, and would have restored him to wholesome soberness. But the fact was that Aschenbach did not want soberness: his intoxication was too precious. Who can explain the stamp and the nature of the artist? Who can understand this deep instinctive welding of discipline and license? For to be unable to want wholesome soberness, is license. Aschenbach was no longer given to self-criticism. His tastes, the mental caliber of his years, his self-respect, ripeness, and a belated simplicity made him unwilling to dismember his motives and to debate whether his impulses were the result of conscientiousness or of dissolution and weakness. He was embarrassed, as he feared that some one or other, if only the guard on the beach, must have observed his pursuit and defeat. He was very much afraid of the ridiculous. Further, he joked with himself about his comically pious distress. "Downed," he thought, "downed like a rooster, with his wings hanging miserably in the battle. It really is a god who can, at one sight of his loveliness, break our courage this way and force down our pride so thoroughly. . . ." He toyed and skirmished with his emotions, and was far too haughty to be afraid of them.

He had already ceased thinking about the time when the vacation period which he had fixed for himself would expire; the thought of going home never even suggested itself. He had sent for an ample supply of money. His only concern was with the possible departure of the Polish family; by a casual questioning of the hotel barber he had contrived to learn that these people had come here only a short time before his own arrival. The sun browned his face and hands, the invigorating salt breezes made him feel fresher. Once he had been in the habit of expending on his work every bit of nourishment which food, sleep, or nature could provide him; and similarly now he was generous and uneconomical, letting pass off as elation and emotion all the daily strengthening derived from the sun, idleness, and sea air.

His sleep was fitful; the preciously uniform days were separated by short nights of happy unrest. He did retire early, for at nine o'clock, when Tadzio had disappeared from the scene, the day seemed over. But at the first gray of dawn he was awakened by a gently insistent shock; he suddenly remembered his adventure, he could no longer remain in bed; he arose and, clad lightly against the chill of morning, he sat down by the open window to await the rising of the sun. Toned by his sleep, he watched this miraculous event with reverence. Sky, earth, and sea still lay in glassy, ghost-like twilight; a dying star still floated in the emptiness of space. But a breeze started up, a winged message from habitations beyond reach, telling that Eos was rising from beside her husband. And that first sweet reddening in the farthest stretches of sky and sea took place by which the sentiency of creation is announced. The goddess was approaching, the seductress of youth who stole Cleitus and Cephalus, and despite the envy of all the Olympians enjoyed the love of handsome Orion. A strewing of roses began there on the edge of the world, an unutterably pure glowing and blooming. Childish clouds, lighted and shined through, floated like busy little Cupids in the rosy, bluish mist. Purple fell upon the sea, which seemed to be simmering, and washing the color towards him. Golden spears shot up into the sky from behind. The splendor caught fire, silently; with godlike power an intense flame of licking tongues broke out—and with rattling hoofs the brother's sacred chargers mounted the horizon. Lighted by the god's brilliance, he sat there, keeping watch alone. He closed his eyes, letting this glory play against the lids. Past emotions, precious early afflictions and yearnings which had been stifled by his rigorous program of living, were now returning in such strange new forms. With an embarrassed, astonished smile, he recognized them. He was thinking, dreaming; slowly his lips formed a name. And still smiling, with his face turned upwards, hands folded in his lap, he fell asleep again in his chair.

But the day which began with such fiery solemnity underwent a strange mythical transformation. Where did the breeze originate which suddenly began playing so gently and insinuatingly, like some whispered suggestion, about his ears and temples? Little white choppy clouds stood in the sky in scattered clumps, like the pasturing herds of the gods. A stronger wind arose, and the steeds of Poseidon came prancing up, and along with them the steers which belonged to the blue-locked god, bellowing and lowering their horns as they ran. Yet among the detritus of the more distant beach, waves were hopping forward like agile goats. He was caught in the enchantment of a sacredly distorted world full of Panic life—and he dreamed delicate legends. Often, when the sun was sinking behind Venice, he would sit on a bench in the park observing Tadzio, who was dressed in a white suit with a colored sash and was playing ball on the smooth gravel—and it was Hyacinth that he seemed to be watching. Hyacinth who was to die because two gods loved him. Yes, he felt Zephyr's aching jealousy of the rival who forgot the oracle, the bow, and the lyre, in order to play for ever with this beauty. He saw the discus, guided by a pitiless envy, strike the lovely head; he too, growing pale, caught the drooping body—and the flower, sprung from this sweet blood, bore the inscription of his unending grief.

Nothing is more unusual and strained than the relationship between people who know each other only with their eyes, who meet daily, even hourly, and yet are compelled, by force of custom or their own caprices, to say no word or make no move of acknowledgment, but to maintain the appearance of an aloof unconcern. There is a restlessness and a surcharged curiosity existing between them, the hysteria of an unsatisfied, unnaturally repressed desire for acquaintanceship and intercourse; and especially there is a kind of tense respect. For one person loves and honors another so long as he cannot judge him, and desire is an evidence of incomplete knowledge.

Some kind of familiarity had necessarily to form itself between Aschenbach and young Tadzio; and it gave the elderly man keen pleasure to see that his sympathies and interests were not left completely unanswered. For example, when the boy appeared on the beach in the morning and was going towards his family's bathing-house, what had induced him never to use the boardwalk on the far side of it any more, but to stroll along the front path, through the sand, past Aschenbach's habitual place, and often unnecessarily close to him, almost touching his table, or his chair even? Did the attraction, the fascination of an overpowering emotion have such an effect upon the frail unthinking object of it? Aschenbach watched daily for Tadzio to approach; and sometimes he acted as though he were occupied when this event was taking place, and he let the boy pass unobserved. But at other times he would look up, and their glances met. They were both in deep earnest when this occurred. Nothing in the elderly man's cultivated and dignified expression betrayed any inner movement; but there was a searching look in Tadzio's eyes, a thoughtful questioning—he began to falter, looked down, then looked up again charmingly, and, when he had passed, something in his bearing seemed to indicate that it was only his breeding which kept him from turning around.

Once, however, one evening, things turned out differently. The Polish children and their governess had been missing at dinner in the large hall; Aschenbach had noted this uneasily. After the meal, disturbed by their absence, Aschenbach was walking in evening dress and straw hat in front of the hotel at the foot of the terrace, when suddenly he saw the nunlike sisters appear in the light of the arc-lamp, accompanied by their governess and with Tadzio a few steps behind. Evidently they were coming from the steamer pier after having dined for some reason in the city. It must have been cool on the water; Tadzio was wearing a dark blue sailor overcoat with gold buttons, and on his head he had a cap to match. The sun and sea air had not browned him; his skin still had the same yellow marble color as at first. It even seemed paler today than usual, whether from the coolness or from the blanching moonlight of the lamps. His regular eyebrows showed up more sharply, the darkness of his eyes was deeper. It is hard to say how beautiful he was; and Aschenbach was distressed, as he had often been before, by the thought that words can only evaluate sensuous beauty, but not re-give it.

He had not been prepared for this rich spectacle; it came unhoped for. He had no time to entrench himself behind an expression of repose and dignity. Pleasure, surprise, admiration must have shown on his face as his eyes met those of the boy—and at this moment it happened that Tadzio smiled, smiled to him, eloquently, familiarly, charmingly, without concealment; and during the smile his lips slowly opened. It was the smile of Narcissus bent over the reflecting water, that deep, fascinated, magnetic smile with which he stretches out his arms to the image of his own beauty—a smile distorted ever so little, distorted at the hopelessness of his efforts to kiss the pure lips of the shadow. It was coquettish, inquisitive, and slightly tortured. It was infatuated, and infatuating.

He had received this smile, and he hurried away as though he carried a fatal gift. He was so broken up that he was compelled to escape the light of the terrace and the front garden; he hastily hunted out the darkness of the park in the rear. Strangely indignant and tender admonitions wrung themselves out of him: "You dare not smile like that! Listen, no one dare smile like that to another!" He threw himself down on a bench; in a frenzy he breathed the night smell of the vegetation. And leaning back, his arms loose, overwhelmed, with frequent chills running through him, he whispered the fixed formula of desire—impossible in this case, absurd, abject, ridiculous, and yet holy, even in this case venerable: "I love you!"

V

During his fourth week at the Lido, Gustav von Aschenbach made several sinister observations touching on the world about him. First, it seemed to him that as the season progressed the number of guests at the hotel was diminishing rather than increasing; and German especially seemed to be dropping away, so that finally he heard nothing but foreign sounds at table and on the beach. Then one day in conversation with the barber, whom he visited often, he caught a word which startled him. The man had mentioned a German family that left soon after their arrival; he added glibly and flatteringly: "But you are staying, sir. You have no fear of the plague." Aschenbach looked at him. "The plague?" he repeated. The gossiper was silent, made out as though busy with other things, ignored the question. When it was put more insistently, he declared that he knew nothing, and with embarrassing volubility he tried to change the subject.

That was about noon. In the afternoon there was a calm, and Aschenbach rode to Venice under an intense sun. For he was driven by a mania to follow the Polish children whom he had seen with their governess taking the road to the steamer pier. He did not find the idol at San Marco. But while sitting over his tea at his little round iron table on the shady side of the square, he suddenly detected a peculiar odor in the air which, it seemed to him now, he had noticed for days without being consciously aware of it. The smell was sweetish and drug-like, suggesting sickness, and wounds, and a suspicious cleanliness. He tested and examined it thoughtfully, finished his luncheon, and left the square on the side opposite the church. The smell was stronger where the street narrowed. On the corners printed posters were hung, giving municipal warnings against certain diseases of the gastric system liable to occur at this season, against the eating of oysters and clams, and also against the water of the canals. The euphemistic nature of the announcement was palpable. Groups of people had collected in silence on the bridge and squares; and the foreigner stood among them, scenting and investigating.

At a little shop he inquired about the fatal smell, asking the proprietor, who was leaning against his door surrounded by coral chains and imitation amethyst jewelry. The man measured him with heavy eyes, and brightened up hastily. "A matter of precaution, sir!" he answered with a gesture. "A regulation of the police which must be taken for what it is worth. This weather is oppressive, the sirocco is not good for the health. In short, you understand—an exaggerated prudence perhaps." Aschenbach thanked him and went on. Also on the steamer back to the Lido he caught the smell of the disinfectant.

Returning to the hotel, he went immediately to the periodical stand in the lobby and ran through the papers. He found nothing in the foreign language press. The domestic press spoke of rumors, produced hazy statistics, repeated official denials and questioned their truthfulness. This explained the departure of the German and Austrian guests. Obviously, the subjects of the other nations knew nothing, suspected nothing, were not yet uneasy. "To keep it quiet!" Aschenbach thought angrily, as he threw the papers back on the table. "To keep that quiet!" But at the same moment he was filled with satisfaction over the adventure that was to befall the world about him. For passion, like crime, is not suited to the secure daily rounds of order and well-being; and every slackening in the *bourgeois* structure, every disorder and affliction of the world, must be held welcome, since they bring with them a vague promise of advantage. So Aschenbach felt a dark contentment with what was taking place, under cover of the authorities, in the dirty alleys of Venice. This wicked secret of the city was welded with his own secret, and he too was involved in keeping it hidden. For in his infatuation he cared about nothing but the possibility of Tadzio's leaving, and he realized with something like terror that he would not know how to go on living if this occurred.

Lately he had not been relying simply on good luck and the daily routine for his chances to be near the boy and look at him. He pursued him, stalked him. On Sundays, for instance, the Poles never appeared on the beach. He guessed that they must be attending mass at San Marco. He hurried there; and, stepping from the heat of the square into the golden twilight of the church, he found the boy he was hunting, bowed over a *prie-dieu*, praying. Then he stood in the background, on the cracked mosaic floor, with people on all sides kneeling, murmuring, and making the sign of the cross. And the compact grandeur of this oriental temple weighed heavily on his senses. In front, the richly ornamented priest was conducting the office, moving about and singing; incense poured forth, clouding the weak little flame of the candle on the altar—and with the sweet, stuffy sacrificial odor another seemed to commingle faintly: the smell of the infested city. But through the smoke and the sparkle Aschenbach saw how the boy there in front turned his head, hunted him out, and looked at him.

When the crowd was streaming out through the opened portals into the brilliant square with its swarms of pigeons, the lover hid in the vestibule; he kept under cover, he lay in wait. He saw the Poles quit the church, saw how the children took ceremonious leave of their mother, and how she turned towards the Piazzetta on her way home. He made sure that the boy, the nunlike sisters, and the governess took the road to the right through the gateway of the clock tower and into the Merceria.

And after giving them a slight start, he followed, followed them furtively on their walk through Venice. He had to stand still when they stopped, had to take flight in shops and courts to let them pass when they turned back. He lost them; hot and exhausted, he hunted them over bridges and down dirty blind-alleys—and he underwent minutes of deadly agony when suddenly he saw them coming towards him in a narrow passage where escape was impossible. Yet it could not be said that he suffered. He was drunk, and his steps followed the promptings of the demon who delights in treading human reason and dignity underfoot.

In one place Tadzio and his companions took a gondola; and shortly after they had pushed off from the shore, Aschenbach, who had hidden behind some structure, a well, while they were climbing in, now did the same. He spoke in a hurried undertone as he directed the rower, with the promise of a generous tip, to follow unnoticed and at a distance that gondola which was just rounding the corner. And he thrilled when the man, with the roguish willingness of an accomplice, assured him in the same tone that his wishes would be carried out, carried out faithfully.

Leaning back against the soft black cushions, he rocked and glided towards the other black-beaked craft where his passion was drawing him. At times it escaped; then he felt worried and uneasy. But his pilot, as though skilled in such commissions, was always able through sly maneuvers, speedy diagonals and shortcuts, to bring the quest into view again. The air was quiet and smelly, the sun burned down strong through the slate-colored mist. Water slapped against the wood and stone. The call of the gondolier, half warning, half greeting, was answered with a strange obedience far away in the silence of the labyrinth. White and purple umbels with the scent of almonds hung down from little elevated gardens over crumbling walls. Arabian window-casings were outlined through the murkiness. The marble steps of a church descended into the water; a beggar squatted there, protesting his misery, holding out his hat, and showing the whites of his eyes as though he were blind. An antiquarian in front of his den fawned on the passer-by and invited him to stop in the hopes of swindling him. That was Venice, the flatteringly and suspiciously beautiful—this city, half legend, half snare for strangers; in its foul air art once flourished gluttonously, and had suggested to its musicians seductive notes which cradle and lull. The adventurer felt as though his eyes were taking in this same luxury, as though his ears were being won by just such melodies. He recalled too that the city was diseased and was concealing this through greed—and he peered more eagerly after the retreating gondola.

Thus, in his infatuation, he wanted simply to pursue uninterrupted the object that aroused him, to dream of it when it was not there, and, after the fashion of lovers, to speak softly to its mere outline. Loneliness, strangeness, and the joy of a deep belated intoxication encouraged him and prompted him to accept even the remotest things without reserve or shame—with the result that as he returned late in the evening from Venice, he stopped on the second floor of the hotel before the door of the boy's room, laid his head in utter drunkenness against the hinge of the door, and for a long time could not drag himself away despite the danger of being caught and embarrassed in such a mad situation.

Yet there were still moments of relief when he came partly to his senses. "Where to!" he would think, alarmed. "Where to!" Like every man whose natural abilities stimulate an aristocratic interest in his ancestry, he was accustomed to think of his forebears in connection with the accomplishments and successes of his life, to assure himself of their approval, their satisfaction, their undeniable respect. He thought of them now, entangled as he was in such an illicit experience, caught in such exotic transgressions. He thought of their characteristic rigidity of principle, their scrupulous masculinity—and he smiled dejectedly. What would they say? But then, what would they have said to his whole life, which was almost degenerate in its departure from theirs, this life under the bane of art—a life against which he himself had once issued such youthful mockeries out of loyalty to his fathers, but which at bottom had been so much like theirs! He too had served, he too had been a soldier and a warrior like many of them—for art was a war, a destructive battle, and one was not equal to it for long, these days. A life of self-conquest and of in-spite-ofs, a rigid, sober, and unyielding life which he had formed into the symbol of a delicate and timely heroism. He might well call it masculine, or brave, and it almost seemed as though the Eros mastering him were somehow peculiarly adapted and inclined to such a life. Had not this Eros stood in high repute among the bravest of people; was it not true that precisely through bravery he had flourished in their cities? Numerous war heroes of antiquity had willingly borne his yoke, for nothing was deemed a disgrace which the god imposed; and acts which would have been rebuked as the sign of cowardice if they had been done for other purposes—prostrations, oaths, entreaties, abjectness—such things did not bring shame upon the lover, but rather he reaped praise for them.

In this way his infatuation determined the course of his thoughts, in this way he tried to uphold himself, to preserve his respect. But at the same time, selfish and calculating, he turned his attention to the unclean transactions here in Venice, this adventure of the outer world which conspired darkly with his own and which fed his passion with vague lawless hopes.

Bent on getting reliable news of the condition and progress of the pestilence, he ransacked the local papers in the city cafés, as they had been missing from the reading-table of the hotel lobby for several days now. Statements alternated with disavowals. The number of the sick and dead was supposed to reach twenty, forty, or even a hundred and more—and immediately afterwards every instance of the plague would be either flatly denied or attributed to completely isolated cases which had crept in from the outside. There were scattered admonitions, protests against the dangerous conduct of foreign authorities. Certainty was impossible. Nevertheless the lone man felt especially entitled to participate in the secret; and although he was excluded, he derived a grotesque satisfaction from putting embarrassing questions to those who did know, and, as they were pledged to silence, forcing them into deliberate lies. One day at breakfast in the large dining-hall he entered into a conversation with the manager, that softly-treading little man in the French frock-coat who was moving amiably and solicitously about among the diners and had stopped at Aschenbach's table for a few passing words. Just why, the guest asked negligently and casually, had disinfectants become so prevalent in Venice recently? "It has to do," was the evasive answer, "with a police regulation, and is intended to prevent any inconveniences or disturbances to the public health which might result from the exceptionally warm and threatening weather." . . . "The police are to be congratulated," Aschenbach answered; and after the exchange of a few remarks on the weather, the manager left.

Yet that same day, in the evening, after dinner, it happened that a little band of strolling singers from the city gave a performance in the front garden of the hotel. Two men and two women, they stood by the iron post of an arc-lamp and turned their whitened faces up towards the large terrace where the guests were enjoying this folk-recital over their coffee and cooling drinks. The hotel personnel, bellboys, waiters, and clerks from the office, could be seen listening by the doors of the vestibule. The Russian family, eager and precise in their amusements, had had wicker chairs placed in the garden in order to be nearer the performers; and they were sitting here in an appreciative semicircle. Behind the ladies and gentlemen, in her turban-like kerchief, stood the old slave.

Mandolin, guitar, harmonica, and a squeaky violin were responding to the touch of the virtuoso beggars. Instrumental numbers alternated with songs, as when the younger of the women, with a sharp trembling voice, joined with the sweetly falsetto tenor in a languishing love duet. But the real talent and leader of the group was undoubtedly the other

of the two men, the one with the guitar. He was a kind of *buffo* bari-
tone, with not much of a voice, although he did have a gift for pan-
tomime, and a remarkable comic energy. Often, with his large instrument under his arm, he would leave the rest of the group and, still acting, would intrude on the platform, where his antics were rewarded
with encouraging laughter. Especially the Russians in their seats down
front seemed to be enchanted with so much southern mobility, and
their applause incited him to let himself out more and more boldly and
assertively.

Aschenbach sat on the balustrade, cooling his lips now and then
with a mixture of pomegranate juice and soda which glowed ruby-red
in his glass in front of him. His nerves took in the miserable notes, the
vulgar crooning melodies; for passion lames the sense of discrimina-
tion, and surrenders in all seriousness to appeals which, in sober moments, are either humorously allowed for or rejected with annoyance.
At the clown's antics his features had twisted into a set painful smile.
He sat there relaxed, although inwardly he was intensely awake; for six
paces from him Tadzio was leaning against the stone hand-rail.

In the white belted coat which he often wore at meal times, he was
standing in a position of spontaneous and inborn gracefulness, his left
forearm on the railing, feet crossed, the right hand on a supporting hip;
and he looked down at the street-singers with an expression which was
hardly a smile, but only an aloof curiosity, a polite amiability. Often he
would stand erect and, expanding his chest, would draw the white
smock down under his leather belt with a beautiful gesture. And then
too, the aging man observed with a tumult of fright and triumph how
he would often turn his head over the left shoulder in the direction of
his admirer, carefully and hesitatingly, or even with abruptness as
though to attack by surprise. He did not meet Aschenbach's eyes, for a
mean precaution compelled the transgressor to keep from staring at
him: in the background of the terrace the women who guarded Tadzio
were sitting, and things had reached a point where the lover had to fear
he might be noticed and suspected. Yes, he had often observed with a
kind of numbness how, when Tadzio was near him, on the beach, in
the hotel lobby, in the Piazza San Marco, they called him back, they
were set on keeping him at a distance—and this wounded him frightfully, causing his pride unknown tortures which his conscience would
not permit him to evade.

Meanwhile the guitar-player had begun a solo to his own accompaniment, a street-ballad popular throughout Italy. It had several stro-
phes, and the entire company joined each time in the refrain, all
singing and playing, while he managed to give a plastic and dramatic
twist to the performance. Of slight build, with thin and impoverished

features, he stood on the gravel, apart from his companions, in an attitude of insolent bravado, his shabby felt hat on the back of his head so that a bunch of his red hair jutted out from under the brim. And to the thrumming of the strings he flung his jokes up at the terrace in a penetrating recitative; while the veins were swelling on his forehead from the exertion of his performance. He did not seem of Venetian stock, but rather of the race of Neapolitan comedians, half pimp, half entertainer, brutal and audacious, dangerous and amusing. His song was stupid enough so far as the words went; but in his mouth, by his gestures, the movements of his body, his way of blinking significantly and letting the tongue play across his lips, it acquired something ambiguous, something vaguely repulsive. In addition to the customary civilian dress, he was wearing a sport shirt; and his skinny neck protruded above the soft collar, baring a noticeably large and active Adam's-apple. He was pale and snub-nosed. It was hard to fix an age to his beardless features, which seemed furrowed with grimaces and depravity; and the two wrinkles standing arrogantly, harshly, almost savagely between his reddish eyebrows were strangely suited to the smirk on his mobile lips. Yet what really prompted the lonely man to pay him keen attention was the observation that the questionable figure seemed also to provide its own questionable atmosphere. For each time they came to the refrain the singer, amid buffoonery and familiar handshakes, began a grotesque circular march which brought him immediately beneath Aschenbach's place; and each time this happened there blew up to the terrace from his clothes and body a strong carbolic smell.

After the song was ended, he began collecting money. He started with the Russians, who were evidently willing to spend, and then came up the stairs. Up here he showed himself just as humble as he had been bold during the performance. Cringing and bowing, he stole about among the tables, and a smile of obsequious cunning exposed his strong teeth, while the two wrinkles still stood ominously between his red eyebrows. This singular character collecting money to live on— they eyed him with a curiosity and a kind of repugnance, they tossed coins into his felt hat with the tips of their fingers, and were careful not to touch him. The elimination of the physical distance between the comedian and the audience, no matter how great the enjoyment may have been, always causes a certain uneasiness. He felt it, and tried to excuse it by groveling. He came up to Aschenbach, and along with him the smell, which no one else seemed concerned about.

"Listen!" the recluse said in an undertone, almost mechanically. "They are disinfecting Venice. Why?" The jester answered hoarsely: "On account of the police. That is a precaution, sir, with such heat, and the sirocco. The sirocco is oppressive. It is not good for the health."

He spoke as though astonished that any one could ask such things and demonstrated with his open hand how oppressive the sirocco was. "Then there is no plague in Venice?" Aschenbach asked quietly, between his teeth. The clown's muscular features fell into a grimace of comical embarrassment. "A plague? What kind of plague? Perhaps our police are a plague? You like to joke! A plague! Of all things! A precautionary measure, you understand! A police regulation against the effects of the oppressive weather." He gesticulated. "Very well," Aschenbach said several times curtly and quietly; and he quickly dropped an unduly large coin into the hat. Then with his eyes he signaled the man to leave. He obeyed, smirking and bowing. But he had not reached the stairs before two hotel employees threw themselves upon him, and with their faces close to his began a whispered cross-examination. He shrugged his shoulders; he gave assurances, he swore that he had kept quiet—that was evident. He was released, and he returned to the garden; then, after a short conference with his companions, he stepped out once more for a final song of thanks and leave-taking.

It was a rousing song which the recluse never recalled having heard before, a "big number" in incomprehensible dialect, with a laugh refrain in which the troupe joined regularly at the tops of their voices. At this point both the words and the accompaniment of the instruments stopped, with nothing left but a laugh which was somehow arranged rhythmically although very naturally done—and the soloist especially showed great talent in giving it a most deceptive vitality. At the renewal of his professional distance from the audience, he recovered all his boldness again, and the artificial laugh that he directed up towards the terrace was derisive. Even before the end of the articulate portion of the strophe, he seemed to struggle against an irresistible tickling. He gulped, his voice trembled, he pressed his hand over his mouth, he contorted his shoulders; and at the proper moment the ungovernable laugh broke out of him, burst into such real cackles that it was infectious and communicated itself to the audience, so that on the terrace also an unfounded hilarity, living off itself alone, started up. But this seemed to double the singer's exuberance. He bent his knees, he slapped his thighs, he nearly split himself; he no longer laughed, he shrieked. He pointed up with his finger, as though nothing were more comic than the laughing guests there, and finally every one in the garden and on the veranda was laughing, even to the waiters, bellboys, and house-servants in the doorways.

Aschenbach was no longer resting in his chair; he sat upright, as if attempting to defend himself, or to escape. But the laughter, the whiffs of the hospital smell, and the boy's nearness combined to put him into a trance that held his mind and his senses hopelessly captive. In the general movement and distraction he ventured to glance across at Tadzio, and as he did so he dared observe that the boy, in reply to his glance, was equally serious, much as though he had modeled his conduct and expression after those of one man, and the prevalent mood had no effect on him since this one man was not part of it. This portentous childish obedience had something so disarming and overpowering about it that the gray-haired man could hardly restrain himself from burying his face in his hands. It had also seemed to him that Tadzio's occasional stretching and quick breathing indicated a complaint, a congestion, of the lungs. "He is sickly, he will probably not grow old," he thought repeatedly with that positiveness which is often a peculiar relief to desire and passion. And along with pure solicitude he had a feeling of rakish gratification.

Meanwhile the Venetians had ended and were leaving. Applause accompanied them, and their leader did not miss the opportunity to cover his retreat with further jests. His bows, the kisses he blew, were laughed at—and so he doubled them. When his companions were already gone, he acted as though he had hurt himself by backing into a lamppost, and he crept through the gate seemingly crippled with pain. Then he suddenly threw off the mask of comic hard luck, stood upright, hurried away jauntily, stuck out his tongue insolently at the guests on the terrace, and slipped into the darkness. The company was breaking up; Tadzio had been missing from the balustrade for some time. But, to the displeasure of the waiters, the lonely man sat for a long while over the remains of his pomegranate drink. Night advanced. Time was crumbling. In the house of his parents many years back there had been an hourglass—of a sudden he saw the fragile and expressive instrument again, as though it were standing in front of him. Fine and noiseless the rust-red sand was running through the glass neck; and since it was getting low in the upper half, a speedy little vortex had been formed there.

As early as the following day, in the afternoon, he had made new progress in his obstinate baiting of the people he met—and this time he had all possible success. He walked from the Piazza of St. Mark's into the English traveling-bureau located there; and after changing some money at the cash desk, he put on the expression of a distrustful foreigner and launched his fatal question at the attendant clerk. He was a Britisher; he wore a woolen suit, and was still young, with close-set eyes, and had that characteristic stolid reliability which is so peculiarly and strikingly appealing in the tricky, nimble-witted South. He began: "No reason for alarm, sir. A regulation without any serious significance. Such measures are often taken to anticipate the unhealthy effects of the heat and the sirocco . . ." But as he raised his blue eyes, he met the stare of the foreigner, a tired and somewhat unhappy stare focused on his lips with a touch of scorn. Then the Englishman blushed. "At least," he continued in an emotional undertone, "that is the official explanation which people here are content to accept. I will admit that there is something more behind it." And then in his frank and leisurely manner he told the truth.

For several years now Indian cholera had shown a heightened tendency to spread and migrate. Hatched in the warm swamps of the Ganges delta, rising with the noxious breath of that luxuriant, unfit primitive world and island wilderness which is shunned by humans and where the tiger crouches in the bamboo thickets, the plague had raged continuously and with unusual strength in Hindustan, had reached eastwards to China, westward to Afghanistan and Persia, and, following the chief caravan routes, had carried its terrors to Astrachan, and even to Moscow. But while Europe was trembling lest the specter continue its advance from there across the country, it had been transported over the sea by Syrian merchantmen, and had turned up almost simultaneously in several Mediterranean ports, had raised its head in Toulon and Malaga, had showed its mask several times in Palermo and Naples, and seemed permanently entrenched through Calabria and Apulia. The north of the peninsula had been spared. Yet in the middle of this May in Venice the frightful vibrions were found on one and the same day in the blackish wasted bodies of a cabin boy and a woman who sold green-groceries. The cases were kept secret. But within a week there were ten, twenty, thirty more, and in various sections. A man from the Austrian provinces who had made a pleasure trip to Venice for a few days, returned to his home town and died with unmistakable symptoms—and that is how the first reports of the pestilence in the lagoon city got into the German newspapers. The Venetian authorities answered that the city's health conditions had never been better, and took the most necessary preventive measures. But probably the food supply had been infected. Denied and glossed over, death was eating its way along the narrow streets, and its dissemination was especially favored by the premature summer heat which made the water of the canals lukewarm. Yes, it seemed as though the plague had got renewed strength, as though the tenacity and fruitfulness of its stimuli had doubled. Cases of recovery were rare. Out of a hundred attacks, eighty were fatal, and in the most horrible manner. For the plague moved with utter savagery, and often showed that most dangerous form which is called "the drying." Water from the blood vessels collected in pockets, and the blood was unable to carry this off. Within a few hours the victim was parched, his blood became as thick as glue, and he stifled amid cramps and hoarse groans. Lucky for him if, as sometimes happened, the attack took the form of a light discomfiture followed by a profound coma from which he seldom or never awakened. At the beginning of June the pest-house of the Ospedale Civico had quietly filled; there was not much room left in the two orphan asylums, and a frightfully active commerce was kept up between the wharf of the Fondamenta Nuove and San Michele, the burial island. But there was the fear of a general drop in prosperity. The recently opened art exhibit in the public gardens was to be considered, along with the heavy losses which, in case of panic or unfavorable rumors, would threaten business, the hotels, and entire elaborate system for exploiting foreigners—and as these considerations evidently carried more weight than love of truth or respect for international agreements, the city authorities upheld obstinately their policy of silence and denial. The chief health officer had resigned from his post in indignation, and been promptly replaced by a more tractable personality. The people knew this; and the corruption of their superiors, together with the predominating insecurity, the exceptional condition into which the prevalence of death had plunged the city, induced a certain demoralization of the lower classes, encouraging shady and antisocial impulses which manifested themselves in license, profligacy, and a rising crime wave. Contrary to custom, many drunkards were seen in the evenings; it was said that at night nasty mobs made the streets unsafe. Burglaries and even murders became frequent, for it had already been proved on two occasions that persons who had presumably fallen victim to the plague had in reality been dispatched with poison by their own relatives. And professional debauchery assumed abnormal obtrusive proportions such as had never been known here before, and to an extent which is usually found only in the southern parts of the country and in the Orient.

The Englishman pronounced the final verdict on these facts. "You would do well," he concluded, "to leave to-day rather than tomorrow. It cannot be much more than a couple of days before a quarantine zone is declared." "Thank you," Aschenbach said; and left the office.

The square lay sunless and stifling. Unsuspecting foreigners sat in front of the cafés or stood among the pigeons in front of the church and watched the swarms of birds flapping their wings, crowding one another, and pecking at grains of corn offered them in open palms. The recluse was feverishly excited, triumphant in his possession of the truth. But it had left him with a bad taste in his mouth, and a weird horror in his heart. As he walked up and down the flagstones of the gorgeous court, he was weighing an action which would meet the situation and would absolve him. This evening after dinner he could approach the woman with the pearls and make her a speech; he had figured it out word for word: "Permit a foreigner, madam, to give you some useful advice, a warning, which is being withheld from you through self-interest. Leave immediately with Tadzio and your daughters! Venice is full of the plague." Then he could lay a farewell hand on the head of this tool of a mocking divinity, turn away, and flee this morass. But he felt at the same time that he was very far from seriously desiring such a move. He would retract it, would disengage himself from it. . . . But when we are distracted we loathe most the thought of retracing our steps. He recalled a white building, ornamented with inscriptions which glistened in the evening ånd in whose transparent mysticism his mind's eye had lost itself—and then that strange wanderer's form which had awakened in the aging man the roving hankerings of youth after the foreign and the remote. And the thought of return, the thought of prudence and soberness, effort, mastery, disgusted him to such an extent that his face was distorted with an expression of physical nausea. "It must be kept silent!" he whispered heavily. And: "I will keep silent!" The consciousness of his share in the facts and the guilt intoxicated him, much as a little wine intoxicates a tired brain. The picture of the diseased and neglected city hovering desolately before him aroused vague hopes beyond the bounds of reason, but with an egregious sweetness. What was the scant happiness he had dreamed of a moment ago, compared with these expectations? What were art and virtue worth to him, over against the advantages of chaos? He kept silent, and remained in Venice.

This same night he had a frightful dream, if one can designate as a dream a bodily and mental experience which occurred to him in the deepest sleep, completely independent of him, and with a physical realness, although he never saw himself present or moving about among the incidents; but their stage rather was his soul itself, and they broke in from without, trampling down his resistance—a profound and spiritual resistance—by sheer force; and when they had passed through, they left his substance, the culture of his lifetime, crushed and annihilated behind them.

It began with anguish, anguish and desire, and a frightened curiosity as to what was coming. It was night, and his senses were on the watch. From far off a grumble, an uproar, was approaching, a jumble of noises. Clanking, blaring, and dull thunder, with shrill shouts and a definite whine in a long-drawn-out u-sound—all this was sweetly, ominously interspersed and dominated by the deep cooing of wickedly persistent flutes which charmed the bowels in a shamelessly penetrative manner. But he knew one word; it was veiled, and yet would name what was approaching: "The foreign god!" Vaporous fire began to glow; then he recognized mountains like those about his summerhouse. And in the scattered light, from high up in the woods, among tree-trunks and crumbling moss-grown rocks—people, beasts, a throng, a raging mob plunged twisting and whirling downwards, and made the hill swarm with bodies, flames, tumult, and a riotous round dance. Women, tripped by overlong fur draperies which hung from their waists, were holding up tambourines and beating on them, their groaning heads flung back. Others swung sparking firebrands and bare daggers, or wore hissing snakes about the middle of their bodies, or shrieking held their breasts in their two hands. Men with horns on their foreheads, shaggy-haired, girded with hides, bent back their necks and raised their arms and thighs, clashed brass cymbals and beat furiously at kettledrums, while smooth boys prodded he-goats with wreathed sticks, climbing on their horns and falling off with shouts when they bounded. And the bacchantes wailed the word with the soft consonants and the drawn-out *u*-sound, at once sweet and savage, like nothing ever heard before. In one place it rang out as though piped into the air by stags, and it was echoed in another by many voices, in wild triumph—with it they incited one another to dance and to fling out their arms and legs, and it was never silent. But everything was pierced and dominated by the deep coaxing flute. He who was fighting against this experience—did it not coax him too with its shameless penetration, into the feast and the excesses of the extreme sacrifice? His repugnance, his fear, were keen—he was honorably set on defending himself to the very last against the barbarian, the foe to intellectual poise and dignity. But the noise, the howling, multiplied by the resonant walls of the hills, grew, took the upper hand, swelled to a fury of rapture. Odors oppressed the senses, the pungent smell of the bucks, the scent of moist bodies, and a waft of stagnant water, with another smell, something familiar, the smell of wounds and prevalent disease. At the beating of the drum his heart fluttered, his head was spinning, he was caught in a frenzy, in a blinding deafening lewdness—and he yearned to join the ranks of the god. The obscene symbol, huge, wooden, was uncovered and raised up; then they howled the magic word with more abandon. Foaming at the mouth, they raged, teased one another with ruttish gestures and caressing hands; laughing and groaning, they stuck the goads into one another's flesh and licked the blood from their limbs. But the dreamer now was with them, in them, and he belonged to the foreign god. Yes, they were he himself, as they hurled themselves biting and tearing upon the animals, got entangled in steaming rags, and fell in promiscuous unions on the torn moss, in sacrifice to their god. And his soul tasted the unchastity and fury of decay.

When he awakened from the affliction of this dream he was unnerved, shattered, and hopelessly under the power of the demon. He no longer avoided the inquisitive glances of other people; he did not care if he was exciting their suspicions. And as a matter of fact they were fleeing, traveling elsewhere. Numerous bathing-houses stood empty, the occupants of the dining-hall became more and more scattered, and in the city now one rarely saw a foreigner. The truth seemed to have leaked out; the panic, despite the reticence of those whose interests were involved, seemed no longer avoidable. But the woman with the pearls remained with her family, either because the rumors had not yet reached her, or because she was too proud and fearless to heed them. Tadzio remained. And to Aschenbach, in his infatuation, it seemed at times as though flight and death might remove all the disturbing elements of life around them, and he stay here alone with the boy. Yes, by the sea in the forenoon when his eyes rested heavily, irresponsibly, unwaveringly on the thing he coveted, or when, as the day was ending, he followed shamelessly after him through streets where the hideous death lurked in secret—at such times the atrocious seemed to him rich in possibilities, and laws of morality had dropped away.

Like any lover, he wanted to please; and he felt a bitter anguish lest it might not be possible. He added bright youthful details to his dress, he put on jewels, and used perfumes. During the day he often spent much time over his toilet, and came to the table strikingly dressed, excited, and in suspense. In the light of the sweet youthfulness which had done this to him, he detested his aging body. The sight of his gray hair, his sharp features, plunged him into shame and hopelessness. It induced him to attempt rejuvenating his body and appearance. He often visited the hotel barber.

Beneath the barber's apron, leaning back in the chair under the gossiper's expert hands, he winced to observe his reflection in the mirror.

"Gray," he said, making a wry face.

"A little," the man answered. "Due entirely to a slight neglect, an indifference to outward things, which is conceivable in people of importance, but it is not exactly praiseworthy. And all the less so since such persons are above prejudice in matters of nature or art. If the moral objections of certain people to the art of cosmetics were to be logically extended to the care of the teeth, they would give no slight offense. And after all, we are just as old as we feel, and under some circumstances gray hair would actually stand for more of an untruth than the despised correction. In your case, sir, you are entitled to the natural color of your hair. Will you permit me simply to return what belongs to you?"

"How is that?" Aschenbach asked.

Then the orator washed his client's hair with two kinds of water, one clear and one dark, and it was as black as in youth. Following this, he curled it with irons into soft waves, stepped back, and eyed his work.

"All that is left now," he said, "would be to freshen up the skin a little."

And like some one who cannot finish, cannot satisfy himself, he passed with quickening energy from one manipulation to another. Aschenbach rested comfortably, incapable of resistance, or rather his hopes aroused by what was taking place. In the glass he saw his brows arch more evenly and decisively. His eyes became longer; their brilliance was heightened by a light touching-up of the lids. A little lower, where the skin had been a leatherish brown, he saw a delicate crimson tint grow beneath a deft application of color. His lips, bloodless a little while past, became full, and as red as raspberries. The furrows in the cheeks and about the mouth, the wrinkles of the eyes, disappeared beneath lotions and cream. With a knocking heart he beheld a blossoming youth. Finally the beauty specialist declared himself content, after the manner of such people, by obsequiously thanking the man he had been serving. "A trifling assistance," he said, as he applied one parting touch. "Now the gentleman can fall in love unhesitatingly." He walked away, fascinated; he was happy as in a dream, timid and bewildered. His necktie was red, his broad-brimmed straw hat was trimmed with a variegated band.

A tepid storm wind had risen. It was raining sparsely and at intervals, but the air was damp, thick, and filled with the smell of things rotting. All around him he heard a fluttering, pattering, and swishing; and under the fever of his cosmetics it seemed to him as though evil wind-spirits were haunting the place, impure sea-birds which rooted and gnawed at the food of the condemned and befouled it with their droppings. For the sultriness destroyed his appetite, and the fancy suggested itself that the foods were poisoned with contaminating substances. Tracking the boy one afternoon, Aschenbach had plunged deep into the tangled center of the diseased city. He was becoming uncertain of where he was, since the alleys, waterways, bridges, and little squares of the labyrinth were all so much alike, and he was no longer even sure of directions. He was absorbed with the problem of keeping the pursued figure in sight. And, driven to disgraceful subterfuges, flattening himself against walls, hiding behind the backs of other people, for a long time he did not notice the weariness, the exhaustion, with which emotion and the continual suspense had taxed his mind and his body. Tadzio walked behind his companions. He always allowed the governess and the nunlike sisters to precede him in the narrow places; and, loitering behind alone, he would turn his head occasionally to look over his shoulder and make sure by a glance of his peculiarly dark-gray eyes that his admirer was following. He saw him, and did not betray him. Drunk with the knowledge of this, lured forward by those eyes, led meekly by his passion, the lover stole after his unseemly hope—but finally he was cheated and lost sight of him. The Poles had crossed a short arching bridge; the height of the curve hid them from the pursuer, and when he himself had arrived there he no longer saw them. He hunted for them vainly in three directions, straight ahead and to either side along the narrow dirty wharf. In the end he was so tired and unnerved that he had to give up the search.

His head was on fire, his body was covered with a sticky sweat, his knees trembled. He could no longer endure the thirst that was torturing him, and he looked around for some immediate relief. From a little vegetable store he bought some fruit—strawberries, soft and overly ripe—and he ate them as he walked. A very charming, forsaken little square opened up before him. He recognized it; here he had made his frustrated plans for flight weeks ago. He let himself sink down on the steps of the cistern in the middle of the square, and laid his head against the stone cylinder. It was quiet; grass was growing up through the pavement; refuse was scattered about. Among the weatherbeaten, unusually tall houses surrounding him there was one like a palace, with little lion-covered balconies, and Gothic windows with blank emptiness behind them. On the ground floor of another house was a drug store. Warm gusts of wind occasionally carried the smell of carbolic acid.

He sat there, he, the master, the artist of dignity, the author of "The Wretch," a work which had, in such accurate symbols, denounced vagabondage and the depths of misery, had denied all sympathy with the engulfed, and had cast out the outcast; the man who had arrived and, victor over his own knowledge, had outgrown all irony and acclimatized himself to the obligations of public confidence; whose reputation was official, whose name had been knighted, and on whose style boys were urged to pattern themselves—he sat there. His eyelids were shut; only now and then a mocking uneasy side-glance slipped out from beneath them. And his loose lips, set off by the cosmetics, formed isolated words of the strange dream-logic created by his half-slumbering brain.

"For beauty, Phædrus, mark me, beauty alone is both divine and visible at once; and thus it is the road of the sensuous; it is, little Phædrus, the road of the artist to the spiritual. But do you now believe, my dear, that they can ever attain wisdom and true human dignity for whom the road to the spiritual leads through the senses? Or do you believe rather (I leave the choice to you) that this is a pleasant but perilous road, a really wrong and sinful road, which necessarily leads astray? For you must know that we poets cannot take the road of beauty without having Eros join us and set himself up as our leader. Indeed, we may even be heroes after our fashion, and hardened warriors, though we be like women, for passion is our exaltation, and our desire must remain love—that is our pleasure and our disgrace. You now see, do you not, that we poets cannot be wise and dignified? That we necessarily go astray, necessarily remain lascivious, and adventurers in emotion? The mastery of our style is all lies and foolishness, our renown and honor are a farce, the confidence of the masses in us is highly ridiculous, and the training of the public and of youth through art is a precarious undertaking which should be forbidden. For how, indeed, could he be a fit instructor who is born with a natural leaning towards the precipice? We might well disavow it and reach after dignity, but wherever we turn it attracts us. Let us, say, renounce the dissolvent of knowledge, since knowledge, Phædrus, has no dignity or strength. It is aware, it understands and pardons, but without reserve and form. It feels sympathy with the precipice, it *is* the precipice. This then, we abandon with firmness, and from now on our efforts matter only by their yield of beauty, or, in other words, simplicity, greatness, and new rigor, form, and a second type of openness. But form and openness, Phædrus, lead to intoxication and to desire, lead the noble perhaps into sinister revels of emotion which his own beautiful rigor rejects as infamous, lead to the precipice—yes, they too lead to the precipice. They lead us poets there, I say, since we cannot force ourselves, since we can merely let ourselves out. And now I am going, Phædrus. You stay here; and when you no longer see me, then you go too."

A few days later, as Gustav von Aschenbach was not feeling well, he left the beach hotel at a later hour in the morning than usual. He had to fight against certain attacks of vertigo which were only partially physical and were accompanied by a pronounced malaise, a feeling of bafflement and hopelessness—while he was not certain whether this had to do with conditions outside him or with his own nature. In the lobby he noticed a large pile of luggage ready for shipment; he asked the doorkeeper who it was that was leaving, and heard in answer the Polish title which he had learned secretly. He accepted this without any alteration of his sunken features, with that curt elevation of the head by which one acknowledges something he does not need to know. Then he asked: "When?" The answer was: "After lunch." He nodded, and went to the beach.

It was not very inviting. Rippling patches of rain retreated across the wide flat water separating the beach from the first long sandbank. An air of autumn, of things past their prime, seemed to lie over the pleasure spot which had once been so alive with color and was now almost abandoned. The sand was no longer kept clean. A camera, seemingly without an owner, stood on its tripod by the edge of the sea; and a black cloth thrown over it was flapping noisily in the wind.

Tadzio, with the three or four companions still left, was moving about to the right in front of his family's cabin. And midway between the sea and the row of bathing-houses, lying back in his chair with a robe over his knees, Aschenbach looked at him once more. The game, which was not being supervised since the women were probably occupied with preparations for the journey, seemed to have no rules, and it was degenerating. The stocky boy with the sleek black hair who was called Jaschu had been angered and blinded by sand flung in his face. He forced Tadzio into a wrestling match which quickly ended in the fall of the beauty, who was weaker. But as though, in the hour of parting, the servile feelings of the inferior had turned to merciless brutality and were trying to get vengeance for a long period of slavery, the victor did not let go of the boy underneath, but knelt on his back and pressed his face so persistently into the sand that Tadzio, already breathless from the struggle, was in danger of strangling. His attempts to shake off the weight were fitful; for moments they stopped entirely and were resumed again as mere twitchings. Enraged, Aschenbach was about to spring to the rescue, when the torturer finally released his victim. Tadzio, very pale, raised himself halfway and sat motionless for several minutes, resting on one arm with rumpled hair and glowering eyes. Then he stood up completely, and moved slowly away. They called him, cheerfully at first, then anxiously and imploringly; he did not listen. The swarthy boy, who seemed to regret his excesses immediately afterwards, caught up with him and tried to placate him. A movement of the shoulder put him at his distance. Tadzio went down obliquely to the water. He was barefoot, and wore his striped linen suit with the red bow. He lingered on the edge of the water with his head down, drawing figures in the wet sand with one toe; then he went into the shallows, which did not cover his knees in the deepest place, crossed them leisurely, and arrived at the sandbank. He stood there a moment, his face turned to the open sea; soon after, he began stepping slowly to the left along the narrow stretch of exposed ground. Separated from the mainland by the expanse of water, separated from his companions by a proud moodiness, he moved along, a strongly isolated and unrelated figure with fluttering hair—placed out there in the sea, the wind, against the vague mists. He stopped once more to look around. And suddenly, as though at some recollection, some impulse, with one hand on his hip he turned the upper part of his body in a beautiful twist which began from the base—and he looked over his shoulder towards the shore. The watcher sat there, as he had sat once before when for the first time those twilight-gray eyes had turned at the doorway and met his own. His head, against the back of the chair, had slowly followed the movements of the boy walking yonder. Now, simultaneously with this glance it rose and sank on his breast, so that his eyes looked out from underneath, while his face took on the loose, inwardly relaxed expression of deep sleep. But it seemed to him as though the pale and lovely lure out there were smiling to him, nodding to him; as though, removing his hand from his hip, he were signaling to come out, were vaguely guiding towards egregious promises. And, as often before, he stood up to follow him.

Some minutes passed before any one hurried to the aid of the man who had collapsed into one corner of his chair. He was brought to his room. And on the same day a respectfully shocked world received the news of his death.

FLAGMAN THIEL

Gerhart Hauptmann

I

EVERY SUNDAY Thiel, the flagman, was to be seen sitting in a pew in the church at Neu Zittau. If he was absent, you might be sure he was on Sunday duty or else—as happened twice in the course of ten years—at home ill in bed. Once a great lump of coal from the tender of a passing locomotive had struck his leg and sent him rolling into the ditch at the bottom of the embankment. The second time the trouble was a wine bottle that had come flying from an express and had hit him in the middle of his chest. Nothing but these two mishaps had ever succeeded in keeping Thiel from church the instant he was off duty.

The first five years he had had to come alone to Neu Zittau from Schön-Schornstein, a small collection of homes on the Spree. Then, one fine day, he appeared in the company of a delicate, sickly looking woman. The people thought she ill suited his herculean build. And on a later Sunday afternoon, at the altar of the church, he solemnly gave her his hand and pledged his troth.

So, for two years, the delicate young creature sat beside him in the pew. For two years her fine, hollow-cheeked face bent over the ancient hymnal beside his weather-tanned face.

And suddenly the flagman was to be seen sitting alone, as of old.

On one of the preceding weekdays the bell had tolled for the dead. That was all.

Scarcely any change, so the people declared, was to be observed in the flagman. The brass buttons of his clean Sunday uniform were as brightly polished as before, his red hair as sleekly pomaded and as neatly parted, military fashion. Only he held his broad, hairy neck a little bent, and sang more eagerly, and listened to the sermon more devoutly. The general opinion was that his wife's death had not hit him very hard. A view that was strengthened when in the course of the year he married again. The second wife was a strong, stout milkmaid from Altegrund.

Even the pastor felt free to express his doubts when Thiel came to announce his engagement.

"So soon again? You really want to marry so soon again?"

"I can't keep my house running, sir, with the wife who's gone."

"To be sure. But I mean—aren't you in a bit of a hurry?"

"It's on account of the boy."

Thiel's wife had died in childbirth. The boy had lived and been named Tobias.

"Yes, yes, to be sure, the boy," said the pastor, with a gesture clearly revealing that he had not thought of the infant until that moment. "That throws a different light on the matter. What have you been doing with him until now while you are at work?"

Thiel explained that he left Tobias in the care of an old woman. Once she had nearly let him get burned, and another time had let him roll from her lap to the floor. Fortunately the child had not been badly hurt—only a big surface bruise. Such a state of things could not continue, the flagman said, especially as the child, being delicate, required particular attention. For that reason and also because he had sworn to his wife on her deathbed that he would always take exceedingly good care of the child, he had decided to marry again.

The people found absolutely nothing to cavil with in the new couple that now visited the church regularly on Sundays. The milkmaid seemed to have been made for the flagman. She was but a few inches shorter than he and exceeded him in girth, while her features were just as coarsely molded as his, though, in contrast, they lacked soul.

If Thiel had cherished the desire for an inveterate worker and paragon of a housewife in his second wife, then his hopes were surprisingly fulfilled. However, without knowing it, he had purchased three other qualities, too, a hard, domineering disposition, quarrelsomeness, and brutal passion.

Within half a year the whole place knew who was lord and master in the flagman's little house. Thiel became the object of general pity. It was a piece of good luck for the "creature," the exercised husbands said, that she had got such a gentle lamb as Thiel for a husband. With other men she wouldn't come off so easy, she'd receive some hard knocks. An animal like that had to be managed—with blows, if need be—a good sound thrashing to make her behave herself.

But Thiel, despite his sinewy arms, was not the man to thrash his wife. What got the people so annoyed seemed to cause him no perturbation. As a rule, he let his wife's endless sermonizings pass without a word, and when he did occasionally make a response, the slow drag of his speech and the quiet coolness of his tone contrasted oddly with her high-pitched bawling.

The outside world seemed scarcely to touch him. It was as though he carried something within him that heavily overbalanced all of the evil it brought by good.

Nevertheless, for all his phlegm, there were occasions on which he would not allow things to pass—when little Toby was concerned. Then his childlike goodness, his yieldingness took on a dash of determination that even so untamed a temperament as Lena's did not dare to oppose.

The moments, however, in which he revealed this side of his character became rarer and rarer, and finally ceased completely. During the first year of his marriage he had shown a certain suffering resistance to Lena's tyranny. In the second year this also ceased completely. After a quarrel he no longer left for his work with his earlier indifference in case he had not previously placated her. Often he even stooped to beg her to be kind again. His solitary post in the heart of the Brandenburg pine forest was no longer, as it had been, the place where he would rather be than anywhere else on earth. The quiet devout thoughts of his dead wife were crossed by thoughts of the living wife. It was not with repugnance, as in the first months of his marriage, that he trod the homeward way, but often with passionate haste, after having counted the hours and minutes till the time of his release.

He who had been united to his first wife by a more spiritual love fell into his second wife's grip through the power of crude impulses. He became almost wholly dependent upon her.

At times he experienced pangs of conscience at this turn and resorted to a number of unusual devices to bring about a change. For one thing, he declared his hut and his beat to be holy ground, dedicated exclusively to the shades of the dead. And he actually succeeded by all sorts of pretexts in preventing Lena from accompanying him there. He hoped he should always be able to keep her off. The very number of his hut and the direction in which it lay were still unknown to her.

Thus, by conscientiously dividing the time at his disposal between the living and the dead, Thiel actually succeeded in soothing his conscience.

Often, to be sure, especially in moments of solitary devotion, when he felt the tie between him and his dead wife deeply and warmly, he beheld his present condition in the light of truth, and he experienced disgust.

If he was doing day duty, his spiritual intercourse with her was limited to dear recollections of their life together. But in the dark, when a snowstorm raged among the pines and along the embankment, his hut at midnight, by the light of his lantern, became a chapel.

With a faded photograph of the departed before him on the table, and the hymnal and the Bible turned open, he alternately read and sang the whole night long, interrupted only at intervals by the trains rushing past. He would attain a <u>state of ecstasy</u> in which he had visions of his wife standing there in person.

In its remoteness this post, which Thiel had held for ten years, contributed to the intensification of his mystic inclinations. To the north, east, south and west, it was separated by a walk of at least three quarters of an hour from the nearest habitation. It lay in the very heart of the forest. But there was a grade crossing there, and Thiel's duty was to lower and raise the gates.

In the summer days passed, in the winter weeks without a single person except other railroad workers setting foot on Thiel's beat. Almost the only changes in the solitude came from the weather and the periodic mutations of the seasons. It was not difficult to recall the events—besides the two mishaps to his body—that had broken into the regular course of the hours of service.

Four years previous the imperial special bearing the Kaiser to Breslau had gone dashing by. Once on a winter's night an express had run over a stag. And once on a hot summer's day, as Thiel was making an inspection of his beat, he had found a <u>corked bottle of wine</u>. It was <u>scorching hot</u> to the touch, and Thiel had esteemed its contents because when he uncorked it a geyser spouted out, showing that the stuff was well fermented. Thiel had laid the bottle on the edge of a pond in the woods to cool off. Somehow it had disappeared from the spot, and even after the passage of years Thiel never thought of that bottle without a pang of regret.

A bit of diversion was provided by a spring behind the hut. From time to time men at work on the road bed or on the telegraph lines came for a drink, and stayed, of course, to talk a while. Sometimes the forest ranger would also come when he was thirsty.

Tobias developed slowly. It was not until he was two years old that he learned to walk and talk. For his father he displayed unusual affection, and as he grew more understanding Thiel's old love for his child was re-awakened. Accordingly Lena's love for the child decreased, turning into unmistakable dislike when the next year a baby boy was born to her, too.

After that bad times began for Tobias. In his father's absence he was particularly made to suffer. He had to dedicate his feeble powers unrewarded to the service of the little cry-baby. He became more and more exhausted. His head grew too large round, and his fiery red hair, with the chalky face beneath, on top of his wretched little body, made an unlovely and pitiful impression. When the backward mite was seen dragging himself down to the Spree with his baby brother bursting with health in his arms, curses were muttered behind the windows of the cottages. But no one ever ventured to utter the curses in the open.

Thiel, who was most of all concerned, seemed to have no eyes for what was going on, and refused to understand the hints of well-meaning neighbors.

II

Once Thiel returned from night duty at seven o'clock of a June morning. Directly Lena had greeted him, she burst into her usual complaining.

A few weeks before notice had been given that they could no longer cultivate the piece of land which they rented for planting potatoes for their own use, and no other land had been found to replace it. Though everything pertaining to the land was part of Lena's duty, Thiel none the less had to listen to a hundred iterations that he would be to blame if they had to buy ten sacks of potatoes for dear money. Thiel merely muttered a word or two. Paying slight attention to Lena's tirade, he went straight over to Tobias's bed, which he shared with the boy on nights when he was off duty.

He sat down and watched the sleeping child with an anxious expression on his good face. For a while he contented himself with chasing away the persistent flies, then he woke him up. A touching joy lighted up the boy's blue, deep-set eyes. He snatched for his father's hand, and a pitiful smile drew the corners of his mouth. Thiel helped him put on his few bits of clothing. Suddenly a shadow chased across his face. He noticed that his son's right cheek was slightly swollen and bore finger marks designed white on red.

At breakfast Lena brought up the same subject again, pursuing it with even more vigor. Thiel cut her off by telling her that the railroad inspector had given him for nothing the use of a stretch of land alongside the tracks not far from his hut, probably because it was too distant for the inspector to use for himself.

Lena was incredulous, then gradually her doubts melted away and she became noticeably good-humored. How big was the lot? How good was the soil? She plied him with questions. And when she learned that there were actually two dwarf fruit trees on the land, she fairly lost her head. At length the questions were all asked, and as the shopkeeper's bell, which could be heard in every house in the place, kept ringing incessantly, Lena ran forth to ferret out the latest news.

While she remained in the dark shop crowded with wares, Thiel occupied himself at home with Tobias, who sat on his knee playing with pine cones that his father had brought from the woods.

"What do you want to be when you grow up?" asked Thiel. The stereotyped question was invariably answered by the equally stereo-typed reply, "Railroad inspector." It was not asked in fun. The flagman's dreams actually soared so high. It was in all seriousness that he cher-ished the hope that with God's help Tobias would become something extraordinary. The instant "railroad inspector" left the child's bloodless lips, Thiel's face brightened, fairly radiated bliss.

"Go play now, Tobias," he said soon afterward, lighting his pipe with a shaving kindled at the hearth fire. The boy showing shy pleasure went out.

Thiel undressed and got into bed. For a long while he lay staring up at the low, cracked ceiling. Finally he fell asleep and woke up shortly before twelve o'clock. While Lena in her noisy fashion prepared the midday meal, he dressed and went out on the street to fetch Tobias, whom he found scratching plaster out of a hole in the wall and stuffing it into his mouth. Thiel led him by the hand past the eight houses that constituted the hamlet down to the Spree. The stream lay dark and glassy between sparsely foliaged populars. Thiel sat down on a block of granite close to the water's edge.

Every fair day the villagers were accustomed to see him on this spot. The children were devoted to him. They called him Father Thiel. He taught them games that he remembered from his own childhood, re-serving, however, the best of his memories for Tobias. He whittled him arrows that flew farther than those of the other boys, he carved him wil-low pipes, and even deigned to sing ditties in his rusty bass, and tap the beat with the horn handle of his knife against the bark of a tree.

The people thought him silly. They blamed him. They could not understand how he could go to so much trouble for the little brats. Though they should have been richly content, seeing that the children were well taken care of when in his charge. Besides, Thiel did more than play with them. He took up serious things, too. He heard the older ones recite their lessons, helped them study their Bible and hymn verses, and spelled out c-a-t and d-o-g with the younger ones.

After the midday meal Thiel rested again a while, drank a cup of cof-fee, and began to prepare for work. It took him a lot of time, as for everything he did. Each move had been regulated for years. The ob-jects carefully spread out on the walnut dresser went into his various pockets always in the same order—knife, notebook, comb, a horse's tooth, an old watch in a case, and a small book wrapped in red paper. The last was handled with especial care. During the night it lay under Thiel's pillow, and by day was carried in his breast-pocket. On a label pasted on the cover was written in Thiel's awkward yet flourishing hand, "Savings Account of Tobias Thiel."

The clock on the wall with the long pendulum and sickly yellow face indicated a quarter to five when Thiel left. A small boat, his own property, ferried him across the Spree. Arrived at the further side, he stood still a moment and listened back in the direction he had come from. Then he turned into a broad path through the woods and within a few moments reached the depths of the deep-booming pine forest, its mass of needles like a dark green undulating sea.

The moist layers of needles and moss made a carpet as inaudible to the tread as felt. Thiel made his way without looking up, now past the rusty brown columns of the older trees, now between the thickly enmeshed younger growth, and farther on across broad stretches of nursery, overshadowed by a few tall slim pines for the protection of the young saplings. A transparent bluish haze rising from the earth laden with mingled fragrances blurred the forms of the trees. A heavy, drab sky hung low over the tops. Flocks of cawing crows seemed to bathe in the gray of the atmosphere. Black puddles filled the depressions in the path and cast a still drearier reflection of a dreary nature.

"Fearful weather," thought Thiel when he roused out of deep reflection and looked up.

Suddenly his thoughts were deflected. A dim feeling came to him that he must have forgotten something. And surely enough, when he searched his pockets, he discovered that he had not brought along the sandwich that he required on account of the long hours on duty. For a while he stood undecided. Then turned and hurried back.

In a short while he reached the Spree, rowed himself across in a few powerful strokes, and without delay, perspiring from every pore, ascended the gradual slope of the village street. The shopkeeper's old, mangy poodle lay in the middle of the road. On the tarred board fence around a cottager's yard perched a hooded crow. It spread its feathers, shook itself, nodded, uttered an ear-splitting caw, caw, and with a slapping sound of its wings rose in the air and let the wind drive it in the direction of the forest.

Nothing was to be seen of the villagers—about twenty fishermen and lumbermen with their families.

The stillness was broken—by a high-pitched voice. The flagman involuntarily stopped. A volley of violent, jangling tones assailed his ears. It seemed to come from the open dormer window of a low house that he knew only too well.

Treading as silently as possible, he glided nearer. Now he quite clearly recognized his wife's voice. Only a few steps more, and he could understand almost everything she said.

"You horrid little beast, you! Is the poor baby to scream its belly inside out from hunger? What? Just you wait—just you wait. I'll teach you to mind. You'll never forget."

For a few moments there was <u>silence</u>. Then a sound could be heard like the beating out of clothes. And the next instant another <u>hailstorm of abuse</u> was let loose.

"You <u>miserable little puppy</u>, you! Do you think I'll let my own child die of hunger because of a <u>mean little thing</u> like you?—Shut your mouth!" A slight whimper had been audible. "If you don't shut your mouth, I'll give you something that'll keep you going a whole week."

The whimpering did not subside.

The flagman felt his heart pounding in irregular beats. He began to tremble slightly. His glance fastened on the ground as though his mind were wandering, and again and again his coarse, hard hand went up to his freckled forehead to brush back a dank strand of hair. For a second he was about to give way. He stood shaken by a convulsion that swelled his muscles and drew his fingers into a clenched ball. The convulsion subsided. He was left in a state of dull exhaustion.

With unsteady steps he entered the narrow, brick-paved vestibule and slowly, wearily mounted the creaking wooden stairs.

"Pugh, pugh, pugh!" You could hear how with every sign of scorn and fury some one spat out three times in succession. "You horrid, mean, sneaking, cowardly, low-down good-for-nothing!" The epithets followed one another in crescendo, the voice that uttered them breaking several times from strain. "<u>You want to hit my boy</u>, do you? You <u>ugly little brat</u> you, don't you dare to hit the poor helpless child on its mouth. What's that? Huh? If I wanted to soil my hands on you, I'd—"

At that moment the door to the living room was opened, and the rest of the sentence remained unspoken on the frightened woman's tongue. She was livid with passion, her lips twitched evilly. Her right hand raised in the air sank and grasped the <u>saucepan with milk</u> in it. She tried to pour some into the baby's bottle, but desisted as the larger part of the milk flowed down the outside of the bottle on to the table. She clutched at various objects without being able to hold them any length of time. Finally she recovered herself sufficiently to address her husband with violence. What did he mean by coming home at this unusual hour? Was he thinking of spying on her? That would be too much. This last was directly followed by the asseveration that she had a clear conscience and need not lower her eyes before any one.

Thiel scarcely heard what she said. He gave a hasty look at Toby, who was crying aloud, and for a few moments he had to restrain forcibly a <u>something dreadful rising within him.</u> Then the old phlegm spread over his taut features, and at the same time a furtive, lustful light came into his eyes. His glance played over his wife's heavy limbs while she with averted face, bustled about still making an effort to be composed. Her full, half-bared breasts swelled with excitement and threatened to burst her corset. Her drawn-up skirts accentuated the width of her broad hips. A force seemed to emanate from the woman, indomitable, inescapable. Thiel felt himself powerless to cope with it. Tightly, like a cobweb, yet firmly as a mesh of steel, it laid itself around him, chaining him down, robbing him of his strength. In this condition he was incapable of saying a word to her, much less a harsh word.

Thus it was that Tobias, bathed in tears, cowering in a corner, saw his father go over to the oven bench without looking round at him, pick up the forgotten sandwich, hold it out to Lena by way of the only explanation, give a short, distraught nod of his head in good-by, and disappear.

III

Thiel made all possible haste back to his solitary post in the woods. Even so he was a quarter of an hour late. The assistant who relieved him, a consumptive, the victim of the unavoidably rapid changes in temperature to which the work subjected one, was waiting prepared to leave on the sanded little platform of the hut, on which the number, black on white, gleamed from a distance between the tree trunks.

The two men shook hands, exchanged a few brief reports, and parted, the one disappearing within the hut, the other taking the continuation of the road by which Thiel had come. His convulsive cough sounded further and further away among the trees, until finally the one human sound in the solitude fell silent.

Thiel as always, after his fashion, set about preparing the small square room for the night. He worked mechanically, his mind occupied with the impression of the past hour.

First he laid his supper on the narrow, brown-painted table beside one of the windows like slits through which the stretch of track could be conveniently viewed. Next he kindled a fire in the small, rusty stove and placed a pot of cold water on top. After that he straightened out his utensils, a shovel, a spade, a wrench and a few other things, and then cleaned his lantern and filled it with fresh oil.

Scarcely were his arrangements completed when the signal rang shrilly, three times, and three times again, to announce that a train from the direction of Breslau was pulling out of the near station. Thiel showed no hurry, allowing a few minutes to pass before emerging from the hut with flag and cartridge case in his hand. And it was with a lazy, dragging shuffle that he walked along the narrow strip of sand to the crossing, about sixty feet away. Though there was scarcely any traffic along the road at that point, still he conscientiously let down and raised the gates before and after the passage of each train.

This operation now concluded, he leaned idly on one of the black-and-white barred anchor-posts.

The tracks cut in a straight line right and left into the green forest stretching beyond the reach of the eye. On each side the mass of needles stood apart to leave, as it were, an avenue free for the reddish-brown graveled embankment. The black tracks running parallel looked like the strands of a huge iron net drawn together to a point on the horizon in the extreme south and north.

The wind had risen, it drove light waves of mist along the edge of the forest into the distance. A humming came from the telegraph poles alongside the tracks. On the wires that stretched from pole to pole like the sustaining cords spun by a huge spider perched swarms of chirping birds. A woodpecker flew with a laugh over Thiel's head. The man did not so much as look up.

The sun hanging from under the edge of vast masses of clouds and about to sink into the dark-green sea of treetops poured streams of purple over the forest. The pillared arcades of the pine trunks on the yon side of the embankment took fire as from within and glowed like metal. The tracks, too, began to glow, turning into the semblance of fiery snakes. They were the first to pale. The glow, leaving the ground, slowly ascended upward, resigning first the bodies of the trees, then the lower tops to the cold light of dissolution. For a while a reddish sheen lingered on the extreme crowns.

Silently and solemnly was the exalted drama enacted.

The flagman still stood at the gates motionless. At length he made a step forward. A dark point on the horizon where the tracks joined, became more than a point. Increasing from second to second it yet seemed to stand still. Then of a sudden it acquired movement, and drew nearer. A vibrating and humming went through the tracks, a rhythmic clang, a muted thunder. It grew louder and louder until at length it sounded not unlike the hoof beats of a storming cavalry regiment. From a distance the air pulsated intermittently with a panting and a blustering. Then suddenly the serenity of the forest snapped. A mad uproar filled the welkin, the tracks curved, the earth shook—a blast of air, a cloud of dust and steam and smoke—and the snorting monster had gone by.

The noises waned as they had waxed. The exhalations thinned away. Shrunken to a point again the train vanished in the distance, and the old solemn hush again settled upon this corner of the forest.

"Minna," whispered the flagman, as if coming out of a dream.

He returned to the hut, where he brewed himself some weak

coffee, then sat down, sipping from time to time and all the while staring at a dirty piece of newspaper that he had picked up on his round.

Gradually a curious unrest came upon him. Attributing it to the heat from the stove, he tore off his coat and waistcoat. That proving to be of no help, he got up, took a spade from a corner, and went out to the lot that the inspector had presented to him.

It was a narrow strip of soil, overgrown with weeds. The blossoms on the two fruit trees were like snowy white foam. Thiel calmed down, a quiet content possessed him.

To work now.

The spade cut into the earth with a crunch. The wet clods flew and crumbled as they fell.

For a long while he dug uninterruptedly. Then he paused and said to himself audibly, shaking his head gravely:

"No, no, it won't do. No, it won't do."

The thought had suddenly struck him that Lena would be coming there often to look after the lot, and his accustomed life would be seriously disturbed. At one blow pleasure on the possession of the bit of ground turned into distaste. Hastily, as if he had been about to do wrong, he ripped the spade out of the earth and carried it back to the hut.

Again he sank into gloomy reflections. Almost without knowing why, he could not endure the prospect of Lena's presence for whole days at a stretch while he was on duty. Much as he might try he could not reconcile himself to the idea. It seemed to him he had something valuable to defend, against some one who was attempting to violate his holiest sanctuary. Involuntarily his muscles tautened in a slight cramp, and a short, defiant laugh escaped him.

The sound of his own laughter was alarming. He looked about and lost the thread of his thoughts. Finding it again he went back to the same dismal broodings.

Then suddenly a heavy black curtain was torn apart, his eyes so long befogged had now a clear view. He had the sensation of awakening from a deathlike sleep that had lasted two years. With an incredulous shake of the head he contemplated all the awful things he must have been guilty of in that condition. The long-suffering of his child, which the impressions of the earlier afternoon should only have confirmed, now were clearly revealed to his soul. Pity and penitence overcame him, and also great shame, that all this long while he had lived in disgraceful resignation, never taking the dear, helpless child's part, not even finding the strength to admit how much the child suffered.

From the self-tormenting contemplation of his sins of omission a great tiredness came over him. He fell asleep, bent over the table with his forehead resting on his hand.

For a long time he lay like that, and several times uttered the name Minna in a choked voice.

A rushing and roaring filled his ears, as of great masses of water. He tore his eyes open and looked about. Darkness enveloped him. His limbs gave way, the sweat of terror oozed from every pore, his pulse beat irregularly, his face was wet with tears.

He wanted to look toward the door, but in the inky darkness did not know which way to turn. He rose reeling. And still terror possessed him. The woods outside boomed like the ocean, the wind drove rain and sleet against the panes. Thiel groped about helplessly. For a moment he felt himself to be drowning. Then suddenly there was a dazzling bluish flare, as of drops of supernatural light falling down into the earth's atmosphere to be instantly extinguished by it.

The moment sufficed to restore the flagman to reason. He fumbled for his lantern and found it. At the same instant the thunder awoke on the farthest edge of the heavens over Brandenburg. At first a dull, re-strained rumble, it rolled nearer in surging metallic waves, until over-head it discharged itself in great peals, menacing roars that shook the earth to its foundations.

The window panes clattered. Thiel lighted the lantern, and his first glance after he regained self-control was at the clock. In a bare five minutes the express was due. Thinking he had failed to hear the signal, he made for the crossing as quickly as the dark and the storm permit-ted. Just as he was letting down the gates the signal rang—the sound was scattered by the wind in all directions.

The pine-trees bent over, their branches scraped against each other with uncanny creakings and squeakings. For a few moments the moon was visible, a pale yellow chalice amid the torn clouds. By its light could be seen the wind's mauling of the black treetops. The foliage of the birches along the embankment waved and fluttered like ghostly horses' tails. Beneath them lay the rails gleaming wet, absorbing the pale moonlight in spots here and there.

Thiel tore the cap from his head. The rain soothed him. It ran down his face mingled with tears.

His brain was in a ferment with confused recollections of his dream. Tobias seemed to be undergoing maltreatment, and such horrible mal-treatment that the mere thought of it stopped his heart. Another vision was clearer, of his dead wife. She had come from somewhere along the railroad tracks. She had looked very ill and was wearing rags for clothes. Without looking round she passed the hut, and then—here his memory became vague—she had great difficulty somehow in proceeding, she even collapsed several times.

Thiel pondered. And then he knew that she was in flight. No doubt of it. Else why those anxious backward glances as she dragged herself forward with her legs giving way under her? Oh, those awful looks of hers!

But there was something that she was carrying, wrapped in cloths, something limp, bloody, pale. And the way she looked down on it reminded him of a past scene.

A dying woman who kept her gaze fixed on her new-born babe with an expression of the deepest pain, intolerable torture. It was an expression he could no more forget than that he had a father and a mother.

Where had she gone? He did not know. But one thing was clear in his soul: she had withdrawn from him, disregarded him, dragged herself further and further away into the dark, stormy night. "Minna, Minna," he had cried, and the sound of his own cry awakened him.

Two round red lights like the staring eyes of a huge monster penetrated the dark. A bloody sheen glided in advance, transforming the drops of rain in its course into drops of blood. A veritable rain of blood seemed to descend from heaven.

Horror fell upon Thiel, mounting and mounting as the train drew nearer. Dream and reality fused into one. He still saw the woman wandering down the tracks. His hand wavered toward the cartridge case, as if to stop the speeding train. Fortunately it was too late. Lights flared before his eyes, the train had rushed past.

The remainder of the night there was little peace for Thiel. He felt a great urgency to be at home, a great longing to see little Toby, from whom, it seemed to him, he had been separated for years. Several times, in his growing anxiety over the child's condition he was tempted to quit duty.

To shorten the hours until his release he determined as soon as day dawned to walk his beat. So, with a cane in one hand and a large iron wrench in the other, he went out into the dirty-gray twilight and stepped along on the spine of a rail, halting every now and then to tighten a bolt with the wrench or to hammer at one of the fish-plates that held the rails together.

The wind and rain had stopped, fragments of a pale blue sky became visible between rifts in the banked clouds. The monotonous tap-tap of his soles on the hard metal and the sleepy drip-drop from the wet trees gradually calmed Thiel.

At six o'clock he was relieved. Without delay he started home.

It was a glorious Sunday morning. The clouds had broken and drifted beyond the horizon. The sun, gleaming like a great blood-red gem, poured veritable masses of light upon the forest. Through the network of the branches the beams shot in sharp straight lines casting a glow upon islets of lacy ferns and here and there turning silvery gray patches on the ground into bits of coral. The tops of the trees, the trunks, the grass shed fire like dew. The world seemed to lie under a deluge of light. And the freshness of the air penetrated to the very core of one's being.

Even in Thiel's brain the fantasies of the night could not but grow pale. And when he entered the room where little Toby was lying in bed with the sun shining on him and more color in his cheeks than usual, they disappeared completely.

To be sure, in the course of the day Lena thought she noticed something odd about him. At church instead of looking in the book he observed her sidewise, and in the middle of the day, when Toby was supposed as usual to carry the baby out on the street, he took it from the boy's arms and laid it in her lap. Otherwise there was nothing conspicuously different about him.

Having no chance to take a nap and as he was to do day duty that week, he went to bed early, at nine o'clock. Exactly as he was about to fall asleep, his wife told him that she intended to accompany him the next morning to dig the lot and plant potatoes.

Thiel winced. He awoke completely, but kept his eyes shut.

Lena went on. If the potatoes were to amount to anything, she said, it was high time to do the planting. And she would have to take the children along because it would probably occupy her the entire day.

Thiel muttered a few unintelligible words, to which she paid no attention. She had turned her back and by the light of a tallow candle was occupied with unfastening her corset and letting down her skirts. Suddenly, without herself knowing why, she turned round and beheld her husband's ashen face distorted by a play of passions. He had raised himself partly, supporting himself by his hands on the edge of the bed, his burning eyes fastened upon her.

"Thiel!" cried the woman, half in anger, half in fear.

Like a somnambulist who hears his name called, Thiel came out of his daze. He stammered something, threw his head back on the pillow, and pulled the quilt over his ears.

Lena was the first to get up the next morning. She went about noiselessly, making the necessary preparations for the excursion. The baby was put into the perambulator, then Tobias was awakened and dressed. He smiled when he was told where he was going.

When everything was ready and even the coffee was made and set on the table, Thiel awoke. His first sensation on seeing the arrangements was of displeasure. He wanted to protest, but the proper opening refused to frame itself. Besides, what arguments could he advance that would weigh with Lena? And there was his child's little face beaming with joy, growing happier and happier each instant, until Thiel, from the sight of his delight in the approaching excursion, could not think of opposing it.

Nevertheless, on the way through the woods, as he pushed the baby-carriage with difficulty through the deep soil, Thiel was not free from anxiety.

Tobias gathered flowers and laid them in the carriage. He was happier than almost any time his father had seen him. In his little brown plush cap he hopped about among the ferns and tried, helplessly to be sure, to catch the glassy winged dragonflies that darted above them.

As soon as they reached the spot, Lena made a survey. She threw the sack of seed potatoes on the grassy edge of a small grove of birches, kneeled down, and let the darkish soil run between her fingers.

Thiel watched her eagerly.

"Well," he said, "how is it?"

"Every bit as good as the corner on the Spree."

A burden fell from the flagman. He contentedly scratched the stubble on his face. He had feared she would be dissatisfied.

After hastily devouring a thick slice of bread the woman tossed aside head cloth and jacket, and began to spade up the earth with the speed and endurance of a machine. At regular intervals she straightened up and took several deep breaths. But the pauses were never for long, except when she had to suckle the baby, which she did quickly, with panting, perspiring breasts.

After a while the flagman called to her from the platform in front of the hut:

"I must inspect the beat. I'm taking Tobias with me."

"What!" she screamed back. "Nonsense! Who'll stay with the baby? You'll come here," she shouted still louder.

But the flagman as if not hearing walked off with Toby. For a moment she considered whether she should not run after the two, then desisted because of the loss of time.

Thiel walked down the tracks with his son. The boy was quite excited, everything was so new and strange. Those narrow black rails warmed by the sun—he could not comprehend what they could be meant for. And he kept up an incessant stream of funny questions. What struck him as strangest of all was the resonance of the telegraph poles.

Thiel knew the sound of each pole on his beat so well that with closed eyes he could tell at exactly what spot he stood. And now he stopped several times, holding Tobias by the hand, to listen to the wonderful tones that came from the wood like sonorous chorals from inside a church. The pole at the extreme south end made a particularly full, beautiful sound. It was a mingling of tones that seemed to come without pausing for breath.

Tobias ran round the weathered post to see if he could not through some hole discover the originators of the lovely music. His father listening sank into a devout mood, as in church. He distinguished a voice that reminded him of his dead wife, and fancied it was a choir of blessed spirits, her voice mingling with the others. A deep emotion, a great yearning brought the tears to his eyes.

Tobias asked to be allowed to gather the flowers in the field alongside the tracks. Thiel as always let the child have his way.

Fragments of the blue sky seemed to have dropped on to the meadow, so thickly was it strewn with small, blue blossoms. Like colored pennants the butterflies fluttered and floated among the shining white trunks of the birches. The delicate green foliage gave forth a soft rustle.

Tobias plucked flowers. His father watched him meditatively. Occasionally the flagman raised his eyes and searched between the leaves for a glimpse of the sky, which held the golden sunlight like a huge, spotless bowl.

"Father," said the child, pointing to a brown squirrel which with small scratching sounds was darting up a solitary pine-tree, "father, is that the good Lord?"

"Silly boy," was all that Thiel could find to reply as bits of loosened bark fell from the trunk of the tree to his feet.

Lena was still digging when Thiel and Tobias returned. She had already spaded up half the plot!

The trains passed at intervals. Each time they rushed by Tobias watched with mouth agape. Even his stepmother was amused by the funny faces he made.

The midday meal, consisting of potatoes and a remnant of roast pork, was consumed inside the hut. Lena was in good spirits. Even Thiel seemed ready to resign himself to the inevitable with good grace. While they ate, he entertained his wife by telling her various things connected with his work. Could she, for instance, imagine that there were forty-six screws in one rail, and more like that.

By mealtime the spading had been done, and in the afternoon Lena was going to sow the potatoes. This time, insisting that Tobias must look after the baby, she took him along.

"Watch out!" Thiel called after her, suddenly gripped by concern. "Watch out that he doesn't go too close to the tracks."

A shrug of Lena's shoulders was her only answer.

The signal rang for the Silesian express. Scarcely had Thiel taken his place in readiness at the gates when the approaching rumble became audible. Within a fraction of a minute he could see the train. On it came, the black funnel spitting steam in countless puffs, one chasing upward after the other. There! One—two—three milk-white geysers gushing up straight as candles—the engine whistling. Three times in succession, short, shrill, alarming.

"They're putting on the brakes," Thiel said to himself. "I wonder why."

He stepped out beyond the gates to look down the tracks, mechanically pulling the red flag from its case and holding it straight in front of him.

Good heavens! Had he been blind? God, O God, what was that? There—between the rails.

"Stop!" he screamed with every atom of breath in his lungs.

Too late. A dark mass had gone down under the train and was being tossed between the wheels like a rubber ball.

Only a few seconds more and with a grating and squeaking of the brakes, the train came to a standstill.

Instantly the lonely stretch became a scene of animation. The conductor and brakeman ran along the gravel path beside the tracks back to the rear end. From every window curious faces peered. And then the crowd that had gathered in the rear formed into a cluster, and moved forward.

Thiel panted. He had to hold on to something not to sink to the ground like a slaughtered steer.

How's that? Were they actually waving to him?

"No!"

A scream came from the spot where the accident had occurred, followed by a howling as from an animal. Who was that? Lena? It was not her voice, yet—

A man came hurrying down the tracks.

"Flagman!"

"What's the matter?"

"An accident."

The messenger shrank before the strange expression in the flagman's eyes. His cap hung on the side of his head, his red hair stood straight up.

"He's still alive. Maybe something can be done."

A rattle in the flagman's throat was the only answer.

"Come quickly—quickly."

With a tremendous effort Thiel pulled himself together. His slack muscles tautened, he drew himself to his full height, his face was empty and dead.

He followed the man at a run, oblivious of the pale, frightened faces at the windows. A young woman looked out, a traveling salesman with a fez on his head, a young couple apparently on their honeymoon. What were they to him? The contents of those rattling, thumping boxes on wheels had never concerned him. His ears were filled with Lena's lamentations.

Yellow dots swam before his eyes, countless yellow dots like fireflies. He shrank back, he stood still. From out of the dance of fireflies it came toward him, pale, limp, bloody—a forehead beaten black and blue, blue lips with dark blood trickling from them. Tobias!

Thiel said nothing. His face went a dirty white. He grinned as if out of his senses. At length he bent over, he felt the limp, dead limbs heavy in his arms. The red flag went round them.

He started to leave.

Where?

"To the railroad doctor, to the railroad doctor," came from all sides.

"We'll take him," called the baggage-master, and turned to prepare a couch of coats and books in his car. "Well?"

Thiel made no move to let go of the boy. They urged him. In vain. The baggage-master had a stretcher handed out from the car and ordered a man to remain with the father. Time was precious. The conductor's whistle shrilled. Coins rained from the windows.

Lena raved like a madwoman. "The poor woman," they said in the coaches, "the poor, poor mother."

The conductor whistled several times, the engine blew a signal, sent white clouds hissing up from its cylinders, and stretched its sinews of iron. In a few seconds, the mail express, with floating flags of smoke, was dashing with redoubled speed through the forest.

The flagman, whose mood had altered, laid the half-dead child on the stretcher.

There he lay with his racked tiny body. Every now and then a long wheeze raised the bony chest, which was visible under the tattered shirt. The little arms and legs, broken not only at the joints, assumed the most unnatural positions. The heel of one small foot was twisted to the front, the arms hung over the sides of the stretcher.

Lena kept up a continuous whimper. Every trace of her former insolence had disappeared. Over and over again she repeated a story to exonerate herself.

Thiel seemed not to notice her. With an expression of awful anxiety he kept his eyes riveted on the child.

A hush had fallen, a deadly hush. The tracks rested hot and black on the glaring gravel. The noon had stifled the wind, and the forest stood motionless, as if carved in stone.

In muffled voices the two men took counsel. The quickest way to reach Friedrichshagen would be to go back to the neighboring station in the direction of Breslau, because the next train, a fast commutation, did not stop at the station that was nearer to Friedrichshagen.

Thiel seemed to consider if he should go along. At the time there was no one there who understood the duties of the position, so with a mute motion of his head he indicated to his wife that she should take hold of the stretcher. She did not dare to refuse though she was concerned about having to leave the baby behind.

Thiel accompanied the cortège of two to the end of his beat, then stood still and looked after them long. Suddenly he clapped his hand to his forehead with a blow that resounded afar. It might wake him up, he thought. Because this was a dream like the one he had had yesterday. No use. Reeling rather than walking he reached his hut. There he fell face downward on the floor. His cap flew into a corner, his carefully kept watch fell from his pocket, the case sprang open, the glass broke. An iron fist seemed to be clamped on his neck, so tight that he could not move no matter how he moaned and groaned and tried to free himself. His forehead was cold, his throat parched.

The ringing of the signal roused him. Under the influence of those three repeated sounds the attack abated. Thiel could rise and do his duty. To be sure, his feet were heavy as lead, and the stretch of rails circled about him like the spokes of an enormous wheel with his head for its axis. But at least he could stand up a while.

The commutation train approached. Tobias must be in it. The nearer it drew the more the pictures before Thiel's eyes blurred. Finally all he saw was the mutilated boy with the bloody mouth. Then darkness fell.

After a while he awoke from the swoon. He found himself lying in the hot sun close to the gates. He rose, shook the sand from his clothes and spat it from his mouth. His head cleared a bit, he could think more quietly.

In the hut he immediately picked his watch up from the floor and laid it on the table. It was still going. For two hours he counted the seconds, then the minutes, while representing to himself what was happening to Tobias. Now Lena was arriving with him, now she stood in front of the doctor. The doctor observed the boy and felt him all over, and shook his head.

"Bad, very bad—but perhaps—who can tell?"

He made a more thorough examination.

"No," he then said, "no, it's all over."

"All over, all over," groaned the flagman. But then he drew himself up, raised his unconsciously clenched fist, rolled his eyes to the ceiling, and shouted as if the narrow little room must burst with the sound of his voice. "He must live, he must. I tell you, he must live."

He flung open the door of the hut—the red glow of evening fell through—and ran rather than walked to the gates. Here he stood still seemingly bewildered. Then suddenly spreading his arms he went to the middle of the road-bed, as if to stop something that was coming from the same direction as the commutation. His wide-open eyes made the impression of blindness. While stepping backward to make way for something, a stream of half-intelligible words came from between his gritted teeth.

"Listen. Don't go. Listen, listen. Don't go. Stay here. Give him back to me. He's beaten black and blue. Yes, yes. All right. I'll beat her black and blue, too. Do you hear? Stay. Give him back to me."

Something seemed to move past him, because he turned and made as if to follow.

"Minna, Minna,"—his voice was weepy like a small child's—"Minna, listen. Give him back to me. I will—" He groped in the air as if to catch and hold some one fast. "My little wife—yes, yes—and I'll—and I'll beat her—so she's black and blue, too—I'll beat her, too—with the hatchet—you see?—with the kitchen hatchet—I'll beat her with the kitchen hatchet. And that'll be the end of her. And then—yes, yes—with the hatchet—yes, with the kitchen hatchet—black blood."

Foam gathered on his lips, his glassy eyeballs rolled incessantly.

A gentle breath of the evening blew steadily over the forest, a rosy cloud mass hung in the western sky.

He had followed the invisible something about a hundred paces when he stood still, apparently having lost courage. With fearful dread in his eyes, he stretched out his arms, pleading, adjuring. He strained his eyes, shaded them with his hand, as if to discern the inessential being in the far distance. Finally his head sank, and the tense expression of his face changed into apathy. He turned and dragged himself the way he had come.

The sunlight laid its final glow over the forest, then was extinguished. The trunks of the pines rose among the tops like pale, decayed bones, and the tops weighed upon them like grayish black layers of mold. The hammering of a woodpecker penetrated the silence. Up above one last dilatory pink cloud traversed the steely blue of the sky. The breath of the wind turned dankly cold as if blowing from a cellar.

The flagman shivered. Everything was new and strange. He did not know what he was walking on, or what was about him. A squirrel hopped along the road-bed. Thiel pondered. He had to think of the Lord. But why? "The Lord is hopping along the tracks, the Lord is hopping along the tracks." He said it several times as if to get at something associated with it. He interrupted himself. A ray of illumination fell upon his brain. "Good heavens! That's madness." He forgot everything else and turned upon this new enemy. He tried to order his thoughts. In vain. They'd come and go and ramble away and shoot off at a tangent. He caught himself in the absurdest fancies, and shuddered at the consciousness of his impotence.

The sound of a child crying came from the birch grove near by. It was the signal for madness. Almost against his will he had to hurry to the spot where the baby, whom everybody had neglected, was crying and kicking on the unblanketed floor of its carriage.

What did he mean to do? What had driven him there? The questions were submerged in a whirling eddy of thoughts and emotions.

"The Lord is hopping along the tracks." Now he knew. Tobias—she had murdered him—Lena—the child had been entrusted to her care. "Stepmother! Beast of a mother!" he hissed between clenched teeth. "And her brat lives."

A red mist enveloped his senses. Two baby eyes penetrated through it. He felt something soft, fleshy between his fingers. He heard gurgling, whistling sounds, mingled with hoarse cries that came from he did not know whom.

Then something fell upon his brain like hot drops of sealing wax, and his spirit was cleared as from a cataleptic trance. Aroused to consciousness, he caught the quiver in the air that was the final reverberation of the signal, and in a trice he realized what he had been about to do. His hand relaxed its grip on the throat, under which the infant had writhed and squirmed. It gasped for breath, then began to cough and bawl.

"It's alive. Thank the Lord, it's alive."

He let it lie and hastened to the crossing. Dark clouds of smoke rolled in the distance, the wind drove them to the ground. He distinguished the panting of an engine that sounded like the intermittent, tortured breathing of a giant.

The stretch was shrouded in a cold twilight. But after a while the clouds of smoke parted, and Thiel recognized the train as being the freight that was returning with open empty cars and bringing home the men who had been working on the road-bed during the day. It had ample running time to stop at each station to drop or pick up the men.

Quite a distance from Thiel's hut the brakes began to be put on, and a loud clanking and clanging and rattling and screeching tore the silence before the train came to a standstill with a single shrill, long-drawn whistle.

About fifty men and women were in the different cars. Nearly all of them stood, some of the men with bared heads. There was a mystifying air of solemnity about them. When they caught sight of the flagman, a whispering began among them, and the old men drew their pipes from between their yellow teeth and held them respectfully in their hands. Here and there a woman would turn to blow her nose.

The conductor descended and advanced toward Thiel. The workmen saw him solemnly shake the flagman's hand, and then saw Thiel with slow steps almost military in their stiffness go back to the rear. None of them dared to address him, though they all knew him.

From the rear wagon they were lifting little Toby.

He was dead.

Lena followed. Her face was a bluish white, brown rings underlined her eyes.

Thiel did not so much as cast a glance at her. She, however, was shocked at sight of her husband. His cheeks were hollow, his eyelashes and beard were plastered, his hair, it seemed to her, was gone grayer. Traces of dried tears all over his face. And an unsteady light in his eyes that made her shudder.

The stretcher had been brought back for transporting the body home.

For a while there was gruesome silence. Thiel lost himself in black depths of awful thoughts. Darkness deepened. A herd of deer started to cross the embankment. The stag stood still between the rails and turned his agile neck curiously. The engine whistled. He and the rest of the herd disappeared in a flash.

At the moment that the train was about to start Thiel collapsed. The train stood still, and counsel was held as to what had now best be done. Since every effort they made to bring the flagman back to his senses, proved futile, they decided to let the child's body lie in the hut temporarily, and use the stretcher for conveying the flagman instead. Two men carried the stretcher, Lena followed, pushing the baby carriage, sobbing the whole way, the tears running down her cheeks.

The great purplish ball of the moon shone low between the trunks of the pine-trees. As it rose it paled and diminished in size until finally it hung high in the heavens like a swinging lamp, and cast a pale sheen over the forest, through every chink and cranny of the foliage, painting the faces of the processionists a livid white.

Cautiously but sturdily they made their way through the close second growth, then past broad nurseries with the larger trees scattered among the younger ones. Here the pale light seemed to have collected itself in great dark bowls.

Occasionally a rattle came from the unconscious man's throat, and occasionally he raved. Several times he clenched his fists and tried to raise himself, his eyes all the time remaining closed. Getting him across the Spree was difficult, and a return trip had to be made to fetch Lena and the baby.

As they ascended the slight eminence on which the hamlet was situated, they met a few of the inhabitants, who forthwith spread the news of the misfortune. The whole colony came running.

Among her gossips Lena broke into fresh lamentations.

Thiel was with difficulty carried up the narrow stairway of his home and put to bed. And the men returned immediately to bring little Toby's body back.

Some of the old, experienced people advised cold compresses. Lena carried out their prescription eagerly, properly, dropping cloths into icy cold spring water and renewing them as soon as the unconscious man's burning forehead had heated them. Anxiously she observed his breathing. It seemed to come more regularly and to continue to improve each minute.

However, the day's excitement had told upon her, and she decided to try to get a little sleep. No use! Whether she held her eyes open or shut, she kept seeing the events of the past hours. The baby slept. Contrary to her wont, she had not paid much attention to it. Altogether she had turned into a different person. Not a trace of her former arrogance. The sick man with the colorless face shining with sweat dominated her even in sleep.

A cloud passed, obscuring the moon and throwing the room into complete darkness. Lena heard nothing but her husband's heavy though regular breathing. She felt creepy in the dark and considered whether she should not rise and kindle a light. But as she attempted to get up, a leaden weight on her limbs pulled her back, her lids drooped, she fell asleep.

Some time later the men returning with the boy's body found the front door wide open. Surprised at this, they mounted and found the upstairs door also open. They called the woman by her name. No answer. They struck a match. The flare of it revealed awful havoc.

"Murder, murder!"

Lena lay in her blood, her face unrecognizable, her skull broken open.

"He murdered his wife, he murdered his wife!"

They ran about witless. Neighbors came. One bumped against the cradle.

"Good heavens!" He shrank back, ashen pale, his eyes fixed in a horrified stare. The baby lay with its throat cut.

The flagman had disappeared. The search made for him that night proved fruitless. The next morning, however, the man who replaced him found him on the tracks at the spot where little Toby had been run over, holding the shaggy brown cap in his arm and caressing it as if it were a living thing.

The block signaler, apprised of his discovery, telegraphed for help. Several men tried with kindly inducements to lure Thiel from the tracks. He was not to be budged. The express then due had to be stopped, and it was only by the united efforts of the entire crew and the use of force that the man, who had begun to rave fearfully, could be removed from the railroad. They had to bind him hands and feet, and the policeman summoned to the spot guarded his transportation the whole way to Berlin, where he was examined in the jail and the next day was sent to a free psychopathic ward. He never let go of the shaggy brown cap. He watched over it with jealous tenderness.

IN THE PENAL COLONY

Franz Kafka

"IT'S A MACHINE like no other," said the officer to the explorer, as he surveyed the machine with a somewhat admiring look, although he was so familiar with it. The explorer seemed to have accepted merely out of courtesy when the governor had invited him to attend the execution of a soldier condemned to death for disobeying and insulting his superior. Even in the penal colony there was no particularly great interest in this execution. At any rate, here in the deep, sandy little valley enclosed on all sides by bare slopes, the only people present, apart from the officer and the explorer, were the condemned man, a dull-witted, wide-mouthed fellow with ungroomed hair and face, and a soldier, who held the heavy chain that gathered together all the small chains, with which the condemned man was fettered at his wrists, ankles and neck, and which were also connected to one another by intermediate chains. Anyway, the condemned man had a look of such doglike devotion that you might picture him being allowed to run around at liberty on the slopes and returning at the beginning of the execution if you just whistled for him.

The explorer had little taste for the machine and walked back and forth behind the condemned man with an almost visible lack of concern, while the officer saw to the final preparations, now crawling under the machine, which was sunk deep into the ground, now climbing a ladder to inspect the upper sections. Those were tasks that could really have been left to a mechanic, but the officer performed them with great enthusiasm, either because he was a special devotee of this machine or because, for some other reasons, the work couldn't be entrusted to anyone else. "All ready now," he finally called, and climbed down the ladder. He was unusually exhausted, breathed with his mouth wide open, and had two delicate lady's handkerchiefs crammed behind the collar of his uniform. "These uniforms are surely too heavy for the tropics," said the explorer, instead of inquiring about the machine, as the officer had expected. "Of course," said the officer, washing the oil and grease off his hands in a bucket that stood ready there, "but they represent our homeland; we don't want to be cut off from our country.—But now you see this machine," he added without a pause, drying his hands on a cloth and simultaneously pointing to the machine. "Up to this point some hand operations were still necessary; from this point on, however, the machine does all the work by itself." The explorer nodded and followed the officer. The latter, attempting to insure himself against all incidents, said: "Naturally, disorders occur; true, I hope none will happen today, but they still have to be reckoned with. You see, the machine needs to keep going for twelve hours uninterruptedly. But if disorders do occur, they will be very minor and will be cleared away at once."

"Won't you have a seat?" he finally asked, pulling a cane-bottomed chair out from a stack of them and offering it to the explorer, who couldn't refuse. He was now sitting on the rim of a pit, into which he cast a fleeting glance. It wasn't very deep. On one side of the pit the excavated earth was heaped up into a mound, on the other side stood the machine. "I don't know," said the officer, "whether the governor has already explained the machine to you." The explorer made a vague sign with his hand; the officer asked for nothing better, for now he could explain the machine himself. "This machine," he said, grasping a cranking rod, on which he supported himself, "is an invention of our previous governor. I participated in the very first experiments and took part in all the other developments until it was perfected. Of course, the credit for the invention is due to him alone. Have you heard about our previous governor? No? Well, I'm not claiming too much when I say that the organization of the entire penal colony is his creation. We, his friends, already knew at the time of his death that his plan for the colony was so perfectly worked out that his successor, even if he had a thousand new schemes in mind, wouldn't be able to change the old arrangements for many years, at least. And our prediction came true; the new governor had to acknowledge it. Too bad you never met the previous governor!—But," the officer interrupted himself, "I'm babbling, and his machine is here before us. It consists, as you see, of three parts. In the course of time each of these parts has acquired a somewhat popular nickname. The lowest one is called the bed, the highest one is called the sketcher and this central, freely hanging part is called the harrow." "The harrow?" the explorer asked. He hadn't been listening too attentively, the sunlight had lodged itself all too strongly in the shadeless valley, it was hard to gather one's thoughts. And so he considered the officer all the more admirable, seeing him in his tight parade jacket, laden with epaulets and covered with braid, expounding his subject with such enthusiasm and, what's more, still busying himself at a screw here and there, while speaking, screwdriver in hand. The soldier seemed to be of the same frame of mind as the explorer. He had wrapped the condemned man's chain around both wrists, and was leaning on his rifle with one hand; his head was sunk on his chest and he was totally unconcerned. The explorer wasn't surprised at this, because the officer was speaking French, and surely neither the soldier nor the condemned man understood French. Which made it all the more curious that the condemned man was nevertheless making an effort to follow the officer's explanation. With a kind of sleepy persistence he always directed his gaze to the spot the officer was pointing out at the moment, and when the latter was now interrupted by a question from the explorer, he, too, as well as the officer, looked at the explorer.

"Yes, the harrow," said the officer, "the name fits. The needles are arranged in harrow fashion, and the whole thing is manipulated like a harrow, although it remains in one place only, and works much more artistically. Anyway, you'll understand it right away. The condemned man is laid here on the bed.—I'm going to describe the machine first, you see, and only after that will I have the procedure itself carried out. Then you'll be better able to follow it. Besides, one cogwheel in the sketcher is worn too smooth, and squeaks a lot when in operation; when that's going on, it's barely possible to understand one another; unfortunately, spare parts are very hard to procure here.—So then, here is the bed, as I was saying. It's completely covered by a layer of absorbent cotton; you'll soon learn the purpose of that. The condemned man is placed stomach down on this cotton, naked, naturally; here are straps for his hands, here for his feet, here for his neck, to buckle him in tight. Here at the head end of the bed, where, as I said, the man's face lies at first, there is this little felt projection, which can easily be adjusted so that it pops right into the man's mouth. Its purpose is to keep him from screaming and chewing up his tongue. Naturally, the man is forced to put the felt in his mouth or else his neck would be broken by the neck strap." "This is absorbent cotton?" the explorer asked, bending forward. "Yes, of course," said the officer with a smile, "feel it yourself." He took the explorer's hand and ran it over the bed. "It's a specially prepared absorbent cotton, that's why it's so hard to recognize; as I continue talking, I'll get to its purpose." The explorer was now a little more interested in the machine; shading his eyes from the sun with his hand, he looked up at the top of the machine. It was a large construction. The bed and the sketcher were of the same size and looked like two dark trunks for clothing. The sketcher was installed about six feet above the bed; the two were connected at the corners by four brass rods, which were practically darting rays in the sunlight. Between the trunks the harrow hung freely on a steel ribbon.

The officer had scarcely noticed the explorer's earlier indifference, but he was fully aware of the interest he was now beginning to feel, so he ceased his exposition in order to give the explorer time to observe unmolestedly. The condemned man mimicked the explorer; since he couldn't raise his hand to his brow, he blinked upward with unshaded eyes.

"Well, then, the man lies there," said the explorer, leaning back in his chair and crossing his legs.

"Yes," said the officer, pushing his cap back a bit and drawing his hand over his hot face. "Now listen! The bed and the sketcher each has its own electric battery; the bed needs it for itself, the sketcher needs it for the harrow. As soon as the man is strapped in tight, the bed is set in motion. It vibrates in tiny, very rapid jerks sideways and up and down at the same time. You may have seen similar machines in sanatoriums, but in our bed all the movements are precisely calculated; you see, they have to be scrupulously synchronized with the movements of the harrow. It is this harrow, however, that actually carries out the sentence."

"What *is* the sentence?" the explorer asked. "You don't know that, either?" said the officer in amazement, biting his lips: "Forgive me if my explanations may appear haphazard; I ask your pardon most humbly. You see, in the past the governor used to give the explanations; but the new governor has exempted himself from the honor of this duty; but that even such a distinguished visitor"—the explorer attempted to forestall this praise with a gesture of both hands, but the officer insisted on the expression—"that he doesn't apprise even such a distinguished visitor of the form of our sentence, is another innovation that—" He had an oath on his lips, but controlled himself and merely said: "I wasn't notified of that, it's no fault of mine. Anyway, I am the one best capable of explaining our types of sentence, because I carry here"—he tapped his breast pocket—"the designs drawn by the previous governor bearing on the matter."

"Designs by the governor himself?" asked the explorer. "Was he a combination of everything, then? Was he a soldier, judge, engineer, chemist and designer?"

"Yes, indeed," said the officer, nodding, his gaze fixed and meditative. Then he looked at his hands searchingly; he didn't consider them clean enough to touch the drawings, so he went over to the bucket and washed them again. Then he pulled out a little leather wallet, saying: "Our sentence isn't severe. The regulation that the condemned man has broken is written on his body with the harrow. This condemned man, for example"—the officer pointed to the man—"will have 'Honor your superior!' written on his body."

The explorer glanced fleetingly at the man; when the officer had pointed to him, he had been standing with lowered head, seeming to concentrate all his powers of hearing in order to find out something. But the movements of his lips, which bulged as he compressed them, clearly showed he couldn't understand a thing. The explorer had wanted to ask this and that, but now, looking at the man, he merely asked: "Does he know his sentence?" "No," said the officer, and wanted to continue his exposition at once, but the explorer interrupted him: "He doesn't know his own sentence?" "No," the officer said again, then stopped short for a moment, as if desiring the explorer to offer some substantial reason for his question, and then said: "It would be pointless to inform him of it. After all, he'll learn it on his body." The explorer was now ready to remain silent, when he felt the condemned man turn his eyes toward him; he seemed to be asking whether he could approve of the procedure that had been described. And so the explorer, who had already leaned back, bent forward again and asked another question: "But he does at least know, doesn't he, that he has been condemned?" "Not that, either," said the officer, and smiled at the explorer, as if he were still expecting a few more peculiar utterances from him. "No," said the explorer, rubbing his forehead, "and so even now the man still doesn't know how his defense was received?" "He had no opportunity to defend himself," said the officer, looking off to the side, as if he were talking to himself and didn't wish to embarrass the explorer by telling him what was so obvious to himself. "But he must have had an opportunity to defend himself," said the explorer, rising from his chair.

The officer realized he was running the risk of being delayed for a long time in the explanation of the machine; so he went over to the explorer, locked his arm in his, pointed to the condemned man, who, now that their attention was so clearly directed toward him, straightened up smartly—the soldier also pulled the chain taut—and said: "The matter is as follows. Here in the penal colony I serve as a judge. Despite my youth. Because in all penal matters I stood side by side with the previous governor, and I also know the machine best. The principle behind my decisions is: Guilt is always beyond doubt. Other courts can't adhere to this principle, because they consist of several judges and have even higher courts over them. That isn't the case here, or at least it wasn't under the previous governor. To be sure, the new one has already shown a desire to meddle with my court, but so far I've managed to fend him off, and I'll continue to manage it.—You wanted an explanation of this case; it's just as simple as all of them. This morning a captain reported that this man, who's assigned to him as an orderly and sleeps in front of his door, slept through his tour of duty. You see, he is obliged to get up every hour on the hour and salute in front of the captain's door. Certainly not an onerous duty, but a necessary one, since he has to stay alert as both a guard and a servant. Last night the captain wanted to verify whether his orderly was doing his duty. At the stroke of two he opened his door and found him curled up asleep. He went for his riding whip and struck him on the face. Now, instead of standing up and asking for forgiveness, the man grasped his master by the legs, shook him and shouted: 'Hey, throw away that whip or I'll gobble you up.' Those are the facts of the matter. An hour ago the captain came to me, I wrote down his declaration and followed it up with the sentence. Then I had the man put in chains. All that was very simple. If I had first summoned the man and interrogated him, that would only have led to confusion. He would have lied; if I had succeeded in disproving those lies, he would have replaced them with new lies, and so on. But, as it is, I've got him and I won't let go of him again. — Does that now explain everything? But time is passing, the execution ought to begin by now, and I'm not finished yet with the explanation of the machine." He urged the explorer to sit down again, stepped up to the machine once more, and began: "As you see, the shape of the harrow corresponds to the human form; here is the harrow for the upper part of the body, here are the harrows for the legs. For the head there is only this small spike. Is that clear to you?" He leaned over to the explorer in a friendly way, ready to give the most comprehensive explanations.

The explorer looked at the harrow with furrowed brow. The information about the judicial procedure had left him unsatisfied. All the same, he had to tell himself that this was, after all, a penal colony, that special regulations were required here, and that a military code had to be followed, even to extreme limits. But, in addition, he placed some hope in the new governor, who obviously, if only slowly, intended to introduce a new procedure that couldn't penetrate this officer's thick head. Pursuing this train of thought, the explorer asked: "Will the governor attend the execution?" "It's uncertain," said the officer, touched on a sore spot by the blunt question, and his friendly expression clouded over: "For that very reason we must make haste. In fact, as sorry as that makes me, I must shorten my explanations. But tomorrow, when the machine has been cleaned again — its getting so very dirty is its only shortcoming — I could fill in the smaller details. And so, for now, only the most essential facts. — When the man is lying on the bed and the bed begins to vibrate, the harrow lowers itself onto the body. It adjusts itself in such a manner that it just barely touches the body with its sharp points; once this adjustment is completed, this steel cable immediately stiffens into a rod. And now the machine goes into play. An uninitiated person notices no outward difference in the punishments. The harrow seems to work in a uniform way. Quivering, it jabs its points into the body, which is already shaken by the bed. Now, to allow everybody to inspect the execution of the sentence, the harrow was made of glass. Several technical difficulties had to be overcome to embed the needles in it firmly, but we succeeded after a number of experiments. We literally spared no effort. And now everyone can watch through the glass and see how the inscription on the body is done. Won't you step closer and take a look at the needles?"

The explorer got up slowly, went over and bent over the harrow. "Here," said the officer, "you see two types of needles in a complex arrangement. Each long one has a short one next to it. You see, the long ones do the writing and the short ones squirt water to wash away the blood and to keep the lettering clear at all times. The bloody water is then channeled here into small grooves and finally runs off into this main groove, whose drainpipe leads into the pit." With one finger the officer indicated the precise route the bloody water had to take. When, in order to give the most graphic demonstration, he made the actual motion of catching it in his two hands at the outlet of the drainpipe, the explorer raised his head and, groping backwards with his hand, attempted to regain his chair. Then he saw, to his horror, that, like him, the condemned man had accepted the officer's invitation to take a close look at the structure of the harrow. He had tugged the drowsy soldier forward a little by the chain and had also stooped over the glass. He could be seen searching with unsure eyes for what the two gentlemen had just been observing, but not succeeding for lack of the explanation. He bent over this way and that way. Again and again he ran his eyes over the glass. The explorer wanted to drive him back, because he was probably committing a punishable offense. But the officer restrained the explorer firmly with one hand, and with the other took a clod of earth from the mound and threw it at the soldier. The latter raised his eyes with a start, saw what the condemned man had dared to do, dropped his rifle, dug his heels into the ground, tore the condemned man back so hard that he fell right over, and then looked down at the writhing man, who was making his chains rattle. "Pick him up!" shouted the officer, because he noticed that the explorer's attention was being distracted far too much by the condemned man. The explorer even leaned forward all the way across the harrow, not caring about it at all, concerned only to discover what was happening to the condemned man. "Handle him carefully!" shouted the officer again. He ran around the machine, seized the condemned man under the arms himself and, with the aid of the soldier, raised him to his feet, although the man's feet slid out from under him several times.

"By now I know everything," said the explorer when the officer came back to him. "Except for the most important thing of all," the latter said, grasping the explorer's arm and pointing upward: "Up there in the sketcher are the cogwheels that regulate the motion of the harrow, and those wheels are pre-set in accordance with the pattern called for by the sentence. I am still using the previous governor's designs. Here they are"—he drew a few sheets out of the leather wallet—"but unfortunately I cannot hand them to you; they're the most precious things I possess. Sit down, I'll show them to you from this distance, then you'll be able to see them all clearly." He showed the first sheet. The explorer would gladly have made some appreciative remark, but all he saw was mazelike lines in complicated crisscrosses, covering the paper so completely that it was hard to see the white spaces between them. "Read it," said the officer. "I can't," said the explorer. "But it's legible," said the officer. "It's very artistic," said the explorer evasively, "but I can't decipher it." "Yes," said the officer, laughed and pocketed the wallet again, "it isn't model calligraphy for schoolboys. One has to study it a long time. Even you would surely recognize it finally. Naturally, it can't be any simple script; you see, it is not supposed to kill at once, but only after a period of twelve hours on the average; the turning point is calculated to occur during the sixth hour. And so there must be many, many ornaments surrounding the actual letters; the real message encircles the body only within a narrow band; the rest of the body is set aside for the decorations. Are you now able to appreciate the work of the harrow and of the whole machine?—Look!" He leaped onto the ladder, turned a wheel and called down: "Careful, step to one side!" and everything went into action. If the cogwheel hadn't been squeaking, it would have been magnificent. As if the officer were surprised by that disturbing wheel, he threatened it with his fist, then, excusing himself, extended his arms toward the explorer and climbed down hastily in order to observe the operation of the machine from below. There was still something out of order which only he noticed; he climbed up again, thrust both hands into the sketcher, then, to get down more quickly, slid down one of the rods instead of using the ladder, and now, to make himself heard over the noise, shouted with extreme tension into the explorer's ear. "Do you understand the process? The harrow begins to write; when it is finished with the first draft of the lettering on the man's back, the layer of absorbent cotton rolls and turns the body slowly onto its side to give the harrow additional space. Meanwhile the areas that are pierced by the writing press against the cotton, which, thanks to its special preparation, stops the bleeding at once and clears the way for the lettering to sink in further. The prongs here at the edge of the harrow then rip the cotton from the wounds as the body continues to turn, fling it into the pit, and the harrow can go on working. In this way it writes more and more deeply for the twelve hours. For the first six hours the condemned man lives almost as he previously did, but suffering pain. After two hours the felt is removed, because the man has no more strength to scream. In this electrically heated bowl at the head end we place hot boiled rice and milk, from which the man, if he feels like it, can take whatever he can get hold of with his tongue. None of them passes up the opportunity. I know of none, and my experience is extensive. Only around the sixth hour does he lose his pleasure in eating. Then I generally kneel down here and observe this phenomenon. The man seldom swallows the last mouthful, he just turns it around in his mouth and spits it out into the pit. Then I have to duck or he'll hit me in the face with it. But then, how quiet the man becomes around the sixth hour! Even the dumbest one starts to understand. It begins around the eyes. From there it spreads out. A sight that could tempt someone to lie down alongside the man under the harrow. Nothing further happens, the man merely begins to decipher the writing; he purses his lips as if listening to something. As you've seen, it isn't easy to decipher the script with your eyes; but our man deciphers it with his wounds. True, it takes a lot of effort; he needs six hours to complete it. But then the harrow skewers him completely and throws him into the pit, where he splashes down into the bloody water and the cotton. Then the execution is over, and we, the soldier and I, bury him."

The explorer had inclined his ear toward the officer and, his hands in his jacket pockets, was watching the machine run. The condemned man was watching it, too, but without understanding. He was stooping a little and following the moving needles, when the soldier, at a sign from the officer, cut through his shirt and trousers in the back with a knife, so that they fell off the condemned man; he wanted to make a grab for the falling garments, in order to hide his nakedness, but the soldier lifted him up in the air and shook the last scraps off him. The officer turned off the machine, and in the silence that ensued the condemned man was placed under the harrow. His chains were removed and replaced by the fastened straps; at the first movement this seemed to be almost a relief for the condemned man. And now the harrow lowered itself a little more, because he was a thin man. When the points touched him, a shudder ran over his skin; while the soldier was busy with his right hand, he stretched out the left, without knowing in what direction; but it was toward the spot where the explorer was standing. The officer uninterruptedly watched the explorer from the side, as if trying to read in his face the impression being made by the execution, which he had now explained to him at least superficially.

The strap intended for the wrist tore; probably the soldier had drawn it up too tightly. The officer was to help, the soldier showed him the torn-off piece of strap. And the officer did go over to him, saying: "The machine is composed of many, many parts; from time to time something has to rip or break; but that shouldn't falsify one's total judgment. Besides, an immediate substitute is available for the strap; I shall use a chain; of course, for the right arm the delicacy of the vibrations will be impaired." And, while he attached the chains, he added: "The means for maintaining the machine are now quite limited. Under the previous governor there was a fund, readily accessible to me, set aside for just that purpose. There was a supply depot here in which all conceivable spare parts were stored. I confess, I was almost wasteful with it, I mean in the past, not now, as the new governor claims; for him everything serves as a mere pretext for combating the old arrangements. Now he has the machine fund under his own management, and, if I send for a new strap, the torn one is requested as evidence, the new one doesn't come for ten days, and then is of poorer quality and isn't worth much. But how I am supposed to run the machine in the meantime without a strap—nobody cares about that."

The explorer thought it over: It's always a ticklish thing to interfere in someone else's affairs in some decisive way. He was neither a citizen of the penal colony nor a citizen of the country it belonged to. If he wished to condemn the execution or even prevent it, they could say to him: "You're a foreigner, keep quiet." He would have no reply to that, but would only be able to add that in this case he didn't even understand his own motives, since he was traveling purely with the intention of seeing things, and by no means that of altering other people's legal codes, or the like. But matters here were truly very tempting. The injustice of the proceedings and the inhumanity of the execution couldn't be denied. No one could assume that the explorer was doing anything self-serving, because the condemned man was unknown to him, not a compatriot and in no way a person who elicited sympathy. The explorer himself had letters of recommendation from high official sources, he had been welcomed here with great courtesy, and the fact that he had been invited to this execution even seemed to indicate that his opinion of this court was desired. Moreover, this was all the more likely since the governor, as he had now heard more than explicitly, was not partial to these proceedings and was almost hostile to the officer.

At that point the explorer heard the officer shout with rage. He had just shoved the felt gag into the condemned man's mouth, not without difficulty, when the condemned man shut his eyes with an uncontrollable urge to vomit, and vomited. Hastily the officer pulled him up and away from the gag, trying to turn his head toward the pit; but it was too late, the filth was already running down the machine. "All the governor's fault!" yelled the officer, beside himself, shaking the brass rods in front, "my machine is getting befouled like a stable." With trembling hands he showed the explorer what had happened. "Haven't I tried for hours on end to get it across to the governor that no more food is to be given a day before the execution? But the new, lenient school of thought is of a different opinion. The governor's ladies stuff the man's mouth with sweets before he's led away. All his life he's lived on stinking fish and now he's got to eat sweets! But it would still be possible, I'd have no objection, if they only supplied me with a new piece of felt, which I've been requesting for three months now. How can anyone put this felt in his mouth without being disgusted, after more than a hundred men have sucked on it and bitten it while they were dying?"

The condemned man had put his head down and looked peaceful, the soldier was busy cleaning the machine with the condemned man's shirt. The officer walked over to the explorer, who with some sort of foreboding took a step backwards, but the officer took him by the hand and drew him to one side. "I want to say a few words to you in confidence," he said; "that is, if I may?" "Of course," said the explorer, and then listened with lowered eyes.

"This procedure and execution, which you now have the opportunity to admire, are no longer openly supported by any one in our colony at the present time. I am their only spokesman, and at the same time the only spokesman for the old governor's legacy. I can no longer contemplate a further extension of the procedure; I consume all my strength to retain what still exists. While the old governor was alive, the colony was full of his followers; I have some of the old governor's power of persuasion, but I lack his authority entirely; as a consequence, his followers have gone underground; there are still a lot of them, but none of them will admit it. If today—that is, on an execution day—you go into the teahouse and keep your ears open, you will perhaps hear nothing but ambiguous utterances. They are all loyal followers, but under the present governor, with his present views, I can't use them at all. And now I ask you. Is it right that, on account of this governor and his women, who influence him, a life's work like this"—he pointed to the machine—"should be wrecked? Is that to be allowed? Even if someone is a foreigner and only staying on our island for a few days? But there's no time to be lost, preparations are under way to combat my jurisdiction; meetings are already being held in the governor's office in which I am not asked to participate; even your visit today seems to me to be characteristic of the whole situation; they're cowardly and send you, a foreigner, out in advance.—How different the execution was in the old times! A day before the punishment was meted out, the whole valley was already crammed with people; they all came only to watch; early in the morning the governor would arrive with his ladies; fanfares roused the whole encampment; I reported that all was in readiness; the guests—no high official was allowed to be absent—grouped themselves around the machine; this stack of cane-bottomed chairs is a pathetic survival from those days. The machine was freshly polished and gleaming; for almost every execution I put in new spare parts. In front of hundreds of eyes—all the spectators stood on their toes all the way up to the heights there—the condemned man was placed under the harrow by the governor himself. What a private soldier is allowed to do today, was then my task, the chief judge's, and was an honor for me. And now the execution began! No false note disturbed the operation of the machine. At this point many people were no longer watching, but were lying on the sand with closed eyes; everybody knew: Now justice will be done. In the silence all that could be heard was the condemned man's sighing, muffled by the felt. Today the machine no longer manages to squeeze a sigh out of the condemned man that's loud enough not to be stifled by the felt; but in those days the writing needles exuded a corrosive fluid that isn't allowed to be used any more. Well, and then the sixth hour arrived! It was impossible to comply with everyone's request to watch from up close. The governor in his wisdom ordered that the children should be considered first and foremost; of course, thanks to my station, I was always allowed to stay right there; often I would squat down, holding two small children in my arms, right and left. How we all captured the transfigured expression on the tortured face, how we held our cheeks in the glow of this finally achieved and already perishing justice! What times those were, my friend!" The officer had obviously forgotten who was in front of him; he had embraced the explorer and had laid his head on his shoulder. The explorer felt extremely awkward, and impatiently looked past the officer. The soldier had finished his cleaning and had just poured boiled rice into the bowl from a jar. The condemned man, who seemed to have recovered completely by this time, had scarcely noticed this when he began snatching at the rice with his tongue. The soldier kept pushing him away again, because the rice was meant for a later time, but surely the soldier also was acting improperly when he dug into the rice with his dirty hands and ate some before the eyes of the covetous condemned man.

The officer quickly regained control of himself. "Please don't think I wanted to play on your sympathy," he said, "I know it's impossible to make anyone understand those times today. Anyway, the machine is still working and speaks for itself. It speaks for itself even when left alone in this valley. And at the end the corpse still falls into the pit with that incomprehensibly gentle sweep, even if hundreds of people are no longer clustered around the pit like flies, as in the past. Then we had to install a strong railing around the pit; it was torn down long ago."

The explorer wanted to move his face out of the officer's gaze, and looked around aimlessly. The officer thought he was contemplating the barrenness of the valley; and so he took his hands, stepped around him to make their eyes meet, and asked: "Do you observe the disgrace?"

But the explorer remained silent. For a while the officer let him alone; with legs planted far apart, his hands on his hips, he stood quietly looking at the ground. Then he smiled at the explorer encouragingly and said: "I was near you yesterday when the governor invited you. I heard the invitation. I know the governor. I immediately understood his purpose in inviting you. Even though his authority may be great enough for him to take steps against me, he still doesn't dare to, but instead he wishes to expose me to your opinion, that of a highly esteemed foreign visitor. He worked it out carefully; this is your second day on the island, you didn't know the old governor and his philosophy, you are prejudiced by European points of view, perhaps you are an opponent on principle of any kind of capital punishment, and of this kind of execution by machine in particular; furthermore, you observe that the execution is performed without the participation of the public, in a dismal atmosphere, on a machine that is already somewhat damaged — now, taking all this together, thinks the governor, wouldn't it be quite possible for you to consider my procedure incorrect? And if you consider it incorrect (I'm still stating the governor's train of thought), you won't keep silent about it, because you must surely trust your tried-and-true convictions. Of course, you've seen and learned to respect many peculiar customs of many nations, and so probably you won't come out against the procedure as openly as you might do at home. But the governor doesn't need that much. A hasty word, merely a careless word, is enough. It doesn't have to be rooted in your convictions, if only it apparently suits his purposes. I'm sure he's going to question you as shrewdly as possible. And his ladies will sit around in a circle, pricking up their ears; you'll say something like 'In our country the judicial procedure is different' or 'In our country the defendant is interrogated before the sentence' or 'In our country there are punishments other than capital punishment' or 'In our country torture was used only in the Middle Ages.' Those are all remarks that are just as correct as they seem self-evident to you, innocent remarks that do not impugn my procedure. But how will the governor take them? I can see him, the good governor, immediately pushing his chair aside and dashing onto the balcony, I can see his ladies pouring after him, I can now hear his voice — his ladies call it a voice of thunder — as he says: 'A great Occidental explorer, sent to investigate judicial procedure all over the world, has just said that our old traditional procedure is inhumane. After this judgment by such a personality, it is naturally impossible for me to tolerate this procedure any longer. As of this date, therefore, I decree — and so on.' You will want to intervene, you didn't say what he is proclaiming, you didn't call my procedure inhumane; on the contrary, in accordance with your profoundest insight, you consider it the most humane and the most fitting for human society, you also admire this machinery—but it's too late; you can't get onto the balcony, which is already full of ladies; you want to call attention to yourself; you want to shout; but a lady's hand shuts your mouth—and I and the achievement of the old governor are lost."

The explorer had to suppress a smile; the task he had considered so hard was thus so easy. He said evasively: "You overestimate my influence; the governor read my letter of recommendation, he knows I'm not an expert on judicial procedure. If I were to express an opinion, it would be the opinion of a private person, no more significant than anyone else's opinion, and at any rate much more insignificant than the opinion of the governor, who, if I'm not misinformed, has very wide-ranging powers in this penal colony. If his opinion of this procedure is as unshakable as you believe, then I'm afraid the end of this procedure has come anyway, without the need of my modest cooperation."

Did the officer understand by this time? No, he still didn't understand. He shook his head vigorously, cast a brief glance back at the condemned man and the soldier, who winced and left the rice alone; then he stepped up close to the explorer, looking not at his face but at a random area of his jacket, and said, more softly than before: "You don't know the governor; to some extent—please forgive the expression—you're an innocent in comparison with him and all of us; believe me, your influence cannot be rated highly enough. In fact, I was overjoyed when I heard that you were to attend the execution alone. That order of the governor's was directed against me, but now I'm turning it around in my favor. Undistracted by false insinuations and contemptuous glances—which couldn't have been avoided if more people had participated in the execution—you have listened to my explanations, you have seen the machine and you are now about to view the execution. Certainly your opinion has been formed; if some small uncertainties still persist, the sight of the execution will remove them. And now I request of you: help me in my dealings with the governor!"

The explorer wouldn't let him continue. "How could I?" he exclaimed, "it's altogether impossible. I can't help you any more than I can harm you."

"Yes, you can," said the officer. With some alarm the explorer saw that the officer was clenching his fists. "Yes, you can," the officer repeated even more urgently. "I have a plan that can't fail. You think your influence isn't enough. I know that it *is* enough. But even granting that you're right, isn't it still necessary to try everything, even measures that are inadequate, in order to preserve this procedure? So listen to my plan. To carry it out, it's necessary above all for you to conceal your opinion of the procedure as much as possible in the colony today. If you're not actually asked, you must by no means make a statement; but if you do make statements, they must be brief and vague; people should notice that it's hard for you to talk about it, that you're bitter, that, in case you were to speak openly, you would actually break out into curses. I'm not asking you to lie; not a bit; you should merely make brief replies, such as 'Yes, I saw the execution' or 'Yes, I heard all the explanations.' Only that, nothing more. Of course, there's enough reason for the resentment that people must see in you, even if it's not in the way the governor thinks. Naturally, he will misunderstand it completely and interpret it in his own fashion. That's the basis of my plan. Tomorrow in the government building, under his chairmanship, a big meeting of all the top administration officials will take place. Naturally, the governor has managed to turn such meetings into a show. A gallery has been built that's always full of spectators. I am compelled to take part in the deliberations, but I tremble with repugnance. Now, in any case, you will surely be invited to the meeting; if you behave today in accordance with my plan, the invitation will become an urgent request. But if, for some inconceivable reason, you're not invited after all, you will have to ask for an invitation; there's no doubt you'll get it then. So then, tomorrow you are sitting with the ladies in the governor's box. He looks upward again and again to make sure you're there. After various indifferent, ridiculous items on the agenda that are just sops for the audience—generally, harbor construction, always harbor construction!—the legal procedure comes up for discussion, too. If it isn't mentioned, or isn't mentioned soon enough, by the governor, I'll make sure that it gets mentioned. I'll stand up and make my report on today's execution. A very brief speech, nothing but the report. True, a report of that nature isn't customary, but I'll make it. The governor thanks me, as always, with a friendly smile, and then he isn't able to restrain himself, he seizes the favorable opportunity. 'Just now,' he'll say, or words to that effect, 'the report of the execution has been made. I would merely like to add to this report the fact that the great explorer whose visit, which honors our colony so immensely, you all know about, was present at that very execution. Our meeting today is also made more significant by his presence. Now, shall we not ask this great explorer for his opinion of this old, traditional style of execution and of the proceedings that lead up to it?' Everyone naturally applauds to indicate approval and general consent, I loudest of all. The governor bows to you and says: 'Then, in the name of all assembled here, I pose the question.' And now you walk up to the railing. Place your hands where everyone can see them, or else the ladies will take hold of them and play with your fingers.—And now finally comes your speech. I don't know how I'll bear the suspense of the hours till then. In your talk you mustn't keep within any bounds; shout out the truth; lean over the railing; roar, yes, roar your opinion, your unalterable opinion, at the governor. But perhaps you don't want to, it doesn't suit your nature, perhaps in your country behavior in such situations is different; that's all right, too, even that is perfectly satisfactory; don't stand up at all, say only a few words, whisper them, so that only the officials right below you can hear; that's enough; you yourself don't need to speak about the lack of attendance at the execution, the squeaking cogwheel, the torn strap, the disgusting felt gag; no, I'll pick up on all the rest, and, trust me, if my speech doesn't actually drive him out of the room, at least it will bring him to his knees, so he'll have to avow: 'Old governor, I bow down before you.'—That's my plan; are you willing to help me carry it out? But of course you're willing; what's more, you must." And the officer grasped the explorer by both arms and looked him in the face, breathing heavily. He had shouted the last few sentences so loud that even the soldier and the condemned man had had their attention aroused; even though they couldn't understand any of it, still they stopped eating and looked over at the explorer as they chewed.

The answer he had to give was unequivocal for the explorer from the very outset; he had experienced too much in his life for him to possibly waver now; he was basically honest and he was fearless. Nevertheless he now hesitated for the space of a moment at the sight of the soldier and the condemned man. But finally he said as he had to: "No." The officer blinked his eyes several times, but didn't avert his gaze from him. "Do you want an explanation?" the explorer asked. The officer nodded in silence. "I'm an opponent of this procedure," the explorer now said; "even before you took me into your confidence—naturally, under no circumstances will I abuse that confidence—I had already considered whether I had any right to take steps against this procedure, and whether my intervention could have even a small chance of succeeding. It was clear to me whom I should turn to first if I wanted to do this: to the governor, of course. You made that even clearer to me, but you didn't plant the seeds of my decision; on the contrary, I sincerely respect your honest conviction, even if it can't lead me astray."

The officer remained silent, turned toward the machine, grasped one of the brass rods and then, bending backwards a little, looked up at the sketcher as if to check whether everything was in order. The soldier and the condemned man seemed to have become friends; difficult as it was to accomplish, being strapped in as tightly as he was, the condemned man made signs to the soldier; the soldier leaned over toward him; the condemned man whispered something to him, and the soldier nodded.

The explorer walked after the officer and said: "You still don't know what I intend to do. Yes, I'll give the governor my views about the procedure, but personally, not at an open meeting; furthermore, I won't be staying here long enough to be drawn into any meeting; by tomorrow morning I'll be sailing away or at least boarding the ship." It didn't look as if the officer had been listening. "So the procedure didn't win you over," he said to himself, and smiled, the way an old man smiles at a child's silliness while pursuing his own real thoughts behind the smile.

"Well, then, it's time," he finally said, and suddenly looked at the explorer with bright eyes that communicated some invitation, some summons to participate.

"Time for what?" asked the explorer uneasily, but received no reply.

"You're free," the officer said to the condemned man in the man's language. At first the man didn't believe it. "Well, you're free," said the officer. For the first time the condemned man's face showed real signs of life. Was it true? Was it only a caprice of the officer that might be only temporary? Had the foreign explorer won him a pardon? What was it? Those were the questions visible in his face. But not for long. Whatever the case might be, he wanted to be really free if he could, and he began to squirm, to the extent that the harrow would permit him to.

"You'll rip the straps on me," shouted the officer; "lie still! We're opening them now." And, along with the soldier, to whom he signaled, he set to work. The condemned man laughed quietly and wordlessly to himself; now he would turn his face to the officer on his left, now to the soldier on his right, nor did he forget the explorer.

"Pull him out," the officer ordered the soldier. To do this, some precautions had to be taken because of the harrow. As a result of his impatience the condemned man already had a few small scratches on his back. But, from this point on, the officer hardly gave him another thought. He walked up to the explorer, drew out the little leather wallet again, leafed through it, finally found the sheet he was looking for and showed it to the explorer. "Read it," he said. "I can't," said the explorer, "I've already told you I can't read these sheets." "But look at the sheet closely," said the officer, and stepped right next to the explorer to read along with him. When even that didn't help, he moved his little finger over the paper—but high above it, as if the sheet was in no case to be touched—in order to make it easier for the explorer to read. The explorer also made an effort, so that he could at least be obliging to the officer in this matter, but it was impossible. Now the officer began to spell out the inscription, and then he read it once more straight through. "It says 'Be just!'" he said, "now surely you can read it." The explorer bent so low over the paper that the officer moved it further away, fearing he might touch it; now the explorer said no more, but it was obvious that he still hadn't been able to read it. "It says 'Be just!'" the officer said again. "Could be," said the explorer, "I take your word for it." "Good," said the officer, at least partially contented, and, holding the sheet, stepped onto the ladder; with great care he inserted the sheet into the sketcher, apparently making a total rearrangement of the wheels; it was a very painstaking task; very small wheels must also have been involved; at times the officer's head disappeared in the sketcher altogether, because he had to examine the wheels so closely.

The explorer watched this labor from below without a pause; his neck grew stiff and his eyes hurt from the sunlight that streamed all over the sky. The soldier and the condemned man were occupied only with each other. The condemned man's shirt and trousers, which were already in the pit, were fished out by the soldier on the point of his bayonet. The shirt was horribly filthy, and the condemned man washed it in the bucket of water. When he put on the shirt and trousers, both the soldier and the condemned man had to laugh out loud, because, after all, the garments were cut in two in the back. Perhaps the condemned man felt obligated to entertain the soldier; in his cut-up clothes he turned around in a circle in front of the soldier, who squatted on the ground and slapped his knees as he laughed. Nevertheless, they still controlled themselves out of regard for the gentlemen's presence.

When the officer was finally finished up above, he once more surveyed the whole thing in every detail, smiling all the while; now he closed the cover of the sketcher, which had been opened up till then, climbed down, looked into the pit and then at the condemned man, noticed with satisfaction that he had taken his clothing out, then went to the bucket of water to wash his hands, realized too late how loathsomely filthy it now was, was sad about not being able to wash his hands, finally dipped them in the sand—he found this substitute inadequate but he had to make do with it—then stood up and started to unbutton his uniform jacket. As he did so, the two lady's handkerchiefs he had crammed behind his collar fell into his hands right away. "Here are your handkerchiefs for you," he said, throwing them to the condemned man. And to the explorer he said, by way of explanation, "Gifts from the ladies."

Despite the obvious haste with which he took off his jacket and then stripped completely, he nevertheless handled each garment very carefully; he even expressly ran his fingers over the silver braid on his jacket and shook a tassel back into place. It seemed inconsistent with this care, however, that, as soon as he was through handling a garment, he immediately threw it into the pit with an angry jerk. The last thing left to him was his short sword with its belt. He drew the sword from its sheath, broke it, then gathered everything together in his hand, the pieces of the sword, the sheath and the belt, and threw them away so violently that they clattered together down in the pit.

Now he stood there naked. The explorer bit his lips and said nothing. Of course, he knew what was going to happen, but he had no right to prevent the officer from doing anything he wanted. If the judicial procedure to which the officer was devoted was really so close to being abolished—possibly as a result of the intervention of the explorer, which the latter, for his part, felt obligated to go ahead with—then the officer was now acting perfectly correctly; in his place the explorer would have acted no differently.

At first the soldier and the condemned man understood nothing; at the beginning they didn't even watch. The condemned man was quite delighted to have gotten the handkerchiefs back, but he wasn't allowed to take pleasure in them long, because the soldier took them away from him in one rapid, unforeseeable grab. Now, in his turn, the condemned man tried to pull the handkerchiefs out of the belt under which he had stowed them, but the soldier was alert. They were fighting that way half-jokingly. Only when the officer was completely naked did they pay attention. The condemned man in particular seemed struck by the presentiment of some great shift in events. What had happened to him was now happening to the officer. Perhaps it would continue that way right up to the bitter end. Probably the foreign explorer had given the order for it. Thus it was revenge. Without having suffered all the way himself, he was nevertheless avenged all the way. A broad, soundless laugh now appeared on his face and no longer left it.

But the officer had turned toward the machine. If it had been clear even earlier that he understood the machine intimately, now it was absolutely astounding how he manipulated it and how it obeyed him. He had merely brought his hand close to the harrow and it rose and sank several times until reaching the proper position for receiving him; he merely clutched the bed by the edge and it already began to vibrate; the felt gag moved toward his mouth; it was evident that the officer didn't really want to use it, but his hesitation lasted only a moment; he gave in right away and closed his mouth around it. Everything was ready, only the straps still hung down along the sides, but they were obviously unnecessary; the officer didn't need to be buckled in. Then the condemned man noticed the loose straps; in his opinion the execution wouldn't be perfect if the straps weren't buckled tight; he made a vigorous sign to the soldier and they ran over to strap in the officer. He had already stretched out one foot to move the crank that was to set the sketcher in motion; then he saw that those two had come, so he pulled back his foot and let himself be strapped in. Now, of course, he could no longer reach the crank; neither the soldier nor the condemned man would be able to find it, and the explorer was determined not to move an inch. It wasn't necessary; the straps were scarcely in place when the machine started running; the bed vibrated, the needles danced on his skin; the harrow moved lightly up and down. The explorer had already been staring at the scene for some time before he recalled that a wheel in the sketcher should have been squeaking; but all was still, not the slightest whir was to be heard.

Because of this quietness, their attention was drawn away from the actual operation of the machine. The explorer looked over at the soldier and the condemned man. The condemned man was the livelier one; everything about the machine interested him; now he bent down, now he stretched upward; his index finger was constantly extended to show the soldier something. It was agonizing for the explorer. He was resolved to stay there to the end, but he knew he couldn't stand the sight of those two very long. "Go home," he said. The soldier may have been prepared to do so, but the condemned man looked on the order as an actual punishment. He asked beseechingly, with clasped hands, to be allowed to remain, and when the explorer shook his head and refused to give in, he even knelt down. The explorer saw that orders were of no use in this instance; he was about to go over and chase the two away. Then he heard a noise up in the sketcher. He looked up. Was that cogwheel creating a hindrance after all? But it was something else. Slowly the cover of the sketcher lifted and then flew wide open with a bang. The cog of a wheel became visible and rose higher, soon the whole wheel could be seen; it was as if some terrific force were compressing the sketcher, so that there was no more room for this wheel; the wheel turned until it reached the rim of the sketcher, fell down and rolled on its edge for some distance in the sand before coming to rest on its side. But up there a second wheel was already rising, followed by many more wheels, large, small and barely discernible ones; the same thing occurred with all of them; every time it seemed the sketcher surely had to be completely empty, a new, particularly numerous group appeared, rose, fell down, rolled in the sand and came to rest. This series of events made the condemned man completely forget the explorer's command; the cogwheels delighted him thoroughly; he kept trying to grab hold of one, at the same time spurring the soldier on to help him, but always drew back his hand in alarm, because that wheel was followed immediately by another wheel that frightened him, at least when it just started to roll.

The explorer, on the other hand, was very uneasy; the machine was obviously falling apart; the quietness of its operation was deceptive; he felt that he now had to do something for the officer, who could no longer take care of himself. But while the falling of the cogwheels had monopolized his entire attention, he had neglected to observe the rest of the machine; now, however, that the last cogwheel had left the sketcher and he bent over the harrow, he had a new, even worse surprise. The harrow wasn't writing, it was merely stabbing, and the bed wasn't turning the body over but merely lifting it, quivering, into the needles. The explorer wanted to intervene and possibly bring the whole thing to a standstill; this was no torture such as the officer wished to achieve, this was outright murder. He extended his hands. But at that moment the harrow was already lifting itself to the side with the skewered body, as it usually did only in the twelfth hour. The blood was flowing in a hundred streams, not mixed with water; the little water pipes had failed to work this time, as well. And now the final failure took place; the body didn't come loose from the long needles; it poured out its blood, but hung over the pit without falling. The harrow was already prepared to return to its former position, but, as if it noticed of its own accord that it was not yet free of its burden, it remained above the pit. "Why don't you help?" shouted the explorer to the soldier and the condemned man, seizing the officer's feet himself. He intended to press himself against the feet on this side, while those two grasped the officer's head on the other side, so he could be slowly removed from the needles. But now those two couldn't make up their minds to come; the condemned man actually turned away; the explorer had to go up to them and forcibly hustle them over to the officer's head. In doing so, he saw the face of the corpse, almost against his will. It was as it had been in life; no sign of the promised redemption could be discovered; what all the others had found in the machine, the officer did not find; his lips were tightly compressed, his eyes were open and had a living expression; his gaze was one of calm conviction; his forehead was pierced by the point of the big iron spike.

When the explorer, with the soldier and the condemned man behind him, arrived at the first houses of the colony, the soldier pointed to one and said: "Here is the teahouse."

On the ground floor of the house was a long, low cavelike room, its walls and ceiling blackened by smoke. On the street side it was open for its entire width. Although the teahouse was not much different from the rest of the houses in the colony, which, except for the governor's palace complex, were all very rundown, it still gave the explorer the impression of a historic survival; and he felt the impact of earlier times. He stepped up closer and, followed by the two who were accompanying him, he walked among the unoccupied tables that stood in the street in front of the teahouse, inhaling the cool, musty air that came from inside. "The Old Man is buried here," said the soldier; "the priest refused to allow him a place in the cemetery. For a while people were undecided about where to bury him, finally they buried him here. I'm sure the officer didn't tell you anything about that, because he was naturally more ashamed of that than of anything else. He even tried a few times to dig the Old Man out at night, but he was always chased away." "Where is the grave?" asked the explorer, who couldn't believe the soldier. At once both of them, the soldier and the condemned man, ran ahead of him and with outstretched hands indicated a spot where they claimed the grave was located. They led the explorer all the way to the back wall, where customers were sitting at a few tables. Probably they were dock workers, powerful men with short beards that were so black they shone. All were jacketless, their shirts were torn, they were poor, downtrodden people. When the explorer approached, a few of them stood up, flattened themselves against the wall and looked in his direction. "It's a foreigner," was the whisper on all sides of the explorer; "he wants to see the grave." They pushed aside one of the tables, beneath which there actually was a gravestone. It was a simple stone, low enough to be concealed under a table. It bore an inscription in very small letters; the explorer had to kneel to read it. It said: "Here lies the old governor. His followers, who may not now reveal their names, dug this grave for him and erected the stone. There exists a prophecy that after a certain number of years the governor will rise again and will lead his followers out of this house to reconquer the colony. Believe and wait!" When the explorer had read this and stood up, he saw the men standing around him and smiling, as if they had read the inscription along with him, had found it ludicrous and were inviting him to share their opinion. The explorer acted as if he didn't notice this, distributed a few coins among them, waited until the table was pushed back over the grave, left the teahouse and went down to the harbor.

In the teahouse the soldier and the condemned man had run into acquaintances who detained them. But they must have torn themselves away from them quickly, because the explorer was still only halfway down the long flight of stairs that led to the boats when he saw they were already running after him. They probably wanted to force the explorer to take them along at the last moment. While the explorer, down below, was negotiating with a boatman to row him over to the steamer, those two dashed furiously down the steps, silently, because they didn't dare shout. But when they arrived down below, the explorer was already in the boat, which the boatman was just shoving off from shore. They might still have been able to jump into the boat, but the explorer picked up a heavy, knotted hawser from the floor, threatened them with it and thus prevented them from jumping.

THE GOLDEN POT

E. T. A. Hoffmann

First Vigil

ON ASCENSION DAY, about three o'clock in the afternoon in Dresden, a young man dashed through the Schwarzthor, or Black Gate, and ran right into a basket of apples and cookies which an old and very ugly woman had set out for sale. The crash was prodigious; what wasn't squashed or broken was scattered, and hordes of street urchins delightedly divided the booty which this quick gentleman had provided for them. At the fearful shrieking which the old hag began, her fellow vendors, leaving their cake and brandy tables, surrounded the young man, and with plebian violence scolded and stormed at him. For shame and vexation he uttered no word, but merely held out his small and by no means particularly well-filled purse, which the old woman eagerly seized and stuck into her pocket.

The hostile ring of bystanders now broke; but as the young man started off, the hag called after him, "Ay, run, run your way, Devil's Bird! You'll end up in the crystal! The crystal!" The screeching harsh voice of the woman had something unearthly in it: so that the promenaders paused in amazement, and the laughter, which at first had been universal, instantly died away. The Student Anselmus, for the young man was no other, even though he did not in the least understand these singular phrases, felt himself seized with a certain involuntary horror; and he quickened his steps still more, until he was almost running, to escape the curious looks of the multitude, all of whom were staring at him. As he made his way through the crowd of well-dressed people, he heard them muttering on all sides: "Poor young fellow! Ha! What a vicious old witch!" The mysterious words of the old woman, oddly enough, had given this ludicrous adventure a sort of sinister turn; and the youth, previously unobserved, was now regarded with a certain sympathy. The ladies, because of his fine figure and handsome face, which the glow of inward anger rendered still more expressive, forgave

105

him his awkwardness, as well as the dress he wore, though it was at variance with all fashion. His pike-gray frock was shaped as if the tailor had known the modern style only by hearsay; and his well-kept black satin trousers gave him a certain pedagogic air, to which his gait and manner did not at all correspond.

The Student had almost reached the end of the alley which leads out to the Linkische Bath; but his breath could no longer stand such a pace. From running, he took to walking; but he still hardly dared to lift an eye from the ground, for he still saw apples and cookies dancing around him, and every kind look from this or that pretty girl seemed to him to be only a continuation of the mocking laughter at the Schwarzthor.

In this mood he reached the entrance of the Bath: groups of holiday people, one after the other, were moving in. Music of wind instruments resounded from the place, and the din of merry guests was growing louder and louder. The poor Student Anselmus was almost ready to weep; since Ascension Day had always been a family festival for him, he had hoped to participate in the felicities of the Linkische paradise; indeed, he had intended even to go to the length of a half portion of coffee with rum and a whole bottle of double beer, and he had put more money in his purse than was entirely convenient or advisable. And now, by accidentally kicking the apple-and-cookie basket, he had lost all the money he had with him. Of coffee, of double or single beer, of music, of looking at the pretty girls—in a word, of all his fancied enjoyments there was now nothing more to be said. He glided slowly past; and at last turned down the Elbe road, which at that time happened to be quite empty.

Beneath an elder-tree, which had grown out through the wall, he found a kind green resting place: here he sat down, and filled a pipe from the Sanitätsknaster, or health-tobacco-box, of which his friend the Conrector Paulmann had lately made him a present. Close before him rolled and chafed the gold-dyed waves of the fair Elbe: on the other side rose lordly Dresden, stretching, bold and proud, its light towers into the airy sky; farther off, the Elbe bent itself down towards flowery meads and fresh springing woods; and in the dim distance, a range of azure peaks gave notice of remote Bohemia. But, heedless of this, the Student Anselmus, looking gloomily before him, blew forth smoky clouds into the air. His chagrin at length became audible, and he said, "In truth, I am born to losses and crosses for all my life! That, as a boy, I could never guess the right way at Odds and Evens; that my bread and butter always fell on the buttered side—but I won't even mention these sorrows. But now that I've become a student, in spite of Satan, isn't it a frightful fate that I'm still as bumbling as ever? Can I put on a new coat without getting grease on it the first day, or without tearing a cursed hole in it on some nail or other? Can I ever bow to a Councillor or a lady without pitching the hat out of my hands, or even slipping on the smooth pavement, and taking an embarrassing fall? When I was in Halle, didn't I have to pay three or four groschen every market day for broken crockery—the Devil putting it into my head to dash straight forward like a lemming? Have I ever got to my college, or any other place that I had an appointment to, at the right time? Did it ever matter if I set out a half hour early, and planted myself at the door, with the knocker in my hand? Just as the clock is going to strike, souse! Some devil empties a wash basin down on me, or I run into some fellow coming out, and get myself engaged in endless quarrels until the time is clean gone.

"Ah, well. Where are you fled now, you blissful dreams of coming fortune, when I proudly thought that I might even reach the height of Geheimrat? And hasn't my evil star estranged me from my best patrons? I had heard, for instance, that the Councillor, to whom I have a letter of introduction, cannot stand hair cut close; with an immensity of trouble the barber managed to fasten a little queue to the back of my head; but at my first bow his unblessed knot comes loose, and a little dog which had been snuffing around me frisks off to the Geheimrat with the queue in its mouth. I spring after it in terror, and stumble against the table, where he has been working while at breakfast; and cups, plates, ink-glass, sandbox crash to the floor and a flood of chocolate and ink covers the report he has just been writing. 'Is the Devil in this man?' bellows the furious Privy Councillor, and he shoves me out of the room.

"What did it matter when Conrector Paulmann gave me hopes of copywork: will the malignant fate, which pursues me everywhere, permit it? Today even! Think of it! I intended to celebrate Ascension Day with cheerfulness of soul. I was going to stretch a point for once. I might have gone, as well as anyone else, into the Linkische Bath, and called out proudly, 'Marqueur, a bottle of double beer; best sort, if you please.' I might have sat till far in the evening; and moreover close by this or that fine party of well-dressed ladies. I know it, I feel it! Heart would have come into me, I should have been quite another man; nay, I might have carried it so far, that when one of them asked, 'What time is it?' or 'What is it they are playing?' I would have started up with light grace, and without overturning my glass, or stumbling over the bench, but with a graceful bow, moving a step and a half forward, I would have answered, 'Give me leave, mademoiselle! it is the overture of the *Donauweibchen*'; or, 'It is just going to strike six.' Could any mortal in the world have taken it ill of me? No! I say; the girls would have looked over, smiling so roguishly; as they always do when I pluck up heart to show them that I too understand the light tone of society, and know how ladies should be spoken to. And now the Devil himself leads me into that cursed apple-basket, and now I must sit moping in solitude, with nothing but a poor pipe of——" Here the Student Anselmus was interrupted in his soliloquy by a strange rustling and whisking, which rose close by him in the grass, but soon glided up into the twigs and leaves of the elder-tree that stretched out over his head. It was as if the evening wind were shaking the leaves, as if little birds were twittering among the branches, moving their little wings in capricious flutter to and fro. Then he heard a whispering and lisping, and it seemed as if the blossoms were sounding like little crystal bells. Anselmus listened and listened. Ere long, the whispering, and lisping, and tinkling, he himself knew not how, grew to faint and half-scattered words:

"'Twixt this way, 'twixt that; 'twixt branches, 'twixt blossoms, come shoot, come twist and twirl we! Sisterkin, sisterkin! up to the shine; up, down, through and through, quick! Sunrays yellow; evening wind whispering; dewdrops pattering; blossoms all singing: sing we with branches and blossoms! Stars soon glitter; must down: 'twixt this way, 'twixt that, come shoot, come twist, come twirl we, sisterkin!"

And so it went along, in confused and confusing speech. The Student Anselmus thought: "Well, it is only the evening wind, which tonight truly is whispering distinctly enough." But at that moment there sounded over his head, as it were, a triple harmony of clear crystal bells: he looked up, and perceived three little snakes, glittering with green and gold, twisted around the branches, and stretching out their heads to the evening sun. Then, again, began a whispering and twittering in the same words as before, and the little snakes went gliding and caressing up and down through the twigs; and while they moved so rapidly, it was as if the elder-bush were scattering a thousand glittering emeralds through the dark leaves.

"It is the evening sun sporting in the elder-bush," thought the Student Anselmus; but the bells sounded again; and Anselmus observed that one snake held out its little head to him. Through all his limbs there went a shock like electricity; he quivered in his inmost heart: he kept gazing up, and a pair of glorious dark-blue eyes were looking at him with unspeakable longing; and an unknown feeling of highest blessedness and deepest sorrow nearly rent his heart asunder. And as he looked, and still looked, full of warm desire, into those kind eyes, the crystal bells sounded louder in harmonious accord, and the glittering emeralds fell down and encircled him, flickering round him in a thousand sparkles and sporting in resplendent threads of gold. The elder-bush moved and spoke: "You lay in my shadow; my perfume flowed around you, but you understood it not. The perfume is my speech, when love kindles it." The evening wind came gliding past, and said: "I played round your temples, but you understood me not. That breath is my speech, when love kindles it." The sunbeam broke through the clouds, and the sheen of it burned, as in words: "I overflowed you, with glowing gold, but you understood me not. That glow is my speech, when love kindles it."

And, still deeper and deeper sank in the view of those glorious eyes, his longing grew keener, his desire more warm. And all rose and moved around him, as if awakening to glad life. Flowers and blossoms shed their odours round him, and their odour was like the lordly singing of a thousand softest voices, and what they sang was borne, like an echo, on the golden evening clouds, as they flitted away, into far-off lands. But as the last sunbeam abruptly sank behind the hills, and the twilight threw its veil over the scene, there came a hoarse deep voice, as from a great distance:

"Hey! hey! what chattering and jingling is that up there? Hey! hey! who catches me the ray behind the hills? Sunned enough, sung enough. Hey! hey! through bush and grass, through grass and stream. Hey! hey! Come dow-w-n, dow-w-w-n!"

So the voice faded away, as in murmurs of a distant thunder; but the crystal bells broke off in sharp discords. All became mute; and the Student Anselmus observed how the three snakes, glittering and sparkling, glided through the grass towards the river; rustling and hustling, they rushed into the Elbe; and over the waves where they vanished, there crackled up a green flame, which, gleaming forward obliquely, vanished in the direction of the city.

Second Vigil

"The gentleman is ill?" said a decent burgher's wife, who, returning from a walk with her family, had paused here, and, with crossed arms, was looking at the mad pranks of the Student Anselmus. Anselmus had clasped the trunk of the elder-tree, and was calling incessantly up to the branches and leaves: "O glitter and shine once more, dear gold snakes: let me hear your little bell-voices once more! Look on me once more, kind eyes; O once, or I must die in pain and warm longing!" And with this, he was sighing and sobbing from the bottom of his heart most pitifully; and in his eagerness and impatience, shaking the elder-tree to and fro; which, however, instead of any reply, rustled quite stupidly and unintelligibly with its leaves; and so rather seemed, as it were, to make sport of the Student Anselmus and his sorrows.

"The gentleman is ill!" said the burgher's wife; and Anselmus felt as if someone had shaken him out of a deep dream, or poured ice-cold water on him, to awaken him without loss of time. He now first saw clearly where he was, and recollected what a strange apparition had assaulted him, nay, so beguiled his senses, as to make him break forth into loud talk with himself. In astonishment, he gazed at the woman, and at last snatching up his hat, which had fallen to the ground in his transport, was about to make off in all speed. The burgher himself had come forward in the meanwhile, and, setting down the child from his arm on the grass, had been leaning on his staff, and with amazement listening and looking at the Student. He now picked up the pipe and tobacco-box which the Student had let fall, and, holding them out to him, said: "Don't take on so dreadfully, my worthy sir, or alarm people in the dark, when nothing is the matter, after all, but a drop or two of christian liquor: go home, like a good fellow, and sleep it off."

The Student Anselmus felt exceedingly ashamed; he uttered nothing but a most lamentable Ah!

"Pooh! Pooh!" said the burgher, "never mind it a jot; such a thing will happen to the best; on good old Ascension Day a man may readily enough forget himself in his joy, and gulp down a thought too much. A clergyman himself is no worse for it: I presume, my worthy sir, you are a *Candidatus*. But, with your leave, sir, I shall fill my pipe with your tobacco; mine was used up a little while ago."

This last sentence the burgher uttered while the Student Anselmus was about to put away his pipe and box; and now the burgher slowly and deliberately cleaned his pipe, and began as slowly to fill it. Several burgher girls had come up: these were speaking secretly with the woman and each other, and tittering as they looked at Anselmus. The Student felt as if he were standing on prickly thorns, and burning needles. No sooner had he got back his pipe and tobacco-box, than he darted off as fast as he could.

All the strange things he had seen were clean gone from his memory; he simply recollected having babbled all sorts of foolish stuff beneath the elder-tree. This was the more frightful to him, as he entertained an inward horror against all soliloquists. It is Satan that chatters out of them, said his Rector; and Anselmus had honestly believed him. But to be regarded as a *Candidatus Theologiæ*, overtaken with drink on Ascension Day! The thought was intolerable.

Running on with these mad vexations, he was just about turning up Poplar Alley, by the Kosel garden, when a voice behind him called out: "Herr Anselmus! Herr Anselmus! for the love of Heaven, where are you running in such a hurry?" The Student paused, as if rooted to the ground; for he was convinced that now some new accident would befall him. The voice rose again: "Herr Anselmus, come back: we are waiting for you here at the water!" And now the Student perceived that it was his friend Conrector Paulmann's voice: he went back to the Elbe, and found the Conrector, with his two daughters, as well as Registrator Heerbrand, all about to step into their gondola. Conrector Paulmann invited the Student to go with them across the Elbe, and then to pass the evening at his house in the suburb of Pirna. The Student Anselmus very gladly accepted this proposal, thinking thereby to escape the malignant destiny which had ruled over him all day.

Now, as they were crossing the river, it chanced that on the farther bank in Anton's Garden, some fireworks were just going off. Sputtering and hissing, the rockets went aloft, and their blazing stars flew to pieces in the air, scattering a thousand vague shoots and flashes around them. The Student Anselmus was sitting by the steersman, sunk in deep thought, but when he noticed in the water the reflection of these darting and wavering sparks and flames, he felt as if it were the little golden snakes that were sporting in the flood. All the wonders that he had seen at the elder-tree again started forth into his heart and thoughts; and again that unspeakable longing, that glowing desire, laid hold of him here, which had agitated his bosom before in painful spasms of rapture.

"Ah! is it you again, my little golden snakes? Sing now, O sing! In your song let the kind, dear, dark-blue eyes again appear to me—Ah! are you under the waves, then?"

So cried the Student Anselmus, and at the same time made a violent movement, as if he was about to plunge into the river.

"Is the Devil in you, sir?" exclaimed the steersman, and clutched him by the lapels. The girls, who were sitting by him, shrieked in terror, and fled to the other side of the gondola. Registrator Heerbrand whispered something in Conrector Paulmann's ear, to which the latter answered at considerable length, but in so low a tone that Anselmus could distinguish nothing but the words: "Such attacks more than once?—Never heard of it." Directly after this, Conrector Paulmann also rose, and then sat down, with a certain earnest, grave, official mien beside the Student Anselmus, taking his hand and saying: "How are you, Herr Anselmus?"

The Student Anselmus was almost losing his wits, for in his mind there was a mad contradiction, which he strove in vain to reconcile. He now saw plainly that what he had taken for the gleaming of the golden snakes was nothing but the reflection of the fireworks in Anton's Garden: but a feeling unexperienced till now, he himself did not know whether it was rapture or pain, cramped his breast together; and when the steersman struck through the water with his helm, so that the waves, curling as in anger, gurgled and chafed, he heard in their din a soft whispering: "Anselmus! Anselmus! do you see how we still skim along before you? Sisterkin looks at you again: believe, believe, believe in us!" And he thought he saw in the reflected light three green-glowing streaks: but then, when he gazed, full of fond sadness, into the water, to see whether those gentle eyes would not look up to him again, he perceived too well that the shine proceeded only from the windows in the neighbouring houses. He was sitting mute in his place, and inwardly battling with himself, when Conrector Paulmann repeated, with still greater emphasis: "How are you, Herr Anselmus?"

With the most rueful tone, Anselmus replied: "Ah! Herr Conrector, if you knew what strange things I have been dreaming, quite awake, with open eyes, just now, under an elder-tree at the wall of Linke's Garden, you would not take it amiss of me that I am a little absent, or so."

"Ey, ey, Herr Anselmus!" interrupted Conrector Paulmann, "I have always taken you for a solid young man: but to dream, to dream with your eyes wide open, and then, all at once, to start up and try to jump into the water! This, begging your pardon, is what only fools or madmen would do."

The Student Anselmus was deeply affected by his friend's hard saying; then Veronica, Paulmann's eldest daughter, a most pretty blooming girl of sixteen, addressed her father: "But, dear father, something singular must have befallen Herr Anselmus; and perhaps he only thinks he was awake, while he may have really been asleep, and so all manner of wild stuff has come into his head, and is still lying in his thoughts."

"And, dearest Mademoiselle! Worthy Conrector!" cried Registrator Heerbrand, "may one not, even when awake, sometimes sink into a sort of dream state? I myself have had such fits. One afternoon, for instance, during coffee, in a sort of brown study like this, in the special season of corporeal and spiritual digestion, the place where a lost *Act* was lying occurred to me, as if by inspiration; and last night, no farther gone, there came a glorious large Latin paper tripping out before my open eyes, in the very same way."

"Ah! most honoured Registrator," answered Conrector Paulmann, "you have always had a tendency to the *Poetica*; and thus one falls into fantasies and romantic humours."

The Student Anselmus, however, was particularly gratified that in this most troublous situation, while in danger of being considered drunk or crazy, anyone should take his part; and though it was already pretty dark, he thought he noticed, for the first time, that Veronica had really very fine dark blue eyes, and this too without remembering the strange pair which he had looked at in the elder-bush. Actually, the adventure under the elder-bush had once more entirely vanished from the thoughts of the Student Anselmus; he felt himself at ease and light of heart; nay, in the capriciousness of joy, he carried it so far, that he offered a helping hand to his fair advocate Veronica, as she was stepping from the gondola; and without more ado, as she put her arm in his, escorted her home with so much dexterity and good luck that he only missed his footing once, and this being the only wet spot in the whole road, only spattered Veronica's white gown a very little by the incident.

Conrector Paulmann did not fail to observe this happy change in the Student Anselmus; he resumed his liking for him and begged forgiveness for the hard words which he had let fall before. "Yes," added he, "we have many examples to show that certain phantasms may rise before a man, and pester and plague him not a little; but this is bodily disease, and leeches are good for it, if applied to the right part, as a certain learned physician, now deceased, has directed." The Student Anselmus did not know whether he had been drunk, crazy, or sick; but in any case the leeches seemed entirely superfluous, as these supposed phantasms had utterly vanished, and the Student himself was growing happier and happier the more he prospered in serving the pretty Veronica with all sorts of dainty attentions.

As usual, after the frugal meal, there came music; the Student Anselmus had to take his seat before the harpsichord, and Veronica accompanied his playing with her pure clear voice: "Dear Mademoiselle," said Registrator Heerbrand, "you have a voice like a crystal bell!"

"That she has not!" ejaculated the Student Anselmus, he scarcely knew how. "Crystal bells in elder-trees sound strangely! strangely!" continued the Student Anselmus, murmuring half aloud.

Veronica laid her hand on his shoulder, and asked: "What are you saying now, Herr Anselmus?"

Instantly Anselmus recovered his cheerfulness, and began playing. Conrector Paulmann gave him a grim look; but Registrator Heerbrand laid a music leaf on the rack, and sang with ravishing grace one of Bandmaster Graun's bravura airs. The Student Anselmus accompanied this, and much more; and a fantasy duet, which Veronica and he now fingered, and Conrector Paulmann had himself composed, again brought everyone into the gayest humour.

It was now pretty late, and Registrator Heerbrand was taking up his hat and stick, when Conrector Paulmann went up to him with a mysterious air, and said: "Hem!—Would not you, honoured Registrator, mention to the good Herr Anselmus himself—Hem! what we were speaking of before?"

"With all the pleasure in the world," said Registrator Heerbrand, and having placed himself in the circle, began, without farther preamble, as follows:

"In this city is a strange remarkable man; people say he follows all manner of secret sciences. But as there are no such sciences, I take him rather for an antiquary, and along with this for an experimental chemist. I mean no other than our Privy Archivarius Lindhorst. He lives, as you know, by himself, in his old isolated house; and when he is away from his office, he is to be found in his library or in his chemical laboratory, to which, however, he admits no stranger. Besides many curious books, he possesses a number of manuscripts, partly Arabic, Coptic, and some of them in strange characters, which do not belong to any known tongue. These he wishes to have copied properly, and for this purpose he requires a man who can draw with the pen, and so transfer these marks to parchment, in Indian ink, with the highest exactness and fidelity. The work is to be carried on in a separate chamber of his house, under his own supervision; and besides free board during the time of business, he will pay his copyist a speziesthaler, or speciedollar, daily, and promises a handsome present when the copying is rightly finished. The hours of work are from twelve to six. From three to four, you take rest and dinner.

"Herr Archivarius Lindhorst having in vain tried one or two young people for copying these manuscripts, has at last applied to me to find him an expert calligrapher, and so I have been thinking of you, my dear Anselmus, for I know that you both write very neatly and draw with the pen to great perfection. Now, if in these bad times, and till your future establishment, you would like to earn a speziesthaler every day, and a present over and above your salary, you can go tomorrow precisely at noon, and call upon the Archivarius, whose house no doubt you know. But be on your guard against blots! If such a thing falls on your copy, you must begin it again; if it falls on the original, the Archivarius will think nothing of throwing you out the window, for he is a hot-tempered man."

The Student Anselmus was filled with joy at Registrator Heerbrand's proposal; for not only could the Student write well and draw well with the pen, but this copying with laborious calligraphic pains was a thing he delighted in more than anything else. So he thanked his patron in the most grateful terms, and promised not to fail at noon tomorrow.

All night the Student Anselmus saw nothing but clear speziesthalers, and heard nothing but their lovely clink. Who could blame the poor youth, cheated of so many hopes by capricious destiny, obliged to take counsel about every farthing, and to forego so many joys which a young heart requires! Early in the morning he brought out his black-lead pencils, his crowquills, his Indian ink; for better materials, thought he, the Archivarius can find nowhere. Above all, he gathered together and arranged his calligraphic masterpieces and his drawings, to show them to the Archivarius, as proof of his ability to do what was desired. Everything went well with the Student; a peculiar happy star seemed to be presiding over him; his neckcloth sat right at the very first trial; no stitches burst; no loop gave way in his black silk stockings; his hat did not once fall to the dust after he had trimmed it. In a word, precisely at half-past eleven, the Student Anselmus, in his pike-gray frock and black satin lower habiliments, with a roll of calligraphic specimens and pen-drawings in his pocket, was standing in the Schlossgasse, or Castle Alley, in Conradi's shop, and drinking one—two glasses of the best stomachic liqueur; for here, thought he, slapping his pocket, which was still empty, for here speziesthalers will soon be chinking.

Notwithstanding the distance of the solitary street where the Archivarius Lindhorst's ancient residence lay, the Student Anselmus was at the front door before the stroke of twelve. He stood there, and was looking at the large fine bronze knocker; but now when, as the last stroke tingled through the air with a loud clang from the steeple clock of the Kreuzkirche, or Church of the Cross, he lifted his hand to grasp this same knocker, the metal visage twisted itself, with a horrid rolling of its blue-gleaming eyes, into a grinning smile. Alas, it was the Applewoman of the Schwarzthor! The pointed teeth gnashed together in the loose jaws, and in their chattering through the skinny lips, there was a growl as of "You fool, fool, fool!—Wait, wait!—Why did you run!—Fool!" Horror-struck, the Student Anselmus flew back; he clutched at the door-post, but his hand caught the bell-rope, and pulled it, and in piercing discords it rang stronger and stronger, and through the whole empty house the echo repeated, as in mockery: "To the crystal, fall!" An unearthly terror seized the Student Anselmus, and quivered through all his limbs. The bell-rope lengthened downwards, and became a gigantic, transparent, white serpent, which encircled and crushed him, and girded him straiter and straiter in its coils, till his brittle paralyzed limbs went crashing in pieces and the blood spouted from his veins, penetrating into the transparent body of the serpent and dyeing it red. "Kill me! Kill me!" he wanted to cry, in his horrible agony; but the cry was only a stifled gurgle in his throat. The serpent lifted its head, and laid its long peaked tongue of glowing brass on the breast of Anselmus; then a fierce pang suddenly cut asunder the artery of life, and thought fled away from him. On returning to his senses, he was lying on his own poor truckle-bed; Conrector Paulmann was standing before him, and saying: "For Heaven's sake, what mad stuff is this, dear Herr Anselmus?"

Third Vigil

"The Spirit looked upon the water, and the water moved itself, and chafed in foaming billows, and plunged thundering down into the abysses, which opened their black throats and greedily swallowed it. Like triumphant conquerors, the granite rocks lifted their cleft peaky crowns, protecting the valley, till the sun took it into his paternal bosom, and clasping it with his beams as with glowing arms, cherished it and warmed it. Then a thousand germs, which had been sleeping under the desert sand, awoke from their deep slumber, and stretched out their little leaves and stalks towards the sun their father's face; and like smiling infants in green cradles, the flowerets rested in their buds and blossoms, till they too, awakened by their father, decked themselves in lights, which their father, to please them, tinted in a thousand varied hues.

"But in the midst of the valley was a black hill, which heaved up and down like the breast of man when warm longing swells it. From the abysses mounted steaming vapours, which rolled themselves together into huge masses, striving malignantly to hide the father's face: but he called the storm to him, which rushed there, and scattered them away; and when the pure sunbeam rested again on the bleak hill, there started from it, in the excess of its rapture, a glorious Fire-lily, opening its fair leaves like gentle lips to receive the kiss of its father.

"And now came a gleaming splendour into the valley; it was the youth Phosphorus; the Lily saw him, and begged, being seized with warm longing love: 'Be mine for ever, fair youth! For I love you, and must die if you forsake me!' Then spoke the youth Phosphorus: 'I will be yours, fair flower; but then, like a naughty child, you will leave father and mother; you will know your playmates no longer, will strive to be greater and stronger than all that now rejoices with you as your equal. The longing which now beneficently warms your whole being will be scattered into a thousand rays and torture and vex you, for sense will bring forth senses; and the highest rapture, which the spark I cast into you kindles, will be the hopeless pain wherein you shall perish, to spring up anew in foreign shape. This spark is thought!'

"'Ah!' mourned the Lily, 'can I not be yours in this glow, as it now burns in me; not still be yours? Can I love you more than now; could I look on you as now, if you were to annihilate me?' Then the youth Phosphorus kissed the Lily; and as if penetrated with light, it mounted up in flame, out of which issued a foreign being, that hastily flying from the valley, roved forth into endless space, no longer heeding its old playmates, or the youth it had loved. This youth mourned for his lost beloved; for he too loved her, it was love to the fair Lily that had brought him to the lone valley; and the granite rocks bent down their heads in participation of his grief.

"But one of these opened its bosom, and there came a black-winged dragon flying out of it, who said: 'My brethren, the Metals are sleeping in there; but I am always brisk and waking, and will help you.' Dashing forth on its black pinions, the dragon at last caught the being which had sprung from the Lily; bore it to the hill, and encircled it with his wing; then was it the Lily again; but thought, which continued with it, tore asunder its heart; and its love for the youth Phosphorus was a cutting pain, before which, as if breathed on by poisonous vapours, the flowerets which had once rejoiced in the fair Lily's presence, faded and died.

"The youth Phosphorus put on a glittering coat of mail, sporting with the light in a thousand hues, and did battle with the dragon, who struck the cuirass with his black wing, till it rung and sounded; and at this loud clang the flowerets again came to life, and like variegated birds fluttered round the dragon, whose force departed; and who, thus being vanquished, hid himself in the depths of the earth. The Lily was freed; the youth Phosphorus clasped her, full of warm longing, of heavenly love; and in triumphant chorus, the flowers, the birds, nay, even the high granite rocks, did reverence to her as the Queen of the Valley."

"By your leave, worthy Herr Archivarius, this is Oriental bombast," said Registrator Heerbrand: "and we beg very much you would rather, as you often do, give us something of your own most remarkable life, of your travelling adventures, for instance; above all, something true."

"What the deuce, then?" answered Archivarius Lindhorst. "True? This very thing I have been telling is the truest I could dish out for you, my friends, and belongs to my life too, in a certain sense. For I come from that very valley; and the Fire-lily, which at last ruled as queen there, was my great-great-great-great-grandmother; and so, properly speaking, I am a prince myself." All burst into a peal of laughter. "Ay, laugh your fill," continued Archivarius Lindhorst. "To you this matter, which I have related, certainly in the most brief and meagre way, may seem senseless and mad; yet, notwithstanding this, it is meant for anything but incoherent, or even allegorical, and it is, in one word, literally true. Had I known, however, that the glorious love story, to which I owe my existence, would have pleased you so little, I might have given you a little of the news my brother brought me on his visit yesterday."

"What, what is this? Have you a brother, then, Herr Archivarius? Where is he? Where does he live? In his Majesty's service too? Or perhaps a private scholar?" cried the company from all quarters.

"No!" replied the Archivarius, quite cool, composedly taking a pinch of snuff, "he has joined the bad side; he has gone over to the Dragons."

"What do you mean, dear Herr Archivarius?" cried Registrator Heerbrand: "Over to the Dragons?"—"Over to the Dragons?" resounded like an echo from all hands.

"Yes, over to the Dragons," continued Archivarius Lindhorst: "it was sheer desperation, I believe. You know, gentlemen, my father died a short while ago; it is but three hundred and eighty-five years ago at most, and I am still in mourning for it. He had left me, his favourite son, a fine onyx; this onyx, rightly or wrongly, my brother would have: we quarrelled about it, over my father's corpse; in such unseemly manner that the good man started up, out of all patience, and threw my wicked brother downstairs. This stuck in our brother's stomach, and so without loss of time he went over to the Dragons. At present, he lives in a cypress wood, not far from Tunis: he has a famous magical carbuncle to watch there, which a dog of necromancer, who has set up a summerhouse in Lapland, has an eye to; so my poor brother only gets away for a quarter of an hour or so, when the necromancer happens to be out looking after the salamander bed in his garden, and then he tells me in all haste what good news there is about the Springs of the Nile."

For the second time, the company burst out into a peal of laughter: but the Student Anselmus began to feel quite dreary in heart; and he could scarcely look at Archivarius Lindhorst's parched countenance, and fixed earnest eyes, without shuddering internally in a way which he could not himself understand. Moreover, in the harsh and strangely metallic sound of Archivarius Lindhorst's voice there was something mysteriously piercing for the Student Anselmus, and he felt his very bones and marrow tingling as the Archivarius spoke.

The special object for which Registrator Heerbrand had taken him into the coffee house, seemed at present not attainable. After that accident at Archivarius Lindhorst's door, the Student Anselmus had withstood all inducements to risk a second visit: for, according to his own heart-felt conviction, it was only chance that had saved him, if not from death, at least from the danger of insanity. Conrector Paulmann had happened to be passing through the street at the time when Anselmus was lying quite senseless at the door, and an old woman, who had laid her cookie-and-apple basket aside, was busied about him. Conrector Paulmann had forthwith called a chair, and so had him carried home. "Think what you will of me," said the Student Anselmus, "consider me a fool or not: I say, the cursed visage of that witch at the Schwarzthor grinned on me from the doorknocker. What happened after I would rather not speak of: but if I had recovered from my faint and seen that infernal Apple-wife beside me (for the old woman whom you talk of was no other), I should that instant have been struck by apoplexy, or have run stark mad."

All persuasions, all sensible arguments on the part of Conrector Paulmann and Registrator Heerbrand, profited nothing; and even the blue-eyed Veronica herself could not raise him from a certain moody humour, in which he had ever since been sunk. In fact, these friends regarded him as troubled in mind, and considered ways for diverting his thoughts; to which end, Registrator Heerbrand thought, there could nothing be so serviceable as copying Archivarius Lindhorst's manuscripts. The business, therefore, was to introduce the Student in some proper way to Archivarius Lindhorst; and so Registrator Heerbrand, knowing that the Archivarius used to visit a certain coffee house almost nightly, had invited the Student Anselmus to come every evening to that same coffee house, and drink a glass of beer and smoke a pipe, at his, the Registrator's charge, till such time as Archivarius Lindhorst should in one way or another see him, and the bargain for this copying work be settled; which offer the Student Anselmus had most gratefully accepted. "God will reward you, worthy Registrator, if you bring the young man to reason!" said Conrector Paulmann. "God will reward you!" repeated Veronica, piously raising her eyes to heaven, and vividly thinking that the Student Anselmus was already a most pretty young man, even without any reason.

Now accordingly, as Archivarius Lindhorst, with hat and staff, was making for the door, Registrator Heerbrand seized the Student Anselmus briskly by the hand, and stepping to meet the Herr Archivarius, he said: "Most esteemed Herr Archivarius, here is the Student Anselmus, who has an uncommon talent in calligraphy and drawing, and will undertake the copying of your rare manuscripts."

"I am most particularly glad to hear it," answered Archivarius Lindhorst sharply, then threw his three-cocked military hat on his head, and shoving Registrator Heerbrand and the Student Anselmus aside, rushed downstairs with great tumult, so that both of them were left standing in great confusion, gaping at the door, which he had slammed in their faces till the bolts and hinges of it rung again.

"He is a very strange old gentleman," said Registrator Heerbrand. "Strange old gentleman," stammered the Student Anselmus, with a feeling as if an ice-stream were creeping over all his veins, and he were stiffening into a statue. All the guests, however, laughed, and said: "Our Archivarius is on his high horse today: tomorrow, you shall see, he will be mild as a lamb again, and won't speak a word, but will look into the smoke-vortexes of his pipe, or read the newspapers; you must not mind these freaks."

"That is true too," thought the Student Anselmus: "who would mind such a thing, after all? Did not the Archivarius tell me he was most particularly glad to hear that I would undertake the copying of his manuscripts; and why did Registrator Heerbrand step directly in his way, when he was going home? No, no, he is a good man at bottom this Privy Archivarius Lindhorst, and surprisingly liberal. A little curious in his figures of speech; but what is that to me? Tomorrow at the stroke of twelve I will go to him, though fifty bronze Apple-wives should try to hinder me!"

Fourth Vigil

Gracious reader, may I venture to ask you a question? Have you ever had hours, perhaps even days or weeks, in which all your customary activities did nothing but cause you vexation and dissatisfaction; when everything that you usually consider worthy and important seemed trivial and worthless? At such a time you did not know what to do or where to turn. A dim feeling pervaded your breast that you had higher desires that must be fulfilled, desires that transcended the pleasures of this world, yet desires which your spirit, like a cowed child, did not even dare to utter. In this longing for an unknown Something, which longing hovered above you no matter where you were, like an airy dream with thin transparent forms that melted away each time you tried to examine them, you had no voice for the world about you. You passed to and fro with troubled look, like a hopeless lover, and no matter what you saw being attempted or attained in the bustle of varied existence, it awakened no sorrow or joy in you. It was as if you had no share in this sublunary world.

If, favourable reader, you have ever been in this mood, you know the state into which the Student Anselmus had fallen. I wish most heartily, courteous reader, that it were in my power to bring the Student Anselmus before your eyes with true vividness. For in these vigils in which I record his singular history, there is still so much more of the marvellous—which is likely to make the everyday life of ordinary mortals seem pallid—that I fear in the end you will believe in neither the Student Anselmus nor Archivarius Lindhorst; indeed, that you will even entertain doubts as to Registrator Heerbrand and Conrector Paulmann, though these two estimable persons, at least, are still walking the pavements of Dresden. Favourable reader, while you are in the faery region of glorious wonders, where both rapture and horror may be evoked; where the goddess of earnestness herself will waft her veil aside and show her countenance (though a smile often glimmers in her glance, a sportive teasing before perplexing enchantments, comparable to mothers nursing and dandling their children)—while you are in this region which the spirit lays open to us in dreams, make an effort to recognize the well-known forms which hover around you in fitful brightness even in ordinary life. You will then find that this glorious kingdom lies much closer at hand than you ever supposed; it is this kingdom which I now very heartily desire, and am striving to show you in the singular story of the Student Anselmus.

So, as was hinted, the Student Anselmus, ever since that evening when he met with Archivarius Lindhorst, had been sunk in a dreamy musing, which rendered him insensible to every outward touch from common life. He felt that an unknown Something was awakening his inmost soul, and calling forth that rapturous pain, which is even the mood of longing that announces a loftier existence to man. He delighted most when he could rove alone through meads and woods; and as if released from all that fettered him to his necessary life, could, so to speak, again find himself in the manifold images which mounted from his soul.

It happened once that in returning from a long ramble, he passed by that notable elder-tree, under which, as if taken with faery, he had formerly beheld so many marvels. He felt himself strangely attracted by the green kindly sward; but no sooner had he seated himself on it than the whole vision which he had previously seen as in a heavenly trance, and which had since as if by foreign influence been driven from his mind, again came floating before him in the liveliest colours, as if he had been looking on it a second time. Nay, it was clearer to him now than ever, that the gentle blue eyes belonged to the gold-green snake, which had wound itself through the middle of the elder-tree; and that from the turnings of its tapering body all those glorious crystal tones, which had filled him with rapture, must have broken forth. As on Ascension Day, he again clasped the elder-tree to his bosom, and cried into the twigs and leaves: "Ah, once more shoot forth, and turn and wind yourself among the twigs, little fair green snake, that I may see you! Once more look at me with your gentle eyes! Ah, I love you, and must die in pain and grief, if you do not return!" All, however, remained quite dumb and still; and as before, the elder-tree rustled quite unintelligibly with its twigs and leaves. But the Student Anselmus now felt as if he knew what it was that so moved and worked within him, nay, that so tore his bosom in the pain of an infinite longing. "What else is it," said he, "but that I love you with my whole heart and soul, and even to the death, glorious little golden snake; nay, that without you I cannot live, and must perish in hopeless woe, unless I find you again, unless I have you as the beloved of my heart. But I know it, you shall be mine; and then all that glorious dreams have promised me of another higher world shall be fulfilled."

Henceforth the Student Anselmus, every evening, when the sun was scattering its bright gold over the peaks of the trees, was to be seen under the elder-bush, calling from the depths of his heart in most lamentable tones into the branches and leaves for a sight of his beloved, of his little gold-green snake. Once as he was going on with this, there suddenly stood before him a tall lean man, wrapped up in a wide light-gray surtout, who, looking at him with large fiery eyes, exclaimed: "Hey, hey, what whining and whimpering is this? Hey, hey, this is Herr Anselmus that was to copy my manuscripts." The Student Anselmus felt not a little terrified at hearing this voice, for it was the very same which on Ascension Day had called: "Hey, hey, what chattering and jingling is this," and so forth. For fright and astonishment, he could not utter a word. "What ails you, Herr Anselmus," continued Archivarius Lindhorst, for the stranger was no one else; "what do you want with the elder-tree, and why did you not come to me and set about your work?"

In fact, the Student Anselmus had never yet prevailed upon himself to visit Archivarius Lindhorst's house a second time, though, that evening, he had firmly resolved on doing it. But now at this moment, when he saw his fair dreams torn asunder, and that too by the same hostile voice which had once before snatched away his beloved, a sort of desperation came over him, and he broke out fiercely into these words: "You may think me mad or not, Herr Archivarius; it is all the same to me: but here in this bush, on Ascension Day, I saw the gold-green snake—ah! the beloved of my soul; and she spoke to me in glorious crystal tones; and you, you, Herr Archivarius, cried and shouted horribly over the water."

"How is this, my dear sir?" interrupted Archivarius Lindhorst, smiling quite inexpressibly, and taking snuff.

The Student Anselmus felt his breast becoming easy, now that he had succeeded in beginning this strange story; and it seemed to him as if he were quite right in laying the whole blame upon the Archivarius, and that it was he, and no one else, who had thundered so from the distance. He courageously proceeded: "Well, then, I will tell you the whole mystery that happened to me on Ascension evening; and then you may say and do, and think of me whatever you please." He accordingly disclosed the whole miraculous adventure, from his luckless upsetting of the apple basket, till the departure of the three gold-green snakes over the river; and how the people after that had thought him drunk or crazy. "All this," ended the Student Anselmus, "I actually saw with my eyes; and deep in my bosom those dear voices, which spoke to me, are still sounding in clear echo: it was in no way a dream; and if I am not to die of longing and desire, I must believe in these gold-green snakes, though I see by your smile, Herr Archivarius, that you hold these same snakes as nothing more than creatures of my heated and overstrained imagination."

"Not at all," replied the Archivarius, with the greatest calmness and composure; "the gold-green snakes, which you saw in the elder-bush, Herr Anselmus, were simply my three daughters; and that you have fallen over head and ears in love with the blue eyes of Serpentina the youngest, is now clear enough. Indeed, I knew it on Ascension Day myself: and as (on that occasion, sitting busied with my writing at home) I began to get annoyed with so much chattering and jingling, I called to the idle minxes that it was time to get home, for the sun was setting, and they had sung and basked enough."

The Student Anselmus felt as if he now merely heard in plain words something he had long dreamed of, and though he fancied he observed that elder-bush, wall and sward, and all objects about him were beginning slowly to whirl around, he took heart, and was ready to speak; but the Archivarius prevented him; for sharply pulling the glove from his left hand, and holding the stone of a ring, glittering in strange sparkles and flames before the Student's eyes, he said: "Look here, Herr Anselmus; what you see may do you good."

The Student Anselmus looked in, and O wonder! the stone emitted a cluster of rays; and the rays wove themselves together into a clear gleaming crystal mirror; in which, with many windings, now flying asunder, now twisted together, the three gold-green snakes were dancing and bounding. And when their tapering forms, glittering with a thousand sparkles, touched each other, there issued from them glorious tones, as of crystal bells; and the midmost of the three stretched forth her little head from the mirror, as if full of longing and desire, and her dark-blue eyes said: "Do you know me, then? Do you believe in me, Anselmus? In belief alone is love: can you love?"

"O Serpentina! Serpentina!" cried the Student Anselmus in mad rapture; but Archivarius Lindhorst suddenly breathed on the mirror, and with an electric sputter the rays sank back into their focus; and on his hand there was now nothing but a little emerald, over which the Archivarius drew his glove.

"Did you see the golden snakes, Herr Anselmus?" said the Archivarius.

"Ah, good heaven, yes!" replied the Student, "and the fair dear Serpentina."

"Hush!" continued Archivarius Lindhorst, "enough for now: for the rest, if you decide to work with me, you may see my daughter often enough; or rather I will grant you this real satisfaction: if you stick tightly and truly to your task, that is to say, copy every mark with the greatest clearness and correctness. But you have not come to me at all, Herr Anselmus, although Registrator Heerbrand promised I should see you immediately, and I have waited several days in vain."

Not until the mention of Registrator Heerbrand's name did the Student Anselmus again feel as if he was really standing with his two legs on the ground, and he was really the Student Anselmus, and the man talking to him really Archivarius Lindhorst. The tone of indifference, with which the latter spoke, in such rude contrast with the strange sights which like a genuine necromancer he had called forth, awakened a certain horror in the Student, which the piercing look of those fiery eyes, glowing from their bony sockets in the lean puckered visage, as from a leathern case, still farther aggravated: and the Student was again forcibly seized with the same unearthly feeling, which had before gained possession of him in the coffee house, when Archivarius Lindhorst had talked so wildly. With a great effort he retained his self-command, and as the Archivarius again asked, "Well, why did you not come?" the Student exerted his whole energies, and related to him what had happened at the street door. .

"My dear Herr Anselmus," said the Archivarius, when the Student was finished; "dear Herr Anselmus, I know this Apple-wife of whom you speak; she is a vicious slut that plays all sorts of vile tricks on me; but that she has turned herself to bronze and taken the shape of a door-knocker, to deter pleasant visitors from calling, is indeed very bad, and truly not to be endured. Would you please, worthy Herr Anselmus, if you come tomorrow at noon and notice any more of this grinning and growling, just be so good as to let a drop or two of this liquor fall on her nose; it will put everything to rights immediately. And now, adieu, my dear Herr Anselmus! I must make haste, therefore I would not advise you to think of returning with me. Adieu, till we meet! — Tomorrow at noon!"

The Archivarius had given the Student Anselmus a little vial, with a gold-coloured fluid in it; and he walked rapidly off; so rapidly, that in the dusk, which had now come on, he seemed to be floating down to the valley rather than walking down to it. Already he was near the Kosel garden; the wind got within his wide greatcoat, and drove its breasts asunder; so that they fluttered in the air like a pair of large wings; and to the Student Anselmus, who was looking full of amazement at the course of the Archivarius, it seemed as if a large bird were spreading out its pinions for rapid flight. And now, while the Student kept gazing into the dusk, a white-gray kite with creaking cry soared up into the air; and he now saw clearly that the white flutter which he had thought to be the retiring Archivarius must have been this very kite, though he still could not understand where the Archivarius had vanished so abruptly.

"Perhaps he may have flown away in person, this Herr Archivarius Lindhorst," said the Student Anselmus to himself; "for I now see and feel clearly, that all these foreign shapes of a distant wondrous world, which I never saw before except in peculiarly remarkable dreams, have now come into my waking life, and are making their sport of me. But be this as it will! You live and glow in my breast, lovely, gentle Serpentina; you alone can still the infinite longing which rends my soul to pieces. Ah, when shall I see your kind eyes, dear, dear Serpentina!" cried the Student Anselmus aloud.

"That is a vile unchristian name!" murmured a bass voice beside him, which belonged to some promenader returning home. The Student Anselmus, reminded where he was, hastened off at a quick pace, thinking to himself: "Wouldn't it be a real misfortune now if Conrector Paulmann or Registrator Heerbrand were to meet me?"— But neither of these gentlemen met him.

Fifth Vigil

"There is nothing in the world that can be done with this Anselmus," said Conrector Paulmann; "all my good advice, all my admonitions, are fruitless; he will apply himself to nothing; though he is a fine classical scholar too, and that is the foundation of everything."

But Registrator Heerbrand, with a sly, mysterious smile, replied: "Let Anselmus take his time, my dear Conrector! he is a strange subject, this Anselmus, but there is much in him: and when I say much, I mean a Privy Secretary, or even a Court Councillor, a Hofrath."

"Hof——" began Conrector Paulmann, in the deepest amazement; the word stuck in his throat.

"Hush! hush!" continued Registrator Heerbrand, "I know what I know. These two days he has been with Archivarius Lindhorst, copying manuscripts; and last night the Archivarius meets me at the coffee house, and says: 'You have sent me a proper man, good neighbour! There is stuff in him!' And now think of Archivarius Lindhorst's influence—Hush! hush! we will talk of it this time a year from now." And with these words the Registrator, his face still wrinkled into the same sly smile, went out of the room, leaving the Conrector speechless with astonishment and curiosity, and fixed, as if by enchantment, in his chair.

But on Veronica this dialogue had made a still deeper impression. "Did I not know all along," she thought, "that Herr Anselmus was a most clever and pretty young man, to whom something great would come? Were I but certain that he really liked me! But that night when we crossed the Elbe, did he not press my hand twice? Did he not look at me, in our duet, with such glances that pierced into my very heart? Yes, yes! he really likes me; and I ——" Veronica gave herself up, as young maidens are wont, to sweet dreams of a gay future. She was Mrs. Hofrath, Frau Hofräthinn; she occupied a fine house in the

Schlossgasse, or in the Neumarkt, or in the Moritzstrasse; her fashionable hat, her new Turkish shawl, became her admirably; she was breakfasting on the balcony in an elegant negligée, giving orders to her cook for the day: "And see, if you please, not to spoil that dish; it is the Hofrath's favourite." Then passing beaux glanced up, and she heard distinctly: "Well, she is a heavenly woman, that Hofräthinn; how prettily the lace cap suits her!" Mrs. Privy Councillor Ypsilon sends her servant to ask if it would please the Frau Hofräthinn to drive as far as the Linke Bath today? "Many compliments; extremely sorry, I am engaged to tea already with the Presidentinn Tz." Then comes the Hofrath Anselmus back from his office; he is dressed in the top of the mode: "Ten, I declare," cries he, making his gold watch repeat, and giving his young lady a kiss. "How are things, little wife? Guess what I have here for you?" he continues in a teasing manner, and draws from his waistcoat pocket a pair of beautiful earrings, fashioned in the newest style, and puts them on in place of the old ones. "Ah! What pretty, dainty earrings!" cried Veronica aloud; and started up from her chair, throwing aside her work, to see those fair earrings with her own eyes in the glass.

"What is this?" said Conrector Paulmann, roused by the noise from his deep study of *Cicero de Officiis*, and almost dropping the book from his hand; "are we taking fits, like Anselmus?" But at this moment, the Student Anselmus, who, contrary to his custom, had not been seen for several days, entered the room, to Veronica's astonishment and terror; for, in truth, he seemed altered in his whole bearing. With a certain precision, which was far from usual in him, he spoke of new tendencies of life which had become clear to his mind, of glorious prospects which were opening for him, but which many did not have the skill to discern. Conrector Paulmann, remembering Registrator Heerbrand's mysterious speech, was still more struck, and could scarcely utter a syllable, till the Student Anselmus, after letting fall some hints of urgent business at Archivarius Lindhorst's, and with elegant adroitness kissing Veronica's hand, was already down the stairs, off and away.

"This was the Hofrath," murmured Veronica to herself: "and he kissed my hand, without sliding on the floor, or treading on my foot, as he used to! He threw me the softest look too; yes, he really loves me!"

Veronica again gave way to her dreaming; yet now, it was as if a hostile shape were still coming forward among these lovely visions of her future household life as Frau Hofräthinn, and the shape were laughing in spiteful mockery, and saying: "This is all very stupid and trashy stuff, and lies to boot; for Anselmus will never, never, be Hofrath or your husband; he does not love you in the least, though you have blue eyes, and a fine figure, and a pretty hand." Then an ice-stream poured over Veronica's soul; and a deep sorrow swept away the delight with which, a little while ago, she had seen herself in the lace cap and fashionable earrings. Tears almost rushed into her eyes, and she said aloud: "Ah! it is too true; he does not love me in the least; and I shall never, never, be Frau Hofräthinn!"

"Romantic idiocy, romantic idiocy!" cried Conrector Paulmann; then snatched his hat and stick, and hastened indignantly from the house. "This was still wanting," sighed Veronica; and felt vexed at her little sister, a girl of twelve years, because she sat so unconcerned, and kept sewing at her frame, as if nothing had happened.

Meanwhile it was almost three o'clock; and now time to tidy up the apartment, and arrange the coffee table: for the Mademoiselles Oster had announced that they were coming. But from behind every work-box which Veronica lifted aside, behind the notebooks which she took away from the harpsichord, behind every cup, behind the coffeepot which she took from the cupboard, that shape peeped forth, like a little mandrake, and laughed in spiteful mockery, and snapped its little spider fingers, and cried: "He will not be your husband! he will not be your husband!" And then, when she threw everything away, and fled to the middle of the room, it peered out again, with long nose, in gigantic bulk, from behind the stove, and snarled and growled: "He will not be your husband!"

"Don't you hear anything, don't you see anything?" cried Veronica, shivering with fright, and not daring to touch anything in the room. Fränzchen rose, quite grave and quiet, from her embroidering frame, and said, "What ails you today, sister? You are just making a mess. I must help you, I see."

But at this time the visitors came tripping in in a lively manner, with brisk laughter; and the same moment, Veronica perceived that it was the stove handle which she had taken for a shape, and the creaking of the ill-shut stove door for those spiteful words. Yet, overcome with horror, she did not immediately recover her composure, and her excitement, which her paleness and agitated looks betrayed, was noticed by the Mademoiselles Oster. As they at once cut short their merry talk, and pressed her to tell them what, in Heaven's name, had happened, Veronica was obliged to admit that certain strange thoughts had come into her mind; and suddenly, in open day a dread of spectres, which she did not normally feel, had got the better of her. She described in such lively colours how a little gray mannikin, peeping out of all the corners of the room, had mocked and plagued her, that the Mademoiselles Oster began to look around with timid glances, and began to have all sorts of unearthly notions. But Fränzchen entered at this moment with the steaming coffeepot; and the three, taking thought again, laughed outright at their folly.

Angelica, the elder of the Osters, was engaged to an officer; the young man had joined the army; but his friends had been so long without news of him that there was too little doubt of his being dead, or at least grievously wounded. This had plunged Angelica into the deepest sorrow; but today she was merry, even to extravagance, a state of things which so much surprised Veronica that she could not but speak of it, and inquire the reason.

"Darling," said Angelica, "do you fancy that my Victor is out of heart and thoughts? It is because of him I am so happy. O Heaven! so happy, so blessed in my whole soul! For my Victor is well; in a little while he will be home, advanced to Rittmeister, and decorated with the honours which he has won. A deep but not dangerous wound, in his right arm, which he got from a sword cut by a French hussar, prevents him from writing; and rapid change of quarters, for he will not consent to leave his regiment, makes it impossible for him to send me tidings. But tonight he will be ordered home, until his wound is cured. Tomorrow he will set out for home; and just as he is stepping into the coach, he will learn of his promotion to Rittmeister."

"But, my dear Angelica," interrupted Veronica. "How do you know all this?"

"Do not laugh at me, my friend," continued Angelica; "and surely you will not laugh, for the little gray mannikin, to punish you, might peep out from behind the mirror there. I cannot lay aside my belief in certain mysterious things, since often enough in life they have come before my eyes, I might say, into my very hands. For example, I cannot consider it so strange and incredible as many others do, that there should be people gifted with a certain faculty of prophecy. In the city, here, is an old woman, who possesses this gift to a high degree. She does not use cards, nor molten lead, nor coffee grounds, like ordinary fortune tellers, but after certain preparations, in which you yourself take a part, she takes a polished metallic mirror, and the strangest mixture of figures and forms, all intermingled rise up in it. She interprets these and answers your question. I was with her last night, and got those tidings of my Victor, which I have not doubted for a moment."

Angelica's narrative threw a spark into Veronica's soul, which instantly kindled with the thought of consulting this same old prophetess about Anselmus and her hopes. She learned that the crone was called Frau Rauerin, and lived in a remote street near the Seethor; that she was not to be seen except on Tuesdays, Thursdays, and Fridays, from seven o'clock in the evening, but then, indeed, through the whole night till sunrise; and that she preferred her customers to come alone. It was now Thursday, and Veronica determined, under pretext of accompanying the Osters home, to visit this old woman, and lay the case before her.

Accordingly, no sooner had her friends, who lived in the Neustadt, parted from her at the Elbe Bridge, than she hastened towards the Seethor; and before long, she had reached the remote narrow street described to her, and at the end of it saw the little red house in which Frau Rauerin was said to live. She could not rid herself of a certain dread, nay, of a certain horror, as she approached the door. At last she summoned resolution, in spite of inward terror, and made bold to pull the bell: the door opened, and she groped through the dark passage for the stair which led to the upper story, as Angelica had directed. "Does Frau Rauerin live here?" cried she into the empty lobby as no one appeared; but instead of an answer, there rose a long clear "Mew!" and a large black cat, with its back curved up, and whisking its tail to and fro in wavy coils, stepped on before her, with much gravity, to the door of the apartment, which, on a second mew, was opened.

"Ah, see! Are you here already, daughter? Come in, love; come in!" exclaimed an advancing figure, whose appearance rooted Veronica to the floor. A long lean woman, wrapped in black rags!—while she spoke, her peaked projecting chin wagged this way and that; her toothless mouth, overshadowed by a bony hawk-nose, twisted itself into a ghastly smile, and gleaming cat's-eyes flickered in sparkles through the large spectacles. From a party-coloured clout wrapped round her head, black wiry hair was sticking out; but what deformed her haggard visage to absolute horror, were two large burn marks which ran from the left cheek, over the nose. Veronica's breathing stopped; and the scream, which was about to lighten her choked breast, became a deep sigh, as the witch's skeleton hand took hold of her, and led her into the chamber. Here everything was awake and astir; nothing but din and tumult, and squeaking, and mewing, and croaking, and piping all at once, on every hand. The crone struck the table with her fist, and screamed: "Peace, ye vermin!" And the meer-cats, whimpering, clambered to the top of the high bed; and the little meer-swine all ran beneath the stove, and the raven fluttered up to the round mirror; and the black cat, as if the rebuke did not apply to him, kept sitting at his ease on the cushioned chair, to which he had leapt directly after entering.

So soon as the room became quiet, Veronica took heart; she felt less frightened than she had outside in the hall; nay, the crone herself did not seem so hideous. For the first time, she now looked round the room. All sorts of odious stuffed beasts hung down from the ceiling: strange unknown household implements were lying in confusion on the floor; and in the grate was a scanty blue fire, which only now and then sputtered up in yellow sparkles; and at every sputter, there came a rustling from above and monstrous bats, as if with human countenances in distorted laughter, went flitting to and fro; at times, too, the flame shot up, licking the sooty wall, and then there sounded cutting howling tones of woe, which shook Veronica with fear and horror. "With your leave, Mamsell!" said the crone, knitting her brows, and seizing a brush; with which, having dipped it in a copper skillet, she then besprinkled the grate. The fire went out; and as if filled with thick smoke, the room grew pitch-dark: but the crone, who had gone aside into a closet, soon returned with a lighted lamp; and now Veronica could see no beasts or implements in the apartment; it was a common meanly furnished room. The crone came up to her, and said with a creaking voice: "I know what you wish, little daughter: tush, you would have me tell you whether you shall wed Anselmus, when he is Hofrath."

Veronica stiffened with amazement and terror, but the crone continued: "You told me the whole of it at home, at your father's, when the coffeepot was standing before you: I was the coffeepot; didn't you know me? Daughterkin, hear me! Give up, give up this Anselmus; he is a nasty creature; he trod my little sons to pieces, my dear little sons, the Apples with the red cheeks, that glide away, when people have bought them, whisk! out of their pockets, and roll back into my basket. He trades with the Old One: it was but the day before yesterday, he poured that cursed Auripigment on my face, and I nearly went blind with it. You can see the burn marks yet. Daughterkin, give him up, give him up! He does not love you, for he loves the gold-green snake; he will never be Hofrath, for he has joined the salamanders, and he means to wed the green snake: give him up, give him up!"

Veronica, who had a firm, steadfast spirit of her own, and could conquer girlish terror, now drew back a step, and said, with a serious resolute tone: "Old woman! I heard of your gift of looking into the future; and wished, perhaps too curiously and thoughtlessly, to learn from you whether Anselmus, whom I love and value, could ever be mine. But if, instead of fulfilling my desire, you keep vexing me with your foolish unreasonable babble, you are doing wrong; for I have asked of you nothing but what you grant to others, as I well know. Since you are acquainted with my inmost thoughts apparently, it might perhaps have been an easy matter for you to unfold to me much that now pains and grieves my mind; but after your silly slander of the good Anselmus, I do not care to talk further with you. Goodnight!"

Veronica started to leave hastily, but the crone, with tears and lamentation, fell upon her knees; and, holding the young lady by the gown, exclaimed: "Veronica! Veronica! have you forgotten old Liese? Your nurse who has so often carried you in her arms, and dandled you?"

Veronica could scarcely believe her eyes; for here, in truth, was her old nurse, defaced only by great age and by the two burns; old Liese, who had vanished from Conrector Paulmann's house some years ago, no one knew where. The crone, too, had quite another look now: instead of the ugly many-pieced clout, she had on a decent cap; instead of the black rags, a gay printed bedgown; she was neatly dressed, as of old. She rose from the floor, and taking Veronica in her arms, proceeded: "What I have just told you may seem very mad; but, unluckily, it is too true. Anselmus has done me much mischief, though it is not his own fault: he has fallen into Archivarius Lindhorst's hands, and the Old One means to marry him to his daughter. Archivarius Lindhorst is my deadliest enemy: I could tell you thousands of things about him, which, however, you would not understand, or at best be too much frightened at. He is the Wise Man, it seems; but I am the Wise Woman: let this stand for that! I see now that you love this Anselmus; and I will help you with all my strength, that so you may be happy, and wed him like a pretty bride, as you wish."

"But tell me, for Heaven's sake, Liese——" interrupted Veronica.

"Hush! child, hush!" cried the old woman, interrupting in her turn: "I know what you would say; I have become what I am, because it was to be so: I could do no other. Well, then! I know the means which will cure Anselmus of his frantic love for the green snake, and lead him, the prettiest Hofrath, into your arms; but you yourself must help."

"Tell me, Liese; I will do anything and everything, for I love Anselmus very much!" whispered Veronica, scarcely audibly.

"I know you," continued the crone, "for a courageous child: I could never frighten you to sleep with the *Wauwau*; for that instant, your eyes were open to what the *Wauwau* was like. You would go without a light into the darkest room; and many a time, with papa's powder-mantle, you terrified the neighbours' children. Well, then, if you are in earnest about conquering Archivarius Lindhorst and the green snake by my art; if you are in earnest about calling Anselmus Hofrath and husband; then, at the next Equinox, about eleven at night, glide from your father's house, and come here: I will go with you to the crossroads, which cut the fields hard by here: we shall take what is needed, and whatever wonders you may see shall do you no whit of harm. And now, love, goodnight: Papa is waiting for you at supper."

Veronica hastened away: she had the firmest purpose not to neglect the night of the Equinox; "for," thought she, "old Liese is right; Anselmus has become entangled in strange fetters; but I will free him from them, and call him mine forever; mine he is, and shall be, the Hofrath Anselmus."

Sixth Vigil

"It may be, after all," said the Student Anselmus to himself, "that the superfine strong stomachic liqueur, which I took somewhat freely in

Monsieur Conradi's, might really be the cause of all these shocking phantasms, which tortured me so at Archivarius Lindhorst's door. Therefore, I will go quite sober today, and so bid defiance to whatever farther mischief may assail me." On this occasion, as before when equipping himself for his first call on Archivarius Lindhorst, the Student Anselmus put his pen-drawings, and calligraphic masterpieces, his bars of Indian ink, and his well-pointed crow-pens, into his pockets; and was just turning to go out, when his eye lighted on the vial with the yellow liquor, which he had received from Archivarius Lindhorst. All the strange adventures he had met again rose on his mind in glowing colours; and a nameless emotion of rapture and pain thrilled through his breast. Involuntarily he exclaimed, with a most piteous voice: "Ah, am not I going to the Archivarius solely for a sight of you, gentle lovely Serpentina!" At that moment, he felt as if Serpentina's love might be the prize of some laborious perilous task which he had to undertake; and as if this task were nothing else but the copying of the Lindhorst manuscripts. That at his very entrance into the house, or more properly, before his entrance, all sorts of mysterious things might happen, as before, was no more than he anticipated. He thought no more of Conradi's strong drink, but hastily put the vial of liquor in his waistcoat pocket, that he might act strictly by the Archivarius' directions, should the bronze Apple-woman again take it upon her to make faces at him.

And the hawk-nose actually did peak itself, the cat-eyes actually did glare from the knocker, as he raised his hand to it, at the stroke of twelve. But now, without farther ceremony, he dribbled his liquor into the pestilent visage; and it folded and moulded itself, that instant, down to a glittering bowl-round knocker. The door opened, the bells sounded beautifully over all the house: "Klingling, youngling, in, in, spring, spring, klingling." In good heart he mounted the fine broad stair; and feasted on the odours of some strange perfume that was floating through the house. In doubt, he paused in the hall; for he did not know at which of these many fine doors he was to knock. But Archivarius Lindhorst, in a white damask nightgown, emerged and said: "Well, it is a real pleasure to me, Herr Anselmus, that you have kept your word at last. Come this way, if you please; I must take you straight into the laboratory." And with this he stepped rapidly through the hall, and opened a little side door, which led into a long passage. Anselmus walked on in high spirits, behind the Archivarius; they passed from this corridor into a hall, or rather into a lordly greenhouse: for on both sides, up to the ceiling, grew all sorts of rare wondrous flowers, indeed, great trees with strangely formed leaves and blossoms. A magic dazzling light shone over the whole, though you could not discover where it came from, for no window whatever was to be seen. As the Student Anselmus looked

in through the bushes and trees, long avenues appeared to open into remote distance. In the deep shade of thick cypress groves lay glittering
marble fountains, out of which rose wondrous figures, spouting crystal
jets that fell with pattering spray into the gleaming lily-cups. Strange
voices cooed and rustled through the wood of curious trees; and sweet-
est perfumes streamed up and down.

The Archivarius had vanished: and Anselmus saw nothing but a
huge bush of glowing fire-lilies before him. Intoxicated with the sight
and the fine odours of this fairy-garden, Anselmus stood fixed to the
spot. Then began on all sides of him a giggling and laughing; and light
little voices railed at him and mocked him: "Herr Studiosus! Herr
Studiosus! how did you get in here? Why have you dressed so bravely,
Herr Anselmus? Will you chat with us for a minute and tell us how
grandmamma sat down upon the egg, and young master got a stain on
his Sunday waistcoat?—Can you play the new tune, now, which you
learned from Daddy Cockadoodle, Herr Anselmus?—You look very
fine in your glass periwig, and brown-paper boots." So cried and chattered and sniggered the little voices, out of every corner, indeed, close
by the Student himself, who now observed that all sorts of multi-
coloured birds were fluttering above him, and jeering at him. At that
moment, the bush of fire-lilies advanced towards him; and he perceived that it was Archivarius Lindhorst, whose flowered nightgown,
glittering in red and yellow, had deceived his eyes.

"I beg your pardon, worthy Herr Anselmus," said the Archivarius,
"for leaving you alone: I wished, in passing, to take a peep at my fine
cactus, which is to blossom tonight. But how do you like my little
house-garden?"

"Ah, Heaven! It is inconceivably beautiful, Herr Archivarius,"
replied the Student; "but these multicoloured birds have been bantering me a little."

"What chattering is this?" cried the Archivarius angrily into the
bushes. Then a huge gray Parrot came fluttering out, and perched itself beside the Archivarius on a myrtle bough, and looking at him with
an uncommon earnestness and gravity through a pair of spectacles that
stuck on its hooked bill, it creaked out: "Don't take it amiss, Herr
Archivarius; my wild boys have been a little free or so; but the Herr
Studiosus has himself to blame in the matter, for——"

"Hush! hush!" interrupted Archivarius Lindhorst; "I know the var-
lets; but you must keep them in better discipline, my friend!—Now,
come along, Herr Anselmus."

And the Archivarius again stepped forth through many a strangely
decorated chamber, so that the Student Anselmus, in following him,
could scarcely give a glance at all the glittering wondrous furniture and

other unknown things with which all the rooms were filled. At last they entered a large apartment, where the Archivarius, casting his eyes aloft, stood still; and Anselmus got time to feast himself on the glorious sight, which the simple decoration of this hall afforded. Jutting from the azure-coloured walls rose gold-bronze trunks of high palm-trees, which wove their colossal leaves, glittering like bright emeralds, into a ceiling far up: in the middle of the chamber, and resting on three Egyptian lions, cast out of dark bronze, lay a porphyry plate; and on this stood a simple flower pot made of gold, from which, as soon as he beheld it, Anselmus could not turn away his eyes. It was as if, in a thousand gleaming reflections, all sorts of shapes were sporting on the bright polished gold: often he perceived his own form, with arms stretched out in longing—ah! beneath the elder-bush—and Serpentina was winding and shooting up and down, and again looking at him with her kind eyes. Anselmus was beside himself with frantic rapture.

"Serpentina! Serpentina!" he cried aloud; and Archivarius Lindhorst whirled round abruptly, and said: "What, Herr Anselmus? If I am not wrong, you were pleased to call for my daughter; she is in the other side of the house at present, and indeed taking her lesson on the harpsichord. Let us go along."

Anselmus, scarcely knowing what he did, followed his conductor; he saw or heard nothing more till Archivarius Lindhorst suddenly grasped his hand and said: "Here is the place!" Anselmus awoke as from a dream and now perceived that he was in a high room lined on all sides with bookshelves, and nowise differing from a common library and study. In the middle stood a large writing table, with a stuffed armchair before it. "This," said Archivarius Lindhorst, "is your workroom for the present: whether you may work, some other time, in the blue library, where you so suddenly called out my daughter's name, I do not know yet. But now I would like to convince myself of your ability to execute this task appointed you, in the way I wish it and need it." The Student here gathered full courage; and not without internal self-complacence in the certainty of highly gratifying Archivarius Lindhorst, pulled out his drawings and specimens of penmanship from his pocket. But no sooner had the Archivarius cast his eye on the first leaf, a piece of writing in the finest English style, than he smiled very oddly and shook his head. These motions he repeated at every succeeding leaf, so that the Student Anselmus felt the blood mounting to his face, and at last, when the smile became quite sarcastic and contemptuous, he broke out in downright vexation: "The Herr Archivarius does not seem contented with my poor talents."

"My dear Herr Anselmus," said Archivarius Lindhorst, "you have indeed fine capacities for the art of calligraphy; but, in the meanwhile, it is clear enough, I must reckon more on your diligence and good-will, than on your attainments."

The Student Anselmus spoke at length of his often-acknowledged perfection in this art, of his fine Chinese ink, and most select crowquills. But Archivarius Lindhorst handed him the English sheet, and said: "Be the judge yourself!" Anselmus felt as if struck by a thunderbolt, to see the way his handwriting looked: it was miserable, beyond measure. There was no rounding in the turns, no hairstroke where it should be; no proportion between the capital and single letters; indeed, villainous schoolboy pot-hooks often spoiled the best lines. "And then," continued Archivarius Lindhorst, "your ink will not last." He dipped his finger in a glass of water, and as he just skimmed it over the lines, they vanished without a trace. The Student Anselmus felt as if some monster were throttling him: he could not utter a word. There stood he, with the unfortunate sheet in his hand; but Archivarius Lindhorst laughed aloud, and said: "Never mind, Herr Anselmus; what you could not do well before you will perhaps do better here. At any rate, you shall have better materials than you have been accustomed to. Begin, in Heaven's name!"

From a locked press, Archivarius Lindhorst now brought out a black fluid substance, which diffused a most peculiar odour; also pens, sharply pointed and of strange colour, together with a sheet of special whiteness and smoothness; then at last an Arabic manuscript: and as Anselmus sat down to work, the Archivarius left the room. The Student Anselmus had often copied Arabic manuscripts before; the first problem, therefore, seemed to him not so very difficult to solve. "How those pot-hooks came into my fine English script, heaven and Archivarius Lindhorst know best," said he; "but that they are not from *my* hand, I will testify to the death!" At every new word that stood fair and perfect on the parchment, his courage increased, and with it his adroitness. In truth, these pens wrote exquisitely well; and the mysterious ink flowed pliantly, and black as jet, on the bright white parchment. And as he worked along so diligently, and with such strained attention, he began to feel more and more at home in the solitary room; and already he had quite fitted himself into his task, which he now hoped to finish well, when at the stroke of three the Archivarius called him into the side room to a savoury dinner. At table, Archivarius Lindhorst was in an especially good humour. He inquired about the Student Anselmus' friends, Conrector Paulmann and Registrator Heerbrand, and of the latter he had a store of merry anecdotes to tell. The good old Rhenish was particularly pleasing to the Student Anselmus, and made him more talkative than he usually was. At the stroke of four, he rose to resume his labour; and this punctuality appeared to please the Archivarius.

If the copying of these Arabic manuscripts had prospered in his hands before dinner, the task now went forward much better; indeed, he could not himself comprehend the rapidity and ease with which he succeeded in transcribing the twisted strokes of this foreign character. But it was as if, in his inmost soul, a voice were whispering in audible words: "Ah! could you accomplish it, if you were not thinking of *her*, if you did not believe in *her* and in her love?" Then there floated whispers, as in low, low, waving crystal tones, through the room: "I am near, near, near! I help you: be bold, be steadfast, dear Anselmus! I toil with you so that you may be mine!" And as, in the fullness of secret rapture, he caught these sounds, the unknown characters grew clearer and clearer to him; he scarcely needed to look at the original at all; nay, it was as if the letter were already standing in pale ink on the parchment, and he had nothing more to do but mark them black. So did he labour on, encompassed with dear inspiring tones as with soft sweet breath, till the clock struck six and Archivarius Lindhorst entered the apartment. He came forward to the table, with a singular smile; Anselmus rose in silence: the Archivarius still looked at him, with that mocking smile: but no sooner had he glanced over the copy, than the smile passed into deep solemn earnestness, which every feature of his face adapted itself to express. He seemed no longer the same. His eyes which usually gleamed with sparkling fire, now looked with unutterable mildness at Anselmus; a soft red tinted the pale cheeks; and instead of the irony which at other times compressed the mouth, the softly curved graceful lips now seemed to be opening for wise and soul-persuading speech. His whole form was higher, statelier; the wide nightgown spread itself like a royal mantle in broad folds over his breast and shoulders; and through the white locks, which lay on his high open brow, there wound a thin band of gold.

"Young man," began the Archivarius in solemn tone, "before you were aware of it, I knew you, and all the secret relations which bind you to the dearest and holiest of my interests! Serpentina loves you; a singular destiny, whose fateful threads were spun by enemies, is fulfilled, should she become yours and if you obtain, as an essential dowry, the Golden Flower Pot, which of right belongs to her. But only from effort and contest can your happiness in the higher life arise; hostile Principles assail you; and only the interior force with which you withstand these contradictions can save you from disgrace and ruin. While labouring here, you are undergoing a season of instruction: belief and full knowledge will lead you to the near goal, if you but hold fast, what you have begun well. Bear *her* always and truly in your thoughts, her who loves you; then you will see the marvels of the Golden Pot, and be happy forevermore. Farewell! Archivarius Lindhorst expects you tomorrow at noon in his cabinet. Farewell!" With these words Archivarius Lindhorst softly pushed the Student Anselmus out of the door, which he then locked; and Anselmus found himself in the chamber where he had dined, the single door of which led out to the hallway.

Completely stupefied by these strange phenomena, the Student Anselmus stood lingering at the street door; he heard a window open above him, and looked up: it was Archivarius Lindhorst, quite the old man again, in his light-gray gown, as he usually appeared. The Archivarius called to him: "Hey, worthy Herr Anselmus, what are you studying over there? Tush, the Arabic is still in your head. My compliments to Herr Conrector Paulmann, if you see him; and come tomorrow precisely at noon. The fee for this day is lying in your right waistcoat pocket." The Student Anselmus actually found the speziesthaler in the pocket indicated; but he derived no pleasure from it. "What is to come of all this," said he to himself, "I do not know: but if it is some mad delusion and conjuring work that has laid hold of me, my dear Serpentina still lives and moves in my inward heart; and before I leave her, I will die; for I know that the thought in me is eternal, and no hostile Principle can take it from me: and what else is this thought but Serpentina's love?"

Seventh Vigil

At last Conrector Paulmann knocked the ashes out of his pipe, and said: "Now, then, it is time to go to bed." "Yes, indeed," replied Veronica, frightened at her father's sitting so late: for ten had struck long ago. No sooner, accordingly, had the Conrector withdrawn to his study and bedroom, and Fränzchen's heavy breathing signified that she was asleep, than Veronica, who to save appearances had also gone to bed, rose softly, softly, out of it again, put on her clothes, threw her mantle round her, and glided out of doors.

Ever since the moment when Veronica had left old Liese, Anselmus had continually stood before her eyes; and it seemed as if a voice that was strange to her kept repeating in her soul that he was reluctant because he was held prisoner by an enemy and that Veronica, by secret means of the magic art, could break these bonds. Her confidence in old Liese grew stronger every day; and even the impression of unearthliness and horror by degrees became less, so that all the mystery and strangeness of her relation to the crone appeared before her only in the colour of something singular, romantic, and so not a little attractive. Accordingly, she had a firm purpose, even at the risk of being missed from home, and encountering a thousand inconveniences, to undertake the adventure of the Equinox. And now, at last, the fateful night, in which old Liese had promised to afford comfort and help, had come; and Veronica, long used to thoughts of nightly wandering, was full of heart and hope. She sped through the solitary streets; heedless of the storm which was howling in the air and dashing thick raindrops in her face.

With a stifled droning clang, the Kreuzthurm clock struck eleven, as Veronica, quite wet, reached old Liese's house. "Are you here, dear! wait, love; wait, love—" cried a voice from above; and in a moment the crone, laden with a basket, and attended by her cat, was also standing at the door. "We will go, then, and do what is proper, and can prosper in the night, which favours the work." So speaking, the crone with her cold hand seized the shivering Veronica, to whom she gave the heavy basket to carry, while she herself produced a little cauldron, a trivet, and a spade. By the time they reached the open fields, the rain had ceased, but the storm had become louder; howlings in a thousand tones were flitting through the air. A horrible heart-piercing lamentation sounded down from the black clouds, which rolled themselves together in rapid flight and veiled all things in thickest darkness. But the crone stepped briskly forward, crying in a shrill harsh voice: "Light, light, my lad!" Then blue forky gleams went quivering and sputtering before them; and Veronica perceived that it was the cat emitting sparks, and bounding forward to light the way; while his doleful ghastly screams were heard in the momentary pauses of the storm. Her heart almost failed; it was as if ice-cold talons were clutching into her soul; but, with a strong effort, she collected herself, pressed closer to the crone, and said: "It must all be accomplished now, come of it what may!"

"Right, right, little daughter!" replied the crone; "be steady, like a good girl; you shall have something pretty, and Anselmus to boot."

At last the crone paused, and said: "Here is the place!" She dug a hole in the ground, then shook coals into it, put the trivet over them, and placed the cauldron on top of it. All this she accompanied with strange gestures, while the cat kept circling round her. From his tail there sputtered sparkles, which united into a ring of fire. The coals began to burn; and at last blue flames rose up around the cauldron. Veronica was ordered to lay off her mantle and veil, and to cower down beside the crone, who seized her hands, and pressed them hard, glaring with her fiery eyes at the maiden. Before long the strange materials (whether flowers, metals, herbs, or beasts, you could not determine), which the crone had taken from her basket and thrown into the cauldron, began to seethe and foam. The crone let go Veronica, then clutched an iron ladle, and plunged it into the glowing mass, which she began to stir, while Veronica, as she directed, was told to look steadfastly into the cauldron and fix her thoughts on Anselmus. Now the crone threw fresh ingredients, glittering pieces of metal, a lock of hair which Veronica had cut from her head, and a little ring which she had long worn, into the pot, while the old woman howled in dread yelling tones through the gloom, and the cat, in quick, incessant motion, whimpered and whined—

I wish very much, favorable reader, that on this twenty-third of September, you had been on the road to Dresden. In vain, when night sank down upon you, the people at the last stage-post tried to keep you there; the friendly host represented to you that the storm and the rain were too bitter, and moreover, for unearthly reasons, it was not safe to rush out into the dark on the night of the Equinox; but you paid no heed to him, thinking to yourself, "I will give the postillion a whole thaler as a tip, and so, at latest, by one o'clock I shall reach Dresden. There in the Golden Angel or the Helmet or the City of Naumburg a good supper and a soft bed await me."

And now as you ride toward Dresden through the dark, you suddenly observe in the distance a very strange, flickering light. As you come nearer, you can distinguish a ring of fire, and in its center, beside a pot out of which a thick vapour is mounting with quivering red flashes and sparkles, there sit two very different forms. Right through the fire your road leads, but the horses snort, and stamp, and rear; the postillion curses and prays, and does not spare his whip; the horses will not stir from the spot. Without thinking, you leap out of the stagecoach and hasten forward toward the fire.

And now you clearly see a pretty girl, obviously of gentle birth, who is kneeling by the cauldron in a thin white nightdress. The storm has loosened her braids, and her long chestnut-brown hair is floating freely in the wind. Full in the dazzling light from the flame flickering from beneath the trivet hovers her sweet face; but in the horror which has poured over it like an icy stream, it is stiff and pale as death; and by her updrawn eyebrows, by her mouth, which is vainly opened for the shriek of anguish which cannot find its way from her bosom compressed with unnamable torment—you perceive her terror, her horror. She holds her small soft hands aloft, spasmodically pressed together, as if she were calling with prayers her guardian angel to deliver her from the monsters of the Pit, which, in obedience to this potent spell are to appear at any moment! There she kneels, motionless as a figure of marble. Opposite her a long, shrivelled, copper-yellow crone with a peaked hawk-nose and glistering cat-eyes sits cowering. From the black cloak which is huddled around her protrude her skinny naked arms; as she stirs the Hell-broth, she laughs and cries with creaking voice through the raging, bellowing storm.

I can well believe that unearthly feelings might have arisen in you, too—unacquainted though you are otherwise with fear and dread—at the aspect of this picture of Rembrandt or Hell-Breughel, taking place in actual life. Indeed, in horror, the hairs of your head might have stood on end. But your eye could not turn away from the gentle girl entangled in these infernal doings; and the electric stroke that quivered through all your nerves and fibres, kindled in you with the speed of lightning the courageous thought of defying the mysterious powers of the ring of fire; and at this thought your horror disappeared; nay, the thought itself came into being from your feelings of horror, as their product. Your heart felt as if you yourself were one of those guardian angels to whom the maiden, frightened almost to death, was praying; nay, as if you must instantly whip out your pocket pistol and without further ceremony blow the hag's brains out. But while you were thinking of all this most vividly, you cried aloud, "Holla!" or "What the matter here?" or "What's going on there?" The postillion blew a clanging blast on his horn; the witch ladled about in her brewage, and in a trice everything vanished in thick smoke. Whether you would have found the girl, for whom you were groping in the darkness with the most heart-felt longing, I cannot say: but you surely would have destroyed the witch's spell and undone the magic circle into which Veronica had thoughtlessly entered.

Alas! Neither you, favourable reader, nor any other man either drove or walked this way, on the twenty-third of September, in the tempestuous witch-favouring night; and Veronica had to abide by the cauldron, in deadly terror, till the work was near its close. She heard, indeed, the howling and raging around her; all sorts of hateful voices bellowed and bleated, and yelled and hummed; but she did not open her eyes, for she felt that the sight of the abominations and the horrors with which she was encircled might drive her into incurable destroying madness. The hag had ceased to stir the pot: its smoke grew fainter and fainter; and at last, nothing but a light spirit-flame was burning in the bottom. Then she cried: "Veronica, my child! my darling! look into the grounds there! What do you see? What do you see?"

Veronica could not answer, yet it seemed as if all sorts of perplexing shapes were dancing and whirling in the cauldron; and suddenly, with friendly look, reaching her his hand, the Student Anselmus rose from the cavity of the vessel. She cried aloud: "It is Anselmus! It is Anselmus!"

Instantly the crone turned the cock fixed at the bottom of the cauldron, and glowing metal rushed forth, hissing and bubbling, into a little mould which she had placed beside it. The hag now sprang aloft, and shrieked, capering about with wild horrific gestures: "It is done! It is done! Thanks, my pretty lad; did you watch?—Pooh, pooh, he is coming! Bite him to death! Bite him to death!" But then there sounded a strong rushing through the air: it was as if a huge eagle were pouncing down, striking round him with his pinions; and there shouted a tremendous voice: "Hey, hey, vermin!—It is over! It is over!—Home with you!" The crone sank down with bitter howling, and Veronica's sense and recollection forsook her.

On her returning to herself, it was broad daylight, she was lying in her bed, and Fränzchen was standing before her with a cup of steaming tea and saying to her: "Tell me, sister, what in all the world ails you? I have been standing here this hour, and you have been lying senseless, as if in a fever, and moaning and whimpering so that we were frightened to death. Father has not gone to his class this morning because of you; he will be here directly with the doctor."

Veronica took the tea in silence: and while she was drinking it, the horrid images of the night rose vividly before her eyes. "So it was all nothing but a wild dream that tortured me? Yet last night, I surely went to that old woman; it was the twenty-third of September too? Well, I must have been very sick last night, and so fancied all this; and nothing has sickened me but my perpetual thinking of Anselmus and the strange old woman who gave herself out for Liese, but was no such thing, and only made a fool of me with that story."

Fränzchen, who had left the room, again came in with Veronica's mantle, all wet, in her hand. "Look, sister," said she, "what a sight your mantle is! The storm last night blew open the shutters and upset the chair where your mantle was hanging; and the rain has come in, and wet it for you."

This speech sank heavy on Veronica's heart, for she now saw that it was no dream which had tormented her, but that she had really been with the witch. Anguish and horror took hold of her at the thought, and a fever-frost quivered through all her frame. In spasmodic shuddering, she drew the bedclothes close over her; but with this, she felt something hard pressing on her breast, and on grasping it with her hand, it seemed like a medallion: she drew it out, as soon as Fränzchen went away with the mantle; it was a little, round, bright-polished metallic mirror. "This is a present from the woman," cried she eagerly; and it was as if fiery beams were shooting from the mirror, and penetrating into her inmost soul with benignant warmth. The fever-frost was gone, and there streamed through her whole being an unutterable feeling of contentment and cheerful delight. She could not but remember Anselmus; and as she turned her thoughts more and more intensely on him, behold, he smiled on her in friendly fashion out of the mirror, like a living miniature portrait. But before long she felt as if it were no longer the image which she saw; no! but the Student Anselmus himself alive and in person. He was sitting in a stately chamber, with the strangest furniture, and diligently writing. Veronica was about to step forward, to pat his shoulder, and say to him: "Herr Anselmus, look round; it is I!" But she could not; for it was as if a fire-stream encircled him; and yet when she looked more narrowly, this fire-stream was nothing but large books with gilt leaves. At last Veronica so far succeeded that she caught Anselmus's eye: it seemed as if he needed, in gazing at her, to bethink himself who she was; but at last he smiled and said: "Ah! Is it you, dear Mademoiselle Paulmann! But why do you like now and then to take the form of a little snake?"

At these strange words, Veronica could not help laughing aloud; and with this she awoke as from a deep dream; and hastily concealed the little mirror, for the door opened, and Conrector Paulmann with Dr. Eckstein entered the room. Dr. Eckstein stepped forward to the bedside; felt Veronica's pulse with long profound study, and then said: "Ey! Ey!" Thereupon he wrote out a prescription; again felt the pulse; a second time said: "Ey! Ey!" and then left his patient. But from these disclosures of Dr. Eckstein's, Conrector Paulmann could not clearly make out what it was that ailed Veronica.

Eighth Vigil

The Student Anselmus had now worked several days with Archivarius Lindhorst; these working hours were for him the happiest of his life; still encircled with lovely tones, with Serpentina's encouraging voice, he was filled and overflowed with a pure delight, which often rose to highest rapture. Every difficulty, every little care of his needy existence, had vanished from his thoughts; and in the new life, which had risen on him as in serene sunny splendour, he comprehended all the wonders of a higher world, which before had filled him with astonishment, nay, with dread. His copying proceeded rapidly and lightly; for he felt more and more as if he were writing characters long known to him; and he scarcely needed to cast his eye upon the manuscript, while copying it all with the greatest exactness.

Except at the hour of dinner, Archivarius Lindhorst seldom made his appearance; and this always precisely at the moment when Anselmus had finished the last letter of some manuscript: then the Archivarius would hand him another, and immediately leave him, without uttering a word; having first stirred the ink with a little black rod, and changed the old pens for new sharp-pointed ones. One day, when Anselmus, at the stroke of twelve, had as usual mounted the stair, he found the door through which he commonly entered, standing locked; and

Archivarius Lindhorst came forward from the other side, dressed in his strange flower-figured dressing gown. He called aloud: "Today come this way, good Herr Anselmus; for we must go to the chamber where the masters of Bhagavadgita are waiting for us."

He stepped along the corridor, and led Anselmus through the same chambers and halls as at the first visit. The Student Anselmus again felt astonished at the marvellous beauty of the garden: but he now perceived that many of the strange flowers, hanging on the dark bushes, were in truth insects gleaming with lordly colours, hovering up and down with their little wings, as they danced and whirled in clusters, caressing one another with their antennae. On the other hand again, the rose and azure-coloured birds were odoriferous flowers; and the perfume which they scattered, mounted from their cups in low lovely tones, which, with the gurgling of distant fountains, and the sighing of the high groves and trees, mingled themselves into mysterious accords of a deep unutterable longing. The mock-birds, which had so jeered and flouted him before, were again fluttering to and fro over his head, and crying incessantly with their sharp small voices: "Herr Studiosus, Herr Studiosus, don't be in such a hurry! Don't peep into the clouds so! They may fall about your ears—He! He! Herr Studiosus, put your powdermantle on; cousin Screech-Owl will frizzle your toupee." And so it went along, in all manner of stupid chatter, till Anselmus left the garden.

Archivarius Lindhorst at last stepped into the azure chamber: the pophyry, with the Golden Flower Pot, was gone; instead of it, in the middle of the room, stood a table overhung with violet-coloured satin, upon which lay the writing gear already known to Anselmus; and a stuffed armchair, covered with the same sort of cloth, was placed beside it.

"Dear Herr Anselmus," said Archivarius Lindhorst, "you have now copied for me a number of manuscripts, rapidly and correctly, to my no small contentment: you have gained my confidence; but the hardest is still ahead; and that is the transcribing or rather painting of certain works, written in a peculiar character; I keep them in this room, and they can only be copied on the spot. You will, therefore, in future, work here; but I must recommend to you the greatest foresight and attention; a false stroke, or, which may Heaven forfend, a blot let fall on the original, will plunge you into misfortune."

Anselmus observed that from the golden trunks of the palm-tree, little emerald leaves projected: one of these leaves the Archivarius took hold of; and Anselmus saw that the leaf was in truth a roll of parchment, which the Archivarius unfolded, and spread out before the Student on the table. Anselmus wondered not a little at these strangely intertwisted characters; and as he looked over the many points, strokes, dashes, and twirls in the manuscript, he almost lost hope of ever copying it. He fell into deep thought on the subject.

"Be of courage, young man!" cried the Archivarius; "if you have continuing belief and true love, Serpentina will help you."

His voice sounded like ringing metal; and as Anselmus looked up in utter terror, Archivarius Lindhorst was standing before him in the kingly form, which, during the first visit, he had assumed in the library. Anselmus felt as if in his deep reverence he could not but sink on his knee; but the Archivarius stepped up the trunk of a palm-tree, and vanished aloft among the emerald leaves. The Student Anselmus perceived that the Prince of the Spirits had been speaking with him, and was now gone up to his study; perhaps intending, by the beams which some of the Planets had despatched to him as envoys, to send back word what was to become of Anselmus and Serpentina.

"It may be too," he further thought, "that he is expecting news from the springs of the Nile; or that some magician from Lapland is paying him a visit: it behooves me to set diligently about my task." And with this, he began studying the foreign characters on the roll of parchment.

The strange music of the garden sounded over him, and encircled him with sweet lovely odours; the mock-birds, too, he still heard giggling and twittering, but could not distinguish their words, a thing which greatly pleased him. At times also it was as if the leaves of the palm-trees were rustling, and as if the clear crystal tones, which Anselmus on that fateful Ascension Day had heard under the elder-bush, were beaming and flitting through the room. Wonderfully strengthened by this shining and tinkling, the Student Anselmus directed his eyes and thoughts more and more intensely on the superscription of the parchment roll; and before long he felt, as it were from his inmost soul, that the characters could denote nothing else than these words: *Of the marriage of the Salamander with the green snake.* Then resounded a louder triphony of clear crystal bells: "Anselmus! dear Anselmus!" floated to him from the leaves; and, O wonder! on the trunk of the palm-tree the green snake came winding down.

"Serpentina! Serpentina!" cried Anselmus, in the madness of highest rapture; for as he gazed more earnestly, it was in truth a lovely glorious maiden that, looking at him with those dark blue eyes, full of inexpressible longing, as they lived in his heart, was slowly gliding down to meet him. The leaves seemed to jut out and expand; on every hand were prickles sprouting from the trunk; but Serpentina twisted and wound herself deftly through them; and so drew her fluttering robe, glancing as if in changeful colours, along with her, that, plying round the dainty form, it nowhere caught on the projecting points and prickles of the palm-tree. She sat down by Anselmus on the same chair, clasping him with her arm, and pressing him towards her, so that he felt the breath which came from her lips, and the electric warmth of her frame.

"Dear Anselmus," began Serpentina, "you shall now be wholly mine; by your belief, by your love, you shall obtain me, and I will bring you the Golden Flower Pot, which shall make us both happy forevermore."

"O, kind, lovely Serpentina!" said Anselmus. "If I have you, what do I care for anything else! If you are but mine, I will joyfully give in to all the wonderful mysteries that have beset me since the moment when I first saw you."

"I know," continued Serpentina, "that the strange and mysterious things with which my father, often merely in the sport of his humour, has surrounded you have raised distrust and dread in your mind; but now, I hope, it shall be so no more; for I came at this moment to tell you, dear Anselmus, from the bottom of my heart and soul, everything, to the smallest detail, that you need to know for understanding my father, and so for seeing clearly what your relation to him and to me really is."

Anselmus felt as if he were so wholly clasped and encircled by the gentle lovely form, that only with her could he move and live, and as if it were but the beating of her pulse that throbbed through his nerves and fibres; he listened to each one of her words till it sounded in his inmost heart, and, like a burning ray, kindled in him the rapture of Heaven. He had put his arm round that daintier than dainty waist; but the changeful glistering cloth of her robe was so smooth and slippery, that it seemed to him as if she could at any moment wind herself from his arms, and glide away. He trembled at the thought.

"Ah, do not leave me, gentlest Serpentina!" cried he; "you are my life."

"Not now," said Serpentina, "till I have told you everything that in your love of me you can comprehend:

"Know then, dearest, that my father is sprung from the wondrous race of the Salamanders; and that I owe my existence to his love for the green snake. In primeval times, in the Fairyland Atlantis, the potent Spirit-prince Phosphorus bore rule; and to him the Salamanders, and other spirits of the elements, were pledged by oath. Once upon a time, a Salamander, whom he loved before all others (it was my father), chanced to be walking in the stately garden, which Phosphorus' mother had decked in the lordliest fashion with her best gifts; and the Salamander heard a tall lily singing in low tones: 'Press down thy little eyelids, till my lover, the Morning-wind, awake thee.' He walked towards it: touched by his glowing breath, the lily opened her leaves: and he saw the lily's daughter, the green snake, lying asleep in the hollow of the flower. Then was the Salamander inflamed with warm love for the fair snake; and he carried her away from the lily, whose perfumes in nameless lamentation vainly called for her beloved daughter throughout all the garden. For the Salamander had borne her into the palace of Phosphorus, and was there beseeching him: 'Wed me with my beloved, and she shall be mine forevermore.' — 'Madman, what do you ask?' said the Prince of the Spirits. 'Know that once the Lily was my mistress, and bore rule with me; but the Spark, which I cast into her, threatened to annihilate the fair Lily; and only my victory over the black Dragon, whom now the Spirits of the Earth hold in fetters, maintains her, that her leaves continue strong enough to enclose this Spark, and preserve it within them. But when you clasp the green snake, your fire will consume her frame; and a new being rapidly arising from her dust, will soar away and leave you.'

"The Salamander heeded not the warning of the Spirit-prince: full of longing ardour he folded the green snake in his arms; she crumbled into ashes; a winged being, born from her dust, soared away through the sky. Then the madness of desperation caught the Salamander; and he ran through the garden, dashing forth fire and flames; and wasted it in his wild fury, till its fairest flowers and blossoms hung down, blackened and scathed; and their lamentation filled the air. The indignant Prince of the Spirits, in his wrath, laid hold of the Salamander, and said: 'Your fire has burnt out, your flames are extinguished, your rays darkened: sink down to the Spirits of the Earth; let them mock and jeer you, and keep you captive, till the Fire-elements shall again kindle, and beam up with you as with a new being from the Earth.' The poor Salamander sank down extinguished: but now the testy old earth-spirit, who was Phosphorus' gardener, came forth and said: 'Master! who has greater cause to complain of the Salamander than I? Had not all the fair flowers, which he has burnt, been decorated with my gayest metals; had I not stoutly nursed and tended them, and spent many a fair hue on their leaves? And yet I must pity the poor Salamander; for it was but love, in which you, O Master, have full often been entangled, that drove him to despair, and made him desolate the garden. Remit his too harsh punishment!' — 'His fire is for the present extinguished,' said the Prince of the Spirits; 'but in the hapless time, when the speech of nature shall no longer be intelligible to degenerate man; when the spirits of the elements, banished into their own regions, shall speak to him only from afar, in faint, spent echoes; when, displaced from the harmonious circle, an infinite longing alone shall give him tidings of the land of marvels, which he once might inhabit while belief and love still dwelt in his soul: in this hapless time, the fire of the Salamander shall again kindle; but only to manhood shall he be permitted to rise, and entering wholly into man's necessitous existence, he shall learn to endure its wants and oppressions. Yet not only shall the remembrance of his first state continue with him, but he shall again rise into the sacred harmony of all Nature; he shall understand its wonders, and the power of his fellow-spirits shall stand at his behest. Then, too, in a lily-bush, shall he find the green snake again: and the fruit of his marriage with her shall be three daughters, which, to men, shall appear in the form of their mother. In the spring season these shall disport themselves in the dark elder-bush, and sound with their lovely crystal voices. And then if, in that needy and mean age of inward stuntedness, there shall be found a youth who understands their song; nay, if one of the little snakes look at him with her kind eyes; if the look awaken in him forecastings of the distant wondrous land, to which, having cast away the burden of the Common, he can courageously soar; if, with love to the snake, there rise in him belief in the wonders of nature, nay, in his own existence amid these wonders, then the snake shall be his. But not till three youths of this sort have been found and wedded to the three daughters, may the Salamander cast away his heavy burden, and return to his brothers.'—'Permit me, Master,' said the earth-spirit, 'to make these three daughters a present, which may glorify their life with the husbands they shall find. Let each of them receive from me a flower pot, of the fairest metal which I have; I will polish it with beams borrowed from the diamond; in its glitter shall our kingdom of wonders, as it now exists in the harmony of universal nature be imaged back in glorious dazzling reflection; and from its interior, on the day of marriage, shall spring forth a fire-lily, whose eternal blossoms shall encircle the youth that is found worthy, with sweet wafting odours. Soon too shall he learn its speech, and understand the wonders of our kingdom, and dwell with his beloved in Atlantis itself.'

"Thou perceivest well, dear Anselmus, that the Salamander of whom I speak is no other than my father. In spite of his higher nature, he was forced to subject himself to the paltriest contradictions of common life; and hence, indeed, often comes the wayward humour with which he vexes many. He has told me now and then, that, for the inward make of mind, which the Spirit-prince Phosphorus required as a condition of marriage with me and my sisters, men have a name at present, which, in truth, they frequently enough misapply: they call it a childlike poetic character. This character, he says, is often found in youths, who, by reason of their high simplicity of manners, and their total want of what is called knowledge of the world, are mocked by the common mob. Ah, dear Anselmus! beneath the elder-bush, you understood my song, my look: you love the green snake, you believe in me, and will be mine for evermore! The fair lily will bloom forth from the Golden Flower Pot; and we shall dwell, happy, and united, and blessed, in Atlantis together!

"Yet I must not hide from you that in its deadly battle with the Salamanders and spirits of the earth, the black Dragon burst from their grasp, and hurried off through the air. Phosphorus, indeed, again holds him in fetters; but from the black quills, which, in the struggle, rained down on the ground, there sprang up hostile spirits, which on all hands set themselves against the Salamanders and spirits of the earth. That woman who hates you so, dear Anselmus, and who, as my father knows full well, is striving for possession of the Golden Flower Pot; that woman owes her existence to the love of such a quill (plucked in battle from the Dragon's wing) for a certain beet beside which it dropped. She knows her origin and her power; for, in the moans and convulsions of the captive Dragon, the secrets of many a mysterious constellation are revealed to her; and she uses every means and effort to work from the outward into the inward and unseen; while my father, with the beams which shoot forth from the spirit of the Salamander, withstands and subdues her. All the baneful principles which lurk in deadly herbs and poisonous beasts, she collects; and, mixing them under favourable constellations, raises therewith many a wicked spell, which overwhelms the soul of man with fear and trembling, and subjects him to the power of those demons, produced from the Dragon when it yielded in battle. Beware of that old woman, dear Anselmus! She hates you, because your childlike pious character has annihilated many of her wicked charms. Keep true, true to me; soon you will be at the goal!"

"O my Serpentina! my own Serpentina!" cried the Student Anselmus, "how could I leave you, how should I not love you forever!" A kiss was burning on his lips; he awoke as from a deep dream: Serpentina had vanished; six o'clock was striking, and it fell heavy on his heart that today he had not copied a single stroke. Full of anxiety, and dreading reproaches from the Archivarius, he looked into the sheet; and, O wonder! the copy of the mysterious manuscript was fairly concluded; and he thought, on viewing the characters more narrowly, that the writing was nothing else but Serpentina's story of her father, the favourite of the Spirit-prince Phosphorus, in Atlantis, the land of marvels. And now entered Archivarius Lindhorst, in his light-gray surtout, with hat and staff: he looked into the parchment on which Anselmus had been writing; took a large pinch of snuff, and said with a smile: "Just as I thought!—Well, Herr Anselmus, here is your speziesthaler; we will now go to the Linkische Bath: please follow me!" The Archivarius walked rapidly through the garden, in which there was such a din of singing, whistling, talking, that the Student Anselmus was quite deafened with it, and thanked Heaven when he found himself on the street.

Scarcely had they walked twenty paces, when they met Registrator Heerbrand, who companionably joined them. At the Gate, they filled their pipes, which they had upon them: Registrator Heerbrand complained that he had left his tinder-box behind, and could not strike fire. "Fire!" cried Archivarius Lindhorst, scornfully; "here is fire enough, and to spare!" And with this he snapped his fingers, out of which came streams of sparks, and directly kindled the pipes. — "Observe the chemical knack of some men!" said Registrator Heerbrand; but the Student Anselmus thought, not without internal awe, of the Salamander and his history.

In the Linkische Bath, Registrator Heerbrand drank so much strong double beer, that at last, though usually a good-natured quiet man, he began singing student songs in squeaking tenor; he asked everyone sharply, whether he was his friend or not? and at last had to be taken home by the Student Anselmus, long after the Archivarius Lindhorst had gone his ways.

Ninth Vigil

The strange and mysterious things which day by day befell the Student Anselmus, had entirely withdrawn him from his customary life. He no longer visited any of his friends, and waited every morning with impatience for the hour of noon, which was to unlock his paradise. And yet while his whole soul was turned to the gentle Serpentina, and the wonders of Archivarius Lindhorst's fairy kingdom, he could not help now and then thinking of Veronica; nay, often it seemed as if she came before him and confessed with blushes how heartily she loved him; how much she longed to rescue him from the phantoms, which were mocking and befooling him. At times he felt as if a foreign power, suddenly breaking in on his mind, were drawing him with resistless force to the forgotten Veronica; as if he must needs follow her whither she pleased to lead him, nay, as if he were bound to her by ties that would not break. That very night after Serpentina had first appeared to him in the form of a lovely maiden; after the wondrous secret of the Salamander's nuptials with the green snake had been disclosed, Veronica came before him more vividly than ever. Nay, not till he awoke, was he clearly aware that he had only been dreaming; for he had felt persuaded that Veronica was actually beside him, complaining with an expression of keen sorrow, which pierced through his inmost soul, that he should sacrifice her deep true love to fantastic visions, which only the distemper of his mind called into being, and which, moreover, would at last prove his ruin. Veronica was lovelier than he had ever seen her; he could not drive her from his thoughts: and in this perplexed and contradictory mood he hastened out, hoping to get rid of it by a morning walk.

A secret magic influence led him on the Pirna gate: he was just turning into a cross street, when Conrector Paulmann, coming after him, cried out: "Ey! Ey!—Dear Herr Anselmus!—*Amice! Amice!* Where, in Heaven's name, have you been buried so long? We never see you at all. Do you know, Veronica is longing very much to have another song with you. So come along; you were just on the road to me, at any rate."

The Student Anselmus, constrained by this friendly violence, went along with the Conrector. On entering the house, they were met by Veronica, attired with such neatness and attention, that Conrector Paulmann, full of amazement, asked her: "Why so decked, Mamsell? Were you expecting visitors? Well, here I bring you Herr Anselmus."

The Student Anselmus, in daintily and elegantly kissing Veronica's hand, felt a small soft pressure from it, which shot like a stream of fire over all his frame. Veronica was cheerfulness, was grace itself; and when Paulmann left them for his study, she contrived, by all manner of rogueries and waggeries, to uplift the Student Anselmus so much that he at last quite forgot his bashfulness, and jigged round the room with the playful girl. But here again the demon of awkwardness got hold of him: he jolted on a table, and Veronica's pretty little workbox fell to the floor. Anselmus lifted it; the lid had flown up; and a little round metallic mirror was glittering on him, into which he looked with peculiar delight. Veronica glided softly up to him; laid her hand on his arm, and pressing close to him, looked over his shoulder into the mirror also. And now Anselmus felt as if a battle were beginning in his soul: thoughts, images flashed out—Archivarius Lindhorst—Serpentina—the green snake—at last the tumult abated, and all this chaos arranged and shaped itself into distinct consciousness. It was now clear to him that he had always thought of Veronica alone; nay, that the form which had yesterday appeared to him in the blue chamber, had been no other than Veronica; and that the wild legend of the Salamander's marriage with the green snake had merely been written down by him from the manuscript, but nowise related in his hearing. He wondered greatly at all these dreams; and ascribed them solely to the heated state of mind into which Veronica's love had brought him, as well as to his working with Archivarius Lindhorst, in whose rooms there were, besides, so many strangely intoxicating odours. He could not help laughing heartily at the mad whim of falling in love with a little green snake; and taking a well-fed Privy Archivarius for a Salamander: "Yes, yes! It is

Veronica!" cried he aloud; but on turning round his head, he looked right into Veronica's blue eyes, from which warmest love was beaming. A faint soft Ah! escaped her lips, which at that moment were burning on his.

"O happy I!" sighed the enraptured Student: "What I yesternight but dreamed, is in very deed mine today."

"But will you really marry me, then, when you are a Hofrath?" said Veronica.

"That I will," replied the Student Anselmus; and just then the door creaked, and Conrector Paulmann entered with the words:

"Now, dear Herr Anselmus, I will not let you go today. You will put up with a bad dinner; then Veronica will make us delightful coffee, which we shall drink with Registrator Heerbrand, for he promised to come here."

"Ah, Herr Conrector!" answered the Student Anselmus, "are you not aware that I must go to Archivarius Lindhorst's and copy?"

"Look, *Amice!*" said Conrector Paulmann, holding up his watch, which pointed to half-past twelve.

The Student Anselmus saw clearly that he was much too late for Archivarius Lindhorst; and he complied with the Conrector's wishes the more readily, as he might now hope to look at Veronica the whole day long, to obtain many a stolen glance, and little squeeze of the hand, nay, even to succeed in conquering a kiss. So high had the Student Anselmus's desires now mounted; he felt more and more contented in soul, the more fully he convinced himself that he should soon be delivered from all these fantasies, which really might have made a sheer idiot of him.

Registrator Heerbrand came, as he had promised, after dinner; and coffee being over, and the dusk come on, the Registrator, puckering his face together, and gaily rubbing his hands, signified that he had something about him, which, if mingled and reduced to form, as it were, paged and titled, by Veronica's fair hands, might be pleasant to them all, on this October evening.

"Come out, then, with this mysterious substance which you carry with you, most valued Registrator," cried Conrector Paulmann. Then Registrator Heerbrand shoved his hand into his deep pocket, and at three journeys, brought out a bottle of arrack, two lemons, and a quantity of sugar. Before half an hour had passed, a savoury bowl of punch was smoking on Paulmann's table. Veronica drank their health in a sip of the liquor; and before long there was plenty of gay, good-natured chat among the friends. But the Student Anselmus, as the spirit of the drink mounted into his head, felt all the images of those wondrous things, which for some time he had experienced, again coming through his mind. He saw the Archivarious in his damask dressing gown, which glittered like phosphorus; he saw the azure room, the golden palm-trees; nay, it now seemed to him as if he must still believe in Serpentina: there was a fermentation, a conflicting tumult in his soul. Veronica handed him a glass of punch; and in taking it, he gently touched her hand. "Serpentina! Veronica!" sighed he to himself. He sank into deep dreams; but Registrator Heerbrand cried quite aloud: "A strange old gentleman, whom nobody can fathom, he is and will be, this Archivarius Lindhorst. Well, long life to him! Your glass, Herr Anselmus!"

Then the Student Anselmus awoke from his dreams, and said, as he touched glasses with Registrator Heerbrand: "That proceeds, respected Herr Registrator, from the circumstance, that Archivarius Lindhorst is in reality a Salamander, who in his fury laid waste the Spirit-prince Phosphorus' garden, because the green snake had flown away from him."

"What?" inquired Conrector Paulmann.

"Yes," continued the Student Anselmus; "and for this reason he is now forced to be a Royal Archivarius; and to keep house here in Dresden with his three daughters, who, after all, are nothing more than little gold-green snakes, that bask in elder-bushes, and traitorously sing, and seduce away young people, like so many sirens."

"Herr Anselmus! Herr Anselmus!" cried Conrector Paulmann, "is there a crack in your brain? In Heaven's name, what monstrous stuff is this you are babbling?"

"He is right," interrupted Registrator Heerbrand: "that fellow, that Archivarius, is a cursed Salamander, and strikes you fiery snips from his fingers, which burn holes in your surtout like red-hot tinder. Ay, ay, you are in the right, brotherkin Anselmus; and whoever says No, is saying No to me!" And at these words Registrator Heerbrand struck the table with his fist, till the glasses rung again.

"Registrator! Are you raving mad?" cried the enraged Conrector. "Herr Studiosus, Herr Studiosus! what is this you are about again?"

"Ah!" said the Student, "you too are nothing but a bird, a screech-owl, that frizzles toupees, Herr Conrector!"

"What?—I a bird?—A screech-owl, a frizzler?" cried the Conrector, full of indignation: "Sir, you are mad, born mad!"

"But the crone will get a clutch of him," cried Registrator Heerbrand.

"Yes, the crone is potent," interrupted the Student Anselmus, "though she is but of mean descent; for her father was nothing but a ragged wing-feather, and her mother a dirty beet: but the most of her power she owes to all sorts of baneful creatures, poisonous vermin which she keeps about her."

"That is a horrid calumny," cried Veronica, with eyes all glowing in anger: "old Liese is a wise woman; and the black cat is no baneful creature, but a polished young gentleman of elegant manners, and her cousin-german."

"Can *he* eat Salamanders without singeing his whiskers, and dying like a snuffed candle?" cried Registrator Heerbránd.

"No! no!" shouted the Student Anselmus, "that he never can in this world; and the green snake loves me, and I have looked into Serpentina's eyes."

"The cat will scratch them out," cried Veronica.

"Salamander, Salamander beats them all, all," hallooed Conrector Paulmann, in the highest fury: "But am I in a madhouse? Am I mad myself? What foolish nonsense am I chattering? Yes, I am mad too! mad too!" And with this, Conrector Paulmann started up; tore the peruke from his head, and dashed it against the ceiling of the room; till the battered locks whizzed, and, tangled into utter disorder, it rained down powder far and wide. Then the Student Anselmus and Registrator Heerbrand seized the punch bowl and the glasses; and, hallooing and huzzaing, pitched them against the ceiling also, and the sherds fell jingling and tingling about their ears.

"*Vivat* the Salamander!—*Pereat, pereat* the crone!—Break the metal mirror!—Dig the cat's eyes out!—Bird, little bird, from the air—*Eheu—Eheu—Evoe—Evoe*, Salamander!" So shrieked, and shouted, and bellowed the three, like utter maniacs. With loud weeping, Fränzchen ran out; but Veronica lay whimpering for pain and sorrow on the sofa.

At this moment the door opened: all was instantly still; and a little man, in a small gray cloak, came stepping in. His countenance had a singular air of gravity; and especially the round hooked nose, on which was a huge pair of spectacles, distinguished itself from all noses ever seen. He wore a strange peruke too; more like a feather-cap than a wig.

"Ey, many good-evenings!" grated and cackled the little comical mannikin. "Is the Student Herr Anselmus among you, gentlemen?—Best compliments from Archivarius Lindhorst; he has waited today in vain for Herr Anselmus; but tomorrow he begs most respectfully to request that Herr Anselmus does not miss the hour."

And with this, he went out again; and all of them now saw clearly that the grave little mannikin was in fact a gray parrot. Conrector Paulmann and Registrator Heerbrand raised a horselaugh, which reverberated through the room; and in the intervals, Veronica was moaning and whimpering, as if torn by nameless sorrow; but, as to the Student Anselmus, the madness of inward horror was darting through him; and unconsciously he ran through the door, along the streets.

Instinctively he reached his house, his garret. Ere long Veronica came in to him, with a peaceful and friendly look, and asked him why, in the festivity, he had so vexed her; and desired him to be upon his guard against figments of the imagination while working at Archivarius Lindhorst's. "Goodnight, goodnight, my beloved friend!" whispered Veronica scarcely audibly, and breathed a kiss on his lips. He stretched out his arms to clasp her, but the dreamy shape had vanished, and he awoke cheerful and refreshed. He could not but laugh heartily at the effects of the punch; but in thinking of Veronica, he felt pervaded by a most delightful feeling. "To her alone," said he within himself, "do I owe this return from my insane whims. Indeed, I was little better than the man who believed himself to be of glass; or the one who did not dare leave his room for fear the hens should eat him, since he was a barleycorn. But so soon as I am Hofrath, I shall marry Mademoiselle Paulmann, and be happy, and there's an end to it."

At noon, as he walked through Archivarius Lindhorst's garden, he could not help wondering how all this had once appeared so strange and marvellous. He now saw nothing that was not common; earthen flowerpots, quantities of geraniums, myrtles, and the like. Instead of the glittering multi-coloured birds which used to flout him, there were nothing but a few sparrows, fluttering hither and thither, which raised an unpleasant unintelligible cry at sight of Anselmus. The azure room also had quite a different look; and he could not understand how that glaring blue, and those unnatural golden trunks of palm-trees, with their shapeless glistening leaves, should ever have pleased him for a moment. The Archivarius looked at him with a most peculiar ironic smile, and asked: "Well, how did you like the punch last night, good Anselmus?"

"Ah, doubtless you have heard from the gray parrot how——" answered the Student Anselmus, quite ashamed; but he stopped short, thinking that this appearance of the parrot was all a piece of jugglery.

"I was there myself," said Archivarius Lindhorst; "didn't you see me? But, among the mad pranks you were playing, I almost got lamed: for I was sitting in the punch bowl, at the very moment when Registrator Heerbrand laid hands on it, to dash it against the ceiling; and I had to make a quick retreat into the Conrector's pipehead. Now, adieu, Herr Anselmus! Be diligent at your task; for the lost day you shall also have a speziesthaler, because you worked so well before."

"How can the Archivarius babble such mad stuff?" thought the Student Anselmus, sitting down at the table to begin the copying of the manuscript, which Archivarius Lindhorst had as usual spread out before him. But on the parchment roll, he perceived so many strange crabbed strokes and twirls all twisted together in inexplicable confu-

sion, offering no resting point for the eye, that it seemed to him well
nigh impossible to copy all this exactly. Nay, in glancing over the
whole, you might have thought the parchment was nothing but a piece
of thickly veined marble, or a stone sprinkled over with lichens.
Nevertheless he determined to do his utmost; and boldly dipped in his
pen: but the ink would not run, do what he liked; impatiently he
flicked the point of his pen against his fingernail, and—Heaven and
Earth!—a huge blot fell on the outspread original! Hissing and foaming, a blue flash rose from the blot; and crackling and wavering, shot
through the room to the ceiling. Then a thick vapour rolled from the
walls; the leaves began to rustle, as if shaken by a tempest; and down
out of them darted glaring basilisks in sparkling fire; these kindled the
vapour, and the bickering masses of flame rolled round Anselmus. The
golden trunks of the palm-trees became gigantic snakes, which
knocked their frightful heads together with piercing metallic clang;
and wound their scaly bodies round Anselmus.

"Madman! suffer now the punishment of what, in capricious irrev-
erence, thou hast done!" cried the frightful voice of the crowned
Salamander, who appeared above the snakes like a glittering beam in
the midst of the flame: and now the yawning jaws of the snakes poured
forth cataracts of fire on Anselmus; and it was as if the fire-streams were
congealing about his body, and changing into a firm ice-cold mass. But
while Anselmus's limbs, more and more pressed together, and contracted, stiffened into powerlessness, his senses passed away. On returning to himself, he could not stir a joint: he was as if surrounded
with a glistening brightness, on which he struck if he but tried to lift his
hand.—Alas! He was sitting in a well-corked crystal bottle, on a shelf,
in the library of Archivarius Lindhorst.

Tenth Vigil

I am probably right in doubting, gracious reader, that you were ever
sealed up in a glass bottle, or even that you have ever been oppressed
with such sorcery in your most vivid dreams. If you have had such
dreams, you will understand the Student Anselmus's woe and will feel
it keenly enough; but if you have not, then your flying imagination, for
the sake of Anselmus and me, will have to be obliging enough to enclose itself for a few moments in the crystal. You are drowned in dazzling splendour; everything around you appears illuminated and begirt
with beaming rainbow hues: in the sheen everything seems to quiver
and waver and clang and drone. You are swimming, but you are powerless and cannot move, as if you were imbedded in a firmly congealed
ether which squeezes you so tightly that it is in vain that your spirit

commands your dead and stiffened body. Heavier and heavier the mountainous burden lies on you; more and more every breath exhausts the tiny bit of air that still plays up and down in the tight space around you; your pulse throbs madly; and cut through with horrid anguish, every nerve is quivering and bleeding in your dead agony.

Favourable reader, have pity on the Student Anselmus! This inexpressible torture seized him in his glass prison: but he felt too well that even death could not release him, for when he had fainted with pain, he awoke again to new wretchedness when the morning sun shone into the room. He could move no limb, and his thoughts struck against the glass, stunning him with discordant clang; and instead of the words which the spirit used to speak from within him he now heard only the stifled din of madness. Then he exclaimed in his despair: "O Serpentina! Serpentina! Save me from this agony of Hell!" And it was as if faint sighs breathed around him, which spread like transparent green elder-leaves over the glass; the clanging ceased; the dazzling, perplexing glitter was gone, and he breathed more freely.

"Haven't I myself solely to blame for my misery? Ah! Haven't I sinned against you, kind, beloved Serpentina? Haven't I raised vile doubts of you? Haven't I lost my belief, and with it, all, all that was to make me so blessed? Ah! You will now never, never be mine; for me the Golden Pot is lost, and I shall not behold its wonders any more. Ah, could I but see you but once more; but once more hear your kind, sweet voice, lovely Serpentina!"

So wailed the Student Anselmus, caught with deep piercing sorrow: then a voice spoke close by him: "What the devil ails you, Herr Studiosus? What makes you lament so, out of all compass and measure?"

The Student Anselmus now perceived that on the same shelf with him were five other bottles, in which he perceived three Kreuzkirche Scholars, and two Law Clerks.

"Ah, gentlemen, my fellows in misery," cried he, "how is it possible for you to be so calm, nay, so happy, as I read in your cheerful looks? You are sitting here corked up in glass bottles, as well as I, and cannot move a finger, nay, not think a reasonable thought, but there rises such a murder-tumult of clanging and droning, and in your head itself a tumbling and rumbling enough to drive one mad. But of course you do not believe in the Salamander, or the green snake."

"You are pleased to jest, Mein Herr Studiosus," replied a Kreuzkirche Scholar; "we have never been better off than at present: for the speziesthalers which the mad Archivarius gave us for all kinds of pothook copies, are chinking in our pockets; we have now no Italian choruses to learn by heart; we go every day to Joseph's or other beer gardens, where the double-beer is sufficient, and we can look a pretty girl in the face; so we sing like real Students, *Gaudeamus igitur*, and are contented!"

"They of the Cross are quite right," added a Law Clerk; "I too am well furnished with speziesthalers, like my dearest colleague beside me here; and we now diligently walk about on the Weinberg, instead of scurvy law-copying within four walls."

"But, my best, worthiest masters!" said the Student Anselmus, "do you not observe, then, that you are all and sundry corked up in glass bottles, and cannot for your hearts walk a hairsbreadth?"

Here the Kreuzkirche Scholars and the Law Clerks set up a loud laugh, and cried: "The Student is mad; he fancies himself to be sitting in a glass bottle, and is standing on the Elbe Bridge and looking right down into the water. Let us go on our way!"

"Ah!" sighed the Student, "they have never seen the kind Serpentina; they do not know what Freedom, and life in Love, and Belief, signify; and so by reason of their folly and low-mindedness, they do not feel the oppression of the imprisonment into which the Salamander has cast them. But I, unhappy I, must perish in want and woe, if she whom I so inexpressibly love does not rescue me!"

Then, waving in faint tinkles, Serpentina's voice flitted through the room: "Anselmus! Believe, love, hope!" And every tone beamed into Anselmus's prison; and the crystal yielded to his pressure and expanded, till the breast of the captive could move and heave.

The torment of his situation became less and less, and he saw clearly that Serpentina still loved him; and that it was she alone, who had rendered his confinement tolerable. He disturbed himself no more about his inane companions in misfortune; but directed all his thoughts and meditations on the gentle Serpentina. Suddenly, however, there arose on the other side a dull, croaking repulsive murmur. Before long he could observe that it came from an old coffeepot, with half-broken lid, standing opposite him on a little shelf. As he looked at it more narrowly, the ugly features of a wrinkled old woman unfolded themselves gradually; and in a few moments the Apple-wife of the Schwarzthor stood before him. She grinned and laughed at him, and cried with screeching voice: "Ey, ey, my pretty boy, must you lie in limbo now? In the crystal you ended! Didn't I tell you so long ago?"

"Mock and jeer me, you cursed witch!" said Anselmus, "you are to blame for it all; but the Salamander will catch you, you vile beet!"

"Ho, ho!" replied the crone, "not so proud, my fine copyist. You have squashed my little sons and you have scarred my nose; but I still love you, you knave, for once you were a pretty fellow, and my little daughter likes you, too. Out of the crystal you will never get unless I help you:

I cannot climb up there, but my friend the rat, that lives close behind you, will eat the shelf in two; you will jingle down, and I shall catch you in my apron so that your nose doesn't get broken or your fine sleek face get injured at all. Then I will carry you to Mamsell Veronica, and you shall marry her when you become Hofrath."

"Get away, you devil's brood!" shouted the Student Anselmus in fury. "It was you alone and your hellish arts that made me commit the sin which I must now expiate. But I will bear it all patiently: for only here can I be encircled with Serpentina's love and consolation. Listen to me, you hag, and despair! I defy your power: I love Serpentina and none but her forever. I will not become Hofrath, I will not look at Veronica; by your means she is enticing me to evil. If the green snake cannot be mine, I will die in sorrow and longing. Away, filthy buzzard!"

The crone laughed, till the chamber rang: "Sit and die then," cried she: "but now it is time to set to work; for I have other trade to follow here." She threw off her black cloak, and so stood in hideous naked-ness; then she ran round in circles, and large folios came tumbling down to her; out of these she tore parchment leaves, and rapidly patch-ing them together in artful combination, and fixing them on her body, in a few instants she was dressed as if in strange multi-coloured armor. Spitting fire, the black cat darted out of the ink-glass, which was stand-ing on the table, and ran mewing towards the crone, who shrieked in loud triumph, and along with him vanished through the door.

Anselmus observed that she went towards the azure chamber; and di-rectly he heard a hissing and storming in the distance; the birds in the garden were crying; the Parrot creaked out: "Help! help! Thieves! thieves!" That moment the crone returned with a bound into the room, carrying the Golden Flower Pot on her arm, and with hideous gestures, shrieking wildly through the air; "Joy! joy, little son!—Kill the green snake! To her, son! To her!"

Anselmus thought he heard a deep moaning, heard Serpentina's voice. Then horror and despair took hold of him: he gathered all his force, he dashed violently, as if every nerve and artery were bursting, against the crystal; a piercing clang went through the room, and the Archivarius in his bright damask dressing gown was standing in the door.

"Hey, hey! vermin!—Mad spell!—Witchwork!—Here, holla!" So shouted he: then the black hair of the crone started up in tufts; her red eyes glanced with infernal fire, and clenching together the peaked fangs of her abominable jaws, she hissed: "Hiss, at him! Hiss, at him! Hiss!" and laughed and neighed in scorn and mockery, and pressed the Golden Flower Pot firmly to her, and threw out of it handfuls of glit-tering earth on the Archivarius; but as it touched the dressing gown, the earth changed into flowers, which rained down on the ground. Then the lilies of the dressing gown flickered and flamed up; and the Archivarius caught these lilies blazing in sparky fire and dashed them on the witch; she howled with agony, but as she leaped aloft and shook her armor of parchment the lilies went out, and fell away into ashes.

"To her, my lad!" creaked the crone: then the black cat darted through the air, and bounded over the Archivarius's head towards the door; but the gray parrot fluttered out against him; caught him by the nape with his crooked bill, till red fiery blood burst down over his neck; and Serpentina's voice cried: "Saved! Saved!" Then the crone, foaming with rage and desperation, darted at the Archivarius: she threw the Golden Flower Pot behind her, and holding up the long talons of her skinny fists, tried to clutch the Archivarius by the throat: but he instantly doffed his dressing gown, and hurled it against her. Then, hissing, and sputtering, and bursting, blue flames shot from the parchment leaves, and the crone rolled around howling in agony, and strove to get fresh earth from the Flower Pot, fresh parchment leaves from the books, that she might stifle the blazing flames; and whenever any earth or leaves came down on her, the flames went out. But now, from the interior of the Archivarius issued fiery crackling beams, which darted on the crone.

"Hey, hey! To it again! Salamander! Victory!" clanged the Archivarius's voice through the chamber; and a hundred bolts whirled forth in fiery circles round the shrieking crone. Whizzing and buzzing flew cat and parrot in their furious battle; but at last the parrot, with his strong wing, dashed the cat to the ground; and with his talons transfixing and holding fast his adversary, which, in deadly agony, uttered horrid mews and howls, he, with his sharp bill, picked out his glowing eyes, and the burning froth spouted from them. Then thick vapour streamed up from the spot where the crone, hurled to the ground, was lying under the dressing gown: her howling, her terrific, piercing cry of lamentation, died away in the remote distance. The smoke, which had spread abroad with penetrating stench, cleared away; the Archivarius picked up his dressing gown; and under it lay an ugly beet.

"Honoured Herr Archivarius, here let me offer you the vanquished foe," said the parrot, holding out a black hair in his beak to Archivarius Lindhorst.

"Very right, my worthy friend," replied the Archivarius: "here lies my vanquished foe too: be so good now as manage what remains. This very day, as a small douceur, you shall have six coconuts, and a new pair of spectacles also, for I see the cat has villainously broken the glasses of these old ones."

"Yours forever, most honoured friend and patron!" answered the parrot, much delighted; then took the withered beet in his bill, and fluttered out with it by the window, which Archivarius Lindhorst had opened for him.

The Archivarius now lifted the Golden Flower Pot, and cried, with a strong voice, "Serpentina! Serpentina!" But as the Student Anselmus, rejoicing in the destruction of the vile witch who had hurried him into misfortune, cast his eyes on the Archivarius, behold, here stood once more the high majestic form of the Spirit-prince, looking up to him with indescribable dignity and grace. "Anselmus," said the Spirit-prince, "not you, but a hostile principle, which strove destructively to penetrate into your nature, and divide you against yourself, was to blame for your unbelief. You have kept your faithfulness: be free and happy." A bright flash quivered through the spirit of Anselmus: the royal triphony of the crystal bells sounded stronger and louder than he had ever heard it: his nerves and fibres thrilled; but, swelling higher and higher, the melodious tones rang through the room; the glass which enclosed Anselmus broke; and he rushed into the arms of his dear and gentle Serpentina.

Eleventh Vigil

"But tell me, best Registrator! how could the cursed punch last night mount into our heads, and drive us to all kinds of *allotria*?" So said Conrector Paulmann, as he next morning entered his room, which still lay full of broken sherds; with his hapless peruke, dissolved into its original elements, soaked in punch among the ruin. For after the Student Anselmus ran out, Conrector Paulmann and Registrator Heerbrand had kept trotting and hobbling up and down the room, shouting like maniacs, and butting their heads together; till Fränzchen, with much labour, carried her dizzy papa to bed; and Registrator Heerbrand, in the deepest exhaustion, sank on the sofa, which Veronica had left, taking refuge in her bedroom. Registrator Heerbrand had his blue handkerchief tied about his head; he looked quite pale and melancholic, and moaned out: "Ah, worthy Conrector, it was not the punch which Mamsell Veronica most admirably brewed, no! but it was simply that cursed Student who was to blame for all the mischief. Do you not observe that he has long been *mente captus*? And are you not aware that madness is infectious? One fool makes twenty; pardon me, it is an old proverb: especially when you have drunk a glass or two, you fall into madness quite readily, and then involuntarily you manoeuvre, and go through your exercise, just as the crack-brained fugleman makes the motion. Would you believe it, Conrector? I am still giddy when I think of that gray parrot!"

"Gray fiddlestick!" interrupted the Conrector: "it was nothing but Archivarius Lindhorst's little old Famulus, who had thrown a gray cloak over himself, and was looking for the Student Anselmus."

"It may be," answered Registrator Heerbrand; "but, I must confess, I am quite downcast in spirit; the whole night through there was such a piping and organing."

"That was I," said the Conrector, "for I snore loud."

"Well, may be," answered the Registrator: "but, Conrector, Conrector! I had reason to raise some cheerfulness among us last night—And that Anselmus spoiled it all! You do not know—O Conrector, Conrector!" And with this, Registrator Heerbrand started up; plucked the cloth from his head, embraced the Conrector, warmly pressed his hand, and again cried, in quite heartbreaking tone: "O Conrector, Conrector!" and snatching his hat and staff, rushed out of doors.

"This Anselmus will not cross my threshold again," said Conrector Paulmann; "for I see very well, that, with this moping madness of his, he robs the best gentlemen of their senses. The Registrator has now gone overboard, too: I have hitherto kept safe; but the Devil, who knocked hard last night in our carousal, may get in at last, and play his tricks with me. So *Apage, Satanas!* Off with thee, Anselmus!" Veronica had grown quite pensive; she spoke no word; only smiled now and then very oddly, and seemed to wish to be left alone. "She, too, has Anselmus in her head," said the Conrector, full of spleen: "but it is well that he does not show himself here; I know he fears me, this Anselmus, and so he will never come."

These concluding words Conrector Paulmann spoke aloud; then the tears rushed into Veronica's eyes, and she said, sobbing: "Ah! how can Anselmus come? He has been corked up in the glass bottle for a long time."

"What? What?" cried Conrector Paulmann. "Ah Heaven! Ah Heaven! she is doting too, like the Registrator: the loud fit will soon come! Ah, you cursed, abominable, thrice-cursed Anselmus!" He ran forth directly to Dr. Eckstein; who smiled, and again said: "Ey! Ey!" This time, however, he prescribed nothing; but added, to the little he had uttered, the following words, as he walked away: "Nerves! Come round of itself. Take the air; walks; amusements; theatre; playing *Sonntagskind, Schwestern von Prag.* Come around of itself."

"I have seldom seen the Doctor so eloquent," thought Conrector Paulmann; "really talkative, I declare!"

Several days and weeks and months passed. Anselmus had vanished; but Registrator Heerbrand did not make his appearance either: not till the fourth of February, when, in a fashionable new coat of the finest cloth, in shoes and silk stockings, notwithstanding the keen frost, and with a large nosegay of fresh flowers in his hand, the Registrator entered precisely at noon the parlour of Conrector Paulmann, who wondered not a little to see his friend so well dressed. With a solemn air, Registrator Heerbrand came forward to Conrector Paulmann; embraced him with the finest elegance, and then said: "Now at last, on the Saint's-day of your beloved and most honoured Mamsell Veronica, I will tell you out, straightforward, what I have long had lying at my heart. That evening, that unfortunate evening, when I put the ingredients of our noxious punch in my pocket, I intended to tell to you a piece of good news, and to celebrate the happy day in convivial joys. I had learned that I was to be made Hofrath; for which promotion I have now the patent, *cum nomine et sigillo Principis*, in my pocket."

"Ah! Herr Registr—Herr Hofrath Heerbrand, I meant to say," stammered the Conrector.

"But it is you, most honoured Conrector," continued the new Hofrath; "it is you alone that can complete my happiness. For a long time, I have in secret loved your daughter, Mamsell Veronica; and I can boast of many a kind look which she has given me, evidently showing that she would not reject me. In one word, honoured Conrector! I, Hofrath Heerbrand, do now entreat of you the hand of your most amiable Mamsell Veronica, whom I, if you have nothing against it, purpose shortly to take home as my wife."

Conrector Paulmann, full of astonishment, clapped his hands repeatedly, and cried: "Ey, Ey, Ey! Herr Registr—Herr Hofrath, I meant to say—who would have thought it? Well, if Veronica does really love you, I for my share cannot object: nay, perhaps, her present melancholy is nothing but concealed love for you, most honoured Hofrath! You know what freaks women have!"

At this moment Veronica entered, pale and agitated, as she now commonly was. Then Hofrath Heerbrand approached her; mentioned in a neat speech her Saint's-day, and handed her the odorous nosegay, along with a little packet; out of which, when she opened it, a pair of glittering earrings gleamed up at her. A rapid flying blush tinted her cheeks; her eyes sparkled in joy, and she cried: "O Heaven! These are the very earrings which I wore some weeks ago, and thought so much of."

"How can this be, dearest Mamsell," interrupted Hofrath Heerbrand, somewhat alarmed and hurt, "when I bought them not an hour ago, in the Schlossgasse, for cash?"

But Veronica paid no attention to him; she was standing before the mirror to witness the effect of the trinkets, which she had already suspended in her pretty little ears. Conrector Paulmann disclosed to her, with grave countenance and solemn tone, his friend Heerbrand's preferment and present proposal. Veronica looked at the Hofrath with a searching look, and said: "I have long known that you wished to marry me. Well, be it so! I promise you my heart and hand; but I must now unfold to you, to both of you, I mean, my father and my bride-groom, much that is lying heavy on my heart; yes, even now, though the soup should get cold, which I see Fränzchen is just putting on the table."

Without waiting for the Conrector's or the Hofrath's reply, though the words were visibly hovering on the lips of both, Veronica contin-ued: "You may believe me, father, I loved Anselmus from my heart, and when Registrator Heerbrand, who is now become Hofrath himself, as-sured us that Anselmus might possibly rise that high, I resolved that he and no other should be my husband. But then it seemed as if alien hos-tile beings tried snatching him away from me: I had recourse to old Liese, who was once my nurse, but is now a wise woman, and a great enchantress. She promised to help me, and give Anselmus wholly into my hands. We went at midnight on the Equinox to the crossing of the roads: she conjured certain hellish spirits, and by aid of the black cat, we manufactured a little metallic mirror, in which I, directing my thoughts on Anselmus, had but to look, in order to rule him wholly in heart and mind. But now I heartily repent having done all this; and here abjure all Satanic arts. The Salamander has conquered old Liese; I heard her shrieks; but there was no help to be given: so soon as the parrot had eaten the beet, my metallic mirror broke in two with a pierc-ing clang." Veronica took out both the pieces of the mirror, and a lock of hair from her workbox, and handing them to Hofrath Heerbrand, she proceeded: "Here, take the fragments of the mirror, dear Hofrath; throw them down, tonight, at twelve o'clock, over the Elbe Bridge, from the place where the Cross stands; the stream is not frozen there: the lock, however, wear on your faithful breast. I here abjure all magic: and heartily wish Anselmus joy of his good fortune, seeing he is wed-ded with the green snake, who is much prettier and richer than I. You dear Hofrath, I will love and reverence as becomes a true honest wife."

"Alack! Alack!" cried Conrector Paulmann, full of sorrow; "she is cracked, she is cracked; she can never be Frau Hofräthinn; she is cracked!"

"Not in the smallest," interrupted Hofrath Heerbrand; "I know well that Mamsell Veronica has had some kindness for the loutish Anselmus; and it may be that in some fit of passion, she has had re-course to the wise woman, who, as I perceive, can be no other than the card-caster and coffee-pourer of the Seethor; in a word, old Rauerin. Nor can it be denied that there are secret arts, which exert their influ-ence on men but too banefully; we read of such in the ancients, and doubtless there are still such; but as to what Mamsell Veronica is pleased to say about the victory of the Salamander, and the marriage of Anselmus with the green snake, this, in reality, I take for nothing but a poetic allegory; a sort of song, wherein she sings her entire farewell to the Student."

"Take it for what you will, my dear Hofrath!" cried Veronica; "perhaps for a very stupid dream."

"That I will not do," replied Hofrath Heerbrand; "for I know well that Anselmus himself is possessed by secret powers, which vex him and drive him on to all imaginable mad escapades."

Conrector Paulmann could stand it no longer; he burst out: "Hold! For the love of Heaven, hold! Are we overtaken with that cursed punch again, or has Anselmus's madness come over us too? Herr Hofrath, what stuff is this you are talking? I will suppose, however, that it is love which haunts your brain: this soon comes to rights in marriage; otherwise, I should be apprehensive that you too had fallen into some shade of madness, most honoured Herr Hofrath; then what would become of the future branches of the family, inheriting the *malum* of their parents? But now I give my paternal blessing to this happy union; and permit you as bride and bridegroom to take a kiss."

This immediately took place; and thus before the soup had grown cold, a formal betrothment was concluded. In a few weeks, Frau Hofräthinn Heerbrand was actually, as she had been in vision, sitting in the balcony of a fine house in the Neumarkt, and looking down with a smile at the beaux, who passing by turned their glasses up to her, and said: "She is a heavenly woman, the Hofräthinn Heerbrand."

Twelfth Vigil

How deeply did I feel, in the centre of my spirit, the blessedness of the Student Anselmus, who now, indissolubly united with his gentle Serpentina, has withdrawn to the mysterious land of wonders, recognized by him as the home towards which his bosom, filled with strange forecastings, had always longed. But in vain was all my striving to set before you, favourable reader, those glories with which Anselmus is encompassed, or even in the faintest degree to shadow them to you in words. Reluctantly I could not but acknowledge the feebleness of my every expression. I felt myself enthralled amid the paltrinesses of everyday life; I sickened in tormenting dissatisfaction; I glided about like a dreamer; in brief, I fell into that condition of the Student Anselmus, which, in the Fourth Vigil, I endeavoured to set before you. It grieved me to the heart, when I glanced over the Eleven Vigils, now happily accomplished, and thought that to insert the Twelfth, the keystone of the whole, would never be permitted me. For whenever, in the night I set myself to complete the work, it was as if mischievous spirits (they might be relations, perhaps cousins-german, of the slain witch) held a polished glittering piece of metal before me, in which I beheld my own mean self, pale, drawn, and melancholic, like Registrator Heerbrand after his bout of punch. Then I threw down my pen, and hastened to bed, that I might behold the happy Anselmus and the fair Serpentina at least in my dreams. This had lasted for several days and nights, when at length quite unexpectedly I received a note from Archivarius Lindhorst, in which he wrote to me as follows:

Respected Sir,—It is well known to me that you have written down, in Eleven Vigils, the singular fortunes of my good son-in-law Anselmus, whilom student, now poet; and are at present cudgelling your brains very sore, that in the Twelfth and Last Vigil you may tell somewhat of his happy life in Atlantis, where he now lives with my daughter, on the pleasant freehold, which I possess in that country. Now, notwithstanding I much regret that hereby my own peculiar nature is unfolded to the reading world; seeing it may, in my office as Privy Archivarius, expose me to a thousand inconveniences; nay, in the Collegium even give rise to the question: How far a Salamander can justly, and with binding consequences, plight himself by oath, as a Servant of the State? and how far, on the whole, important affairs may be intrusted to him, since, according to Gabalis and Swedenborg, the spirits of the elements are not to be trusted at all?—notwithstanding, my best friends must now avoid my embrace; fearing lest, in some sudden anger, I dart out a flash or two, and singe their hair-curls, and Sunday frocks; notwithstanding all this, I say, it is still my purpose to assist you in the completion of the work, since much good of me and of my dear married daughter (would the other two were off my hands also!) has therein been said.

If you would write your Twelfth Vigil, descend your cursed five flights of stairs, leave your garret, and come over to me. In the blue palmtreeroom, which you already know, you will find fit writing materials; and you can then, in few words, specify to your readers, what you have seen; a better plan for you than any long-winded description of a life which you know only by hearsay. With esteem,

Your obedient servant,
The Salamander Lindhorst,
P. T. Royal Archivarius.

This somewhat rough, yet on the whole friendly note from Archivarius Lindhorst, gave me high pleasure. It seemed clear enough, indeed, that the singular manner in which the fortunes of his son-in-law had been revealed to me, and which I, bound to silence, must conceal even from you, gracious reader, was well known to this peculiar old gentleman; yet he had not taken it so ill as I might have apprehended. Nay, here was he offering me a helping hand in the completion of my work; and from this I might justly conclude, that at bottom he was not averse to having his marvellous existence in the world of spirits thus divulged through the press.

"It may be," thought I, "that he himself expects from this measure, perhaps, to get his two other daughters married sooner: for who knows but a spark may fall in this or that young man's breast, and kindle a longing for the green snake; whom, on Ascension Day, under the elderbush, he will forthwith seek and find? From the misery which befell Anselmus, when he was enclosed in the glass bottle, he will take warning to be doubly and trebly on his guard against all doubt and unbelief."

Precisely at eleven o'clock, I extinguished my study lamp; and glided forth to Archivarius Lindhorst, who was already waiting for me in the lobby.

"Are you there, my worthy friend? Well, this is what I like, that you have not mistaken my good intentions: follow me!"

And with this he led the way through the garden, now filled with dazzling brightness, into the azure chamber, where I observed the same violet table, at which Anselmus had been writing.

Archivarius Lindhorst disappeared: but soon came back, carrying in his hand a fair golden goblet, out of which a high blue flame was sparkling up. "Here," said he, "I bring you the favourite drink of your friend the Bandmaster, Johannes Kreisler. It is burning arrack, into which I have thrown a little sugar. Sip a little of it: I will doff my dressing gown, and to amuse myself and enjoy your worthy company while you sit looking and writing, I shall just bob up and down a little in the goblet."

"As you please, honoured Herr Archivarius," answered I: "but if I am to ply the liquor, you will get none."

"Don't fear that, my good fellow," cried the Archivarius; then hastily throwing off his dressing gown, he mounted, to my no small amazement, into the goblet, and vanished in the blaze. Without fear, softly blowing back the flame, I partook of the drink: it was truly precious!

Stir not the emerald leaves of the palm-trees in soft sighing and rustling, as if kissed by the breath of the morning wind? Awakened from their sleep, they move, and mysteriously whisper of the wonders, which from the far distance approach like tones of melodious harps! The azure rolls from the walls, and floats like airy vapour to and fro; but dazzling beams shoot through it; and whirling and dancing, as in jubilee of childlike sport, it mounts and mounts to immeasurable height, and vaults over the palm-trees. But brighter and brighter shoots beam upon beam, till in boundless expanse the grove opens where I behold Anselmus. Here glowing hyacinths, and tulips, and roses, lift their fair heads; and their perfumes, in loveliest sound, call to the happy youth: "Wander, wander among us, our beloved; for you understand us! Our perfume is the longing of love: we love you, and are yours for evermore!" The golden rays burn in glowing tones: "We are fire, kindled by love. Perfume is longing; but fire is desire: and do we not dwell in your bosom? We are yours!" The dark bushes, the high trees rustle and sound: "Come to us, beloved, happy one! Fire is desire; but hope is our cool shadow. Lovingly we rustle round your head: for you understand us, because love dwells in your breast!" The brooks and fountains murmur and patter: "Loved one, do not walk so quickly by: look into our crystal! Your image dwells in us, which we preserve with love, for you have understood us." In the triumphal choir, bright birds are singing: "Hear us! Hear us! We are joy, we are delight, the rapture of love!" But anxiously Anselmus turns his eyes to the glorious temple, which rises behind him in the distance. The fair pillars seem trees; and the capitals and friezes acanthus leaves, which in wondrous wreaths and figures form splendid decorations. Anselmus walks to the Temple: he views with inward delight the variegated marble, the steps with their strange veins of moss. "Ah, no!" cries he, as if in the excess of rapture, "she is not far from me now; she is near!" Then Serpentina advances, in the fullness of beauty and grace, from the Temple; she bears the Golden Flower Pot, from which a bright lily has sprung. The nameless rapture of infinite longing glows in her meek eyes; she looks at Anselmus, and says: "Ah! Dearest, the Lily has opened her blossom: what we longed for is fulfilled; is there a happiness to equal ours?" Anselmus clasps her with the tenderness of warmest ardour: the lily burns in flaming beams over his head. And louder move the trees and bushes; clearer and gladder play the brooks; the birds, the shining insects dance in the waves of perfume: a gay, bright rejoicing tumult, in the air, in the water, in the earth, is holding the festival of love! Now sparkling streaks rush, gleaming over all the bushes; diamonds look from the ground like shining eyes: strange vapours are wafted hither on sounding wings: they are the spirits of the elements, who do homage to the lily, and proclaim the happiness of Anselmus. Then Anselmus raises his head, as if encircled with a beamy glory. Is it looks? Is it words? Is it song? You hear the sound: "Serpentina! Belief in you, love of you has unfolded to my soul the inmost spirit of nature! You have brought me the lily, which sprang from gold, from the primeval force of the world, before Phosphorus had kindled the spark of thought; this lily is knowledge of the sacred harmony of all beings; and in this I live in highest blessedness for evermore. Yes, I, thrice happy, have perceived what was highest: I must indeed love thee forever, O Serpentina! Never shall the golden blossoms of the lily grow pale; for, like belief and love, this knowledge is eternal."

For the vision, in which I had now beheld Anselmus bodily, in his freehold of Atlantis, I stand indebted to the arts of the Salamander; and it was fortunate that when everything had melted into air, I found a paper lying on the violet-table, with the foregoing statement of the matter, written fairly and distinctly by my own hand. But now I felt myself as if transpierced and torn in pieces by sharp sorrow. "Ah, happy Anselmus, who has cast away the burden of everyday life, who in the love of kind Serpentina flies with bold pinion, and now lives in rapture and joy on your freehold in Atlantis! while I—poor I!—must soon, nay, in few moments, leave even this fair hall, which itself is far from a Freehold in Atlantis; and again be transplanted in my garret, where, enthralled among the pettinesses of existence, my heart and my sight are so bedimmed with thousand mischiefs, as with thick fog, that the fair lily will never, never be beheld by me."

Then Archivarius Lindhorst patted me gently on the shoulder, and said: "Softly, softly, my honoured friend! Do not lament so! Were you not even now in Atlantis; and have you not at least a pretty little copyhold farm there, as the poetical possession of your inward sense? And is the blessedness of Anselmus anything else but a living in poesy? Can anything else but poesy reveal itself as the sacred harmony of all beings, as the deepest secret of nature?"

HOW OLD TIMOFEI DIED WITH A SONG

Rainer Maria Rilke

WHAT A REAL joy it is to tell stories to a paralyzed person! Healthy people are so unreliable; they look at things, now from one viewpoint, now from another, and after you've been walking with them for an hour and they've always been to the right of you, they sometimes answer you from the left all of a sudden, merely because it occurs to them that it's more polite and shows better breeding. With a paralyzed man one need have no fear of that. His immobility makes him resemble inanimate objects, with which he actually has many cordial relationships; it makes him, so to speak, an object far superior to all the rest, an object that not only listens with its taciturnity, but also with its very few, quiet phrases and with its gentle, respectful feelings.

I like best of all to tell stories to my friend Ewald. And I was very happy when he called to me from his daily window: "I must ask you something."

I walked over to him quickly and said hello. "What is the source of the story you told me recently?" he finally asked. "Did it come from a book?" "Yes," I replied sadly, "the scholars have buried it in one ever since it died, which isn't very long ago. A hundred years ago it was still alive, and certainly quite carefree, on many lips. But the words that people now use, these heavy words that are hard to sing to, were hostile to it and stole one mouth after another from it, so that finally it lived on, but very withdrawn and impoverished, only on a few dry lips, as if on a poor widow's farm. There it also died, without leaving any descendants, and, as I mentioned, was buried with all honors in a book, where others of its lineage already lay." "And was it very old when it died?" my friend asked, picking up my metaphor. "Four or five hundred years old," I reported truthfully; "several of its relatives have attained an immeasurably greater age." "What, without ever reposing in a book?" Ewald asked in surprise. I explained: "As far as I know, they were journeying from mouth to mouth the whole time." "And they never slept?" "Oh, yes; arising from the lips of the singer, they surely remained occasionally in someone's heart, where it was warm and dark." "Then, were people so tranquil that songs could sleep in their hearts?" Ewald seemed quite incredulous to me. "It must have been that way. It's claimed that they spoke less, performed slowly accelerating dances that had a cradling motion, and above all, didn't laugh loudly the way you can often hear people do today despite our universally loftier social graces."

Ewald prepared himself to ask another question, but he repressed it and said with a smile: "I keep on asking things—but perhaps you have a story in mind?" He looked at me expectantly.

"A story? I don't know. I merely wanted to say: Those songs were the heirlooms in certain families. That inherited property had been received and handed down again, not quite as good as new, showing the traces of daily use, but nevertheless undamaged, just as an old Bible, let's say, goes from forefather to grandchild. The man without inheritance differed from his siblings who had received their rightful due in that he couldn't sing, or else at least he knew only a small part of his father's and grandfather's songs, and, losing the rest of the songs, he lost that large segment of experience which all those *byliny* and *skazki* mean to the people. And so, for example, Yegor Timofeievich had married a young, beautiful woman against the wishes of his father, old Timofei, and had moved with her to Kiev, the holy city, in which the tombs of the great martyrs of the holy orthodox church have gathered. His father Timofei, who was reputed to be the most knowledgeable singer in a radius of ten days' journey, cursed his son and told his neighbors that he was often convinced that he had never had one. All the same, he grew mute in his grief and sorrow. And he rejected all the young men who crowded into his hut in order to fall heir to the many songs that were shut away in the old man, as in a dust-covered violin. 'Father, little father of ours, just give us one song or another. You see, we'll take it to the villages, and you'll hear it from every courtyard as soon as evening comes and the cattle have become quiet in their stables.' The old man, who constantly sat on the heated platform, shook his head all day long. His hearing was no longer good, and since he didn't know whether one of the lads who were now forever listening around his house had just made another request, he would signal no, no, no with his trembling white head until he fell asleep, and even kept doing it for a while in his sleep. He would gladly have done what the lads wanted; he himself was sorry that his mute, dead dust would lie upon these songs, perhaps very soon now. But if he had tried to teach one of them anything, it would surely have reminded him of his Yegorushka, and then, who knows what might have happened?

Because it was only his perpetual silence that kept anyone from seeing him cry. Behind each word of his lay a sob, and he always had to shut his mouth very quickly and carefully to keep it from escaping at the same time.

"From early on, old Timofei had taught his only son, Yegor, a few songs, and when a boy of fifteen he was already able to sing more songs more correctly than any of the fully grown lads in the village or in its vicinity. All the same, the old man used to say to the lad, generally on holidays, when he was slightly drunk: 'Yegorushka, my little dove, I've already taught you to sing many songs, many *byliny*, and also the legends of the saints, one for nearly every day. But, as you know, I'm the most knowledgeable in the whole *guberniya*,[1] and my father knew every song in Russia, so to speak, and Tatar stories, besides. You're still very young, and so I have not yet told you the best *byliny*, in which the words are like icons and can't be compared with everyday words, and you have not yet learned how to sing those melodies which no one yet, be he a Cossack or a peasant, has ever been able to hear without weeping.' Timofei would repeat this to his son on every Sunday and all the many feast days in the Russian calendar; that is, fairly often. Until, after a violent scene with the old man, the boy had vanished together with the beautiful Ustyonka, the daughter of a poor peasant.

"In the third year after that incident, Timofei fell ill, just at the time when one of those numerous bands of pilgrims which constantly converge on Kiev from all sections of the extensive empire was about to set out. Then the sick man's neighbor Osip came to see him: 'I'm leaving with the pilgrims, Timofei Ivanich; permit me to embrace you once again.' Osip wasn't friendly with the old man, but now that he was undertaking that distant journey, he felt it needful to take leave of him, as if of a father. 'I've hurt your feelings at times,' he sobbed; 'forgive me, dear heart, it happened while I was drunk and no one can help that, as you know. Now, I'll pray for you and light a candle for you; farewell, Timofei Ivanich, little father; perhaps you'll get well again, if God wishes, then you'll sing to us again. Yes, yes, it's been a long time since you've sung. What songs those were! The one about Dyuk Stepanovich,[2] for instance: do you think I've forgotten it? How foolish you are! I still know it all by heart. Of course, not like you; *you* really and truly knew it, I've got to say! God gave you *that*, to another man he gives other gifts. To me, for example—'

"The old man, who was lying on the heated platform, turned around with a groan and made a gesture as if he wanted to say something. It

---

[1] A large administrative district.
[2] One of the principal *bylina* heroes.

was as if the name of Yegor could be faintly heard. Perhaps he wanted to send him some news. But when his neighbor, already at the door, asked: 'Did you say something, Timofei Ivanich?' he was already lying there perfectly still and merely shaking his white head gently. Nevertheless, God knows how it happened, scarcely a year after Osip's departure Yegor returned quite unexpectedly. The old man didn't recognize him immediately because it was dark in the hut and his aged eyes didn't easily accept a strange new figure. But after Timofei heard the stranger's voice, he became alarmed and leaped off the heated platform onto his shaky old legs. Yegor caught him, and they hugged each other. Timofei was weeping. The young man kept on asking: 'Have you been sick long, father?' After the old man calmed down a bit, he crept back onto his heated platform and inquired, in a different, severe tone: 'And your wife?' A pause. Yegor spat out the words: 'I've chased her away, you know, along with the child.' He was silent for a while. 'Osip came to see me once. "Osip Nikiforovich?" I said. "Yes," he answered, "it's me. Your father is sick, Yegor. He can't sing anymore. It's completely quiet in the village now, as if it had no more soul, our village. No one knocks, no one budges, no one cries anymore, and there's no real reason for laughing, either." I thought about it. What was to be done? So I called over my wife. "Ustyonka," I said, "I must go home, no one else sings there anymore, it's up to me. My father is sick." "All right," said Ustyonka. "But I can't take you along," I explained to her, "as you know, my father doesn't want you. And I probably won't come back to you, either, once I'm back there singing." Ustyonka understood me: "Well, then, God go with you! There are many pilgrims here now, so people give lots of alms. God will help me, Yegor." And so I left. And now, father, tell me all your songs!'

"Word got around that Yegor had returned and that old Timofei was singing again. But that autumn the wind blew so violently through the village that no passerby could ascertain with any assurance whether there was really singing in Timofei's house or not. And the door wasn't opened to anyone who knocked. The two men wanted to be alone. Yegor sat on the edge of the heated platform on which his father lay, and at times brought his ear right up to the old man's lips; for he was indeed singing. His old voice, somewhat stooped and trembling, carried all the best songs over to Yegor, who often waved his head or moved his dangling feet, exactly as if he were already singing them himself. Things went on that way for many days. Timofei kept finding some even lovelier song in his memory; often he'd awaken his son at night and, while making indistinct gestures with his withered, twitching hands, he'd sing a short song and then another and yet another, until the lazy morning began to stir. Soon after the most beautiful one he died. In the last days he had frequently lamented that he still had a vast number of songs inside him and had no more time to impart them to his son. He lay there with furrowed brow, in strained, anxious thought, and his lips trembled with expectancy. From time to time he sat up, waved his head to and fro for a while, and moved his lips, and finally some quiet song was added to the sum; but now he generally kept repeating the same stanzas about Dyuk Stepanovich that were his special favorites, and his son had to act amazed, as if he were hearing them for the first time, to avoid getting him angry.

"After old Timofei Ivanich died, the house, in which Yegor now lived alone, still remained locked for a time. Then, in early spring, Yegor Timofeievich, who now had a fairly long beard, stepped out of his door and began to wander through the village singing. Afterward he visited the neighboring villages, too, and the peasants were already telling one another that Yegor had become a singer at least as knowledgeable as his father Timofei, for he knew a large number of religious and heroic songs and all those melodies which no one, be he a Cossack or a peasant, could hear without weeping. In addition, he was said to have a soft, sad tone that no other singer had yet possessed. And this tone was always to be heard, quite unexpectedly, in the refrains, which made him particularly effective emotionally. At least, that's what I heard tell."

"So he didn't learn that tone from his father?" my friend Ewald asked after a while. "No," I replied, "no one knows where he got it from." After I had already stepped away from the window, the paralyzed man made another gesture and called after me: "Perhaps he was thinking about his wife and child. Besides, did he never send for them, seeing that his father was now dead?" "No, I don't think so. At any rate, when he died afterward he was alone."

THE EARTHQUAKE IN CHILE

Heinrich von Kleist

IN SANTIAGO, the capital of the kingdom of Chile,[1] at the very moment of the great earthquake of the year 1647, in which many thousands of people perished, a young Spaniard accused of a crime, Jerónimo Rugera by name, was standing by a pillar of the prison in which he had been confined and was about to hang himself. About a year previously, Don Enrique Asterón, one of the richest noblemen in the city, had dismissed him from his house, where he was employed as a tutor, because Jerónimo and Doña Josefa, Asterón's only daughter, had fallen in love. A secret tryst, which had been revealed to the old Don—after he had expressly warned his daughter—by the malicious vigilance of his haughty son, so infuriated him that he placed her in the Carmelite convent of Our Lady of the Mountain in that city. Here, through a lucky accident, Jerónimo had been able to resume the relationship and, one night, had secretly made the convent garden the scene of his highest bliss.

It was Corpus Christi day, and the solemn procession of the nuns, whom the novices followed, was just setting out when the unfortunate Josefa sank down on the cathedral steps in labor pains as the bells began to ring. This incident created an unusual sensation; the young sinner, with no regard to her condition, was immediately thrown in prison, and scarcely had she arisen from childbed when, by order of the archbishop, she was subjected to the most harrowing trial.

This scandal was discussed in the city with so much animosity, and people's tongues dealt so harshly with the entire convent in which it had taken place, that neither the intercession of the Asterón family nor even the request of the abbess herself—who had grown fond of the young girl because of her otherwise irreproachable conduct—was able to palliate the severity with which the monastic laws threatened her. All

---

[1]Chile was never a kingdom; in 1647, when an earthquake did occur, it was a Spanish colony, part of the viceroyalty of Peru; the viceroy resided in Lima.

that could be done was to have the death by fire, to which she had been condemned, commuted to beheading by decree of the viceroy, much to the indignation of the matrons and maidens of Santiago. In the streets along which the execution procession would pass, windows were rented, the roofs of the houses were leveled, and the pious daughters of the city invited their girl friends to attend the spectacle offered to divine vengeance at their sisterly side.

Jerónimo, who meanwhile had also been clapped in prison, thought he would go out of his mind when he heard about this horrible turn of events. In vain did he ponder ways of rescuing her: wherever the wings of even the most unbridled notions carried him, he came up against bolts and walls; and an attempt to file through the window grating only gained him a still more cramped dungeon when he was discovered. He flung himself down before the image of the Mother of God, and prayed to her with tremendous ardor, believing her to be the only one from whom salvation could still come.

But the dreaded day arrived, and with it, in his heart, a conviction of the total hopelessness of his situation. The bells that accompanied Josefa to her place of execution rang out, and despair took hold of his soul. Life seemed hateful to him, and he decided to kill himself with a rope that had been left to him by chance. He was just standing, as mentioned above, by a wall pillar and was securing the rope that was to snatch him from this world of sorrow to an iron clamp that was inserted into the pillar molding, when suddenly the greater part of the city sank with a roar as if the sky were falling, and buried all living things beneath its ruins.

Jerónimo Rugera was rigid with terror; and, as if all his presence of mind had been wiped out, he now held on to the pillar on which he had intended to die, in order not to fall over. The ground shook beneath his feet, all the walls of the prison were cleft, the whole structure threatened to collapse onto the street, and only the subsidence of the building opposite, occurring at the same time as the prison was slowly falling apart, prevented its complete leveling with the ground by creating an accidental supporting vault.

Trembling, his hair on end, and with knees about to buckle under him, Jerónimo slid across the now tilted floor toward the opening that the collision of the two buildings had torn in the front wall of the prison. Scarcely was he out in the open when a second earth tremor caused the entire street, already badly shaken, to cave in altogether. Unable to think how he could escape from this universal destruction, he hastened away over debris and timbers toward one of the nearest city gates, while death attacked him from all sides.

Here yet another house collapsed and, flinging its ruins far and wide, forced him into a side street; here flames were already shooting out of every gable, flashing in clouds of smoke, driving him in terror into another street; here the Mapocho River, shifting from its bed, rolled toward him, sweeping him with a roar into a third street. Here lay a heap of corpses, here a voice was still groaning beneath the debris, here people were shouting from burning rooftops, here humans and animals were struggling with the waves, here a courageous rescuer was making an effort to help; here stood another man, pale as death, speechlessly extending his trembling hands toward heaven.

When Jerónimo reached the gate and had ascended a hill outside it, he fell down there in a faint. He had probably lain there completely unconscious for a quarter of an hour when he finally awoke again and partly raised himself from the ground, his back turned toward the city. He felt his forehead and chest, not knowing what to make of his condition, and an immense feeling of bliss came over him when a westerly breeze from the sea quickened his recovering senses, and his eyes roved in all directions over the flourishing countryside of Santiago. Only the clusters of agitated people that were everywhere to be seen saddened his heart; he could not comprehend what had brought him and them to this place, and only when he turned around and saw the city in ruins behind him, did he recall the fearful moment he had lived through. He bowed his head so low that his forehead touched the ground, in order to thank God for his miraculous rescue; and, as if the one terrible impression that had been stamped on his mind had driven all earlier ones from it, he wept for happiness because he still enjoyed the charms of life with all its manifold phenomena.

Then, noticing a ring on his finger, he suddenly recalled Josefa as well; and, along with her, his prison, the bells he had heard there, and the moment preceding its collapse. Deep melancholy filled his heart again; he began to regret having prayed, and the Being that rules above the clouds seemed fearsome to him. He mingled with the people who were dashing out of the gates on all sides, busy saving their belongings, and timidly risked asking about Asterón's daughter and whether her execution had been carried out; but no one was able to give him detailed information. A woman bent over almost to the ground under an enormous load of utensils she was carrying on her shoulders and two children who were clutching her bosom, said as she passed by—speaking as if she had been an eyewitness—that Josefa had been beheaded.

Jerónimo turned aside; and, since, on calculating the time elapsed, he himself had no doubts that the execution had taken place, he sat down in a lonely wood and abandoned himself fully to his grief. He wished that the destructive power of nature would come down upon him again. He could not comprehend why he had escaped death, which his miserable soul now sought, at the time when it was offering itself to him freely on all sides. He resolved firmly not to waver even if the oaks were now uprooted and their tops were to tumble down upon him.

So, after he had wept his fill and, in the midst of his hottest tears, hope had returned to him, he arose and walked back and forth over the area in all directions. He visited every hilltop on which people had gathered; he met them on every path on which the stream of refugees still flowed; his trembling feet bore him wherever a women's garment fluttered in the breeze, but no garment clad the beloved daughter of Asterón.

The sun was again setting, and with it his hope, when he stepped to the edge of a cliff and obtained a view of a broad valley to which very few people had come. Undecided what he should do, he hurried from one to another of the individual groups, and was about to turn away again when he suddenly saw, by a brook that watered the valley, a young woman busy bathing a child in its stream. And his heart leaped at that sight: full of presentiment, he sprang down over the rocks, shouting "O Holy Mother of God!" and recognized Josefa when she timidly looked about on hearing the sound.

With what rapture they embraced, that unfortunate pair whom a miracle of heaven had saved! On her march to death, Josefa had already been quite close to the place of execution when suddenly the entire procession had been scattered by the resounding collapse of the buildings. Then her first terrified steps brought her to the nearest gate; but she soon recovered her presence of mind and turned back in haste to the convent, where her helpless little boy had been left behind.

She found the entire convent already in flames; the abbess, who in those moments which were to have been Josefa's last, had promised to care for the infant, was standing in front of the gates calling for help to save him. Josefa, undaunted by the smoke that billowed toward her, dashed into the building, which was already collapsing all around her, and, as if all the angels in heaven were protecting her, carried him out through the entrance again, unharmed. She was just about to sink into the arms of the abbess, who clasped her hands together over her head, when the abbess, together with almost all her nuns, was ignominiously killed by a falling gable of the building.

At this horrible sight Josefa stepped back, trembling; she hastily closed the abbess' eyes and, filled with terror, ran off to save from destruction her dear boy, whom heaven had restored to her. She had taken only a few more steps when she came across the crushed corpse of the archbishop as well, which had just been pulled out of the debris of the cathedral. The viceroy's palace had disappeared, the court in which her sentence had been pronounced was in flames, and on the spot where her father's house had stood there was a boiling lake emitting reddish vapors. Josefa summoned up all her strength in order to go on.

Banishing sorrow from her heart, she courageously proceeded from street to street with her prize and was already near the gate, when she also saw lying in ruins the prison in which Jerónimo had languished. At that sight she tottered and thought she would faint away at a street corner; but at the same moment the collapse of a building behind her, which the tremors had already totally shaken apart, frightened her into renewed vigor and propelled her forward; she kissed the child, squeezed the tears from her eyes and, no longer heeding the horrors that surrounded her, reached the gate.

When she found herself outside, she soon realized that not everyone who had lived in a ruined building had necessarily been crushed beneath it. At the next crossroads she stopped and waited to see whether the one who, after little Felipe, was dearest to her in the world, might still appear. She went on, since no one came and the crowd of people grew, and turned around again and waited again; and, shedding many tears, she stole into a dark, pine-shaded valley to pray for his soul, which she thought had departed; and found him here in the valley, that beloved man, and found bliss, as if it had been the valley of Eden.

She now told Jerónimo all this with great emotion, and, when she had finished, held the boy out for him to kiss. Jerónimo took him, dandled him with immense paternal joy and, when the child started to cry on seeing a strange face, stopped his mouth with endless kisses and caresses.

Meanwhile, a most beautiful night had fallen, full of wonderfully soft fragrance, as silvery-bright and calm as only poets dream of. Everywhere along the brook in the valley people had settled down in the glimmer of the moonlight and were preparing soft beds of moss and leaves to rest upon after such a painful day. And because the poor people were still lamenting—one because he had lost his house, another because he had lost wife and child, and a third because he had lost everything—Jerónimo and Josefa stole into a denser thicket so as not to sadden anyone with the secret rejoicing of their souls. They found a splendid pomegranate tree with wide-spreading branches full of aromatic fruit; and the nightingale sang its song of delight in the top of the tree.

Here Jerónimo sat down by the tree trunk and, with Josefa in his lap and Felipe in hers, they sat, covered by his cloak, and rested. The shadow of the tree, with its scattering of light, moved over them, and the moon was already growing pale again in anticipation of dawn before they fell asleep. For they had an infinite number of things to talk about, the convent garden, and the prisons, and what they had gone through for each other; and they were very moved when they thought of how much misery had to come upon the world for them to be happy!

They decided to go to Concepción, where Josefa had an intimate woman friend, as soon as the earth tremors ended; with a small loan that she hoped to receive from her they would take ship for Spain, where Jerónimo's maternal relatives lived, and remain happily there to the end of their days. Then, exchanging many kisses, they fell asleep.

When they awoke the sun was already high in the sky, and they noticed several families near them busy preparing a small breakfast by the fire. Jerónimo, too, was just thinking how he could procure food for his own family, when a well-dressed young man with a child in his arms came over to Josefa and discreetly asked her whether she would not briefly nurse the poor infant whose mother was lying injured under the trees there.

Josefa was a little confused when she recognized him as an acquaintance; but when, misinterpreting her confusion, he continued, "It would be just for a few minutes, Doña Josefa, and this child has had no nourishment since the moment that was calamitous for us all," she replied: "My silence—was for a different reason, Don Fernando; in these terrible times no one refuses to give a share of whatever he possesses." She took the little stranger, giving her own child to his father, and laid him to her breast.

Don Fernando was very grateful for this kindness and asked whether they did not wish to accompany him to that group of people who were just preparing a small breakfast by the fire. Josefa replied that she would accept that invitation with pleasure, and, since Jerónimo had no objection either, she followed Don Fernando to his family and was received most heartily and tenderly by his two sisters-in-law, whom she knew to be very respectable young ladies.

When Doña Elvira, Don Fernando's wife, who was lying on the ground with severe foot wounds, saw her hungry child at Josefa's breast, she drew her down toward herself with great friendliness. Don Pedro, too, Fernando's father-in-law, who was wounded in the shoulder, nodded to her kindly.

Thoughts of a strange kind stirred in the hearts of Jerónimo and Josefa. If they found themselves treated with so much familiarity and goodness, they did not know in what light to consider the past, the place of execution, the prison and the bell; had they merely dreamed all that? It was as if all minds were reconciled since the fearsome blow that had stunned them. They could go no farther back in their memory than to the catastrophe.

Only Doña Isabel, who had been invited to stay with a lady friend in order to see the previous morning's spectacle, but had not accepted the invitation, let her dreamy gaze occasionally rest on Josefa; but an account that was made of some ghastly new misfortune jerked her mind back into the present, from which it had barely escaped. It was reported that right after the first main tremor the city had been full of women who went into labor in the sight of all the men; that the monks had run about, crucifixes in their hands, shouting that the end of the world was at hand; that a guard who had requested the evacuation of a church by order of the viceroy received the reply that there was no longer any viceroy of Chile; that at the most fearful moments the viceroy had been compelled to have gallows erected to put a halt to looting; and that an innocent man who had entered a burning house from the back to save himself had been seized by the overhasty owner and immediately hanged.

Doña Elvira, to whose wounds Josefa was busily attending, had at one point—just when these stories were arriving most quickly, each interrupting the other—taken the opportunity to ask her how *she* had fared on that terrible day. And when, with anguished heart, Josefa recounted some of the main features of her story, she was delighted to see tears well up in that lady's eyes; Doña Elvira seized her hand and squeezed it and gestured to her to be silent.

Josefa counted herself among the blessed. With a feeling she could not suppress, she began to consider the previous day—despite all the misery it had brought to the world—a benefaction greater than any yet vouchsafed her by heaven. And, indeed, in the midst of these awful moments, in which all the earthly goods of man were destroyed and all of nature was threatened with burial, the human spirit itself seemed to open out like a beautiful flower.

In the fields, as far as the eye could reach, people of all ranks could be seen mingled together, princes and beggars, matrons and peasant women, bureaucrats and day laborers, monks and nuns. They sympathized with one another, assisted one another and cheerfully shared whatever they had been able to save to keep themselves alive, as if the universal calamity had made a single family of all who had escaped it.

Instead of the usual meaningless tea-table chitchat based on mundane events, now they narrated examples of extraordinary feats: people who had normally been of low esteem in society had shown greatness worthy of ancient Romans; there were examples in plenty of fearlessness, of cheerful disregard of danger, of self-denial and godlike self-sacrifice, of the unhesitating casting away of one's own life as if, like the most worthless possession, it might be recovered the next minute. Yes, since there was no one who had not had some emotional experience on that day, or who had not himself done something magnanimous, the sorrow in every heart was mingled with so much sweet pleasure that Josefa felt it could not be determined whether the sum of universal welfare had not increased on the one hand just as much as it had been diminished on the other.

Jerónimo took Josefa by the arm, after the two of them had silently dwelt on these thoughts for as long as they wished, and led her to and fro beneath the leafy shade of the pomegranate grove with enormous cheerfulness. He told her that, in view of this general frame of mind and this revolution in the entire social order, he was abandoning his decision to take ship for Europe; that he would risk prostrating himself before the viceroy (should he still be alive), who had always favored his cause; and that he had hopes—and here he kissed her—of remaining in Chile with her.

Josefa replied that similar thoughts had occurred to her; that, were her father only still alive, she too no longer doubted she could be reconciled with him; but that, instead of the personal petition to the viceroy, she advised going to Concepción and corresponding with the viceroy from there with the aim of reconciliation; in Concepción they would be close to the harbor in any case, and in the best case—if the affair should take the desired turn—they could easily return to Santiago. After considering the wisdom of these measures briefly, Jerónimo gave them his approval, walked around with her a little more on the forest paths, speaking about the happy times they would have in the future, and returned to their group with her.

Meanwhile it had become afternoon, and the minds of the refugees who were roving about had barely become a little calmer again—now that the tremors were abating—when the news spread that in the Dominican church, the only one spared by the earthquake, a solemn Mass would be read by the prior of the monastery himself, to beseech heaven to prevent further disaster. People were already starting out all over the countryside and hastening to the city in throngs.

In Don Fernando's party the question was raised whether or not to participate in this solemnity and join the general procession. Doña Isabel, with some anguish, reminded them what a calamity had occurred in the church the day before; she remarked that thanksgiving celebrations like this one would be repeated, and that at a later date, when the danger would be clearly past, they could give vent to their feelings all the more cheerfully and calmly.

Josefa, standing up quickly with a degree of enthusiasm, stated that she had never felt a livelier urge to lay her face in the dust before her Creator than she did right then, when He was thus manifesting His incomprehensible and lofty power. Doña Elvira declared with vivacity that she shared Josefa's opinion. She insisted upon hearing the Mass, and called upon Don Fernando to lead their group; whereupon everyone stood up, including Doña Isabel.

But when Isabel, her breast heaving violently, lagged back upon observing their little preparations for departure and, on being asked what was wrong with her, replied that she had a strange foreboding of disaster, Doña Elvira calmed her and invited her to stay behind with her and her wounded father. Josefa said: "In that case, Doña Isabel, perhaps you would take my little darling, who, as you see, is with me once again." "Very gladly," answered Doña Isabel, and made as if to take hold of him; but when he screamed lamentably over the injustice being done him and would in no way consent to it, Josefa said with a smile that she would keep him, and she kissed him until he was quiet again.

Then Don Fernando, who was very pleased with all the dignity and grace of her demeanor, offered her his arm; Jerónimo, who carried little Felipe, escorted Doña Constancia; the other people who had become members of the group followed; and in this order they proceeded to the city.

They had scarcely gone fifty paces when Doña Isabel, who had meanwhile been engaged in vehement secret conversation with Doña Elvira, was heard to call: "Don Fernando!" and was seen hastening toward the walking group with agitated steps. Don Fernando halted and turned around; he tarried for her without releasing his hold on Josefa and—when she stopped at some distance as if waiting for him to meet her partway—he asked her what she wished.

Then Doña Isabel approached him, although with reluctance as it seemed, and murmured a few words in his ear, too low for Josefa to hear. "Well," asked Don Fernando, "and what calamity can arise from that?" Doña Isabel continued to whisper in his ear with a haggard expression on her face. Don Fernando's face grew red with displeasure; he replied: "All right! Please tell Doña Elvira to calm down," and continued to escort Josefa onward.

When they arrived at the Dominican church, they could already hear the musical splendor of the organ, and a countless number of people were surging inside. Outside the doors the crowd stretched far out over the forecourt of the church, and high up on the walls, in the frames of the paintings, boys were perched, holding their caps in their hands with an expectant gaze. Light poured down from all the chandeliers; the pillars cast mysterious shadows in the twilight that was falling; the great stained-glass rose window at the far back of the church glowed like the very evening sun that illuminated it; and, now that the organ had fallen silent, silence reigned in the whole congregation as if no one had a word to say. Never did a flame of ardor leap up to heaven from a Christian church as on that day from the Dominican church in Santiago; and no human heart added a warmer glow to the whole than Jerónimo's and Josefa's!

The celebration began with a sermon spoken from the pulpit by the oldest prebendary, dressed in ceremonial robes. Raising to heaven his trembling hands, which were encircled by his surplice, he began immediately with praise, glorification and thanks that in that part of the world, which was falling into ruins, there were still people able to stammer their thanks to God. He described what had occurred at the beck of the Almighty; the Last Judgment could not be more awesome; and when, pointing to a crack that the church had sustained, he called the previous day's earthquake merely a foretaste, as it were, a shudder ran through the entire congregation.

Next, in the flow of his sacerdotal eloquence, he turned to the moral depravity of the city; he castigated the city for abominations unknown to Sodom and Gomorrah; and he ascribed it only to the infinite forbearance of God that Santiago had not yet been totally wiped out by the earthquake. But the hearts of our two unfortunates, already deeply wounded by this sermon, were stabbed as by a dagger when the prebendary took this opportunity to mention circumstantially the sin that had been committed in the Carmelites' convent garden; he termed the indulgence it had received from society "godless" and, in a parenthetical passage filled with curses, consigned the souls of the perpetrators, mentioned by name, to all the princes of hell!

Doña Constancia, tugging Jerónimo's arm, cried out: "Don Fernando!" But the latter replied, as forcefully as was consonant with his secret tones: "Doña, be silent, don't move a muscle, and pretend to faint; then we will leave the church." But before Doña Constancia had taken these ingeniously conceived measures for escape, a voice, loudly interrupting the prebendary's sermon, was already exclaiming: "Stand well back, citizens of Santiago, here are these godless people!" And when another voice fearfully asked "Where?"—while a wide circle of horror formed around them—"Here!" replied a third and, with vileness prompted by religion, dragged Josefa down by the hair so that she would have reeled to the floor with Don Fernando's son if the Don had not been holding onto her.

"Are you insane?" shouted the young man, putting his arm around Josefa: "I am Don Fernando Ormez, son of the commandant of the city, whom you all know." "Don Fernando Ormez?" shouted a cobbler, standing directly in front of him; this cobbler had done work for Josefa and knew her at least as well as he knew her dainty feet. "Who is the father of this child?" he said, turning with insolent defiance toward Asterón's daughter.

Don Fernando turned pale at that question. Now he looked timidly at Jerónimo, now he glanced quickly over the congregation to see if there was anyone who knew him. Josefa, urged on by the frightening situation, cried out: "This is not my child as you think, Master Pedrillo," and, looking at Don Fernando in extreme anguish of soul, "this young gentleman is Don Fernando Ormez, son of the commandant of the city, whom you all know." The cobbler asked: "Citizens, who among you knows this young man?" And several of those standing near repeated: "Who can recognize Jerónimo Rugera? Let him step forth!"

Now, it happened that at the same moment little Juan, frightened by the uproar, strained to leave Josefa's breast for Don Fernando's arms. Whereupon, "He *is* the father!" a voice shouted; a second voice called, "He *is* Jerónimo Rugera!"; a third, "They *are* the blasphemous people!"; and "Stone them! Stone them!" cried all the Christians assembled in the temple of Jesus!

Then Jerónimo said, "Stop, you inhuman people! If you seek Jerónimo Rugera, he is here! Release that man, who is innocent!" The furious mob, confused by Jerónimo's statement, hesitated; several hands loosed their grip on Don Fernando; and when at the same moment a naval officer of high rank rushed over and, pushing through the press of people, asked, "Don Fernando Ormez, what has happened to you?," Don Fernando, now completely free, answered with truly heroic self-possession: "Just look at these assassins, Don Alonzo! I would have been lost if this estimable man had not pretended to be Jerónimo Rugera to pacify the raging crowd. Be so good as to take him as well as this young lady into custody for the protection of both; and," seizing Master Pedrillo: "Arrest this scoundrel, who instigated the whole uproar!"

The cobbler shouted: "Don Alonzo Onoreja, I ask you on your conscience, is this girl not Josefa Asterón?" When Don Alonzo, who knew Josefa very well, hesitated to answer, and several bystanders, in whom this kindled new rage, called: "It is she, it is she!" and "Death to her!," Josefa placed little Felipe, whom Jerónimo had been carrying up to then, in Don Fernando's arms together with little Juan, and said: "Go, Don Fernando, save your two children and leave us to our fate!"

Don Fernando took the two children and said that he would rather be killed than allow harm to befall his party. After requesting the naval officer's sword, he offered Josefa his arm and invited the couple behind him to follow him. The crowd, impressed by this procedure, made way for them with a sufficient show of respect, and they actually managed to leave the church, thinking they were safe.

But scarcely had they stepped into the forecourt, which was just as crowded with people, when a man from the frenzied throng that had dogged their steps called: "Citizens, this is Jerónimo Rugera, for I am his own father!" and knocked him to the ground at Doña Constancia's side with a mighty cudgel blow. "Jesus and Mary!" shouted Doña Constancia, fleeing to her brother-in-law; but there were already cries of "Convent whore!" and from another side came a second cudgel blow that laid her lifeless alongside Jerónimo.

"Monsters!" shouted an unidentified man, "that was Doña Constancia Xares!" "Why did they lie to us?" replied the cobbler; "find the right woman and kill her!" When Don Fernando caught sight of Constancia's body, he burned with anger; he drew the sword, swung it and aimed a stroke at the fanatical assassin who had caused these abominations, a furious stroke that would have cut him in two had he not eluded it by a twist of his body.

But when she saw that the Don could not overpower the mob crowding in on him, Josefa cried: "Farewell Don Fernando, you and the children!" and "Here, murder me, you bloodthirsty tigers!" and voluntarily threw herself into their midst, to put an end to the combat. Master Pedrillo felled her with his cudgel. Then, spattered all over with her blood, he cried: "Send her bastard to hell after her!" and, his blood lust still unsated, pushed forward again.

Don Fernando, that godlike hero, now stood with his back leaning on the church; with his left hand he held the children, in his right hand the sword. With every flash of his weapon an opponent fell to the ground; a lion does not defend itself better. Seven ravenous dogs lay dead before him, even the prince of the satanic horde was wounded. But Master Pedrillo could not rest until he had pulled one of the children away from his bosom by the legs and, swinging it through the air in a circle, had shattered it against the corner of a church pillar.

Then all became quiet and everyone withdrew. Don Fernando, seeing little Juan lying before him with his brains oozing out, raised his eyes to heaven in inexpressible sorrow. The naval officer rejoined him, attempted to console him and assured him that he regretted his lack of participation in those unhappy events, although it was excusable because of the circumstances; but Don Fernando said that he was not at all to blame and merely asked him to help carry away the bodies now.

In the darkness of the night that was falling they were all brought to Don Alonzo's residence; Don Fernando followed them there, shedding many tears on little Felipe's face. He spent the night at Don Alonzo's, too, and, misrepresenting the true situation to his wife, hesitated a long time before informing her of the whole extent of the tragedy—for one thing, because she was ill, and another, because he did not know how she would judge his conduct during those events. But shortly afterward, happening to be apprised by a visitor of all that had occurred, that excellent lady quietly wept her fill over her maternal sorrow and, one morning, with the last tears still glistening in her eyes, fell about his neck and kissed him. Then Don Fernando and Doña Elvira adopted the little stranger as their own son; and when Don Fernando compared Felipe to Juan and thought of how he had acquired both, he felt almost as if he should rejoice.

LIEUTENANT GUSTL

Arthur Schnitzler

HOW LONG is this going to last, anyhow? I must look at my watch . . . probably not polite at such a serious concert. But who's to see it? If someone sees it, then he's paying just as little attention as I am, and I don't have to bother on *his* account . . . Only a quarter to ten? I feel as if I'd been sitting at this concert for three hours now. I guess I'm not used to it . . . What is it, actually? I'll have to look at the program . . . Yes, that's it: oratorio. I thought it was a Mass. But surely things like that only belong in church! Also, the good thing about church is that you can leave any time.—If I at least had a corner seat!

Well, then, patience, patience! Even oratorios come to an end. Maybe it's very beautiful, and I'm just not in the mood. And why *should* I be in the mood? When I think that I came here to have a good time . . . I wish I'd given the ticket to Benedek instead, *he* gets a treat out of things like this; after all, he plays the violin himself. But then Kopetzky would have been insulted. Of course, it was very nice of him, at least he meant well. A good guy, Kopetzky! The only one you can rely on . . . Of course, his sister is one of the chorus singing up there. At least a hundred girls, all dressed in black; how could I pick her out? Because she's one of the singers, that's why he got the ticket, that Kopetzky . . . Then, why didn't he go himself?

By the way, they sing very nicely. It's very edifying—I'm sure! Bravo! Bravo! . . . Yes, let's join in the applause. That guy next to me is clapping like a lunatic. Does he really like it that much?—The girl in the box over there is really cute. Is she looking at me or at that man over there with the blonde beard? . . . Ah, a solo! Who is it? Alto: Miss Walker; soprano: Miss Michalek . . . this is probably the soprano . . . It's a long time since I was at the opera. At the opera I always have a good time, even if it's boring. Actually, the day after tomorrow I could go again, to *Traviata*. Yes, the day after tomorrow I may be dead and cold! Oh, nonsense, I don't believe that myself! Just wait, Doctor, you're

187

going to lose your taste for making such remarks! I'm going to slice off the tip of your nose . . .

If I could only get a good look at that girl in the box! I'd like to borrow the opera glasses from the man next to me, but he's sure to bite my nose off if I disturb him at his devotions . . . In what area is Kopetzky's sister standing? Would I recognize her? I've only seen her two or three times, the last time in the officers' mess . . . I wonder if they're all respectable girls, all hundred of them? Oh, my! . . . "With the cooperation of the Singers' Association"! Singers' Association . . . funny! Actually, I've always thought of that as something like the Vienna Dancing and Singing Girls—of course, I really knew it was something else! . . . Wonderful memories! That time at the Green Gate . . . What *was* her name? And then she once sent me a picture postcard from Belgrade . . . Another nice area!—Kopetzky is having fun, he's been sitting in the tavern for a while now smoking his Virginia cigar! . . .

Why does that guy there keep staring at me? I bet he's noticed that I'm bored and don't fit in here . . . I'd advise you not to make such impudent faces at me, or I'll meet you later on in the foyer!—Now he's looking away! . . . Why is everyone so afraid when I look at them? . . . "You have the most beautiful eyes I've ever come across!" Steffi said recently . . . Oh, Steffi, Steffi, Steffi!—Steffi is really to blame for my sitting here and having people wail at me for hours on end.

Ah, this way Steffi has of always standing me up is really beginning to get on my nerves! How nice this evening could have been. I have a great urge to read Steffi's note. There it is. But if I take out my wallet, the guy next to me will get steamed up!—Of course, I know what it says . . . she can't come because she has to go to supper with "him" . . . Ah, that was funny a week ago, when she was at the "Horticultural Society" with him and I was sitting opposite with Kopetzky; and she kept on signaling to me with her eyes, making a date. He didn't notice a thing— unbelievable! Anyway, he must be a Jew! Sure, he works in a bank, and that black mustache . . . They say he's also a lieutenant in the reserve! Well, he'd better not come to *my* regiment on active duty! And anyway, why do they always make so many Jews officers—all that talk about anti-Semitism is just a story! Lately at the party where that incident with the Doctor occurred, at the Mannheimers' . . . they say the Mannheimers are Jews themselves, converted, of course . . . but you can't tell by looking at *them*—especially the woman . . . so blonde, her figure pretty as a picture . . . It was very entertaining, all told. Terrific meal, wonderful cigars . . . So tell me, who's got the money? . . .

Bravo, bravo! It'll surely be over soon now?—Yes, now the whole crowd up there on the stage is standing up . . . they look very good— impressive!—An organ, too? . . . I really like organ music . . . Well, that's my style—very nice! It's really true, I ought to go to concerts more often . . . "It was marvelous," I'll tell Kopetzky . . . Will I meet him in the coffeehouse tonight? Oh, I really don't feel at all like going to the coffeehouse; I got into such a foul mood there last night! A hundred and sixty gulden lost at one card game—what a calamity! And who won the pot? Ballert—just the one who doesn't need it . . . Ballert is actually to blame for my having to go to this stupid concert . . . Sure, otherwise I could have played again tonight, maybe I could have won some of it back. But it's really a good thing that I gave myself my word of honor not to touch a card for a whole month . . . Mama is going to pull a long face again when she gets my letter!—

Oh, she ought to go to Uncle, he's got money to burn; a few hundred gulden wouldn't matter to him. If I could only arrange it for him to give me a regular allowance . . . but no, I've got to beg for each and every additional kreuzer. Then I get the old story: last year the harvest was bad! . . . Should I visit Uncle again this summer for two weeks? To tell the truth, I'm bored to death there . . . But if she . . . what was her name again? . . . It's odd, I can't remember names! . . . Oh, yes: Etelka! She didn't understand a word of German, but that wasn't necessary anyway . . . I didn't need to talk at all! . . . Yes, it'll be fine, fourteen days of country air and fourteen nights of Etelka or whoever . . . But I really ought to spend a week again with Papa and Mama . . . She looked bad this past Christmas . . . Well, by this time she'll be over her ailment. In her place, I'd be glad that Papa retired.—And Klara will still get a husband . . . Uncle can shell out something . . . Twenty-eight, that's not so very old . . . Steffi is certainly no younger . . . But it's odd: *that* kind of female keeps young longer. When you think about it: Maretti, who acted in *Madame Sans-Gêne*[1] lately, is surely thirty-seven, and looks like . . . Well, I wouldn't have said no!—Too bad she didn't ask me . . .

It's getting hot! Not over yet? Oh, how I look forward to the fresh air! I'll take a little walk, across the Ring . . . Motto for tonight: early to bed, be well-rested tomorrow afternoon! Funny how little I think about it, I really couldn't care less about it! Yes, the first time I did get a bit excited. Not that I was afraid; but I *was* nervous the night before . . . Of course, First Lieutenant Bisanz was a serious opponent.—And yet nothing happened to me! . . . And that was a year and a half ago. How time flies! And if Bisanz did nothing to me, the Doctor certainly won't! Although it's just these untrained fencers who are sometimes the most dangerous. Doschintzky told me that a guy who was holding a saber for the first time came within a hair of thrusting him through; and today

[1]A popular play by Victorien Sardou and others, 1893.

Doschintzky teaches fencing in the militia. Of course, I wonder if he was already that skilled at the time . . .

The most important thing is to keep cool. I don't even feel rightly angry any more, and it certainly was a piece of insolence—unbelievable! He certainly wouldn't have gone that far if he hadn't been drinking champagne previously . . . What insolence! He must be a socialist! After all, nowadays the pettifoggers are all socialists! A gang . . . what they'd like best of all is to do away with the whole military at once; but they don't stop to think about who would help them then if the Chinese attacked them. Dumbbells!—From time to time a man has to serve as an example. I was completely in the right. I'm glad that I never let him off the hook after that remark. When I think about it, I really get wild! But I behaved terrifically; the Colonel says, too, that I handled myself just as one should. All in all, this affair will help me out.

I know many people who would have let the fellow get away. Müller, surely; he would have been "objective" again or something like that. Everyone who's tried to be objective has made a fool of himself . . . "Lieutenant!" . . . even the way he said "Lieutenant" was brazen! . . . "You will surely have to admit" . . . How did we get into the situation, anyway? Why did I allow myself to get into a conversation with a socialist? How did it start? . . . I think the dark-haired lady I escorted to the buffet was also there . . . and then that youngster who paints hunting scenes—what's his name, now? . . . God bless me, he was to blame for the whole matter! He spoke about maneuvers; and it was only then that this Doctor came by and said something I didn't care for, about playing at war or something like that—but that was before I was able to say anything . . . Yes, and then they spoke about military academies . . . yes, that's how it was . . . and I told about a patriotic festival . . . and then the Doctor said—not right away, but as a spin-off from that festival— "Lieutenant, you will surely have to admit that not all your comrades joined the service solely to defend their country!" What insolence! A person like that dares to say such a thing to an officer! If I could only remember how I replied to that . . . Oh, yes, something about people who meddle with things they don't understand . . . Yes, that's right . . . and then there was someone there who wanted to settle the matter amicably, an older gentleman with a heavy cold . . . But I was too furious! The Doctor definitely said it as if he meant me personally. All he needed to add was that I was thrown out of high school and that's why I was placed in a military academy . . . People just can't understand our sort, they're too dumb to . . .

When I recall the first time I put on the uniform—that's an experience that not everyone has . . . Last year during maneuvers—what I wouldn't have given if it had suddenly become the real thing . . . And

Mirovic told me he felt the same way. And then, when His Highness rode past the front, and the Colonel's speech—a man would have to be a real bum if his heart didn't beat stronger . . . And then an inkslinger like that comes along, who's never done a thing all his life but sit behind books, and feels free to make an insolent remark! . . . Ah, just wait, my good man—till you're put out of action . . . yes, sir, you'll be so far out of action . . .

What's going on? Surely it must be almost over now? . . . "You, His angels, praise the Lord" . . . Of course, that's the closing chorus . . . Very beautiful, you can't deny it. Very beautiful!—Now I've completely forgotten that girl in the box who started to flirt before. Where is she? . . . Gone already . . . That one over there also seems to be very pretty . . . What a nuisance not to have opera glasses with me! Brunnthaler is really clever, he always has his glasses at the cashier's booth in the coffeehouse, that way you can't go wrong . . . If that girl there in front of me would turn around just once! She's been sitting there so well-behaved. The one next to her must be her Mama.

Shouldn't I start to think seriously about getting married? Willy wasn't older than I when he took the plunge. There's something to be said for always having a pretty little wife on hand at home . . . What a shame that Steffi has no time tonight of all nights! If I at least knew where she was, I could sit opposite her again. That would be a fine predicament, if that guy caught on to her, then I would be saddled with her . . . When I think what Fliess's affair with the Winterfeld woman costs him! And at the same time she cheats on him left and right. One of these days it'll end up in a disaster . . . Bravo, bravo! Ah, it's over! There, that feels good, to be able to stand up, to move . . . Well, maybe! How long is that guy going to take to put his glasses into their case?

"Pardon, pardon, would you let me out, please?" . . .

What a crush! Better let the people pass by . . . Elegant lady . . . I wonder if those are genuine diamonds? . . . That girl is cute . . . The way she looks at me! . . . Oh, yes, miss, I'm ready and willing! . . . Oh, her nose!—a Jewess . . . Another one . . . But this is amazing, half of the audience are Jews . . . you can't even enjoy an oratorio in peace any more . . . There, now let's join the procession . . . But why is that idiot shoving in back of me? I'll teach him better manners . . . Ah, an older gentleman! . . . And who is greeting me from up there? . . . Good night, good night! I have no idea who it is . . . The simplest thing would be to go right over to Leidinger's for supper . . . or should I go to the "Horticultural Society"? Maybe Steffi is there too? Really, why didn't she write to tell me where she was going with him? She probably didn't know yet herself. Really awful, such a dependent existence! . . . Poor thing!

Now, there's the exit . . . Ah, but *she* is gorgeous! All alone? The way she's smiling at me! That's an idea, I'll go after *her*! . . . There, down the steps now: Oh, a major of the Ninety-fifth . . . Very charming, the way he returned my salute . . . So I wasn't the only officer here . . . But where's the pretty girl? Ah, there . . . she's standing by the balustrade . . . Well, now I just have to get to the cloakroom . . . I don't want that girl to get away . . . That's done it! What a miserable brat! She has a man come to meet her, and now she's still smiling at me!—After all, not one of them is any good . . . Lord, what a crowd at the cloakroom! . . . Better wait a little bit longer . . . There! Is the dumbbell going to take my ticket? . . .

"You there, No. 224! It's hanging *there*! Well, are you blind? It's hanging *there*! Well, thank God! . . . Come on, now!" . . . That fat man there is blocking almost the whole cloakroom . . . "Excuse me, please!" . . .

"Patience, patience!"

What did the guy say?

"Just have a little patience!"

I just have to answer *him* . . . "Let me through!"

"You're not going to miss anything!"

What did he say? Did he say that to me? That's going too far! I can't put up with that! "Quiet!"

"What do you mean?"

What a tone of voice! That's the limit!

"Don't push!"

"Shut up, you!" I shouldn't have said that, I was too rude . . . Well, what's done is done!

"How was that?"

Now he's turning around . . . I know him!—Damn it, it's the master baker who always comes to the coffeehouse . . . But what is he doing here? He must also have a daughter or something in the chorus . . . But what's this? Yes, what is he doing? It even seems . . . yes, damn me, he's got the hilt of my saber in his hand . . . Is the guy crazy? . . . "You, sir . . ."

"You, Lieutenant, just keep still now."

What did he say? For the love of God, I hope nobody heard! No, he's speaking very low . . . But why doesn't he let go of my saber? . . . Damn it again . . . He's got me raving . . . I can't get his hand off the hilt . . . no uproar now! . . . Could the Major be behind me? . . . Does anyone notice that he's holding the hilt of my saber? But he's talking to me! What is he saying?

"Lieutenant, if you make the slightest disturbance, I'll put your saber out of its scabbard, smash it and send the pieces to your regimental headquarters. Do you understand, you fool?"

What did he say? I must be dreaming! Is he really talking to me? I ought to make some reply . . . But the guy is really serious—he's actually pulling out the saber. Good Lord—he's doing it! . . . I can feel it, he's already tugging at it! What is he saying? For God's sake, no uproar——what does he keep on saying?

"But I don't want to ruin your career . . . So, behave! . . . There, there, don't be afraid, no one heard anything . . . everything's all right now . . . there! And so that no one thinks we had a quarrel, I'll be very friendly to you now!—Good night, Lieutenant, it was a pleasure—good night!"

For God's sake, was I dreaming? . . . Did he really say that? . . . Where is he? . . . There he goes . . . I really ought to have drawn my saber and cut him down——For God's sake, I hope no one heard it . . . No, he was speaking very low, in my ear . . . But why don't I go over and split his skull open? . . . No, that wouldn't do, it wouldn't do . . . I ought to have done it right away . . . Why *didn't* I do it right away? . . . I just wasn't able to . . . he didn't let go of the hilt, and he's ten times stronger than I am . . . If I had said one more word, he would really have broken my saber . . . I ought to be happy that he wasn't speaking out loud! If anyone had heard it, I would have had to shoot myself *stante pede*[2] . . .

Maybe it was a dream after all . . . But why is that man there by the column staring at me like that?—Perhaps he heard something . . . I'll ask him . . . Ask him?—I'm crazy!—How do I look?—Can anyone notice anything from my appearance? I must be very pale.—Where is the dog? . . . I must kill him! . . . He's gone . . . The place is already completely empty . . . But where's my cloak? . . . I've put it on already . . . I didn't even notice . . . Who helped me on with it? . . . Oh, that one . . . I must give him a six-kreuzer piece . . . There! . . .

But what's going on? Did it really happen? Did someone really talk to me that way? Did someone really call me "fool"? And I didn't cut him down on the spot . . . But I wasn't able to . . . he had a fist like iron . . . I stood there as if nailed down . . . No, I must have lost my wits, or else with my other hand I would have . . . But then he would have pulled out my saber and broken it, and it would have been all up with me—I would have been completely finished! And later, when he went away, it was too late . . . after all, I couldn't have run him through from behind with my saber . . .

---

[2]Latin for "on the spot." The use of the phrase does not indicate scholarship on Gustl's part.

What, I'm out on the street already? How did I get outside?—It's so cool . . . ah, the breeze, that feels good . . . But who's that over there? Why are they looking my way? Maybe they heard something . . . No, no one could have heard anything . . . I know, because I looked around right away! No one was paying any attention to me, no one heard anything . . . But he did say it even if no one heard it; he did say it. And I stood there and let him, as if I had been hit over the head! . . . But I couldn't say anything or do anything; the only thing left for me to do was to keep still, keep still . . . it's horrible, it's not to be borne; I must kill him whenever I find him! . . .

That someone should talk that way to me! That a guy like that, a dog like that should speak to me like that! And he knows me . . . Lord, oh Lord, he knows me, he knows who I am! . . . He can tell anybody that he said that to me! . . . No, no, he won't do that, otherwise he wouldn't have spoken so low . . . he only wanted *me* to hear! . . . But who can guarantee that he won't eventually tell it, today or tomorrow, to his wife, his daughter, his friends in the coffeehouse?——For God's sake, I'll see him again tomorrow! When I arrive at the coffeehouse tomorrow, he'll be sitting there again, just like every day, playing his game of tarok with Mr. Schlesinger and the artificial-flower dealer . . . No, no, it's no good, it's no good . . . When I see him, I'll cut him down . . . No, I can't . . . I ought to have done it right away, right away! . . . If it had only worked out! . . .

I'll go to the Colonel and report the matter to him . . . yes, to the Colonel . . . The Colonel is always very friendly—and I'll say to him: Colonel, I beg to report, he held on to the hilt, he didn't let go of it; it was exactly as if I were weaponless . . . What will the Colonel say?— What he'll say?—But there's only one thing he can say: resign in disgrace—resign! . . .

Are those volunteers[3] over there? . . . Disgusting! at night they look like officers . . . they're saluting!—If they knew—if they knew! . . . There's the Café Hochleitner . . . There must be a couple of my fellow officers in there now . . . maybe someone or other that I know . . . What if I told it to the first one I meet, but as if it had happened to someone else? . . . I'm completely off my head by now . . .

Where have I got to? What am I doing out on the street?—Yes, but where should I head? Didn't I want to go to Leidinger's? Ha, ha, to sit down among people . . . I'm sure everybody would see it from my face . . . Yes, but *something* has to happen . . . What should happen? . . . Nothing, nothing—because no one heard anything . . . no one knows anything . . . at this moment no one knows anything . . . Should I go to

---

[3]Men in the service for one year with a certificate of educational proficiency.

his home now and implore him not to tell anyone about it? . . . Ah, better to blow my brains out at once than do something like that! . . . That would be the most sensible thing! . . . The most sensible? The most sensible?—There just isn't any other way . . . no other way . . . If I were to ask the Colonel, or Kopetzky—or Blany—or Friedmaier—everyone would say: There's no other way out for you! . . .

What if I spoke to Kopetzky? . . . Yes, that would be the most rational thing . . . about tomorrow, if for no other reason . . . Yes, of course, about tomorrow . . . at four, in the cavalry barracks . . . yes, I'm to fight a duel tomorrow at four o'clock . . . and I absolutely can't, I'm unqualified to give satisfaction . . . Nonsense! Nonsense! Nobody knows anything, nobody knows anything!—Plenty of men are running around who had worse things happen to them than this . . . All the things they said about Deckener and his pistol fight with Rederow . . . and the court of honor decided the duel ought to take place . . . But how would the court decide in my case?—"Fool—fool" . . . and I stood there—!

God in heaven, it makes no difference if anyone else knows! . . . *I* know, and that's the main thing! *I* realize that I'm not the same man I was an hour ago—*I* know that I'm unfit to fight a duel, and therefore I've got to shoot myself . . . I wouldn't have another peaceful moment in my life . . . I would always be afraid that someone might find out, one way or another . . . and that one day someone would tell me to my face what happened tonight!

What a fortunate person I was an hour ago . . . Then Kopetzky had to go and give me the ticket—and Steffi had to stand me up, the slut!—Things like that control your fate . . . In the afternoon everything was still perfectly all right, and now I'm a ruined man and have to shoot myself . . . Why am I dashing along like this? None of my trouble is running away . . . What is the clock striking now? . . . 1, 2, 3, 4, 5, 6, 7, 8, 9, 10, 11 . . . eleven, eleven . . . I really should go to supper! I've got to go somewhere eventually . . . I could sit down in some saloon where no one knows me—after all, a man has to eat, even if he shoots himself immediately afterward . . . Ha, ha, death isn't child's play . . . who was it said that recently? . . . But that makes no difference . . .

I'd like to know who will be most upset? . . . Mama or Steffi? . . . Steffi . . . God, Steffi . . . she won't even be able to let anything show, or else "he" will send her packing . . . Poor girl!—In the regiment—no one would have any idea why I did it . . . they'd all rack their brains . . . but why did Gustl kill himself?—No one would guess that I had to shoot myself because a miserable baker, a low-down creature like that, who just by chance has stronger fists . . . it's too bad, too bad! Just for that a fellow like me, such a young, nice guy . . .

Yes, later on everyone would surely say: he really didn't have to do that on account of such a trivial incident; it's really a shame! . . . But if I were to ask anyone at all now, everyone would give me the same answer . . . and when I ask myself . . . isn't it the damndest thing? . . . we're completely helpless against civilians . . . People think we're better off because we've got a saber . . . and when an occasion arises for one of us to use his weapon, we catch hell as if we were all born murderers . . .

It would be in the paper too . . . "Suicide of a young officer" . . . How do they always phrase it? . . . "The motives are veiled in obscurity" . . . Ha, ha! . . . "Mourners by the grave were . . ."—But it's real . . . I still feel as if I were telling myself a story . . . but it's real . . . I have to kill myself, there's no other way out for me—I can't take the chance that tomorrow morning Kopetzky and Blany will give me back their commission and say: we can't be your seconds! . . . I'd really be a blackguard if I expected it of them . . . A guy like me, who stands there and lets someone call him a fool . . . tomorrow everyone will know about it . . . it's stupid of me to imagine for a minute that a person like that isn't going to pass the story along . . . he'll tell it everywhere . . . his wife knows already . . . tomorrow the whole coffeehouse will know . . . the waiters will know . . . Mr. Schlesinger—the lady cashier——And even if he has made up his mind not to talk about it, he'll come out with it the day after tomorrow . . . and if he doesn't tell the day after tomorrow, in a week's time . . . And even if he were to have a stroke tonight, *I* still know . . . *I* know . . . and I'm not a man to continue wearing the uniform and the saber with such a disgrace on his head! . . .

There, I must do it, and that's that!—What is there to it, anyway?—Tomorrow afternoon the Doctor could kill me with his saber . . . things like that *have* happened . . . And Bauer, the poor guy, got a brain fever and was gone in three days . . . and Brenitsch fell off his horse and broke his neck . . . and finally, once and for all: there's no other way—not for me, not for me!—Of course, there are people who wouldn't take it so hard . . . God, the kinds of people there are! . . . Ringeimer was slapped in the face by a pork butcher who caught him with his wife, and he resigned and is living somewhere in the country and got married . . . To think there are women who would marry such a person! . . . Damn me, I wouldn't shake hands with him if he came back to Vienna . . .

So, you've heard, Gustl:—it's over, over, your life is finished! Totally finished! . . . There, now I know, it's quite a simple story . . . There! Now I'm actually quite calm . . . Anyway, I always knew that if it ever came to it, I'd be calm, quite calm . . . but that it would come to it in such a way, *that* I never thought . . . that I'd have to kill myself because such a . . . Maybe I didn't understand him correctly . . . maybe he said something completely different . . . I was all numb from the yowling and the heat . . . maybe I was crazy and none of it is true? . . . Not true, ha, ha, not true!—I can still hear it . . . it's still ringing in my ears . . . and I feel it in my fingers, how I wanted to get his hand off my saber hilt . . . He's a strongman, a Jagendorfer[4] . . . Though I'm no weakling, either . . . Franziski is the only one in the regiment stronger than I am . . .

The Aspern Bridge . . . How far will I keep going?—If I go on like this, I'll be in Kagran around midnight . . . Ha, ha!—Lord God, weren't we happy when we pulled in there last September? Only two more hours, and Vienna . . . I was dead tired when we arrived . . . I slept like a log all afternoon, and in the evening we were already at Ronacher's . . . Kopetzky, Ladinser and . . . who else was with us?—Yes, that's right, the volunteer who told us the Jewish jokes on the march . . . Sometimes they're really fine fellows, the one-year men . . . but they all should become only substitutes—because what's the sense of it? We have to drudge for years, and a guy like that serves for a year and has exactly the same rank as we do . . . it's an injustice!—But what does all that matter to me?—Why should I care about such things? A commissariat private counts more now than I do; I'm no longer in the world at all . . . I'm over and done with . . . lose honor, lose everything! . . . I have nothing left to do but load my revolver and . . .

Gustl, Gustl, it seems you still don't seriously believe it? Come to your senses . . . there's no other way . . . even if you rack your brains, there's no other way!—Now all that counts is to behave decently at the end, to be a man, to be an officer, so that the Colonel will say: He was a brave fellow, we'll be sure to remember him! . . . Now, how many companies march out for a lieutenant's funeral? . . . I really ought to know that . . . Ha, ha! Even if the whole battalion marches out, or the whole garrison, and they fire twenty salvos, it'll never wake me up!

In front of the coffeehouse—I was sitting there last summer with Mr. von Engel, after the army steeplechase . . . Funny, I've never seen the man since then . . . Why did he have his left eye bandaged? I kept wanting to ask him about it, but it wouldn't have been proper . . . There go two artillerymen . . . they must think I'm following that tart . . . Anyway, I want to have a look at her . . . Oh, horrible!—I'd like to know how someone like her makes a living . . . I'd sooner . . . And yet, any old port in a storm . . . in Przemysl—I was so disgusted later that I thought I'd never touch another female . . . That was a ghastly time up there in Galicia . . . really a great stroke of luck that we came to Vienna. Bokorny is still in Sambor and may be there for ten more years and grow old and gray . . . But if I had stayed there, what happened to me

---

[4]An athlete and wrestler popular in Vienna at the time.

tonight wouldn't have happened to me . . . and I'd rather grow old and gray in Galicia than . . . than what? Than what?

Yes, what's going on? What's going on?—Am I crazy that I keep forgetting?—Yes, damn me, I forget it every minute . . . has anyone ever heard the like?—that someone has to blow his brains out in a couple of hours and thinks about all conceivable things that don't concern him any more! Damn me, I'm acting exactly as if I were drunk! Ha, ha! Really drunk! Dead drunk! Suicidally drunk!

Ha! I'm making jokes, that's just fine!—Yes, I'm in quite a good mood—something like that surely must be part of your nature . . . Honestly, if I were to tell this to someone, he wouldn't believe it.—I think, if I had the thing with me . . . I'd pull the trigger now—it's all over in a second . . . Not everyone comes off so well—other people have to suffer for months . . . my poor cousin, she was in bed for two years, couldn't move, had the most horrible pains—what a pity! . . . Isn't it better to arrange it by yourself? All that counts is to be careful, to aim well, so no misfortune happens to you, as with that cadet substitute last year . . . Poor devil, he didn't die but went blind . . . I wonder what became of him? Where is he living now?—Terrible, to go around like that—that is: he *can't* go around, he has to be led—such a young man, he can't be twenty yet . . . he took better aim at his sweetheart . . . she was dead on the spot . . .

Unbelievable, the things people shoot themselves over! How can people be jealous, anyhow? . . . I've never had such a feeling in my life . . . Steffi is enjoying herself now at the "Horticultural Society"; then she'll go home with "him" . . . It means nothing to me, nothing! She's got a nicely furnished place—the little bathroom with the red lamp.— The way she came in recently with the green silk robe . . . I'll never see the green robe again, either—nor all of Steffi, either . . . and I'll never again walk up the fine broad stairs on Gusshausstrasse . . . Miss Steffi will go on having good times as if nothing had happened . . . she won't even be able to tell anyone that her dear Gustl killed himself . . . But she *will* cry—oh, yes, she *will* cry . . . All in all, a lot of people will cry . . . For God's sake—Mama!—No, no, I mustn't think of that.—Oh, no, that is definitely not to be thought about . . . No thinking about the family, Gustl, is that understood?—Not the slightest thought . . .

That's not bad, now I'm in the Prater . . . in the middle of the night . . . I wouldn't have imagined this morning that I'd be strolling in the Prater tonight . . . Wonder what that policeman there is thinking? . . . Well, let's keep going . . . it's a lovely night . . . Forget about supper, and about the coffeehouse, too; the air is pleasant and it's quiet . . . very . . . It's true, I'll soon have all the peace and quiet I could ask for. Ha, ha!— But I'm all out of breath . . . I've been walking like a lunatic . . . slower,

slower, Gustl, you aren't missing out on anything, you have nothing left to do—nothing, absolutely nothing left!—Is that right, am I shivering?—It must be the excitement . . . besides that, I haven't eaten . . .

What's that unusual smell? . . . Surely, nothing is in blossom . . . What day is today?—April fourth . . . it did rain a lot the last few days . . . but the trees are still almost completely bare . . . and it's dark, wow! You could almost get scared . . . That was really the only time in my life that I was frightened, as a small boy, in the woods that time . . . but I wasn't all that small, either . . . fourteen or fifteen . . . How long ago is that now?—Nine years . . . right—at eighteen I was a substitute, at twenty a lieutenant . . . and next year I'll be . . . What will I be next year? What does that mean, anyway: next year? What does "next week" mean? What does "the day after tomorrow" mean? . . . What? Your teeth chattering? Oho!—Well, let them chatter a little . . . Lieutenant, you're alone now, you don't need to put on a show for anybody . . . it's bitter, it's bitter . . .

I'll sit down on this bench . . . Ah!——How far have I come?—How dark it is! That, behind me there, must be the "Second Coffeehouse" . . . I was in there once last summer when our band gave a concert . . . with Kopetzky and with Rüttner—a few more were also there . . .—But I'm tired . . . no, I'm as tired as if I had put in a ten-hour march . . . Yes, that would be something, to fall asleep here.—Ha! A homeless lieutenant . . . Yes, I really should get back home . . . what will I do at home? But what am I doing in the Prater?—Ah, what I'd like best is not to have to get up at all—to fall asleep here and never wake up . . . yes, that would really be convenient!—No, things aren't so convenient for you, Lieutenant . . .

But how and when?—Now I could finally think the matter over properly . . . everything has to be thought over, you know . . . that's the way life is . . . So, let's think things over . . . Think what over? . . . No, the air is really nice . . . I ought to come to the Prater at night more often . . . Yes, I should have thought of that sooner, now it's all over with the Prater, with the air and with taking walks . . . Yes, what's going on? Ah, off with the cap; I feel as if it's pressing into my brain . . . I can't think straight . . . Ah . . . there! . . . Now then, pull your thoughts together, Gustl . . . make your final arrangements!

So, tomorrow morning will be the end . . . tomorrow morning at seven o'clock . . . seven o'clock is a nice hour. Ha, ha!—So, at eight, when classes begin, it'll be all over . . . But Kopetzky won't be able to give classes, because he'll be too broken up . . . But maybe he won't know yet . . . there won't be any need for them to have heard . . . They didn't find Max Lippay till the afternoon, and he shot himself in the morning, and no one heard anything about it . . . But what does it matter to me whether Kopetzky gives classes or not? . . . Ha!—At seven o'clock, then!—Yes . . . well, what else? . . . There's nothing else to think over. I'll shoot myself in my room and that's that! Funeral on Monday . . . I know one person who'll be happy: the Doctor . . . Duel cannot take place owing to suicide of one party . . .

What will they say at the Mannheimers'?—Well, *he* won't be very upset by it . . . but the wife, the pretty blonde . . . I had some hopes for her . . . Oh, yes, I think I would have been lucky with her if I had only concentrated my efforts a bit . . . yes, that would have been a little different than that slut Steffi . . . But you just can't be lazy . . . you've not to flirt, send flowers, talk sensibly . . . you can't come out and say: Come see me in the barracks tomorrow afternoon! . . . Yes, a respectable lady like her, that would have been something . . . My captain's wife in Przemysl, she was no respectable lady . . . I could swear: Libitzky and Wermutek and that shabby substitute, he had her, too . . . But Mrs. Mannheimer . . . yes, that would have been different, that would also have moved me into good society, that could almost have made me a new man—I would have gotten a new polish—I would have gained some respect for myself.——But always these tarts . . . and I started so young—I was still a boy when I had my first leave that time and was home in Graz with my parents . . . Riedl was there, too—it was a Bohemian woman . . . she must have been twice my age—I didn't get home until morning . . . The way my father looked at me . . . and Klara . . . I was ashamed in front of Klara most of all . . . She was engaged at the time . . . why did nothing come of it? To tell the truth, I didn't care very much . . . Poor little thing, she never had any luck—and now, on top of that, she's losing her only brother . . .

Yes, you'll never see me again, Klara—finished! You never imagined, did you, sister, when you accompanied me to the station on New Year's Day, that you would never see me again?—And Mama . . . Lord God, Mama . . . no, I mustn't think about that . . . if I think about it, I'm capable of acting ignobly . . . Ah . . . if I could only go home first . . . tell them it's a one-day leave . . . see Papa, Mama, Klara again before I sign off . . . Yes, I could take the first train to Graz at seven, I'd be there at one . . . Hello, Mama . . . Hi, Klara! Well, how are things? . . . No, what a surprise! . . . But they might notice something . . . even if no one else does . . . Klara . . . Klara, certainly . . . Klara is such a clever girl . . .

What a nice letter she sent me lately, and I still owe her an answer—and the good advice she always gives me . . . such a truly good creature . . . I wonder whether everything would have been different if I had stayed home? I would have studied agriculture, would have gone to Uncle's . . . that's what they all wanted when I was still a boy . . . Maybe I'd already be married now to some good, sweet girl . . . maybe to Anna, who liked me so much . . . I still noticed it the last time I was home, even though she already has a husband and two children . . . I saw the way she looked at me . . . And she still calls me "Gustl" the way she used to . . . *She'll* get a real shock when she finds out how I came to die—but her husband will say: I always knew it—a bum like that!

Everyone will think it's because I had debts . . . and that's just not true, it's all paid up . . . only the last hundred sixty gulden—yes, and they'll be there tomorrow . . . Yes, I must still arrange for Ballert to get the hundred sixty gulden . . . I must write that down before I shoot myself . . . It's awful, it's awful! . . . If I were to run away instead—to America, where no one knows me . . . In America not a soul knows what happened here tonight . . . not a soul cares about it there . . . Lately there was a bit in the paper about a Count Runge, who had to decamp on account of some unsavory affair, and now he has a hotel there and doesn't give a damn about the whole business . . . And in a few years I could come back . . . not to Vienna, of course . . . and not to Graz . . . but I could go to the farm . . . and Mama and Papa and Klara would prefer it a thousand times if I just stayed alive . . .

And what do the other people matter to me? Who else cares about my welfare?—Outside of Kopetzky, no one would mind if I disappeared . . . Kopetzky is the only one . . . And *he* was the one who had to go and give me the ticket today . . . and the ticket is to blame for everything . . . without the ticket I wouldn't have gone to the concert, and none of this would have happened . . . But what did happen? . . . It's just as if a hundred years had gone by since then, and it can't be two hours yet . . . Two hours ago somebody called me a fool and wanted to break my saber . . . Lord God, on top of everything, I'm starting to shout in the middle of the night!

Why did this all happen? Couldn't I have waited longer, until the cloakroom was empty? And why did I tell him to shut up? How did that slip out of me? After all, I'm usually a courteous person . . . usually I'm not that rude even to my orderly . . . but, of course, I was nervous—all those things combined . . . bad luck at cards and Steffi constantly standing me up—and the duel tomorrow afternoon—and I haven't been getting enough sleep lately—and the drudgery in the barracks—you can't put up with that forever! . . . Yes, sooner or later I would have gotten sick—I would have had to apply for a leave . . . Now it's no longer necessary—a long leave is coming now—without pay—ha, ha! . . .

How long will I keep sitting here? It must be past midnight . . . didn't I hear it striking before?—What's this . . . a carriage driving there? At this hour? One with rubber wheels—I can imagine . . . They're better off than I am—maybe it's Ballert with his Bertha . . . Why should it be Ballert of all people?—Drive on!—His Highness had a nice carriage in Przemysl . . . he always traveled down into town in it to visit that Rosenberg woman . . . His Highness was very sociable—a real buddy, on close terms with everybody . . . That *was* a fine time . . . even though . . . the district was cheerless and you could pass out there in the summertime . . . once three men got sunstroke on one afternoon . . . also the corporal of my platoon—such a useful man . . . Afternoons we would lie down on the bed naked.—Once Wiesner came into my room suddenly; I must have been dreaming, and I stood up and drew the saber, which was lying next to me . . . I must have looked a sight . . . Wiesner laughed himself half to death—he's a cavalry captain by now . . .—Too bad I didn't go into the cavalry . . . but the old man wasn't willing—it would have been too expensive—but now it's all one . . . Why?—Oh, yes, now I know: I must die, that's why it's all one—I must die . . .

So, what then?—Look, Gustl, after all you came down here to the Prater on purpose, in the middle of the night, with not a soul to disturb you—now you can think it all over calmly . . . That's pure nonsense about America and resigning, and you're much too stupid to make a new start—and if you live to be a hundred and think about the time when someone wanted to break your saber and called you a fool, and you stood there unable to do anything—no, there's nothing to think over—what's done is done—that stuff, too, about Mama and Klara is nonsense—they'll get over it—people get over everything . . . The way Mama mourned when her brother died—and four weeks later she hardly thought about it any more . . . she rode out to the cemetery . . . at first, every week, then every month—and now only on the anniversary of his death.——Tomorrow is the date of *my* death—April fifth.——Will they ship me to Graz? Ha, ha! Then the worms in Graz will have a treat!—But that doesn't concern me—other people can rack their brains about that . . .

So, what *does* really concern me? . . . Yes, the hundred sixty gulden for Ballert—that's all—I don't need to make any further dispositions.—Write letters? What for? To whom? . . . Say goodbye?—Yes, damn it, that's surely clear enough when you shoot yourself!—Then the others can't fail to notice that you've said goodbye . . . If people knew how little I care about the whole matter, they wouldn't feel sorry for me—I'm not at all to be pitied . . . And what did I get out of my whole life?—I would gladly still have done certain things: fight in a war—but I might have waited a long time . . . And I know all the rest . . . Whether such and such a tart is named Steffi or Kunigunde is all the same.—— And I also know the prettiest operettas—and I've gone to see *Lohengrin* a dozen times—and tonight I was even at an oratorio—and a baker called me a fool—damn me, that's plenty!—And I'm not inquisitive

. . . —So let's go home, slowly, very slowly . . . I have no reason at all to rush. —Rest here in the Prater another few minutes, on a bench— homeless. —I definitely won't go to bed—I have enough time for get- ting a good sleep. ——Ah, the air! —That, I'm going to miss . . .

What's going on? —Hey, Johann, bring me a glass of cold water . . . What's this? . . . Where . . . Yes, am I dreaming? . . . my head . . . damn . . . Fischamend[5] . . . I can't open my eyes! —But I'm dressed! —Where am I sitting? —Holy God, I dozed off! How was I able to sleep? It's dawn already! —How long did I sleep? —I must look at my watch . . . I don't see anything? . . . Where are my matches? . . . Well, is one going to light? . . . Three . . . and I'm supposed to fight a duel at four—no, not a duel—I'm supposed to shoot myself! —The duel is nothing any more; I must shoot myself because a baker called me a fool . . . Yes, did that really happen? —My head feels so peculiar . . . my neck seems to be in a vise—I can't move at all—my right leg has gone to sleep.

Get up! Get up! . . . Ah, that's better! —It's getting lighter now . . . and the air . . . just like that morning when I was on outpost duty and camped in the woods . . . that was a different awakening—I had a dif- ferent day before me then . . . I think I still don't completely believe it. —There is the street, gray, empty—I'm surely the only human being in the Prater now. —I was down here once at four in the morning, with Pausinger—we were riding—I was on Captain Mirovic's horse and Pausinger on his own nag—that was in May, last year—everything was already in blossom—everything was green. Now it's still bare—but the spring is coming soon—in a few days it'll be here. —Lilies of the valley, violets—too bad I'll get nothing out of it—every rotten fellow will get something out of it, and I have to die! That's miserable! And the others will sit at supper in the wine garden as if nothing had happened—the way we all sat in the wine garden on the very evening of the day they carried out Lippay . . . And Lippay was so popular . . . they liked him better than me in the regiment—why shouldn't they sit in the wine gar- den when I snuff it?

It's good and warm—much warmer than yesterday—and so fra- grant—there must be some blossoms, after all . . . Will Steffi bring me flowers? —It will never occur to her! She'll just take a ride . . . Yes, if it were still Adele . . . No, Adele! I believe I haven't thought about her for two years . . . What a fuss she kicked up when it was over . . . in my whole life I've never seen a broad cry like that . . . That was really the nicest moment I ever lived through . . . So modest, so undemanding, as she was—she loved me, I could swear. —She was altogether different

---

[5]A village near Vienna; pun with "Fisch am End"—"a fish at the end of its rope."

than Steffi . . . I'd like to know why I gave her up . . . what a stupid thing to do! It got too monotonous for me, yes, that was the whole thing . . . To go out with one and the same girl every night . . . Besides, I was afraid that I'd never get rid of her—such a crybaby——Well, Gustl, you could have waited a little longer—she was the only one who loved you . . . What is she doing now? Well, what *could* she be doing?—She must have another man now . . . Really, my arrangement with Steffi is more convenient—if you're tied up only once in a while and someone else has all the unpleasantness and I have only the pleasure . . . Yes, you can't really expect her to come out to the cemetery . . . Anyway, who'd go along if he didn't have to!—Maybe Kopetzky, and that would be all!—It's sad, after all, not to have anybody . . .

But what nonsense! Papa and Mama and Klara . . . Yes, after all I'm the son, the brother . . . but what more is there between us? Sure, they like me—but what do they know about me?—That I fulfill my military obligations, that I play cards and that I run around with sluts . . . but otherwise?—I've never written them that sometimes I'm disgusted with myself—in fact, I believe I didn't rightly know it myself.—Come now, are you bringing up things like that now, Gustl? All you need now is to start crying . . . Ugh!—Keep in step . . . there! Whether you're going to a rendezvous or on sentry duty or into battle . . . who said that, now? . . . Oh, yes, Major Lederer, in the canteen, when they were talking about Wingleder, who got so pale before his first duel—and threw up . . . Yes: whether you're going to a rendezvous or to certain death, a real officer doesn't let it show in his gait or in his face!—So, Gustl—Major Lederer said so! Ha!—

Lighter all the time . . . by now you could read . . . What's that whistle there? . . . Oh, that's the North Station over there . . . The Tegetthoff Column . . . it never looked so high before . . . There are carriages standing over there . . . But only street cleaners on the street . . . my last street cleaners—ha! I have to laugh when I think of it . . . I don't understand it at all . . . Does this happen to everyone when they finally know for sure? Half-past three by the North Station clock . . . the only question now is, should I shoot myself at seven railroad time or Vienna time? . . . Seven . . . yes, why at seven in particular? . . . As if it couldn't be any other time . . . I'm hungry—damn it, I'm hungry—no wonder . . . how long is it since I ate? . . . Since—since six last evening in the coffeehouse . . . yes! When Kopetzky gave me the ticket—a café au lait and two croissants.

What will the baker say when he hears? . . . The dirty dog!—Oh, *he'll* know why—he'll see the light—he'll find out what it means to be an officer!—A guy like that can let himself be thrashed on the public street and there are no consequences, and one of us is insulted privately and he's a dead man . . . If a crook like that could fight a duel—but no, then he'd be more careful, then he wouldn't risk anything in that line . . . And the guy goes on living in peace and quiet while I—have to croak!—He's the one who killed me . . . Yes, Gustl, do you get that?— He's the one who's killing you! But he won't get away scot-free!—No, no, no! I'll write a letter to Kopetzky telling him everything, I'll write down the whole story . . . or even better: I'll write it to the Colonel, I'll make a report to regiment headquarters . . . just like an official report . . . Yes, wait, you think something like this can remain secret?—You're wrong—it'll be written down as a permanent record, and then I'd like to see whether you still dare to go to the coffeehouse!—Ha!—"I'd like to see that": that's a good one! . . . There's a lot more I'd like to see, but unfortunately it won't be possible—it's all over!—

At this time Johann must be entering my room, now he notices that the Lieutenant hasn't slept at home.—Well, he'll think of all sorts of things; but that the Lieutenant spent the night in the Prater, damn me, he won't think of that! . . . Ah, the Forty-fourth! They're marching out to the firing range—better let them pass by . . . let's stand over here, then . . .—Someone's opening a window up there—good-looking tart—well, I'd at least wrap something around me if I went to the window . . . This past Sunday was the last time . . . I never dreamed that Steffi, of all women, would be my last.—Oh, God, that's the only real pleasure . . . Yes, the Colonel will ride after them in high style in a couple of hours . . . the fine gentlemen enjoy life—yes, yes, eyes right!—Fine . . . If you knew how little I care about you!

Ah, that's not bad: Katzer . . . since when did he transfer to the Forty-fourth?—Hi, hi!—What a face he's making . . . Why is he pointing to his head?—My good man, I'm not much interested in your cranium . . . Oh, that's it! No, my good man, you're wrong: I spent the night in the Prater . . . You'll read all about it in this evening's paper.— "Impossible!" he'll say: "just this morning when we marched out to the firing range I met him on Praterstrasse!" Who will take over my platoon?—Will they give it to Walterer?—Well, that'll be a fine kettle of fish—a guy with no class, who should have become a shoemaker instead . . .

What, is the sun coming up already?—Today will be a nice day—a real spring day . . . Damn it all again!—At eight in the morning the cabbies will still be alive, and I . . . now, what's all this? Hey, wouldn't that be something—to lose my self-control at the last moment on account of a cabbie . . . Now why is my heart starting to pound so stupidly all at once?—It's surely not because . . . No, oh, no . . . it's because I've been without food for so long.——But, Gustl, be honest with yourself: you're afraid—afraid because you've never been through it . . . But that doesn't help you, fear has never done anybody any good, everyone has to go through it once, one man sooner, another man later, and it just so happens your turn is sooner . . . You never amounted to much, so at least behave properly at the very end, that's what I ask of you!—So, then, what counts now is to think things over—but what? . . . I keep wanting to think something over . . . but it's perfectly simple: it's in the drawer of my night table, it's loaded also, all I need to do is squeeze— there's no trick to that!——

She's going to work already . . . poor girls! Adele worked in a shop, too—a couple of times I picked her up after work in the evening . . . When they're in a shop, they don't become such sluts . . . If Steffi belonged to me alone, I'd make her be a milliner or something like that . . . How is she going to find out?—In the newspaper! . . . She'll be annoyed that I didn't write to her about it . . . I think I'll go crazy yet . . . What do I care if she gets annoyed? . . . How long has the whole affair lasted, anyway? . . . Since January? . . . Oh, no, it must have been before Christmas . . . I brought her back candy from Graz, and at New Year's she sent me a note . . .

That's right, the letters that I have at home—are there any I should burn? . . . Hm, the one from Fallsteiner—if they find that letter . . . it might cause the fellow some unpleasantness . . . But what does that mean to me?—Well, it takes no great effort . . . but I can't go hunting for that one scrap of paper . . . The best thing is to burn up everything . . . who needs it? It's nothing but wastepaper.——And I could leave my handful of books to Blany.—*Through Night and Ice* . . . too bad, I'll never get to finish it . . . I haven't had much time for reading lately . . . an organ—oh, from the church . . . early Mass—I haven't been to one for a long time . . . the last time was in February, when my platoon was ordered to go . . . But that didn't count—I kept an eye on my men to see if they were attentive and behaved properly . . .—I'd like to go into the church . . . maybe there's something to it . . .—Well, after my meal today I'll know exactly . . . Ah, "after my meal" is a good one! . . . Well, what about it, should I go in?—I think it would be a comfort to Mama if she knew! . . . Klara sets less store by it . . . Well, let's go in—it can't hurt!

Organ music—singing—hm!—What's this?—I'm all dizzy . . . Oh, God, oh, God, oh, God! I'd like to have a person to talk to before I die!—That would be something—to go to confession! The priest would be surprised if at the end I said: Goodbye, Father; now I'm off to kill myself! . . .—I'd like best of all to lie down here on the stone floor and cry my heart out . . . Oh, no, that just isn't done! But crying sometimes helps so much . . . Let's sit down for a moment—but not fall asleep again as in the Prater! . . .—People who believe are better off, after all . . . Say, now even my hands are starting to tremble! . . . If it keeps on like this, I'll finally become so repulsive to myself that I'll kill myself purely from shame!—The old woman there—what can she still be praying for? . . . It might be an idea if I said to her: You, include me too . . . I never learned how to do it properly . . . Ha! I think dying makes you dumb!—Get up!—Now, what does that melody remind me of?—Holy God! Last night!—Out of here, out! I can't stand this! . . . Sh! Not so much noise, don't let your saber rattle—don't disturb the people at their devotions—there!—it *is* better outdoors . . .

Light . . . Ah, it's getting nearer all the time—if it were only over already!—I should have done it right away—in the Prater . . . I should never go out without my revolver . . . If I had had one last night . . . Damn it again!—I could go and have breakfast in the coffeehouse . . . I'm hungry . . . I always used to think it was strange that condemned prisoners still drank their coffee and smoked their cigar in the morning . . . Hell, I haven't smoked at all! I don't feel at all like smoking!—It's funny; I *would* like to go to my coffeehouse . . . Yes, it's already open, and surely none of our crowd is there now—and even so . . . at best, it shows that you kept cool. "At six he still had breakfast in the coffeehouse, and at seven he shot himself" . . .

I'm completely calm again . . . walking is so pleasant—and the nicest thing about it is that no one is forcing me.—If I wanted, I could still throw up the whole kit and caboodle . . . America . . . What is "caboodle"? What's a "caboodle"? I think I have sunstroke! . . . Oho, can it be that I'm so calm because I still imagine I don't have to go through with it? . . . I must! I must! No, I want to!—Anyway, can you picture yourself, Gustl, taking off your uniform and deserting? And that dirty dog would roar with laughter—and even Kopetzky wouldn't shake hands with you any more . . . I feel as if I've turned red.

The policeman is saluting me . . . I must return the salute . . . "Hi!" Now I've even said "Hi"! . . . That always gives pleasure to a poor devil like that . . . Well, no one has had to complain about me—off duty I was always friendly.—When we were on maneuvers, I gave Britannika cigars to the company officers and NCOs—I once heard a man behind me at rifle drill say something about "damned drudgery," and I didn't report him—I only said to him: "You, watch out, someone else might hear that sometime—then you'd be in for it!" . . . The Burghof . . . Who's on guard today?—The Bosnians—they look good—the Lieutenant Colonel said lately: When we were down there in '78, no one thought *they* would ever knuckle under to us like this! . . . Lord God, I would have liked to be in on something like that!—Now they're all getting up from the bench—Hi, hi!

It's really sickening that none of us can see combat.—Surely it would have been finer to die on the field of honor, for my country, than this way . . . Yes, Doctor, you're really getting off lightly! . . . Could someone take over for me?—Damn me, I should leave instructions for Kopetzky or Wymetal to fight the guy in my place . . . Ha, he wouldn't get out of it that easily!—What the hell! Isn't it all the same what happens later on? I'll never find out about it!—The trees here are in leaf . . . In the Volksgarten I once picked up a tart—she was wearing a red dress—she lived on Strozzigasse—later Rochlitz took her over . . . I think he still has her, but he doesn't talk about it any more—maybe he's ashamed . . . Steffi is still sleeping now . . . she looks so sweet when she sleeps . . . as if butter wouldn't melt in her mouth!—Well, when they sleep they all look that way!—I really should still write her a note . . . and why not? Everybody does it— writes letters beforehand.—I should write to Klara, too, telling her to console Papa and Mama—and the usual things one writes!—and to Kopetzky, too . . . Damn me, I think it must be much easier if you've said goodbye to a few people . . . And the notification to regiment headquarters—and the hundred sixty gulden for Ballert . . . really still a lot to do . . . Well, nobody made me do it at seven . . . from eight on is still plenty of time to be dead! . . . To be dead, yes—that's what it's called—nothing you can do about it . . .

Ringstrasse—not long now before I'm in my coffeehouse . . . I think I'm even looking forward to breakfast . . . it's unbelievable.——Yes, after breakfast I'll light up a cigar, and then I'll go home and write . . . Yes, first of all I'll do the notification for headquarters; then comes the letter to Klara—then to Kopetzky—then to Steffi . . . but what should I write to that tramp? . . . "My dear child, you probably didn't think" . . . Ah, nonsense!—"My dear child, I thank you very much" . . .—"My dear child, before I depart this life, I do not wish to neglect" . . .—Well, letter writing was never my strong point . . . "My dear child, a last farewell from your Gustl" . . .—What a surprise she'll get! It's really lucky I wasn't in love with her . . . it must be sad to love somebody and then . . . Well, Gustl, behave: even this way it's sad enough . . . After Steffi there would have been many others, you know, and maybe one that was worth something—a young girl from a good family with a dowry—it would have been very nice . . .

I must tell Klara in detail that I had no other way out . . . "You must forgive me, dear sister, and please console our dear parents, too. I know that I gave you all a lot of worries and caused you a lot of pain; but believe me, I always loved you all very much, and I hope you will still be happy some day, my dear Klara, and that you won't altogether forget your unfortunate brother" . . . Oh, it's better if I don't write to her! . . . No, it makes me want to cry . . . my eyes start pricking as soon as I think of it . . . I'll write just to Kopetzky—a chummy farewell, and ask him to give the news to the others . . .

Is it six already?—Oh, no: a half-hour to go—a quarter to.—What a cute face that is! . . . The little charmer with dark eyes I run into so often on the Florianigasse!—What will she say?—But *she* doesn't even know who I am—she'll just be surprised that she never sees me . . . The day before yesterday I made up my mind to speak to her the next time.—She's flirted enough . . . she was so young—maybe she was even still a virgin! . . . Yes, Gustl! Don't put off till tomorrow what you can do today! . . . I'm sure that guy there didn't sleep all night, either.—Well, now he'll go comfortably home and go to bed—so will I!—Ha, ha! Now it's getting serious, Gustl, yes! . . . Well, if it weren't for the little bit of fear, there would be nothing to it—and all in all, if I say so myself, I'm behaving well . . . Ah, where to now? That's my coffeehouse . . . they're still sweeping out . . . Well, let's go in . . .

Back there is the table where they always play tarok. Strange, I can't get it into my head that the guy who always sits in back against the wall is the same one who . . . —Not a soul here yet . . . Where's the waiter? . . . Hey! Here he comes out of the kitchen . . . he's slipping quickly into his coat . . . It's really not necessary! . . . Oh, for him it is . . . he'll have to wait on other people today!—

"How do you do, Lieutenant?"

"Good morning."

"So early today, Lieutenant?"

"Oh, don't bother—I don't have much time, I can sit with my cloak on."

"What would you like, Lieutenant?"

"Café au lait with a skin of milk."

"Right away, Lieutenant!"

Ah, newspapers are lying there . . . today's papers already? . . . Anything in them yet? . . . What am I doing?—I think I want to look and see whether they have the story of my suicide! Ha, ha!—Why am I still standing? . . . Let's sit down there by the window . . . He's already set down my café au lait . . . There, I'll draw the curtain: I hate it when people look in . . . Not that anyone is passing by yet . . . Ah, the coffee tastes good—after all, having breakfast wasn't a foolish idea! . . . Ah, you become a totally new man—all those muddled thoughts came from having no supper . . . Why is the fellow already here again?—Ah, he's brought me the rolls . . .

"Have you heard yet, Lieutenant?" . . .

"What?" For the love of God, does he know something already? . . . No, nonsense, that's impossible!

"Mr. Habetswallner . . ."

What? That's the name of the baker . . . what will he say now? . . . Maybe he's already been here. Maybe he was already here last night and told the story . . . Why doesn't he continue speaking? . . . But he *is* speaking . . .

". . . had a stroke last night at twelve."

"What?" . . . I shouldn't shout like that . . . no, I shouldn't let anything show . . . but maybe I'm dreaming . . . I must ask him again . . . "*Who* had a stroke?"—Terrific, terrific!—I said that as innocently as possible!—

"The baker, Lieutenant! . . . You must know him, Lieutenant . . . you know, the fat man who plays tarok every afternoon alongside the officers . . . with Mr. Schlesinger and Mr. Wasner from the artificial-flower store sitting opposite!"

I'm fully awake—everything tallies—and yet I still can't quite believe it—I must ask him again . . . but very innocently . . .

"He had a stroke? . . . Yes, but how was it? How do you know?"

"But, Lieutenant, who should know before we do?—the rolls you're eating there were made by Mr. Habetswallner. The boy who brings us the baked goods at half past four in the morning told us."

For the love of God, I mustn't give myself away . . . I'd really like to shout . . . I'd like to laugh . . . I'd like to give Rudolf a kiss . . . But I still must ask him more! . . . To have a stroke doesn't necessarily mean that he's dead . . . I must ask whether he's dead . . . but very calmly, because what's the baker to me?—I must look at the paper while I ask the waiter . . .

"Is he dead?"

"Well, of course, Lieutenant; he was dead on the spot."

Oh, wonderful, wonderful!—maybe all this is because I went to church . . .

"In the evening he was at the theater; he fell over on the stairs—the concierge heard the crash . . . well, and then they carried him into his apartment, and when the doctor got there it was already long over."

"But that's sad. He was still in the prime of life."—It was terrific, the way I just said that—nobody could tell a thing . . . and I really have to restrain myself to keep from shouting or jumping onto the billiard table . . .

"Yes, Lieutenant, very sad; he was such a charming man, and he'd been coming to us for twenty years—he was a good friend of our proprietor. And his poor wife . . ."

I think I've never been so happy in my entire life . . . He's dead—he's dead! No one knows a thing, and nothing has happened!—And what a great stroke of luck that I came to the coffeehouse . . . otherwise I would have shot myself for nothing at all—after all, it's like a dispensation of destiny . . . Where is Rudolf?—Ah, he's talking to the furnace man . . .—So he's dead—he's dead—I still can't believe it! I'd really like to go over and see for myself.——Maybe he had a stroke from rage, from pent-up anger . . . Ah, the reason makes no difference! The main thing is that he's dead, and I can live, and I've got everything back again! . . . Funny how I keep on crumbling the rolls into the coffee—rolls that Mr. Habetswallner baked for me! They taste very good, Mr. von Habetswallner! Terrific!—There, now I'd like to smoke a cigar . . .

"Rudolf! You there, Rudolf! Leave the furnace man there in peace!"

"Yes, Lieutenant?"

"A Trabucco cigar" . . .—I'm so happy, so happy! . . . What shall I do? . . . What shall I do? . . . Something's got to happen, or I'll have a stroke myself from pure happiness! . . . In a quarter of an hour I'll go over to the barracks and get a cold rubdown from Johann . . . half past seven is rifle drill, and half past nine is formation.—And I'll write to Steffi that she must make herself available for tonight, even if all of Graz is at stake! And at four in the afternoon . . . just wait, my good man, just wait, my good man! I happen to be in good form . . . I'll make mincemeat out of you!

THE STORY OF THE JUST CASPER
AND FAIR ANNIE

Clemens Brentano

IT WAS EARLY summer. The nightingales had only just begun to sing, but on this cool night they were silent. The breath of distant storms was in the air. The night-watchman called out the eleventh hour. Homeward bound I saw before the door of a large building a group, just out of the taverns, gathered about someone, who was sitting on the doorsteps. The bystanders seemed to show such lively concern, that I augured a mishap and joined the group.

On the steps sat an old peasant woman. Despite the animated concern the onlookers displayed, she turned a deaf ear to the inquisitive questions and good-natured proposals, that came from all quarters. There was something quite uncanny, yes, even a touch of majesty about the way the good old woman knew just what she wanted; while she was making herself comfortable for a night under the open sky, as little abashed by her audience, as though she were at home in her own little bedroom. She threw her apron about her as a protection, drew her large, black, lacker hat over her eyes, placed the bundle containing her belongings under her head, and was silent at all questions.

"What ails the old woman?" I asked one of the onlookers. Hereupon replies came from every hand: "She has walked in eighteen miles from the country; she is exhausted; she doesn't know her way about in the city; she has acquaintances at the other end of town, but can't get there alone."—"I was going to take her," said one, "it's a long way though, and I've left my housekey at home. Besides she wouldn't know the house she's looking for."—"Still, the woman can't stay here over night," remarked a newcomer. "But she insists," replied the first; "I told her more than once, that I'd take her home, but she talks only nonsense, she must be drunk."—"I think she's weak-minded. At any rate, she can't stay here," repeated the former, "the night is cool and long."

During all this chatter the old woman, just as if she were deaf and blind, had gone on unconcerned with her preparations for the night.

When the last speaker again stressed the point: "At all events she can't stay here," she replied in a strangely deep and earnest tone:

"Why am I not to stay here? is this not a ducal house? I am eighty-eight years old, and the duke certainly won't drive me from his threshold. Three of my sons have died in his service, and my only grandson has taken his leave.—God, I'm sure will forgive him, and I want to live until he is honorably buried."

"Eighty-eight years old and has walked in eighteen miles!" exclaimed the bystanders. "She is tired and childish; at that advanced age one weakens."

"But, mother, you might catch cold and take sick here; then too, how lonesome you'll be," said one of the group as he bent down to her.

Then the old woman spoke again in her deep voice, half entreating, half commanding:

"Oh leave me in peace and be sensible! I'm in no need of a cold, nor need I be lonely; it is already late, I am eighty-eight years old, morning will dawn soon, then I'll pick up and go to my friends. If one is pious, has his own cross to bear, and can pray, he can surely live through these few short hours too."

Gradually the crowd had dispersed. The last who had remained now hastened away also, because the nightwatchman was approaching and they wanted him to unlock their doors for them. I alone remained. The street-noises died away. Under the trees of the square lying opposite I paced back and forth thoughtfully. The manner of the peasant woman, her certain, earnest way of expressing herself, her self-reliance, despite her eighty-eight years; all this made it appear as though she considered this long span of life but as the vestibule to the sanctuary. I was greatly moved. "What are all the pangs, all the desires of the heart? Unmindful the stars continue in their course. To what purpose do I seek meat and drink, and from whom do I seek to secure them and for whom? Whatever I may strive for here, and love, and gain, will it ever teach me so to live that I can with as much composure as this good pious soul, spend the night on a doorstep? There to await the morrow? And will I then find my friend, as she is certain to find hers? Ah, I'll not have the strength to get as far as the city; footsore and exhausted I'll collapse in the sands before the gates, or perchance fall into the hands of robbers." Thus I spoke to myself. A bit later, when I was walking under the linden trees in the direction of the old woman, I heard her praying half aloud to herself with head bowed. I was strangely affected, stepped to her side and said: "Good mother, include me in your prayers, just an entreaty for me!" With these words I slipped a silver coin into her apron.

Perfectly composed, the old woman exclaimed: "A thousand thanks, my dear Master, that you have answered my prayer."

I thought that she was speaking to me and said: "Mother, did you ask me for something? if so, I wasn't aware of it."

Surprised the old woman raised herself and spoke: "Good sir, do go home, say your prayers and lie down to sleep. Why are you roaming the streets at this hour? That's not good for young fellows, for the enemy goeth about and looketh, where he may seize upon you. Many a one has come to grief through being abroad at such hours of the night. Whom are you seeking? The Lord? He is in the hearts of men, if they be righteous, and not on the streets. But if you seek the enemy, be assured, you have him already. Go home now and pray that you may be rid of him. Good night."

At these words she turned quietly on her other side and put the coin in her bundle. Whatever the old woman did made a peculiar, serious impression on me. Again I addressed myself to her: "Good mother, what you say is perfectly true, but it is you yourself that keep me here. I overheard you praying, so I made bold to beg you to include me in your prayers."

"That's already done," said she. "When I noticed you walking back and forth under the linden trees, I prayed to God, that He grant you clean thoughts. Now you have them, go home and sleep well."

Instead I sat down upon the steps beside her, seized her wrinkled hand and spoke: "Let me sit here beside you through the night, while you tell me all about your home, and what brought you so far to the city. Here you have no one to stand by you, at your age one is nearer God than men. The world has greatly changed since you were young." —

"I'm aware of it," replied the old woman, "my life long I have found it pretty much the same. You are still young; at your age everything seems new and strange. I have lived and relived so much, that I look upon life now only with pleasure, because God is so faithful in all things. But one should never turn goodwill away, even though one doesn't stand in need of it, lest the good friend fail to appear another time when he would be most welcome. Sit where you are, perhaps you can be of some help. I'll tell you what has urged me over these long miles into the city. I never thought I should see this place again. Seventy years ago I served as a maid in this very house, on the doorstep of which I now sit. Since then I have never again been in the city. How time flies, like the turn of a hand. How often did I sit here of an evening seventy years ago waiting for my sweetheart, who was then serving as a soldier. Here we became engaged. If he — but shh —, the guard is making the rounds."

Then she began in a subdued voice to sing, as young maids and ser-

vants are wont on bright moonlight nights before the doors, and I heard
with great delight this old sweet song from her lips:

> "When the last Great Day shall be,
> The stars shall fall on land and sea.
> Ye dead, ye dead shall then arise,
> And stand before the Last Assize;
> There, far in front your feet shall go
> Where blesséd angels sit in row;
> God, newly come, shall wait you there,
> A beauteous rainbow round His chair.
> There those false Jews shall trembling stand,
> Who gave the Christ to Pilate's hand.
> Tall trees shall shed a glory near,
> Hard stones shall crush their hearts with fear.
> Who then can pray this simple prayer
> Will surely pray it then and there,
> The soul before its God is tried,
> When Heaven's doors shall open wide."

When the guard came nearer, the good old woman exclaimed with
a show of emotion: "Ah, to-day is the sixteenth of May; there's but little
difference, it's just as in the past, only they wear different caps now, and
the cues are gone. What matters that, if the heart is pure!" The officer
of the guard stopped at the doorstep. Just as he was on the point of asking what was our business here at that late hour, I recognized in him
an acquaintance, corporal, Count Grossinger. I explained the situation
to him briefly; whereupon he replied, signally stirred: "Take this coin
for the old woman and a rose too"—he held it in his hand—"old peasants of her type are fond of flowers. To-morrow ask the old woman to
repeat the song so that you may write it down and bring it to me. I have
searched far and near for that song, but never have I been able to come
upon the complete version." Then we parted, for from the headquarters toward which I had accompanied him over the square, the nearby
guard shouted: "Who's there!" As Grossinger turned, he told me that
he was in command of the guard at the castle, I should look him up
there. I returned to the old woman, and gave her the rose and the coin.

She seized the rose with a touching impetuousness and fastened it in
her hat, while in a low voice almost weeping she repeated:

> "Roses as flowers on the cap I wear,
> Had I but gold I'd have no care,
> Roses and my dear one."

I said to her: "Come, mother, you have grown quite merry," and she
recited:

"Merry, merry,
Reckless, very,
Much did dare he,
High did fare he,
Then miscarry.
Wherefore stare ye?"

"See, dear sir, is it not well that I remained here? It's all the same, you may well believe. It is seventy years ago to-day, I was sitting here on the doorstep. I was an hard-working maid and was fond of singing all the old songs. I was just in the midst of the Judgment Day song that I sang to-night, when the guard went by. A grenadier in passing threw a rose into my lap—I have it now between the pages of my Bible—. That was the beginning of my acquaintance with my husband long since dead. Next morning I wore the rose to church; he saw me there, and soon we were on good terms. How great is my pleasure, that again I hold a rose on this anniversary day. It is a sign, I'm to come to him! How happy it makes me to be invited this way! Four sons and a daughter have gone on before me; day-before-yesterday my grandson took his leave—may God help him and have mercy on him!—To-morrow another good soul will leave me; but why do I say to-morrow, is it not already past midnight?"

"The clock has indeed struck twelve," I replied, astonished at her words.

"God grant her comfort and peace these four short hours to come!" said the old woman, and waxed silent, folding her hands as in prayer. I too was speechless; her words and her behavior had gripped me so. Since, however, the silence became prolonged and the coin of the officer still lay in her lap, I addressed her again: "Mother, put the coin away, lest you lose it."

"I'll not put this one away, I'm going to give it to my friend in her last great suffering," she replied. "The first coin, I'll take home with me to-morrow, my grandson shall have it, it's his to enjoy. You see, he was always a splendid boy; he had a deal of pride in his person and in his soul—Oh, God, in his soul!—The whole long way to the city I prayed for him; the dear Lord certainly will have mercy on him. Of the lads at school he was always the cleanest and most hard-working, but the astonishing thing was his sense of honor. His lieutenant often remarked: 'If my company has a high sense of honor, then Casper Finkel's responsible.' He was a lancer. The first time he returned from France he had a great deal to tell, but rarely did he venture a story that did not savor of honor. His father and step-brother served with the militia. There was many a quarrel about honor, for where he had an excess of it, they had not enough. God forgive me my great sin, I don't mean to speak evil of them. Everyone has his burden to bear; but my dead daughter, his mother, worked herself to death for that sluggard. Try as she might, she couldn't pay off his debts. The lancer said his bit about the Frenchmen, and when his father and step-brother had not a good word to utter for them, the lancer said with emphasis: 'Father, you don't understand, they do have a high sense of honor.' Angrily the step-brother retorted: 'Why babble so much about honor to your father? Wasn't he a petty-officer of company N? He ought to know more about it than you, you private!' — 'Yes,' old Finkel chimed in, 'to be sure I was a petty-officer, and many an insolent fellow got his twenty-five stripes; if I'd had Frenchmen in the company, they'd have felt them even more, with their sense of honor!' These remarks irritated the lancer, and he said: 'I'll tell you an incident of a French petty-officer, that's more to my taste. During the reign of the former king there was much talk of introducing corporal punishment into the French army. An order of the war minister was proclaimed at Strassburg on the occasion of a large parade, and the troops in rank and file listened grimly to the proclamation. Now at the close of the parade a private did something against military rules, so his petty-officer was ordered to advance and administer twelve blows to him. Sternly he was commanded to perform his duty, so there was no getting around it. But scarcely had he finished when he grasped the musket of the private, whom he had just finished beating, placed the butt of it on the ground before him, and discharged it with his foot, so that the bullet raced through his head and he fell dead to the pavement. The incident reached the ears of the king, who immediately ordered that corporal punishment be discontinued. Mind, father, that chap had a real sense of honor!' — 'He was a fool,' exclaimed the brother. — 'Eat your honor, if you're hungry,' grumbled the father. Then my grandson took his sabre, left the house and came straight to tell me the incident, tears of anger rolling down his cheeks. I couldn't cheer him up, although I didn't entirely discredit his story; still I always came back to the same conclusion: 'to God alone be honor!' I gave him my blessing, for his furlough expired on the day following, and it was his wish to ride away a mile to the place where a god-child of mine was in service on an estate. He thought a good deal of this girl and wanted to see her once more: — they'll soon be united, if God hears my prayers. He has already taken his leave, my god-child will get hers to-day. Her dower I have brought with me. No one shall be present at her marriage but me." Here the old woman lapsed into silence and seemed to be praying. My mind was confused through sheer meditation on honor. Would a Christian consider the death of the petty-officer noble and proper? How I wished some one would tell me a sufficient solution to this problem!

When the watchman sang out one o'clock, the old woman remarked: "Two hours more! Ah, you're still here, why don't you go home to bed? To-morrow you'll not be fit to work and you'll not get on well with your employer. What's your trade, friend?"

The thought of explaining to her that I was an author put me to some embarrassment. I couldn't very well tell her that I was a scholar without lying. It is remarkable that a German always feels a bit ashamed to call himself an author (*Schriftsteller*); especially wary is he in using this term when speaking with the lower classes, because it so readily conjures up in their minds the scribes and the Pharisees of the Bible. The word *Schriftsteller* has not been so generally accepted among the Germans, as the *homme de lettres* among the French. In France there exists a sort of author's guild, and in their works one traces a good deal of professional tradition. Not infrequently the question is asked: *Où avez vous fait votre Philosophie?*—where have you "made" your philosophy?—which leads us to venture the pun, that there is a good deal of the "made" man about the Frenchman. But it isn't this un-German custom alone, that makes it so embarrassing to pronounce this word when at the city-gate you are asked your occupation. A certain inner humiliation makes us reticent, a feeling that comes over all those who barter in free spiritual capital, the immediate heavenly gifts. Scholars are less embarrassed than poets, for as a rule they have paid their tuition, are for the most part state officials, and perform such tasks as produce more or less tangible results. But the so-called poet is verily in a bad way, because as a rule he has played truant from school to climb Parnassus. Thus suspicion enshrouds the poet by vocation; perhaps he who writes as an avocation is a shade the better. It is an easy matter to say reproachfully to the former: "Sir, every mother's son has a bit of poetry in his make-up as he has brains, a heart, a stomach, a spleen, a liver and the like; but he who feels it to excess, pampers or fattens one of these members, and develops it at the expense of the others, or even goes to the length of making it a means of livelihood; he has cause to be ashamed of himself in the presence of his fellow men. One who lives by poetry, has lost his balance; and an enlarged goose's liver, no matter how delicate to the taste, does posit a sick goose. Every one who does not earn his bread by the sweat of his brow must feel a measure of humiliation. That humiliation is especially felt by one who has not yet been dubbed a knight of the quill, when he is forced to speak of himself as a *Schriftsteller*." Such thoughts passed through my mind, as I bethought myself what my reply to the old woman should be. She was surprised at my hesitancy, looked me in the face, and said:

"What's your trade? I ask. Why don't you tell me? If your trade be not honest, then apprentice yourself properly; an honest trade has its own reward. I trust you're not a hangman or a spy, who is on my trail. For my part you may be what you may be; speak, who are you! If you were lounging about this way by day, I'd think you a sluggard or a do-nothing, who props himself against the houses, not to fall over from sheer laziness."

At that a word came to me, that might perhaps bridge the gap between us: "Good mother," said I, "I am a clerk."—"Well," she replied, "you might have told me that sooner; you're a man of the quill then. You must have a good hand, nimble fingers and a good heart, otherwise you wouldn't get far. So you're a clerk? Fine! In that case you can write a petition to the duke for me, but such a petition as will surely come to his notice and find favor with him. Most such writings are bandied about in the antechambers."

"Indeed, I'll write a petition for you, good mother," said I, "and I'll take great pains, to make it as forceful as possible."

"That's good of you," she replied, "God reward you for it. May you arrive at a riper old age than I, and in your old age may He grant you a like composure, as happy a night with roses and coins, as I; and in addition a friend, who will write a petition for you, if there be need of it. But do go home now, good sir, and get some paper so that you may write the petition. I'll wait here for you one hour longer before I go to my god-child. You can go with me to witness her pleasure in the petition. Her heart is pure, but God's judgments are incomprehensible."

After these words the old woman said no more; she bowed her head and appeared to be praying. When she began to weep, I enquired: "Mother, what has come over you? What brings the tears to your eyes?"

"Why shouldn't I weep? The coin, the petition, everything has moved me to tears. But to what purpose? The world is still much, much better than we deserve, and tears as bitter as gall are still much too sweet. Just look at that golden camel over there on the apothecary's sign! How strange and glorious God has created everything, only man is not mindful of it, and a camel like that can sooner pass through the eye of a needle than man enter the kingdom of heaven.—But you're still sitting here, why don't you go get the paper and fetch me the petition?"

"Good mother," I rejoined, "how can I frame this petition for you, if you don't tell me what I'm to put in it?"

"I'm to tell you that?" she replied; "then petition-writing isn't an art, and I'm no longer surprised that you were ashamed to call yourself a clerk, if I have to tell you all that. Well, I'll do my best. Put into the petition, that two lovers are to be laid to rest side by side; that the one of them is not to be dissected but left so that his limbs shall be assembled

at the cry: 'Ye dead, ye dead, shall arise, ye shall come to judgment!'"
Then she began weeping bitterly again.

I augured that a great sorrow was crushing her, but despite the burden of her years she broke down only for brief intervals. Her weeping
was devoid of complaint, her utterance was at all times calm and dis-
passionate. Once more I begged her to tell me the full purpose of her
mission to the city, and she spoke:

"My grandson, the lancer, of whom I made mention before, loved
my god-child, as you will recall. He was constantly speaking to the fair
Annie—so people called her because of her beauty—about honor, and
he repeatedly told her that she must cherish her honor, and his too. As
a result, the girl took on a something quite distinctive in feature and in
her dress. She was more genteel and better mannered than all the other
girls of her class. She grew more sensitive, and if a lad clasped her too
tightly at the dance, or swung her higher than the bridge of the bass-
viol, then she came to me in tears repeating over and over, that such
things were contrary to her honor. Ah, Annie was always a peculiar girl.
Sometimes when no one was aware of it, she seized upon her apron
with both hands and tore it off, as though it were ablaze, and then burst
into violent tears. But there's a reason for that; teeth tore at it; the fiend
won't rest. Would that the child had not been so possessed of honor and
had put a stronger trust in the dear Lord; would that she had clung to
Him in all tribulation, had suffered disgrace and contempt for His sake,
instead of laying such store by worldly honor. The Lord would have
had mercy, and will still show mercy. Ah, I know they'll meet; God's
will be done!

The lancer had returned to France. Never a line did he write, so we
quite believed him dead and shed many a hot tear for him. In a hospital he lay, sick of a dangerous wound, but when he returned to his comrades and was advanced to a petty-officer, he remembered how his step-
brother had insulted him two years before, calling him nothing but a
private and his father a corporal. Then he reflected on the story of the
French petty-officer, and his many, many urgings to Annie about
honor, when he was on the point of saying good-bye. Then his peace
was gone; home-sickness seized upon him. He said to his commanding
officer, who had noticed the change that had come over him: 'Ah sir, I
feel as though I were being drawn home by the teeth!' He was granted
leave to ride home on his horse, for all his officers trusted him. Three
months was his furlough; he was to return when the cavalry got its fresh
quota of horses. Now he hastened as fast as was possible, without harm
to his mount, of which he was more chary than ever, because it had
been entrusted to him. One day he felt a special urge to hasten homeward; it was the day before the anniversary of his mother's death, and

he seemed to see her running alone before his horse crying: 'Casper, do me the honor!' Ah, on that very day I sat on her grave all alone and thought, if Casper were only here too. I had woven forget-me-nots into a wreath and had hung it on the sunken cross. Then I measured the space round about and thought to myself: 'I'd like to rest here, and there let Casper be buried, if God grant him a grave at home. Then we could all be together when it shall be said: 'Ye dead, ye dead, shall arise, ye shall come to judgment!' But Casper didn't come. I couldn't know that he was so near at hand and might have arrived. He felt an unusually urgent desire for haste, for while in France he had often thought of the day. He had brought along a little wreath of everlasting, to decorate the grave of his mother, and also a wreath for Annie, which she was to keep against her day of honor."

Here the old woman ceased and shook her head; but when I repeated her last words: "which she was to keep against her day of honor,"—she continued: "Who knows, perhaps they will let me have it still. Ah, if I might but wake the duke!"—"To what purpose?" I queried, "what is your request, mother?" Then she continued seriously: "Oh, what were there to life, if one's days were not numbered; what were there to life, if it were not eternal!" She went on:

"Casper could well have been in our village at noon, but that morning the hostler had pointed out to him that he had ridden his horse sore, and added: 'My friend, that runs contrary to the honor of horsemanship.' Casper felt the force of the reproof, loosened the girth and did everything to heal the wound. Afoot, leading the horse by the bridle, he continued his journey. So he came late at night to a mill, three miles from our village. Since he knew the miller as an old friend of his father, he put up there for the night, and was received as a welcome guest just come from distant parts. Casper led his horse into the stable, placed the saddle and his valise in a corner and entered the living-room of the miller. Then he asked after his relatives and was told that I, his old grandmother, was still alive, that his father and step-brother were well and were prospering. Yesterday they had brought grain to the mill. The father had turned a hand to trading in horses and oxen and was doing well at the business. As a result he had some regard for his honor and had laid aside his torn and patched clothing. Casper was delighted to hear this. When he asked about fair Annie, the miller replied he didn't know her, but if his guest had reference to the girl who had been in service at Roseacres, he had heard that she had taken a place in the capital, because she could get much more experience there, and more honor went with such service. This he had learned a year ago from a hand at Roseacres. That too was pleasant news for Casper. He grieved at the postponement of seeing her, but he hoped to find her in the capital very soon, pretty and neat, so that it would prove a real honor for him, an officer, to go walking with her of a Sunday. Then he told the miller this and that about France, they ate and drank together, and he helped his host pour in some grain. Finally the miller took him upstairs to bed, while he himself lay down to rest on some sacks on the floor below. The clatter of the mill and his great desire to be home kept Casper awake, even though he was very tired. He was restless, thinking much of his dead mother and of fair Annie, and about the honor, that he anticipated, when he came back as an officer. At last he fell off into a light slumber, but started up often out of disturbing dreams. Time and again he saw his dead mother approach him and, wringing her hands, implore him for aid. Then he dreamed that he had died and was about to be buried, but as a corpse he himself walked along to his burial, fair Annie beside him. He wept bitter tears that his comrades did not escort him, and when he had arrived at the church-yard, he saw that his grave was beside his mother's. Annie's grave was there too, and he gave Annie the wreath he had brought for her, and he hung his mother's on the cross over her grave. Then he looked about him and saw no one there but me. Then he saw Annie dragged into her grave by the apron, and after that he too climbed down into his grave exclaiming: 'Isn't there anyone here, who'll do me the last honors, and shoot into my grave as becomes a brave soldier?' Then he drew his pistol and himself shot into his grave.

At the ring of the shot he awoke in great fear, for it seemed to him that the windows rattled. He peered about the room, then he heard another shot, then a tumult in the mill and cries through the mill's clatter. With a bound he was out of bed and seized his sabre; his door opened, and in the full moon-shine he saw two men with blackened faces, armed with cudgels, rush on him, but he defended himself and struck one of them a blow on the arm. Then both fled, bolting the door, that opened outwards, behind them. Casper tried in vain to pursue them. Finally he succeeded in kicking out one of the door-panels. Hastily he crept through the hole and ran down the stairs, where he heard the miller whimpering, gagged and lying among the grain sacks. Casper loosed him and hurried off into the stable in search of his horse and valise. Both were gone. In great anguish he hastened back to the miller and lamented to him his misfortune, that all his belongings were gone, and the horse entrusted to him had been stolen. That the horse had been taken drove him to distraction. Then the miller appeared with a great bag of money; he had fetched it from a closet in the room above and now said to the lancer: 'Dear Casper, be content, to you I owe it that my entire fortune was not carried away. The robbers had laid their plans to make off with this bag, which was up in your room. The bold defence you put up has saved me all; I have lost nothing. The thieves who took your horse and valise from the stable must have been a part of the look-out, for they gave warning by their shots that danger was near, because in all probability they saw by your saddle that a cavalryman was lodging with me. On my account then you shall not come to grief. I shall take every pains and spare no money to get back your horse, and if I do not find this one, I'll buy you another, cost what it may.' Casper replied: 'I'll take no presents, that runs counter to my honor, but if in these hard strâits you will advance me seventy thalers, I'll give you my note, to return you the sum within two years.' This was agreed; and the lancer took his leave so that he could hasten to his village and report the matter to a magistrate who represented the nobility of the surrounding region. The miller staid at home awaiting his wife and son, who had gone to a wedding in one of the neighboring places. As soon as they had returned, he would follow the lancer with his statement for the magistrate too.

You can well imagine, my dear Mr. Clerk, with what a heavy heart poor Casper hastened on his way to our village, on foot and poor, where it had been his ambition to make his appearance proudly riding a-horseback. He had been robbed of fifty-one thalers, which he had saved, his letter-patent as petty-officer, his furlough and the wreaths for his mother's grave and for fair Annie. He was desperate. In this state of mind he arrived at one in the morning in his home village. No time did he waste, but immediately knocked at the door of the justice, whose house is the first as you enter the town. The minute he was let in, he reported the robbery and carefully listed everything that had been taken from him. The justice advised him to go at once to his father, who was the only peasant in the place that kept horses. With him and his brother he might patrol the region, to see whether some trace of the robbers could not be found. Meanwhile the justice himself would send others out on foot, and interview the miller for any further evidence. Casper now turned his back on the justice's house and proceeded toward his father's farm. His way led past my hut where through the window he heard me singing a religious song. I had not been able to close an eye for thoughts of his dear, dead mother, so he tapped on the window and said: 'Praise be to Jesus Christ, dear grandmother, Casper is here.' Ah, how those words struck into the marrow of my bones. I hastened to the window, opened it, and kissed and embraced him with unending tears. Briefly he told me of his misfortune, then of the commission he had to his father from the justice. This errand would brook no delay, the sooner they got on the trail of the thieves the better, for he would forfeit his honor, if he did not recover his horse.

Strange, but that word honor shook me from head to foot, for I knew the trials he had to face. 'Do your duty, and to God alone be the honor,' I said, as he left me to hurry away to Finkel's farm at the other end of the village. When he had gone, I sank on my knees to pray God, He might protect my Casper. Ah, I prayed with a fear as never before, and repeated over and over: 'Lord, Thy will be done on earth even as it is in heaven.'

Casper, mad with fear, ran toward his father's place. He climbed in over the garden wall; he heard the creaking of the pump, and a neighing in the stall, that chilled his blood. He stopped stone-still. By the light of the moon he saw two men washing themselves. Casper thought his heart would break. One of them exclaimed: 'This confounded stuff won't come off!' Then the other said: 'Let's go into the stall first to bob the nag's tail and trim its mane. Did you bury the valise deep enough in the dung-heap?'—'Yes,' replied the first. Then both went into the stable; and Casper, mad for sheer misery, rushed up, locked the stable-door behind them and shouted: 'In the name of the duke, surrender! If you resist, I'll shoot you dead!' Ah, so he had caught his father and his step-brother as the robbers of his horse. 'My honor! my honor! it's gone!' he cried, 'I am the son of a dishonorable horse-thief!' When the two within heard those words they were greatly frightened. 'Casper, dear Casper,' they shouted, 'for God's sake don't bring ruin upon us! Casper, we'll give up everything on the spot; for your dear mother's sake, whose death-day's to-day, have mercy on your father and brother!' But Casper was desperate. He kept on exclaiming: 'My honor, my duty!' Then as they tried to force the door and had kicked a hole in the dirt wall in order to escape, Casper shot his pistol into the air as he cried out: 'Help, help, thieves, help!' The peasants awakened by the justice were approaching in order to make their plans as how best to pursue the thieves. At the sound of the shot and the cries they rushed to the scene. Old Finkel was still pleading with his son to open, but he persisted: 'I am a soldier, and must act as the law commands.' Here the justice, surrounded by peasants, came up. Casper cried: 'God's mercy, justice, my own father, my own brother are the thieves. Oh, that I had never been born! I have locked them here in the barn, my valise lies buried in the dung-heap.' Then the peasants made their way into the stall, bound old Finkel and his son and dragged them into the house. But Casper dug up his valise, took from it the two wreaths, and did not go into the house; he went to the church-yard to the grave of his mother. Dawn was in the east; I had been out upon the meadow and had woven for me and for Casper two wreaths of forget-me-nots. I thought to myself, 'we two shall decorate his mother's grave when he returns from his search.' Strange noises came from the village; and since every hub-bub is unpleasant to me, and I prefer to be alone, I skirted the village and went toward the church-yard. I heard a shot, the smoke rose up before me. I hurried toward it. Oh, Lord of Heaven! have mercy on him! Casper lay dead on his mother's grave. He had sent a bullet through his heart over which he had fastened to a button the wreath he had brought for fair Annie,—through this wreath he had sent the bullet into his heart. The wreath for his mother hung on the cross. I felt as though the earth yawned under my feet at sight of this. On to his dead body I threw myself and cried out: 'Casper, poor boy, what have you done? Ah, who acquainted you with your misery; oh, why did I let you go before I told you all! Oh God! what will your poor father, your brother say, when they find you so?' I didn't know that he had taken this step on account of them; I was thinking of quite another matter. But worse was in store. The justice and the peasants brought old Finkel and his son bound with ropes. Misery made me dumb, I couldn't utter a sound. The justice asked me whether I had seen my nephew. I pointed to the spot where he lay. The justice drew nearer, for he thought that Casper was weeping on his mother's grave. He shook the prostrate form, then he saw the blood gush forth. 'Jesus, Mary!' he exclaimed, 'Casper has done away with himself.' At these words the two captives looked at one another in horror. Casper's corpse was now lifted and carried along beside his father and brother to the house of the justice. The village resounded with cries of lament; good peasant women helped me to follow. Ah, that was the most woeful journey of my life!"

Here the old woman ceased, and I said to her: "Good mother, your sorrow is great, but God loves you; whom he tries sorely, they are His dearest children. Tell me now, good mother, what has induced you to make the long journey hither, and what is the purpose of your petition to the duke?"

"Ay, you must have an inkling of that by now," she continued calmly, "to get an honorable burial for Casper and fair Annie. This wreath, I have brought along, she shall have; it was meant for her day of honor; it is drenched with Casper's blood. Just look at it, sir!"

Here she drew a little wreath of gold tinsel out of her bundle and held it before me. By the faint light of the dawn I could see that it was blackened with powder and spattered with blood. My heart ached at the great trials of this dear old woman, and the dignity and steadfastness with which she bore up under them filled me with awe. "Ah, dear mother," said I, "how will you acquaint poor Annie with her sorrow lest she fall down dead of fright, and what manner of day of honor is it for which you are bringing Annie this woeful wreath?"

"Good sir," spoke she, "come with me, you may take me there. I can't walk very fast, and so we shall find her just in time. On the way I'll tell you about her."

Then she rose, said her morning prayer very calmly, and arranged her clothing. But her bundle she hung over my arm. It was two o'clock in the morning, the day was dawning as we walked along through the quiet streets together.

"You see," the old woman continued her story, "when Finkel and his son were locked up, the justice summoned me into court. Casper's body was laid upon a table and, covered with his lancer's coat, carried into the court-room. Then I had to tell the justice all I knew about my nephew, also what he had said to me through the window that morning. Every word of mine went down on the paper that lay before the official. When he had finished with me, he examined the memorandum book that had been found among Casper's effects. There were records of his expenses in it, several stories about honor, among them that one about the French petty-officer—and just after it something written in pencil." Here the old woman gave me the booklet, and I read these last words of poor Casper: "I too cannot outlive my disgrace; my father and my brother are thieves, they have robbed me, their nearest of kin. My heart was sore, yet what could I do but seize them and bind them over to justice, for I am a soldier of my duke, and my sense of honor will allow of no leniency. I have given my father and my brother over to vengeance for honor's sake. Ah, may many lips intercede for me that I be granted an honorable burial, here beside my mother, where I have fallen. I ask my grandmother to send fair Annie the wreath through which I shot myself, and my greetings too. Ah, her sad lot chills me to the bone, but she shall not become the wife of a horse-thief's son, for honor has always been most dear to her. Dear, fair Annie, I hope you will not take my death too hard; it has to be, and if ever you liked me, then don't speak evil of me now. My disgrace is not of my doing! I tried so hard my life long to keep myself honorable. I had already been advanced to a petty-officer and was well thought of by every one. Surely I would have become an officer sometime, and Annie, truly I would not have given you up to court a grand lady—but the son of a horse-thief, who for honor's sake must have his own father seized and convicted, cannot outlive his disgrace. Annie, dear Annie, do accept the little wreath; I have always kept the faith with you, as surely as God will have mercy on me! I give you your freedom again, but do me the honor never to marry anyone who might be considered inferior to me. And if it is in your power, then intercede for me, that I may be granted honorable burial beside my mother, and should you die here in our village, ask that your grave be beside ours. My dear grandmother will rest here too, then we'll all be together. I have fifty thalers in my valise, they shall be let out at interest for your first baby. The pastor shall have my silver watch, if I receive honorable burial. My horse, the uniform and the arms belong to the duke, this my brief-case is for you. Farewell, dearly beloved; farewell, dear grandmother, pray for me and to all farewell — God have mercy on me — ah, my despair is great!"

The last words of an assuredly noble, afflicted human being I could not read without shedding bitter tears. — "Casper must have been a very good person, dear mother," I said to the old woman. At these words she stopped still, pressed my hand, and replied in a deeply moved voice: "Yes, he was the best person on earth. But he shouldn't have written those last few words about despair; they'll rob him of his honorable burial; they'll put him on the dissecting table. Ah, dear Clerk, if you could only be of help on this point!"

"How, of help, dear mother?" I asked, "of what weight can these last few words be?" — "Yes, yes," she replied, "the justice told me quite plainly. An order has gone out to all courts that only suicides out of melancholy shall have honorable burial, but all such as lay hands on themselves from despair shall be used for dissection. And the justice told me that he should have to send Casper to the laboratory as one who had admitted his despair in so many words."

"That is certainly a strange law," I said, "for in the case of every suicide a suit could easily be brought, as to whether death resulted from melancholy or despair, and the suit might be of such long duration that the judge and the advocates would be brought to melancholy and despair, and themselves be sent to the laboratory. But be of good cheer, dear mother, our duke is a kind and just ruler; if the whole matter is brought to his attention he will most certainly grant Casper a resting place beside his mother."

"God grant that!" replied the old woman. "You see, dear sir, when the justice had written down all the evidence, he gave me the brief-case and the wreath for fair Annie, and with these I came the long way here yesterday, so that on her day of honor I might give her this comfort for her journey. — Casper died just in time; had he known all, he would have grown mad with grief."

"Do tell me what has happened to fair Annie?" I asked the old woman. "Now you say that she has but a few hours more, now you mention her day of honor, and that she will have comfort from your sad message. Do tell me plainly, is she about to marry another, is she dead, or incurably sick? All this I must know if I am to write out the petition."

To this the old woman replied: "Ah, dear Clerk, these are the facts; God's will be done! You see, when Casper returned I was not as happy as might be. When Casper took his life I wasn't as sad as I should have been. I should never have survived if God had not had mercy on me and sent me even a greater sorrow. Yes, hear me, a stone had been placed before my heart like an icebreaker, and all the pangs which like floating ice rushed upon me and would most certainly have torn my heart away, they broke against the stone and drifted by almost without notice. I'll tell you now a sad story.

When my god-child, the fair Annie, lost her mother, a cousin of mine, who lived some twenty-one miles from our place, I was taking care of the sick woman. She was the widow of a poor peasant. In her youth she had fallen in love with a huntsman, but had rejected him because of his wild ways. Finally the huntsman had come to such a pass that he was jailed because of a murder and sentenced to die. This news came to my cousin upon her sick bed, and she grieved so deeply at this that from day to day she grew worse. Just before she passed away she intrusted dear, fair Annie to me as my god-child, and then in her last moments with parting breath she said to me: 'Dear Anna Margaret, when you pass through the city where the huntsman is held captive, send a message to him through the jailor, that on my death-bed I entreat him to turn to God, and that with my last breath I have prayed for him fervently, and that I send him my greetings.'—Not long after these words my good cousin died. When she had been buried I lifted little Annie—she was only three then—on to my arm and started on my homeward journey.

At the edge of the city, through which our way led, I came to the house of the headsman. He had some skill in doctoring cattle, so our burgomaster had asked me to bring back a medicine that the headsman prepared. When I entered his house and told him what I wanted he said that I should go up to the attic with him, where he kept his store of herbs, and help him select. I left little Annie below in the living-room and followed him up. On our return little Annie was standing before a small cabinet that was fastened to the wall, and kept saying: 'Grandmother, there's a mouse in there, listen, how it rattles; there's a mouse in there!'

These words of the child made the headsman look very serious. He opened the cabinet and said: 'God have mercy on us!' for he saw his headsman's sword, which hung quite alone in the cabinet on a nail, sway back and forth. He took down the sword. I was all atremble. 'Good woman,' he continued, 'if you love the dear little Annie, then do not start if I slit the skin a bit all around her neck with my sword. The sword, you see, set itself in motion in her presence. It thirsts for her blood, and if I don't slit her neck with it, the child will face grave misery in her life.' Then he took hold of the child, who began to cry unmercifully. I too cried out and clasped Annie to me. Here the burgomaster of the city came in; he was just returning from the hunt and had brought a sick dog to be cured. He asked the cause of the outcry. Annie screamed in reply: 'He's going to kill me!' I was beside myself with fear.

The headsman told the burgomaster what had happened. The latter re-
proved him for his superstition, as he called it, and added some threats.
The headsman, however, did not lose his composure and said: 'So was
the custom of my fathers, I shall not depart from it.' To this the burgomaster made reply: 'Headsman Franz, if you had believed that your
sword moved because I here and now give you notice, that to-morrow
morning at six the huntsman Jürge shall be beheaded by you, then I
would see some reason in it; but when you set out to draw conclusions
as regards this child, that is quite unreasonable and the part of madness.
An experience such as this might drive one to despair should he recall
later in life that it had occurred in his youth. You should lead no one
into temptation.'—'The like is true of a headsman's sword,' murmured
Franz, and hung the sword back in the cabinet. Then the burgomaster
kissed little Annie and gave her a roll out of his hunting-pouch. Next
he turned to me and asked who I was, where I had come from, and
whither I was going. When I had informed him of my cousin's death
and her message to the huntsman Jürge, he said to me: 'You shall deliver your greeting in person. I myself will take you to him. His heart is
hard, it may be, the memory of this good woman dying will touch his
heart in his last moments.' The good gentleman then took us into his
cart that was before the door and drove us into the city.

He bade me go to his cook, where we got a good meal, and toward
evening he accompanied me to the poor sinner. When I had brought
the condemned man my cousin's last message, bitter tears began to
flow from his eyes as he cried: 'Ah, God, if she had become my wife I
should never have ended so.' Then he begged that the pastor be sent
for after all, he wished to pray with him. The burgomaster promised to
do his bidding, praised him for his change of heart, and asked him
whether he had one last wish that might be granted. To this the huntsman Jürge exclaimed: 'Ah, do beg this good old mother to be present
to-morrow at my execution. That will give me strength in my dying
hour.' Then the burgomaster put this last wish to me, and gruesome as
it was, I could not refuse the poor miserable man. He begged my hand
in pledge, and as I solemnly promised he sank back weeping on the
straw. From there the burgomaster took me to his friend, the pastor.
Before this good man could be prevailed upon to visit the jail, I had to
tell him all that had happened.

That night I spent with the child in the mayor's house, and on the
next morning I went the hard road to the execution of the huntsman
Jürge. I stood beside the burgomaster in the circle and saw how he
broke the little staff. Now the huntsman Jürge said a few parting words,
all the people wept; and, deeply touched, the condemned man looked
at me and little Annie, who was standing just in front of me. Then he

kissed the headsman Franz, the pastor prayed with him, his eyes were
blinded, and he knelt down. In a flash the headsman gave him the
deathblow. 'Jesus, Mary, Joseph!' I cried; for Jürge's head bounded
along right toward little Annie and set its teeth in the little girl's apron.
She shrieked with fear. I tore off my apron and threw it over the gruesome head. As I did this Franz rushed up, tore the head loose and said:
'Mother, mother, what did I tell you this morning? I know my sword, it
has life.'—I was unnerved with fear; little Annie never stopped crying.
The burgomaster was completely bewildered and had me and the child
driven to the house, where his wife gave each of us a change of clothing. After dinner the burgomaster made us a present of some money,
and many people of the city, who were curious to see the girl, did like-
wise, so that I came away with twenty thaler and many clothes for her.
In the evening the pastor visited the house and solemnly charged me
to bring little Annie up in the fear of the Lord, and as a comfort bade
me pay no attention to all these ominous signs. They were clearly the
snares of Satan which must be scorned. At parting he gave me a fine
Bible for little Annie, which she has kept to this day. On the following
morning the burgomaster saw us on our way some nine miles in the direction of home in his own horse and cart.—Ah, Thou my God, and
now all has come just as predicted!" the old woman concluded and was
silent.

A fearful premonition was upon me; the old woman's narration
made my heart bleed. "In the name of God, mother," I cried, "what has
become of poor Annie; is there no help for her?"

"She was drawn to her fate with teeth," said the old woman, "to-day
she must die; but it was an act of despair. Honor, honor, was back of it
all! A passion for worldly honor brought her disgrace. She was seduced
by one in high standing; he left her; she strangled her child in the very
apron that I had thrown over the head of Jürge, the huntsman. Secretly
she had taken it from me. Ah, fate dragged her to it with teeth! She was
not in her right mind when she did it. The seducer had promised to
marry her. He had won her by saying that Casper lay buried in France.
Gradually despair clutched her poor soul, and she smothered the babe.
She gave herself up to the law. At four she will be executed. She wrote
me to come to her. That's what I'm about now. The wreath and poor
Casper's last greetings I am taking to her—and the rose, that I got tonight; these will be of some comfort. Ah, dear Clerk, if only you can
bring it about through your petition, that her body and Casper's too
may find their last resting place in our church-yard."

"Everything, everything in my power, I'll do," I cried. "Without a
moment's delay I'll hasten to the castle. My friend, who gave you the
rose, is in charge of the guard there to-night; I'll beg him to waken the

duke. I'll sink on my knees beside the royal bed and beg a pardon for Annie."

"Pardon?" said the old woman coldly. "You don't understand; fate dragged her to it with teeth. Listen, good sir, justice is better than pardon. Of what profit is pardon on earth? We must all appear before the final Judgment:

> Ye dead, ye dead shall then arise,
> And stand before the Last Assize.

You see, she doesn't seek a pardon; she was offered that if she would name the father, but Annie replied: 'I have murdered his child and I want to die, but he must not suffer. I'll bear the penalty, to be with my babe, but all will go wrong, if I name its father.' Then she was convicted to die by the sword. But make haste to the duke and beg him for Casper and Annie, that they may rest in an honorable grave. Go! Go now! See there, the pastor's just entering the jail, I'll ask him to take me in with him to the fair Annie. If you are spry, maybe you can meet us out at the place of execution with the comforting news that honorable burial has been granted to the just Casper and fair Annie."

Now we had come up with the pastor. As soon as the old woman told him her relationship to the condemned, he readily allowed her to accompany him into the jail. But I ran as never before to the castle. On the way I got an inkling of comfort; it seemed like a hopeful sign, as I dashed by the house of Count Grossinger, to hear out of an open window of the garden-house a sweet voice singing to the accompaniment of a lute:

> Though Mercy went a-wooing,
> Yet Honor watches well,
> Respectful love renewing,
> She breathes to-night farewell.
> If Love gives roses to her
> The veil let Mercy take,
> Then Honor greets the wooer,
> With love for Mercy's sake.

Ah, and there were further good omens! A hundred paces on I found a white veil in the street; I picked it up, it was filled with fragrant roses. I clasped it tightly in my hand and hurried on, thrilled with the thought: "Ah God, this is Mercy." As I turned the corner, I saw a man who drew his coat up around him as I hastened past and swiftly turned his back on me in order not to be seen! These were unnecessary precautions, for I saw nothing and heard nothing. My heart alone cried out: "Mercy! mercy!" I rushed in through the iron gate into the courtyard. God be praised, corporal Count Grossinger, who was pacing up and down under the blooming chestnut trees before the guard-house, came forward to meet me.

"Dear Count," I cried impetuously, "you must lead me to the duke immediately, on the spot, or it will be too late. All will be lost!"

He seemed embarrassed at this request and said: "Are you in your right mind? See the duke at this unaccustomed hour! It can't be. Return when the duke reviews the guard, then I'll present you."

The ground burned like coals under my feet. "Now," I shouted, "or never! You must! A life hangs in the balance!"

"It's impossible now," replied Grossinger sharply in a tone of finality. "My honor is at stake. I have strict orders to-night to let nobody up."

The word honor brought me close to desperation. I thought of Casper's honor and fair Annie's honor and exclaimed: "Damn this honor! I must to the duke as a last resort in a case where just such honor has failed. You must announce me or I'll cry out for the duke."

"If you so much as stir," said Grossinger sternly, "I'll have you thrown into the guard-house. You are a dreamer. You have no sense of conditions."

"Oh, I know conditions, frightful conditions! I must speak to the duke. Every moment is precious!" I retorted. "If you'll not announce me now, I'll find my way to him alone."

This said, I was on the point of making for the steps that led up to the duke's apartments when I espied the same muffled figure which I had just encountered hastening toward them. Grossinger forced me about so that I might not see the person. "What are you up to, rashling?" he whispered into my ear. "Be still, quiet, I say, or you will bring me to grief."

"Why didn't you halt that man, who just went up to the duke?" I asked. "He can have no request more urgent than mine. Ah, it is so urgent. I must, I must see the duke! The fate of a poor, deceived, unhappy creature is at stake."

Grossinger replied: "You saw that man ascend those steps; if you ever breathe a word about it you will face the blade of this sword. Just because he went up you cannot; the duke has business with him."

A light shot forth from the duke's windows. "God, there's a light, he's up!" I cried. "I must speak with him. In the name of heaven let me go, or I'll cry for help."

Grossinger seized me by the arm and said: "You're drunk, come into the guard-house. I'm your friend, come, sleep it off. Give me the song that the old woman sang to-night at the doorstep as I marched by with the guard. I'm burning to hear it."

"It's of the old woman and her kin, that I must speak to the duke!" I said.

"Of the old woman?" asked Grossinger. "Tell me about her. Those higher up take no interest in such matters. Come, come to the guard-house!"

He was on the point of pulling me along when the castle-clock pealed down three-thirty. The sound pierced my soul like a cry of anguish, and I shouted with all my strength up to the duke's windows: "Help! in God's name help! for a miserable, deceived creature!" Grossinger flew into a rage, he tried to clasp his hand over my lips, but I freed myself. He thumped me in the back of the neck. He cursed. I felt and heard none of it. He called the guard. A corporal rushed up with several soldiers to seize me. The duke's window was thrown open, and a voice called out:

"Corporal Count Grossinger, what's all the noise? Bring the person up, without delay!"

I did not wait for the corporal. Up the steps I rushed and prostrated myself at the feet of the duke. Embarrassed and out of sorts he bade me arise. He had on his boots and his spurs, although he was still in a bathrobe, which he carefully drew together at the breast.

As briefly as possible I related to the duke all that the old woman had told me of the suicide of the lancer and of fair Annie's history. I entreated him to delay the execution a few short hours and begged for an honorable burial for the two unfortunates, in case a pardon could not be had. — "Ah, mercy, mercy!" I cried as I drew forth from my bosom the white veil filled with roses. "This veil, that I found on the way, seemed to give promise of mercy."

Impetuously and shaken with emotion, the duke seized upon the veil, he clasped it between his palms. I pressed my advantage. When in terse phrases I added that the poor girl was the victim of a false sense of honor; that a person in high standing had deceived her and promised to wed her; that her nobleness was such that she preferred death to exposing the father — then with tears in his eyes the duke interrupted and cried: "Cease, in the name of Heaven, cease!" — Abruptly he turned to the corporal, who stood at the door, with quick sharp commands: "Go! both of you ride. Don't spare the horses! Away to the place of execution! Fasten the veil to your sword, wave it and shout, Mercy! mercy! I follow."

Grossinger took the veil. An utter change had come over him. Like a ghost he looked for fear and haste. We ran into the stall, mounted, and off we were in a gallop. He charged out of the gate like one possessed. As he fastened the veil to the point of his sword he exclaimed: "Lord Jesus, my sister!" These words were dark to me. He rose in his stirrups, waved the veil and kept shouting: "Mercy! mercy!" On the hill-top we saw the crowd assembled for the execution. My horse shied at the streaming veil. I am a poor horseman. I couldn't catch up with Grossinger. He sped along his wild course. I bent every effort. Evil Chance! The artillery was holding morning practice near by. The thunder of cannon drowned our cries so that they could not be heard from a distance. Grossinger was thrown. Before me I could see the crowd draw back. The circle opened to my vision. I saw a gleam of steel glitter in the rising sun—ah God, it was the gleam of the headsman's sword!—I charged up only to hear the moans of the bystanders. "Pardon, pardon!" shouted Grossinger like a madman as he lunged with the waving veil into the circle, but the headsman held out toward him the bleeding head of fair Annie, that smiled at him dolefully. Then he cried out: "God have mercy on me!" and fell over the corpse. "Kill me! Kill me, you people. I have betrayed her. I am the murderer!"

An avenging fury seized the crowd. The women and maidens surged up, tore him from the corpse and spurned him with their feet, but he did nothing to defend himself. The guard could not hold the angry crowd in check. A shout was raised: "The duke, the duke!" He came up in an open carriage, a youth with hat deep over his face, wrapped in a cloak, sat beside him. The crowd dragged Grossinger to where the duke was. "Jesus, my brother!" the youthful officer exclaimed from the carriage in the most feminine tones. The duke, embarrassed, bade him be still and sprang from the carriage. The youth was about to follow when the duke pushed him back not too gently. But the disguise was lifted; it was the sister of Count Grossinger clothed as an officer. The duke commanded that the maltreated, bleeding, fainting Grossinger be placed in his carriage. The sister threw all caution to the winds, she cast her cloak over him. There she stood in woman's apparel. The duke was clearly taken aback; but he soon collected himself and ordered the carriage immediately to turn back, taking the countess and her brother to her dwelling. This had somewhat quelled the rage of the crowd. Then the duke said to the officer in command in a loud voice: "The Countess Grossinger saw her brother gallop past her house to bring the pardon. She wished to be present at this glad event. As I drove by, bent on the same mission, she stood at her window and begged me to take her into my carriage. I could not refuse the dear child. In order to prevent any stir, she quickly donned a hat and a cloak of her brother; now, surprised by an unfortunate accident, she has put on the whole matter the appearance of a romantic scandal. But, lieutenant, were you not able to protect the unfortunate Count Grossinger from the crowd? It is indeed a misfortune that he was thrown, and came too late, but that is scarcely his fault. See to it that the count's assailants are taken and properly punished."

Barely had the duke finished when a general outcry arose: "He is a villain; he is the seducer, the murderer of fair Annie. He confessed to it himself, the wretch, the low-down fellow!"

When the accusations came pouring in from all sides and were confirmed by the pastor, the officer, and the officials, the duke was so thoroughly aroused that he kept repeating: "Revolting, revolting, oh, the miserable fellow!"

Now the duke, pale as a ghost, stepped into the circle to look at the corpse of fair Annie. Upon the green turf she lay, clad in a white dress trimmed with black ribbon. The old woman, who was completely oblivious of all that was going on around her, had laid the head to the body and had covered the terrible cleavage with her apron. She was now engaged in folding fair Annie's hands over the Bible which the pastor of the little city had given her. The golden wreath she bound upon the severed head, and pinned to the lifeless bosom the rose that Grossinger had presented to her in the night, little knowing for whom it might be.

When the duke saw what the old woman had done he spoke: "Ill-fated Annie! Disgraceful seducer, you arrived too late!—Poor old mother, you alone have remained faithful to her 'till death." Now as his eyes fell upon me he remarked: "You told me of a last will of Corporal Casper. Have you it here?" I turned then to the old woman: "Poor mother, let me have Casper's brief-case, the duke wants to read his last will."

The old woman, whose attention up to this point had been riveted upon what she was doing, said sullenly: "You're here too? You might just as well have staid home. Have you the petition? It's too late now. No, I wasn't able to give the poor child the last comfort, that she and Casper should rest in an honorable grave. Ah, I lied to her when I said it had been granted. No, she wouldn't believe me."

Here the duke interrupted: "You did not lie to her, good mother. My messenger did all in his power. The fall of the horse must here bear the blame. She shall have honorable burial beside her mother and Casper, who was a brave fellow. The pastor shall preach a funeral-sermon for them both on the text: 'To God alone be honor!' Casper shall be buried as a corporal, his company shall shoot three times into his grave, and the sword of the corrupter Grossinger shall be laid on his coffin."

After these words he took Grossinger's sword, that with the veil was still lying on the ground, removed the veil, covered Annie with it and said: "This ill-fated veil, that should have brought her pardon, from my heart shall restore her honor. She had died in honor and pardoned; as token of this it shall be buried with her."

Then he handed the sword to the officer with the remark: "To-day at review I shall give you my further orders in regard to the burial of the lancer and this poor girl."

Now he read aloud Casper's last words in a voice choked with emotion. The old grandmother clasped his feet, her eyes filled with tears of joy as though she had been immeasurably blessed. The Duke spoke: "Contain yourself, mother! You shall have a pension until the end of your days. A monument shall be raised to the memory of your grandson and Annie." Then he ordered the pastor to take the old woman and the coffin, in which the body was laid, to his dwelling, and later escort her home, where she should have full charge of the burial. As his adjutant arrived in the meantime with horses, he said to me in parting: "Give your name to my officer, later I'll send for you. You have shown a splendid charitable zeal." The adjutant took down my name and bowed graciously. As the duke galloped off toward the city, he took with him the blessings of the crowd. The body of fair Annie and the good old grandmother were brought to the house of the pastor, and in the following night he took her back home. The next evening the officer with Grossinger's sword and a squadron of lancers arrived. Then the just Casper, with Grossinger's sword on his bier and the corporal's patent, was buried with fair Annie beside the grave of his mother. I too was there to escort the old mother, who seemed childish for joy, but said little. As the lancers fired the third salute into the grave she fell back dead in my arms. Beside her kin she lies buried. God grant them all a blessed resurrection!

> There, far in front, their feet shall go,
> Where blesséd angels sit in row,
> Where, newly come, God waits them there,
> A beauteous rainbow round His chair.
> There souls by God shall now be tried,
> When Heaven's doors shall open wide.

When I returned to the capital, I learned that Count Grossinger was dead. He had poisoned himself. On my desk I found a letter from him which read:

"I owe you much. You revealed my disgrace, which long had been eating out my heart. Well did I know that song of the old woman. Annie had told it to me many and many a time. She was an exceptionally noble being. I was a base criminal—I had given her a written promise of marriage—she burned it. She was in service in the home of an old aunt of mine. Melancholy often seized her. Through certain medicinal preparations of a magic content, I ensnared her soul.—God have mercy on me!—You have saved my sister's honor too.—The duke loves her.—I

stood high in his favor.—This tragedy has stirred him to the depths.—
God help me.—I have taken poison.

JOSEPH, COUNT GROSSINGER."

Fair Annie's apron, to which the head of Jürge, the huntsman, clung at the beheading, has been preserved in the ducal museum. It is rumored that the duke will elevate the sister of Count Grossinger to a princess with the name, *Voile de Grace*, in English, Veil of Mercy, and make her his wife. At the coming review in the neighborhood of D—— the monument over the graves of the two ill-fated victims to honor is to be unveiled and dedicated in the church-yard of the village. The duke and the princess will be there in person. He is exceptionally pleased with the design of this monument. The duke and the princess together, it is said, worked out the theme. It sets forth the true and the false honor. Both figures are deeply bowed, one on either side of a cross, Justice with high-swung sword on the one hand and Mercy on the other casting a veil. Some find in the head of Justice a similarity to the duke, in the head of Mercy a likeness to the princess.

DOVER · THRIFT · EDITIONS

POETRY

LA VITA NUOVA, Dante Alighieri. 56pp. 41915-0

101 GREAT AMERICAN POEMS, The American Poetry & Literacy Project (ed.). (Available in U.S. only.) 96pp. 40158-8

ENGLISH ROMANTIC POETRY: An Anthology, Stanley Appelbaum (ed.). 256pp. 29282-7

DOVER BEACH AND OTHER POEMS, Matthew Arnold. 112pp. 28037-3

SELECTED POEMS FROM "FLOWERS OF EVIL," Charles Baudelaire. 64pp. 28450-6

BHAGAVADGITA, Bhagavadgita. 112pp. 27782-8

THE BOOK OF PSALMS, King James Bible. 128pp. 27541-8

IMAGIST POETRY: AN ANTHOLOGY, Bob Blaisdell (ed.). 176pp. (Available in U.S. only.) 40875-2

IRISH VERSE: AN ANTHOLOGY, Bob Blaisdell (ed.). 160pp. 41914-2

BLAKE'S SELECTED POEMS, William Blake. 96pp. 28517-0

SONGS OF INNOCENCE AND SONGS OF EXPERIENCE, William Blake. 64pp. 27051-3

THE CLASSIC TRADITION OF HAIKU: An Anthology, Faubion Bowers (ed.). 96pp. 29274-6

TO MY HUSBAND AND OTHER POEMS, Anne Bradstreet (Robert Hutchinson, ed.). 80pp. 41408-6

BEST POEMS OF THE BRONTË SISTERS (ed. by Candace Ward), Emily, Anne, and Charlotte Brontë. 64pp. 29529-X

SONNETS FROM THE PORTUGUESE AND OTHER POEMS, Elizabeth Barrett Browning. 64pp. 27052-1

MY LAST DUCHESS AND OTHER POEMS, Robert Browning. 128pp. 27783-6

POEMS AND SONGS, Robert Burns. 96pp. 26863-2

SELECTED POEMS, George Gordon, Lord Byron. 112pp. 27784-4

JABBERWOCKY AND OTHER POEMS, Lewis Carroll. 64pp. 41582-1

SELECTED CANTERBURY TALES, Geoffrey Chaucer. 144pp. 28241-4

THE RIME OF THE ANCIENT MARINER AND OTHER POEMS, Samuel Taylor Coleridge. 80pp. 27266-4

WAR IS KIND AND OTHER POEMS, Stephen Crane. 64pp. 40424-2

THE CAVALIER POETS: An Anthology, Thomas Crofts (ed.). 80pp. 28766-1

SELECTED POEMS, Emily Dickinson. 64pp. 26466-1

SELECTED POEMS, John Donne. 96pp. 27788-7

SELECTED POEMS, Paul Laurence Dunbar. 80pp. 29980-5

"THE WASTE LAND" AND OTHER POEMS, T. S. Eliot. 64pp. (Available in U.S. only.) 40061-1

THE CONCORD HYMN AND OTHER POEMS, Ralph Waldo Emerson. 64pp. 29059-X

THE RUBÁIYÁT OF OMAR KHAYYÁM: FIRST AND FIFTH EDITIONS, Edward FitzGerald. 64pp. 26467-X

A BOY'S WILL AND NORTH OF BOSTON, Robert Frost. 112pp. (Available in U.S. only.) 26866-7

THE ROAD NOT TAKEN AND OTHER POEMS, Robert Frost. 64pp. (Available in U.S. only.) 27550-7

HARDY'S SELECTED POEMS, Thomas Hardy. 80pp. 28753-X

"GOD'S GRANDEUR" AND OTHER POEMS, Gerard Manley Hopkins. 80pp. 28729-7

A SHROPSHIRE LAD, A. E. Housman. 64pp. 26468-8

LYRIC POEMS, John Keats. 80pp. 26871-3

GUNGA DIN AND OTHER FAVORITE POEMS, Rudyard Kipling. 80pp. 26471-8

SNAKE AND OTHER POEMS, D. H. Lawrence. 64pp. 40647-4

DOVER·THRIFT·EDITIONS

POETRY

DOVER·THRIFT·EDITIONS

FICTION

A Journal of the Plague Year, Daniel Defoe. 192pp. 41919-3

Six Great Sherlock Holmes Stories, Sir Arthur Conan Doyle. 112pp. 27055-6

Short Stories, Theodore Dreiser. 112pp. 28215-5

Silas Marner, George Eliot. 160pp. 29246-0

Joseph Andrews, Henry Fielding. 288pp. 41588-0

This Side of Paradise, F. Scott Fitzgerald. 208pp. 28999-0

"The Diamond as Big as the Ritz" and Other Stories, F. Scott Fitzgerald. 29991-0

Madame Bovary, Gustave Flaubert. 256pp. 29257-6

The Revolt of "Mother" and Other Stories, Mary E. Wilkins Freeman. 128pp. 40428-5

A Room with a View, E. M. Forster. 176pp. (Available in U.S. only.) 28467-0

Where Angels Fear to Tread, E. M. Forster. 128pp. (Available in U.S. only.) 27791-7

The Immoralist, André Gide. 112pp. (Available in U.S. only.) 29237-1

Herland, Charlotte Perkins Gilman. 128pp. 40429-3

"The Yellow Wallpaper" and Other Stories, Charlotte Perkins Gilman. 80pp. 29857-4

The Overcoat and Other Stories, Nikolai Gogol. 112pp. 27057-2

Chelkash and Other Stories, Maxim Gorky. 64pp. 40652-0

Great Ghost Stories, John Grafton (ed.). 112pp. 27270-2

Detection by Gaslight, Douglas G. Greene (ed.). 272pp. 29928-7

The Mabinogion, Lady Charlotte E. Guest. 192pp. 29541-9

"The Fiddler of the Reels" and Other Short Stories, Thomas Hardy. 80pp. 29960-0

The Luck of Roaring Camp and Other Stories, Bret Harte. 96pp. 27271-0

The House of the Seven Gables, Nathaniel Hawthorne. 272pp. 40882-5

The Scarlet Letter, Nathaniel Hawthorne. 192pp. 28048-9

Young Goodman Brown and Other Stories, Nathaniel Hawthorne. 128pp. 27060-2

The Gift of the Magi and Other Short Stories, O. Henry. 96pp. 27061-0

The Nutcracker and the Golden Pot, E. T. A. Hoffmann. 128pp. 27806-9

The Aspern Papers, Henry James. 112pp. 41922-3

The Beast in the Jungle and Other Stories, Henry James. 128pp. 27552-3

Daisy Miller, Henry James. 64pp. 28773-4

The Turn of the Screw, Henry James. 96pp. 26684-2

Washington Square, Henry James. 176pp. 40431-5

The Country of the Pointed Firs, Sarah Orne Jewett. 96pp. 28196-5

The Autobiography of an Ex-Colored Man, James Weldon Johnson. 112pp. 28512-X

Dubliners, James Joyce. 160pp. 26870-5

A Portrait of the Artist as a Young Man, James Joyce. 192pp. 28050-0

The Metamorphosis and Other Stories, Franz Kafka. 96pp. 29030-1

The Man Who Would Be King and Other Stories, Rudyard Kipling. 128pp. 28051-9

You Know Me Al, Ring Lardner. 128pp. 28513-8

Selected Short Stories, D. H. Lawrence. 128pp. 27794-1

Green Tea and Other Ghost Stories, J. Sheridan LeFanu. 96pp. 27795-X

The Call of the Wild, Jack London. 64pp. 26472-6

Five Great Short Stories, Jack London. 96pp. 27063-7

The Sea-Wolf, Jack London. 248pp. 41108-7

White Fang, Jack London. 160pp. 26968-X

Death in Venice, Thomas Mann. 96pp. (Available in U.S. only.) 28714-9

In a German Pension: 13 Stories, Katherine Mansfield. 112pp. 28719-X

The Necklace and Other Short Stories, Guy de Maupassant. 128pp. 27064-5

Bartleby and Benito Cereno, Herman Melville. 112pp. 26473-4

The Oil Jar and Other Stories, Luigi Pirandello. 96pp. 28459-X

The Gold-Bug and Other Tales, Edgar Allan Poe. 128pp. 26875-6

Tales of Terror and Detection, Edgar Allan Poe. 96pp. 28744-0

DOVER · THRIFT · EDITIONS

FICTION

THE QUEEN OF SPADES AND OTHER STORIES, Alexander Pushkin. 128pp. 28054-3

THE STORY OF AN AFRICAN FARM, Olive Schreiner. 256pp. 40165-0

FRANKENSTEIN, Mary Shelley. 176pp. 28211-2

THE JUNGLE, Upton Sinclair. 320pp. (Available in U.S. only.) 41923-1

THREE LIVES, Gertrude Stein. 176pp. (Available in U.S. only.) 28059-4

THE BODY SNATCHER AND OTHER TALES, Robert Louis Stevenson. 80pp. 41924-X

THE STRANGE CASE OF DR. JEKYLL AND MR. HYDE, Robert Louis Stevenson. 64pp. 26688-5

TREASURE ISLAND, Robert Louis Stevenson. 160pp. 27559-0

GULLIVER'S TRAVELS, Jonathan Swift. 240pp. 29273-8

THE KREUTZER SONATA AND OTHER SHORT STORIES, Leo Tolstoy. 144pp. 27805-0

THE WARDEN, Anthony Trollope. 176pp. 40076-X

FIRST LOVE AND DIARY OF A SUPERFLUOUS MAN, Ivan Turgenev. 96pp. 28775-0

FATHERS AND SONS, Ivan Turgenev. 176pp. 40073-5

ADVENTURES OF HUCKLEBERRY FINN, Mark Twain. 224pp. 28061-6

THE ADVENTURES OF TOM SAWYER, Mark Twain. 192pp. 40077-8

THE MYSTERIOUS STRANGER AND OTHER STORIES, Mark Twain. 128pp. 27069-6

HUMOROUS STORIES AND SKETCHES, Mark Twain. 80pp. 29279-7

AROUND THE WORLD IN EIGHTY DAYS, Jules Verne. 160pp. 41111-7

CANDIDE, Voltaire (François-Marie Arouet). 112pp. 26689-3

GREAT SHORT STORIES BY AMERICAN WOMEN, Candace Ward (ed.). 192pp. 28776-9

"THE COUNTRY OF THE BLIND" AND OTHER SCIENCE-FICTION STORIES, H. G. Wells. 160pp. (Not available in Europe or United Kingdom.) 29569-9

THE ISLAND OF DR. MOREAU, H. G. Wells. 112pp. (Not available in Europe or United Kingdom.) 29027-1

THE INVISIBLE MAN, H. G. Wells. 112pp. (Not available in Europe or United Kingdom.) 27071-8

THE TIME MACHINE, H. G. Wells. 80pp. (Not available in Europe or United Kingdom.) 28472-7

THE WAR OF THE WORLDS, H. G. Wells. 160pp. (Not available in Europe or United Kingdom.) 29506-0

ETHAN FROME, Edith Wharton. 96pp. 26690-7

SHORT STORIES, Edith Wharton. 128pp. 28235-X

THE AGE OF INNOCENCE, Edith Wharton. 288pp. 29803-5

THE PICTURE OF DORIAN GRAY, Oscar Wilde. 192pp. 27807-7

JACOB'S ROOM, Virginia Woolf. 144pp. (Not available in Europe or United Kingdom.) 40109-X

MONDAY OR TUESDAY: Eight Stories, Virginia Woolf. 64pp. (Not available in Europe or United Kingdom.) 29453-6

NONFICTION

POETICS, Aristotle. 64pp. 29577-X

POLITICS, Aristotle. 368pp. 41424-8

NICOMACHEAN ETHICS, Aristotle. 256pp. 40096-4

MEDITATIONS, Marcus Aurelius. 128pp. 29823-X

THE LAND OF LITTLE RAIN, Mary Austin. 96pp. 29037-9

THE DEVIL'S DICTIONARY, Ambrose Bierce. 144pp. 27542-6

THE ANALECTS, Confucius. 128pp. 28484-0

CONFESSIONS OF AN ENGLISH OPIUM EATER, Thomas De Quincey. 80pp. 28742-4

THE SOULS OF BLACK FOLK, W. E. B. Du Bois. 176pp. 28041-1

DOVER·THRIFT·EDITIONS

NONFICTION

NARRATIVE OF THE LIFE OF FREDERICK DOUGLASS, Frederick Douglass. 96pp. 28499-9

SELF-RELIANCE AND OTHER ESSAYS, Ralph Waldo Emerson. 128pp. 27790-9

THE LIFE OF OLAUDAH EQUIANO, OR GUSTAVUS VASSA, THE AFRICAN, Olaudah Equiano. 192pp. 40661-X

THE AUTOBIOGRAPHY OF BENJAMIN FRANKLIN, Benjamin Franklin. 144pp. 29073-5

TOTEM AND TABOO, Sigmund Freud. 176pp. (Not available in Europe or United Kingdom.) 40434-X

LOVE: A Book of Quotations, Herb Galewitz (ed.). 64pp. 40004-2

PRAGMATISM, William James. 128pp. 28270-8

THE STORY OF MY LIFE, Helen Keller. 80pp. 29249-5

TAO TE CHING, Lao Tze. 112pp. 29792-6

GREAT SPEECHES, Abraham Lincoln. 112pp. 26872-1

THE PRINCE, Niccolò Machiavelli. 80pp. 27274-5

THE SUBJECTION OF WOMEN, John Stuart Mill. 112pp. 29601-6

SELECTED ESSAYS, Michel de Montaigne. 96pp. 29109-X

UTOPIA, Sir Thomas More. 96pp. 29583-4

BEYOND GOOD AND EVIL: Prelude to a Philosophy of the Future, Friedrich Nietzsche. 176pp. 29868-X

THE BIRTH OF TRAGEDY, Friedrich Nietzsche. 96pp. 28515-4

COMMON SENSE, Thomas Paine. 64pp. 29602-4

SYMPOSIUM AND PHAEDRUS, Plato. 96pp. 27798-4

THE TRIAL AND DEATH OF SOCRATES: Four Dialogues, Plato. 128pp. 27066-1

A MODEST PROPOSAL AND OTHER SATIRICAL WORKS, Jonathan Swift. 64pp. 28759-9

CIVIL DISOBEDIENCE AND OTHER ESSAYS, Henry David Thoreau. 96pp. 27563-9

SELECTIONS FROM THE JOURNALS (Edited by Walter Harding), Henry David Thoreau. 96pp. 28760-2

WALDEN; OR, LIFE IN THE WOODS, Henry David Thoreau. 224pp. 28495-6

NARRATIVE OF SOJOURNER TRUTH, Sojourner Truth. 80pp. 29899-X

THE THEORY OF THE LEISURE CLASS, Thorstein Veblen. 256pp. 28062-4

DE PROFUNDIS, Oscar Wilde. 64pp. 29308-4

OSCAR WILDE'S WIT AND WISDOM: A Book of Quotations, Oscar Wilde. 64pp. 40146-4

UP FROM SLAVERY, Booker T. Washington. 160pp. 28738-6

A VINDICATION OF THE RIGHTS OF WOMAN, Mary Wollstonecraft. 224pp. 29036-0

PLAYS

PROMETHEUS BOUND, Aeschylus. 64pp. 28762-9

THE ORESTEIA TRILOGY: Agamemnon, The Libation-Bearers and The Furies, Aeschylus. 160pp. 29242-8

LYSISTRATA, Aristophanes. 64pp. 28225-2

WHAT EVERY WOMAN KNOWS, James Barrie. 80pp. (Not available in Europe or United Kingdom.) 29578-8

THE CHERRY ORCHARD, Anton Chekhov. 64pp. 26682-6

THE SEA GULL, Anton Chekhov. 64pp. 40656-3

THE THREE SISTERS, Anton Chekhov. 64pp. 27544-2

UNCLE VANYA, Anton Chekhov. 64pp. 40159-6

THE WAY OF THE WORLD, William Congreve. 80pp. 27787-9

BACCHAE, Euripides. 64pp. 29580-X

MEDEA, Euripides. 64pp. 27548-5

DOVER · THRIFT · EDITIONS

PLAYS

ELECTRA, Sophocles. 64pp. 28482-4

MISS JULIE, August Strindberg. 64pp. 27281-8

THE PLAYBOY OF THE WESTERN WORLD AND RIDERS TO THE SEA, J. M. Synge. 80pp. 27562-0

THE DUCHESS OF MALFI, John Webster. 96pp. 40660-1

THE IMPORTANCE OF BEING EARNEST, Oscar Wilde. 64pp. 26478-5

LADY WINDERMERE'S FAN, Oscar Wilde. 64pp. 40078-6

BOXED SETS

FAVORITE JANE AUSTEN NOVELS: *Pride and Prejudice, Sense and Sensibility* and *Persuasion* (Complete and Unabridged), Jane Austen. 800pp. 29748-9

BEST WORKS OF MARK TWAIN: Four Books, Dover. 624pp. 40226-6

EIGHT GREAT GREEK TRAGEDIES: Six Books, Dover. 480pp. 40203-7

FIVE GREAT ENGLISH ROMANTIC POETS, Dover. 496pp. 27893-X

FIVE GREAT PLAYS, Dover. 368pp. 27179-X

47 GREAT SHORT STORIES: Stories by Poe, Chekhov, Maupassant, Gogol, O. Henry, and Twain, Dover. 688pp. 27178-1

GREAT AFRICAN-AMERICAN WRITERS: Seven Books, Dover. 704pp. 29995-3

GREAT AMERICAN NOVELS, Dover. 720pp. 28665-7

GREAT ENGLISH NOVELS, Dover. 704pp. 28666-5

GREAT IRISH WRITERS: Five Books, Dover. 672pp. 29996-1

GREAT MODERN WRITERS: Five Books, Dover. 720pp. (Available in U.S. only.) 29458-7

GREAT WOMEN POETS: 4 Complete Books, Dover. 256pp. (Available in U.S. only.) 28388-7

MASTERPIECES OF RUSSIAN LITERATURE: Seven Books, Dover. 880pp. 40665-2

SEVEN GREAT ENGLISH VICTORIAN POETS: Seven Volumes, Dover. 592pp. 40204-5

SIX GREAT AMERICAN POETS: Poems by Poe, Dickinson, Whitman, Longfellow, Frost, and Millay, Dover. 512pp. (Available in U.S. only.) 27425-X

38 SHORT STORIES BY AMERICAN WOMEN WRITERS: Five Books, Dover. 512pp. 29459-5

26 GREAT TALES OF TERROR AND THE SUPERNATURAL, Dover. 608pp. (Available in U.S. only.) 27891-3

All books complete and unabridged. All 5³⁄₁₆" x 8¹⁄₄," paperbound. Available at your book dealer, online at **www.doverpublications.com**, or by writing to Dept. GI, Dover Publications, Inc., 31 East 2nd Street, Mineola, NY 11501. For current price information or for free catalogs (please indicate field of interest), write to Dover Publications or log on to **www.doverpublications.com** and see every Dover book in print. Dover publishes more than 500 books each year on science, elementary and advanced mathematics, biology, music, art, literary history, social sciences, and other areas.